D1488152

Presented By Friends of the Plantation Library

TREASURED

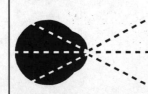

TREASURED

CANDACE CAMP

THORNDIKE PRESS

A part of Gale, Cengage Learning

GALE
CENGAGE Learning·

Farmington Hills, Mich • San Francisco • New York • Waterville, Maine
Meriden, Conn • Mason, Ohio • Chicago

LIBRARY OF CONGRESS CATALOGING-IN-PUBLICATION DATA

Camp, Candace.
    Treasured / by Candace Camp. — Large print edition.
      pages ; cm. — (Thorndike Press large print core) (Secrets of the Loch)
    ISBN 978-1-4104-7568-8 (hardcover) — ISBN 1-4104-7568-9 (hardcover)
    1. Large type books. I. Title.
PS3553.A4374T74 2015
813'.54—dc23   2014036167

Published in 2015 by arrangement with Pocket Books, a division of Simon & Schuster, Inc.

Printed in Mexico
1 2 3 4 5 6 7 19 18 17 16 15

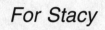

For Stacy

ACKNOWLEDGMENTS

Many thanks to:

Colin, who told us about the Highland Clearances, and to all the wonderful people we met in Scotland. I had never before thought of setting a book there, and I am sure I could never do justice to this beautiful land and its tumultuous and often tragic history. But one look at the ruins of a castle in the mist, and I knew I had my next story.

Anastasia Hopcus, for all her support and help. I couldn't have written *Treasured* without you.

Abby Zidle, editor extraordinaire, the wonderful folks at Pocket, and especially Steve Boldt, who caught all my mistakes.

My wonderful agent, Maria Carvainis, who always has my back.

PROLOGUE

April 1746

He walked swiftly, footsteps muffled on the dirt path, barely noticing the damp stone walls around him. He had taken care of the gold, putting it in safe hands — hands in which he would entrust his very life. Now he was free to find the prince and his fleeing Highlanders. Despite the crushing defeat, he was certain that they could recover, given time and fierce resolve . . . and the fortune he had brought back for them. He had no doubts that he could find them. This land was his, and he knew every cleft, every cave, every bramble that might offer shelter. If he could not evade the Redcoats and find the men they so zealously pursued, then he was not worthy of the name Laird of Baillannan.

But that search was for tomorrow. Right now, Malcolm Rose had a far different quarry. His mind was on only one person.

9

One place. One night before they must part again. His heart sped up as he neared the end of the tunnel, wanting, as it always did, to burst out of his chest at the thought of seeing her. Even after all these years, even though he had been with her only yesterday, he was still as eager as a lad.

He opened the low wooden door at the end of the tunnel and bent to step through it. As he raised his head, the sight that met him was so unexpected that for a moment he could not speak, could not think. "You!"

"Yes. Me." The smile that accompanied the words held a bitter triumph.

"What the devil are you doing here?" His secrets were shattered. He knew that. Yet there was a relief in having it known. Over and done with.

He took a step forward, and so intent was he on the confrontation before him that he did not hear the whisper of movement behind him until the thin blade of Toledo steel slipped between his ribs and into his heart.

1

April 1807

It was raining. It had been doing so, Jack thought in disgust, ever since he set foot in this benighted land. Sometimes the water fell in slanted sheets, lashing him like bits of iron; other times, it subsided into a steady, miserable drizzle. But even when the rain stopped briefly, mist still hung over everything, as if the very air were so laden with moisture it could not hold it.

A cold drop of water slid between cloth and skin, trickling down his back, and Jack turned up the collar of his greatcoat as he gazed out across the bleak landscape. The road — if this rutted, narrow path could be termed that — cut across thick mats of heather and disappeared into the distance. There were few trees between him and the gray curtain of mist, only the brown and green land and a few scrubby bushes. Off to his right, a trench had been dug into the

11

ground, exposing a straight wall of black earth. Rocks of all sizes dotted the lumpy, irregular ground, adding to the image of desolation.

What had possessed him to come to Scotland?

He had asked himself that question last night as he'd lain on the thin straw mattress in the grim little inn in Kinclannoch — indeed he'd asked it almost nightly for the past week, and had still not come up with a satisfactory answer. There was no reason to see the house that was now his or to talk to the people who worked on the estate. His only desire was to sell the place, which fortune had dropped in his lap like an overripe plum. Whatever little tickle of proprietary instinct had made him want to see it, whatever odd pull he'd felt at the thought of being a landed gentleman, the truth was his impulsive journey up here to claim the estate made him as big a fool as the bird-witted Scotsman who had wagered his home on the turn of a card.

Still, it made even less sense to turn back now, when he had drawn so close to his destination. If he had understood the innkeeper's thick brogue, the house could not be much farther.

His horse whickered and shifted as a gust

of wind whipped through them, driving the rain into Jack's face and nearly taking his hat with it. He grabbed the once elegant, now sodden hat, jamming it more firmly down on his head, and leaned over to stroke a soothing hand down the horse's neck. "Steady on, Pharaoh."

Now, blown by the wind, the mist receded, and he could see the narrow loch and, at last, the house. It lay on a shelf of rock beside the water, a long, straight line of stone unbroken by curve or ornamentation. As gray and dreary as the loch and the sky above it, the house might have been formed out of this bleak landscape itself.

Baillannan.

If Jack had harbored some hope that the sight of his new home would lighten his mood, he knew now he was doomed to disappointment. Nothing could have looked less welcoming. Suppressing a sigh, he dug in his heels and started forward.

Isobel was carefully pulling out the last few stitches in her embroidery when her aunt startled her by exclaiming, "We have a visitor! How nice! Barbara, did you know someone was coming?"

"Isobel," she corrected automatically, and her aunt nodded vaguely.

13

"Yes, dear, of course."

"Who is it?" Isobel set aside her needlework and stood up, suddenly hopeful. "Is it Andrew?"

Aunt Elizabeth squinted down at the courtyard below. "I don't think it's anyone I recognize."

"A stranger?" Isobel joined her aunt at the window, but their visitor had already disappeared, and she saw nothing but the groom leading off an unfamiliar bay horse.

"He looked soaked, poor man," Elizabeth went on sympathetically. "Perhaps he's a traveler seeking shelter from the rain."

"A traveler to where?" Isobel asked pragmatically. "It's my guess he's gone astray. No doubt Hamish will set him straight."

"It would have been nice to have a visitor," her aunt said wistfully. "So many people have left, one hardly sees anyone anymore."

"Yes, since the Clearances began, our closest neighbors are now sheep," Isobel agreed tartly.

"The MacKenzies would not have sold if Ronald was still alive. Poor Agnes; she will not enjoy living in Edinburgh, however much her son may have profited."

Agnes MacKenzie had been Elizabeth's closest friend, and Isobel's aunt had been lonely with her gone. Isobel could not help but feel that the loss had affected Aunt Elizabeth's mind as well as her spirits; she had grown more forgetful the last few months.

Isobel murmured a vague agreement, not wanting to set her aunt off on that unpleasant path. She returned to the sofa and picked up her embroidery hoop, saying, "I fear I've made a shambles of my stitches. What do you think I should do?"

Elizabeth was distracted by Isobel's plea for help, and she started toward her niece. But she had scarcely taken a step when the quiet was interrupted by the sound of a voice rising in agitation downstairs. Surprised, both women glanced toward the door. A moment later, there was the clatter of feet on the stairs, and one of the maids burst into the room.

"Miss Isobel!" The girl's face was flushed and her voice trembled with excitement. "Hamish says come quick. There's a man here, claiming Baillannan is his!"

"What?" Isobel stared at the girl. Her words were so absurd that Isobel thought she must not have heard the maid correctly.

"A man, miss, at the door. An Englishman. He says he owns Baillannan. Then Hamish says he maun be daft, but the man says, 'Nae, it's mine,' and shows him a paper, and Hamish sends me to fetch you."

"Isobel . . ." Aunt Elizabeth turned toward her, frowning. "I don't understand. An Englishman, here? Who is he? What does he mean?"

"I have no idea. It's nonsense, of course." Isobel started toward the hall. "Don't worry, Auntie, I will straighten it out."

At the foot of the staircase Isobel was met by the sight of Hamish, the man who had been the Rose family butler all her life, standing, arms crossed, as if he would bar the man from the stairs physically. His weathered face, usually set in stoic, even grim, lines, was red as a beet, bushy brows drawn together, dark eyes glittering with dislike.

Opposite him stood a stranger, tall and dark-haired, his face creased in frustration. He would have been a handsome man, she thought, if he had not been soaked to the skin, his cravat a soggy lump around his neck, starched collar points utterly wilted, and his fine wool jacket stretched out of shape by the weight of the water it had absorbed. He held a waterlogged hat in one hand and a many-caped, gray greatcoat hung over the same arm, both of them puddling water on the stone floor beneath him. His boots were caked with mud, and between the sides of his open jacket, his wet shirt clung to his chest. It was made of fine lawn and the water had turned it almost transparent, so that she could see every line and curve of his chest and stomach. As she watched, he reached up and shoved the mop of hair back from his face, stripping water from it. His hair was thick, and slicked back as it now was, it left his face in sharp relief, emphasizing the square set of his jaw and the high slant of his cheekbones. An errant drop of water trickled from his temple, sliding down his cheek and curving over his jaw to disappear in the cloth of his cravat.

Isobel realized that she was staring, and she quickly averted her eyes, a faint flush rising in her cheeks. "Hamish? Is there a problem?"

The stranger looked up at her, relief flooding his face, and burst out, "Ma'am! Thank heavens, you speak English."

Isobel raised her brows, her voice faintly amused. "I do indeed, sir. I believe you will find that most of us do."

"Not so I could tell," he responded with a dark look at the butler.

"I canna help it if you dinna understand clear speech." Hamish set his jaw mulishly.

The stranger ignored his retort, addressing his words to Isobel. "If I might be so bold as to introduce myself, I am Jack Kensington, ma'am, at your service." He swept her a polite bow, elegant in spite of his drenched condition.

He was clearly a gentleman, his speech and manners as refined as those of her brother or cousin — perhaps more so — and she suspected that his clothes were equally sophisticated when not soaked by the rain.

Isobel was as intrigued as she was puzzled, and she came down the last few steps and held out her hand to him. "I am Isobel Rose, sir. I'm pleased to make your acquaintance."

Mr. Kensington looked taken aback, but he recovered quickly and took her hand, bending over it politely. "Mrs. Rose. An apt name for such a lovely woman."

"Miss Rose," Isobel corrected him, pulling her hand back. His words were too forward and no doubt meaningless flattery, but she could not deny the lift of pleasure at his compliment.

"Dinna trust him, Miss Isobel," the butler warned, taking a step toward her protectively. "This Englishman is trying to swick you. Or he's daft. He says he owns Baillannan."

"I'm sure his intent is not to swindle us,"

Isobel replied. "Perhaps he has been misled." She turned to Kensington. "I am sorry, sir, but you are mistaken. Baillannan belongs to the Rose family."

"It did," Kensington responded tersely, his courteous manner giving way to irritation. "But it is mine now. I have it from Sir Andrew Rose."

"No!" Isobel stared at him in astonishment. "Andrew would never have sold Baillannan."

"He did not sell it, ma'am. He wagered it on a game of whist. And lost."

"No," she repeated, but the blood drained from her face, and for an instant she thought she might faint. "I don't believe you."

"Then believe this." He shoved a piece of paper into her hand. "It is Sir Andrew's chit."

Isobel stared at the familiar writing, the bold swoop of the *A,* and this time she did have to reach for the newel to stay upright.

"Miss Isobel?" Hamish stepped forward anxiously and took her arm to support her. "What is it? The young laird never —"

"Yes." Isobel kept her gaze on the words, now swimming before her eyes. "I fear he did. 'Tis Andrew's hand. He wagered Baillannan," she finished bitterly.

"I have the deed, as well," the Englishman

added mildly.

"No doubt." Her stomach was roiling. She wanted to scream and shred the note, to toss it back in the stranger's face and tell her men to toss *him* back out into the rain. But she was a Rose, and so she must put iron into her spine. Isobel blinked back her tears — she refused to let him see her cry.

He was holding out the deed to her, and she took it, running her eyes down it as if she were reading it, when in truth she could not take in any of the words, her mind overwhelmed by something close to terror. She had no idea what to do, so she clung to the behavior that one expected from the lady of Baillannan, a stoicism that hid the turmoil inside.

"Welcome to Baillannan, Mr. Kensington," she said tightly as she handed him back the papers, though she could not manage to look him in the face. "Hamish, show Mr. Kensington to a room. I am sure he would like to get dry. And no doubt he would appreciate a cup of tea, as well."

"Miss Izzy!" Hamish went an even deeper shade of red, and his eyes bulged. "You canna mean to give him your home! Your father . . . your grandfather . . ."

"Hamish," Isobel said firmly. "I cannot undo what Andrew has done. Baillannan

20

apparently belongs to Mr. Kensington now."

Hamish set his face mutinously, but finally he bobbed his head. "Aye, miss."

He seized Kensington's coat and hat, grabbed up the satchel at his feet, then went to speak to the servants, shooing them toward the kitchen.

Isobel turned back to their visitor in awkward silence, then rushed to speak. "I apologize that your room is not ready."

"No, no need to apologize. Indeed, I should do so for the shock I have given you. I thought Sir Andrew would have written, but no doubt his letter has not had time to reach you."

"No doubt. If you will excuse me . . ." She gave him as close to a smile as she could muster and turned away.

"No, wait." He followed her to the foot of the staircase. "Please."

Isobel stopped on the stairs and turned reluctantly to face him. He was a step below her, so that his head was level with hers, only inches away. His eyes, she realized, were not black or brown as she had thought, but a dark blue, shadowed by thick black lashes. The odd color, combined with the high slash of his cheekbones, gave his face a faintly exotic look. She found it unsettling.

"Are you — I'm not entirely sure I understood what that fellow said, but it seemed — are you related in some way to Sir Andrew?"

"I am his sister."

"His sister!" His eyes widened. "I'm sorry. Sir Andrew never mentioned . . . I didn't know . . ."

"There is no reason you should." This time she could not manage even an attempt at a smile. Whirling, she ran up the stairs.

"Isobel?" Her aunt stood outside the door of the sitting room, looking a trifle lost.

Isobel pulled up short, barely suppressing a groan. Aunt Elizabeth's memory had been growing hazier the last few months, and Isobel had found that any unexpected occurrence tended to make her condition worse. But Isobel was not sure she could explain the situation calmly when she felt as if she might shatter into a storm of tears herself.

"Isobel, who was that man? Was he talking about Andrew?" Her aunt's face brightened. "Is Andrew here?"

"No. Andrew is in London. Or at least I suppose he is, since he has not bothered to write."

"He is so careless that way." Aunt Elizabeth smiled indulgently. "Of course, young men have better things to do than write home."

"He might have thought of something besides himself for once."

"Isobel? Are you angry with Andrew?"

"Yes, I am." She added, softening her tone, "A bit." She couldn't give in to her feelings in front of Elizabeth.

"But why was Hamish upset? Who is that man?"

"He knows Andrew. I — he is staying here for a time."

"Oh. How nice — a visitor. He was quite a handsome young man, I thought." Elizabeth's eyes gleamed speculatively, and for a moment she seemed like her old self. "It will be good for you to have someone your own age here."

"Don't." Isobel felt as if she might choke. "Please, don't try to matchmake. It's impossible."

"Nonsense. Now come in and sit down and tell me all about him."

"I cannot." Isobel pulled away, ignoring the faint hurt in her aunt's eyes. "I will come back later and tell you everything I know. But right now I must go. I — I have to fetch something. From Meg."

Her aunt frowned. "Meg?"

"Meg Munro, Auntie; you know Meg. Coll's sister. Their mother Janet was Andy's wet nurse."

"Of course I know Meg."

The vagueness in Elizabeth's gray eyes made Isobel doubt her aunt's words. I cannot bear it, she thought.

"I must go," she repeated, and fled down the hall without looking back.

Inside her bedroom, Isobel closed the door and sagged against it. She wasn't sure how she had gotten through it without breaking down. Her knees were jelly, her hands trembling. She heard the sound of footsteps and voices in the hall outside her door as Hamish and the Englishman walked past, a bitter reminder that her home was gone.

Not just the house she had grown up in, but the loch, the earth, the rocks and caves, every inch of this land and its wild, harsh beauty. Her very life was tumbling down around her, ripped away by her young brother's folly. Even her beloved aunt was being taken from her bit by bit each day, her mind retreating.

She could not hold back a sob. Grabbing up her cloak, she ran from the room, tearing down the stairs and out into the yard as if pursued by devils.

2

Jack looked around the unprepossessing bedchamber. The room to which Hamish had led him was large, he would give it that — large and cold and sparsely furnished. At the far end was an unlit fireplace. A massive wardrobe loomed against the wall opposite, its dark walnut and plain lines at odds with the decoratively carved oaken bed's delicate — indeed, one could call them spindly — posts. A few more lumps of furniture were hidden under covers, and a faint but distinctly unpleasant odor hung in the air.

Hamish dropped Jack's bag unceremoniously on the floor beside the bed, muttering something beneath his breath. Could this growling gnome of a man really be the butler? Jack did not expect a butler to be friendly, for they could be chilling in their courtesy, but he had never encountered another so surly or so lacking in dignity.

"I take it this room has not been occupied

in a while," Jack commented, and the butler cast an unfriendly glance his way.

"We wurnae expecting ye." Hamish's accent, if possible, seemed even thicker than it had before.

Jack peeled off his sodden jacket and began to unknot his equally wet neckcloth. He wondered if the estate was in as bad a shape as the state of this room suggested. He did not know Sir Andrew well, but the lad had always sported plenty of blunt, a bird of paradise on his arm, the wine flowing freely, as he gambled away the night.

Hamish ripped the covers from the one set of windows, sending dust flying and revealing velvet curtains that might once have been dark green or blue or perhaps even red. Their nap was worn so thin that in spots the afternoon light, weak as it was, glowed through the material. Hamish shoved the draperies open, alleviating the gloom somewhat, then clumped about the room, yanking off the rest of the covers.

"Will ye be wanting anything else?" The butler gave Jack a look that was more challenge than inquiry.

"I believe a fire in the grate might be appropriate," Jack snapped, nettled. "And what the devil is that smell?"

"Smell?" The butler gazed at him blankly.

"I widna know, sir. The sheuch, mebbe, below."

Jack felt sure his own expression was now as lacking in comprehension as the other man's. Did these people not speak English? "The what?"

"The sheuch." The butler made a careless gesture toward the window. "A lass will be in to licht the fire for ye. Dinner's at acht."

Jack was unsure whether all Scots were this unintelligible or Hamish was simply determined to be difficult, but in either case Jack was not about to give the butler the satisfaction of asking for clarification. Jack nodded briefly in dismissal, ignoring the glint of animosity in the man's eyes.

Jack had barely finished pulling on a set of clean and blessedly dry clothes when there was a soft tap on the door, and at his response, a maid entered, carrying a hod of coal. Shooting him a sullen glance even as she bobbed a curtsy, she set about laying coal in the fireplace and lighting it. Jack strolled to the window.

The vista before him was enough to make him wish the fog had not lifted. In the distance he could see a green swell of land strewn with boulders and what seemed to be a building that had fallen into a jumble of stones. Closer to the house a large, muddy yard led to outbuildings of various sizes, as well as some wooden pens. Directly beneath his window was a ditch. This, he surmised, was the "sheuch" Hamish had mentioned as the source of the malodorous scent in the room.

Behind him, the maid uttered a little squeak, and Jack swung around to see black smoke billowing into the room from the fireplace. The girl, coughing, hastened to pull the handle of the flue, and Jack swung back to the window. The ancient catch stuck, but after a few moments of struggle, it screeched open, and he shoved up the window.

The smoke wafted out, but the odor from outside increased, mingling with the smell of the smoke to render the room even more wretched. Muttering a curse, Jack left the room. If he had not already been planning to sell Baillannan, this day would have convinced him to do so. He stalked down the corridor, no purpose in his movement, just an itching need to get away. Every door along the way was shut, and the only noise was the sound of his own footsteps, imbuing the place with an eerie emptiness.

The corridor ended at the long main hallway, and he stopped before the set of double windows, contemplating his folly in coming here. These windows looked out over the side yard, a slightly more pleasant prospect than the drainage ditch behind his own bedchamber. As he watched, a woman emerged from the house. She wore a cloak, the hood shoved back since it was no longer raining, and the light caught the dark blond of her hair. It was Isobel Rose. He straightened and leaned forward. Miss Rose intrigued him.

It seemed absurd that such a beauty should be languishing away in this godforsaken spot. But it was more than her creamy-white skin and thick, honey-colored hair that drew him, something that went beyond the swift, strong tug of lust he'd felt when he'd looked up and seen her standing above him on the stairs. He would have expected tears, even hysteria, from any woman who'd received the blow she'd been dealt. Astonishment had lit her face, followed an instant later by a fierce flash of anger, then fear, in those deep-gray eyes, but she had reined her emotions in, settling her expression into one of studied calm. She did not hide her feelings, a talent Jack himself was well acquainted with, but she exercised a strength of will, a control, that interested him. He could not help but wonder what it would take to shatter that control. And whether any man had ever been able to do so.

As he watched Isobel, he saw a tall, blond man striding toward her across the yard. She hesitated for an instant before she continued toward the man, her steps slower. Reaching up, she ran her hand across her cheeks, and Jack suspected with a pang of compunction that she was wiping away tears.

He frowned, irritated by his reaction. He was no gentleman, no man of sensibility or refinement. No matter how much he might appear to be one, it was mere trappings — all clothes and speech and manner, learned at the feet of an adventurer with a heart as cold as stone. Sutton Kensington had never shown an ounce of compassion for the victims of his swindles, and he would have scorned any such feeling of pity in his son. Even though Jack had escaped both the man and his schemes, he knew that he remained, like his father, merely a carefully crafted shell of a gentleman. He had no inbred code of honor, no inclination toward pity. He was not a man to be afflicted with guilt.

Besides, he had no reason to feel guilty, he reminded himself. It was not *his* fault the woman had lost her home. He had not cheated her brother; he had won fairly. If

Jack had not accepted Baillannan as payment, it would only mean that Sir Andrew would have lost it at some later time.

The devil take the man! What had the fool been thinking, tossing his home into a wager as if it were a mere bagatelle? Until Jack saw the house, he had assumed it was Sir Andrew's lodge, a place where he retreated to hunt or fish or have a bit of quiet — though, Lord knows, Jack could not envision that young wastrel doing any of those. Jack had not realized Baillannan was Rose's ancestral estate. Even less had he imagined that he would be turning a young woman out of her home.

Shaking the thought from his mind in irritation, he watched the couple in the yard below. They were deep in conversation, the man bending solicitously over Miss Rose. Who was the fellow and what was he to her? He was dressed in the plain, rough trousers and shirt of a worker, not the clothes of a gentleman, so he could not be a suitor. But a closeness in their pose denoted familiarity, even affection, and tenderness was in the man's face as he gazed down at her. Could the lovely and genteel Miss Rose have taken a plebeian lover?

He should have found the thought amusing, but somehow it only added to his an-

31

noyance, and he turned away from the window with an impatient gesture, glaring down the long, inhospitable hallway. This damnable place! The belligerent servants . . . the unpleasant room . . . the wet, bleak landscape. There was nothing here to please the eye or lighten the spirit.

Worst of all, it seemed he could not get rid of the image of Isobel Rose, her face paling, her eyes stark, when he'd told her that her home was no longer hers.

Isobel rushed out the side door, her cloak billowing around her. Her cheeks were wet with tears, and she brushed them aside impatiently as she strode toward the loch — and the comfort that the still, gray water always brought. She had taken only a few steps before she saw Coll Munro coming toward her, his face drawn into a black scowl. Well, at least she would not have to put up a brave front with Coll.

"Izzy!" In a sign of Coll's own agitation, he called her a childhood nickname rather than the formal "Miss Isobel" that he deemed appropriate for their stations now. He had come out without his jacket or cap, and his shaggy blond hair was wind tossed, his cheeks flushed. She wasn't sure whether the cold had put the red in his cheeks or anger, for his square jaw was pugnaciously set and his blue eyes were bright, as if he'd been lit from within. "Where is the blackguard? I'll throw him out."

"No." Isobel shook her head, but she felt warmed by his anger on her account. She could always count on Coll. "There is no use."

"What do you mean, no use? Katie said some Sassenach scoundrel was claiming to own Baillannan." Coll half turned as though he were about to go on to the house.

"It's not just a claim." She put her hand on his arm. "It's real. He owns it."

"What? How could that be? You're not making sense, lass." Coll bent toward her, his anger turning to a gentler concern.

"Andrew gave it to him!" she burst out. "He wagered Baillannan and lost."

Her words effectively silenced Coll, who could do no more than gape at her. Finally he said, "Can he do that? Surely it has to stay in the Rose family."

"Baillannan is not entailed; Papa left it to Andrew freehold. He had no way of knowing that Andrew would turn out to be so feckless. The estate was Andrew's, free and clear; he could bequeath it or sell it or do whatever he wished, including throwing it all away on a hand of cards!"

Her voice broke on the last words.

"That fool! That stupid, selfish bastard —" Coll broke off and swung away, slamming his fist into his palm. He cursed, his voice low and vicious, and Isobel was glad he had spared her the names he was calling her brother — though, frankly, at the moment, she would have liked to say some of the same things to Andrew. "I dinna think he would do something like this," Coll went on, in his emotion his voice slipping deeper into a soft burr. "I should have made him stay here last time. . . ."

"How would you have done that? Locked him in his room? Tied him down? He's a grown man now, Coll, not some lad off at school, having a lark. He's not green as grass in his first year in London. He is twenty-five years old. And he still can think of nothing but drinking and gambling!" She could not hold back her bitter words; they tumbled out of her, too long denied and pent up.

"I should have knocked some sense into him," Coll growled.

"I'm not sure that is possible." She sighed, her outburst draining her anger and leaving her weary. "He came into his inheritance too young, only seventeen when our father died, and Cousin Robert was so strict a guardian, kept him on too short a leash. It was no wonder he kicked over the traces when he turned twenty-one. I told myself he would get tired of spending his days in idleness, that he would have his fling, then settle down. That he'd come back home and be the Laird of Baillannan."

Coll let out a snort. "You are more the laird than Andy'll ever be."

Isobel gave him a faint smile. "I did not say mine was a realistic hope." The flash of humor left her face. "Oh, Coll! How could Andy have so little care for Baillannan? The land and the people and our family. It's his inheritance!"

"How could he have so little thought for you, I'd say!" Coll flared.

"It's not just me," Isobel reminded him softly.

"Aye, I know." He let out a weary sigh. " 'Tis your aunt and the servants and all the crofters, too. Baillannan will be like Duncally and the others — they'll throw the crofters out of their homes. No doubt this Englishman will bring in a steward like MacRae, as the earl did."

"I heard one of MacRae's men was tossed in Ferguson's lochan two days ago." Isobel studied her friend's face.

"So I heard." Amusement lit his eyes. "It's

said he decided to go back to Edinburgh."

"Coll, have a care."

"You know me. I am a cautious man."

His words pulled a chuckle from her. "Indeed. I am well aware of the kind of caution you exercise. I've seen you swinging down into some cave you've discovered, nothing but a light and a rope and a prayer." She sobered. "I know you hate the Clearances; I do, too. I cannot bear that so many families are losing their homes. But these men who are fighting the landlords will go to gaol if they are caught. Promise me you won't do anything rash. I worry about you."

"And I appreciate that." Neatly sidestepping her entreaty, he went on, "But right now, you are the one we must worry about. Are you sure this Englishman is telling the truth? He really holds title to Baillannan?"

"He showed me the note of hand Andrew had given him. It was Andrew's writing. He has the deed, as well."

"What will you do? You know I will help you in whatever way you want. And my sister will, as well; that goes without saying."

"I know." Isobel smiled faintly. "You are a true friend, you and Meg both. But what can I do except take Aunt Elizabeth and leave Baillannan?"

"You should not have to go anywhere. This is your home. Come, Isobel, this isn't like you. Would you not fight for Baillannan?"

"Of course I would!" Isobel planted her hands on her hips and glared up at him. "How can you say such a thing?"

"Ah, there's the Isobel I know." His mouth quirked up at the corner. "You always were a fighter — just quieter about it than Meg."

She grimaced at him. "You needn't insult me to get my dander up. Of course I'm angry. I would fight to the end if I had the slightest idea how."

"Och, lass, I have faith in you. You'll think of some way around this scoundrel."

"I don't know that he's a scoundrel. He seemed a gentleman — quite pleasant, really. It was clear that he was surprised to find he would have to turn Andrew's sister out on the streets."

"And would a 'pleasant' gentleman let a callow lad like Andy wager his home on a hand of whist? Whether he knew of your presence here or not, anyone could see that Andrew is a plum ripe for the taking. A real gentleman would not take advantage of that."

"No. You are right. A man of conscience would not. No matter how much Andrew believes he is awake on every suit, in truth he would be easy prey for any sharp. Perhaps Mr. Kensington even fuzzed the cards to ensure the outcome. I cannot help but be suspicious, but it matters not. I've no way of knowing that and even less of proving it." She paused, thinking. "Still . . . I did give in too easily. I was so shocked I could scarcely even read what he showed me." She squared her shoulders, determination settling on her face. "I cannot just run. I must do what I can to fight this. I shall demand to see Andrew's vowel again. Perhaps I missed something. And . . . I can delay. It will take some time, after all, to make arrangements to leave. In the meanwhile, I shall write Papa's solicitor in Inverness for advice. Perhaps I can come up with some way to thwart Mr. Kensington."

"You will. I am sure of it." Coll took her hand in his own work-scarred one and gave it an encouraging squeeze. "And remember what Ma always told you: 'You worry too much, wee one. Dinna fash yourself.' "

" 'It will all be better come the morn,' " Isobel said, supplying the rest of Janet Munro's admonition. "I know. I only hope she's right."

"Ma was never wrong, don't you remember?"

Isobel smiled. "Thank you. I must go back and explain all this to Aunt Elizabeth. No doubt she is worrying herself sick."

"Go." Coll pressed her hand again, then released it. "And remember — I'm here if you need me."

"Thank you." Isobel walked back to the house, planning the best way to tell her aunt. As she entered the side door and started toward the stairs, however, she heard a sound from the direction of the drawing room. She paused, casting a glance upstairs, then turned and walked down the hall to the drawing room.

Jack Kensington was inside, standing before the fireplace, his hands outstretched toward the flames. He turned at the sound of her steps and smiled. "Miss Rose. It's a pleasure to see you again. Pray join me."

"I trust you are settled in," Isobel began formally, ignoring the odd little flip inside her at the sight of his smile.

"Yes. But I could see that it would take some time for the fire to overcome the chill, so I came downstairs." He cast a glance toward the huge stone fireplace behind him. "This seemed ample warmth."

"Yes. One would think they were accustomed to roasting an ox here," Isobel said lightly as she walked over to join him.

"My ancestors tended to build on a grand scale."

"I can see that. But 'tis lovely." He gestured toward the carved rosettes that adorned the mantel and marble surrounds.

"Yes, they were enamored with their own name as well." Kensington was absurdly easy to talk to; she had to remind herself that he was not in any way her friend. His charm was too easy, too practiced to be real, and the warmth of his smile did not change the cool calculation in his eyes. Beneath his pleasant manner lived the cold, hard man who had taken advantage of her brother's foolishness.

Isobel stiffened her spine and tried to recapture her formal tone. "Mr. Kensington . . . I should like to take another look at the papers you showed me earlier. I fear I was too taken aback to give them a sufficient perusal."

He studied her for a moment, his handsome face unreadable. It was no surprise that he was adept at card games. Unlike her brother, whose every emotion and thought showed on his face, Jack Kensington gave away nothing. "Of course." He reached into an inner pocket of his coat and withdrew the folded papers, extending them to her. "I think you will still find that they are quite in order."

Isobel took the documents, unfolding them, and was struck with despair at the familiarity of her brother's handwriting. She had made no mistake. The flourish of the *A* in his signature, the bold, careless stroke of the pen, the misspelling of *their* as Andrew always did — it was his hand. Still, she read through the transfer of deed as well and the repetition of her brother's signature.

"Yes. I see." She lifted her head, keeping her gaze flat and even. "Still, I should like my solicitor to go over the papers."

"Of course. Whenever he wishes." He lifted the documents from her cold fingers, refolding them and settling them back in his pocket.

"How could you?" Isobel snapped, stung by the indifference of his manner. "How could you have taken advantage of a naive, foolish boy like that?"

"Foolish?" His eyebrows rose fractionally. "I will grant you Sir Andrew is that. But he is a man, I think, not a boy, and far from naive. I fear you see him through a sister's fond eyes."

"I see my brother quite clearly," Isobel retorted. "I realize that it takes little to lead him into gambling."

41

"I did not *lead* him anywhere." For the first time, a touch of asperity was in Jack's well-modulated voice. "He was already deep into play before I joined the game."

"And you saw that he was ready for the fleecing?"

"If you are accusing me of cheating your brother, Miss Rose, I can assure you that I did not." Unlike Isobel's voice, flaring with heat, Kensington's was cold as a winter's night. "Sir Andrew is an inept cardplayer, and he amplifies his poor play by being convinced that he is quite clever at it. It is a common failing among the young blades of London. I won Baillannan fairly, and the fault for dispossessing you from your home lies squarely with Sir Andrew."

Isobel clenched her fists, and her cheeks flamed with color. She wanted to rage, to fly at this man with her fists, but years of courtesy — and the truth of his statement — kept her still. She swallowed hard against the anger clogging her throat, reminding herself that she could not afford to antagonize this man. At the moment she was too furious to care if he tossed her out the door, but she had to think of her aunt. "I beg your pardon. You are right, of course. I should not blame you for my brother's failings. Pray excuse me. I must go inform my aunt."

"Your aunt? There is another —"

"Yes, Aunt Elizabeth lives at Baillannan as well. No doubt you will meet her tonight at supper." Isobel could not bear to stay here and discuss her deplorable situation any further. Giving him an abrupt nod, she turned and strode from the room.

She was in too ill a humor to speak with her aunt, but neither could she just walk past the sitting room where Elizabeth sat, so she turned in to the room, forcing her face into more pleasant lines.

"Isobel!" Aunt Elizabeth looked up, relieved. "Dearest, what is happening? I saw a strange man just now walking down the hall. Who is he? Do I — I don't know him, do I?"

"No, Auntie, you've never met him. He is the man who arrived earlier this afternoon."

"Oh, yes, of course. The friend of Andrew's. What was his name?"

"Kensington. Jack Kensington."

"Not a Scotsman, then."

"No. He is English."

"Ah, well, I am sure he is quite nice anyway."

"Aunt Elizabeth . . . he is not a friend of Andrew's. He met him at a club. A gambling den. He — Andrew wagered Baillannan,

43

and he lost. Mr. Kensington owns our home now."

Her aunt said nothing, merely stared at her in white-faced shock. After a long moment, she said, "Oh." She looked away, her hands knotting in her lap. "Oh, dear. I . . . I cannot think quite what to do."

"For the moment we are doing nothing. I will ask Mr. Kensington for leave to stay here a time so that we can get our things together." Isobel debated whether she should tell her aunt of her plans to write their solicitor. Would it be worse to get her aunt's hopes up or to leave her worrying? Finally, she went on, "Do not trouble yourself over this. I will find a way, work it out somehow. We will be all right."

"Of course you will, dear." Elizabeth gave her a wan smile. "Poor Andrew. He must be heartsick over this."

"He should be," Isobel snapped. "Since he threw away our home on a card game."

"I am sure he did not mean to lose it. He has always been too impulsive."

"Unthinking is more like it. Or uncaring." Isobel drew in a calming breath. It would do her aunt no good to see Isobel's distress — or to hear criticism of her beloved nephew.

"Don't worry." Aunt Elizabeth reached

out to take her hand. "We will come about. I am sure of it. You have always been a clever girl. God does not close one door without opening another." She smiled.

"Well, I wish I knew where it was."

"We shall just have to put our minds to it." Elizabeth glanced toward the clock. "Oh, my, 'tis getting late. We must get dressed for dinner. We should look our best, you know, to face Mr. — what did you say his name was, dear?"

"Kensington, Auntie. Mr. Kensington."

"A very nice name." Her aunt rose, then said softly, "I wish your father were still here. John always knew just what to do."

"I wish he were, too, Auntie." Isobel squeezed her aunt, her heart aching at the sight of tears welling in her aunt's eyes. "But you are right. We will come about."

Isobel was late going down to supper, having spent several minutes composing a note to her father's lawyer — and another few minutes giving in to the tears that had been threatening to overwhelm her ever since Mr. Kensington's arrival. She changed into a more formal evening dress, draping her best shawl over her arms against the chill, but she did not waste time trying to improve her appearance as her aunt had suggested. She could not imagine Mr. Kensington would be any more amenable if she looked prettier, and she was not about to try to charm the man who was taking away her home.

Her stomach was a nest of nerves as she hurried to the dining room. She found herself growing increasingly on edge in social situations with her aunt, for she had to be on alert to smooth over any mistakes Elizabeth might make, and tonight would be even worse, for Isobel could not bear to have this strange man witness her aunt's confusion or distress. And the strained, even antagonistic conversation between her and Kensington this afternoon could make polite dinner conversation awkward.

When she stepped into the dining room, she saw with a sinking heart that both Kensington and her aunt were already there. She could only hope that Elizabeth had not said anything untoward. Isobel sneaked a look at Kensington as she took her seat, but she could see nothing in his face to indicate his mood. Her insides clenched even tighter.

"My, don't you look lovely, dear." Elizabeth smiled at Isobel. "Don't you agree, Mr. Kensington?"

"Indeed, Miss Rose. Your niece is a vision well worth waiting for." His compliment was swift and practiced, as was the smile he aimed at Elizabeth. "Of course, it is clear that beauty runs in the family."

Her aunt's cheeks flushed at the compliment, and Isobel realized, startled, that Aunt Elizabeth was actually enjoying her conversation with Kensington. Isobel could not help but wonder if Elizabeth had truly understood what Isobel had said to her earlier.

"Mr. Kensington and I have been having a lovely talk," Elizabeth told her niece. "One forgets how pleasant it is to have visitors. Did you know that this is Mr. Kensington's first trip to Scotland? You should show him around the estate tomorrow, Isobel."

"Um, yes, of course." Isobel affixed a courteous smile to her face. "If Mr. Kensington would like that." She glanced toward him, sure that he would turn down the offer. He must find it strange that Aunt Elizabeth was talking as if he were a guest in his house.

"Indeed, I should be most grateful." Kensington smiled affably. Obviously he felt none of Isobel's unease after their confrontation.

"When you see some of the beauty Baillannan has to offer, Mr. Kensington," Elizabeth said almost coquettishly, "perhaps you will decide not to depart so quickly."

"You are leaving?" Isobel's heart lifted in hope. Maybe the man would simply go away. He clearly had no liking for the place. A new thought struck her. What if she could convince him that she could maintain the estate, sending him the profit? After all, that was essentially what she had been doing for Andrew all these years. It would not be her home any longer, but at least she would not have to uproot her aunt. Her mind worked feverishly as the other two continued to talk.

"Yes." Kensington nodded. "My intent was merely to see Baillannan and return to London."

"Of course, perhaps you are married and have a wife to whom you wish to return posthaste," Elizabeth went on, her tone studiedly casual. Isobel's eyes widened in alarm. Surely her aunt was not still bent on matchmaking?

"No, Miss Rose, I am not married," Kensington replied politely. "I fear it is a state for which I am not destined; I have never been romantically inclined."

"You must not give up hope," Elizabeth told him as though he had expressed regret about his marital state. "You will find the right woman. I am sure of it." Their guest seemed to have no answer for that, and Elizabeth continued to chatter. "No doubt there are other things in London that draw you back. I know the city holds a great allure for young men." Elizabeth sighed. "Sadly, Andrew never stays long with us, either. It is too bad of him not to accompany you on your journey here. I shall have to scold him in my next letter."

Kensington looked nonplussed at this remark, and Isobel hastened to smooth over her aunt's words. "Yes, Andrew would have done better to have introduced you to us and explained the situation. It would have been much easier all around, I am sure."

"No doubt he was distraught," Jack replied drily.

"Distraught?" Aunt Elizabeth frowned. "Is Andy in some scrape at school again? Are you at Christ's College as well, Mr. Kensington? Or perhaps you are one of Andrew's tutors?"

To Kensington's credit, he did not turn a hair at Aunt Elizabeth's odd statement, but simply said, "No, Miss Rose, I was an Oxford man myself. I met Sir Andrew in London."

"Andrew isn't in school anymore, Aunt Elizabeth," Isobel reminded her gently. "You remember, he is in London now."

"Yes, of course. How foolish of me." Elizabeth gave an embarrassed laugh. "You must forgive me, Mr. Kensington. I sometimes forget how grown-up our Andrew is."

"Easily understood, Miss Rose. Sir Andrew is still quite young."

"So true." Elizabeth smiled at him, the faint confusion clearing from her expression.

Isobel could not help but warm a little to the man for the easy way he responded to her aunt. She steered the conversation back to a safe path. "It is a shame you have had such a rude introduction to our Highland weather, Mr. Kensington."

Kensington followed her lead, and they made it through the meal by touching on London, Edinburgh, and the state of the roadways, as well as the rain. Still, it was nerve-racking picking a delicate way through the conversational pitfalls, avoiding anything that would highlight her aunt's failing memory or their coming homeless state at the hands of Mr. Kensington. It did not help matters that supper consisted mostly of a strangely tasteless and watery mutton stew, along with a wedge of haggis, which Kensington gave a dubious look and set aside without tasting.

When supper finally ended and the women rose to leave Mr. Kensington to his post-meal port, Isobel hung back for a moment after her aunt left the room. She had planned what she would say. But Kensington's announcement at the beginning of the meal that he would soon be leaving Baillannan had changed the situation — or had at least changed her view of it. Now, as he stood politely, gazing at her with those oddly dark blue eyes, his brows raised the faintest bit in inquiry, she felt tongue-tied and awkward.

"I wanted to ask you," she began at last. "That is, when you said that you were returning to London, do you not mean to live at Baillannan?"

"No." He looked at her as if she had suggested he might live on the moon. "Of course not. I merely wanted — well, I'm not sure what. To see the place, I suppose."

"Then you will need someone to manage the estate for you, as I have the past several years for Andrew. Someone experienced and trustworthy." She laid the groundwork for her appeal, knowing how difficult it would be to convince him that a woman could do the job.

"No, wait." Kensington held out his hand as if to stop her. "If you are leading up to suggesting a man you think would suit the position, I must tell you that I won't need a

51

manager. I intend to sell Baillannan."

"Oh." Her stomach dropped. "I see."

"I am a city dweller, Miss Rose. And I find the trip a trifle long to visit with any frequency."

"I see." It was hopeless, obviously, but she made another push. "If you kept Baillannan, the estate would provide you with income."

"Scarcely as much as one would receive in a sale. And while I am sure that this friend of yours is an admirable person, there is the uncertainty that comes with letting another handle one's accounts."

"Of course." Isobel nodded, the brief spark of hope extinguished. She took a breath and began again. "I wanted to ask you . . . if you would be so kind . . . that is, I must make arrangements for my aunt and me to move. And the house is so, well, there are so many family things that I am sure you would wish me to remove. I fear it will take me a few days to get it all in order. I hoped — I would ask you the favor of remaining here until I have it settled."

"Naturally. Please, take as much time as you need." He took a step toward her, then stopped and, with an awkwardness she had not seen before in him, said, "Miss Rose . . . I assure you, I did not know — that is, it was never my intent to turn you out of your home. I am truly sorry."

"Yes." Isobel forced a smile. "So am I."

3

Jack Kensington stared down at the meal laid out before him. The gray porridge in the large bowl was so thick he was sure it could have been used for glue. The plate beside it was loaded with several meats and two fried eggs, leaking their yellow yolks in an unappetizing way. The meats were fried, as well. One he recognized as the kind of indigestible-looking dark wedge he had avoided at supper the evening before — indeed, it could have been the same one, for all he knew. The other meat was in the shape of a sausage and had the color and consistency of a piece of charcoal. A smaller plate held a flat, roundish bread product.

He had better leave here soon or he might starve to death. Deciding that the bread appeared the only thing remotely palatable, he tore off a piece and found that it snapped in his hand like wood. Putting it in his mouth, he tentatively began to chew. Somewhat to his surprise, the thing did not crack a tooth, but it was bland and unsweetened and seemed to grow larger as he chewed it. He swallowed and washed the lump down with a sip of the bitterly dark tea.

The breakfast matched the rest of his stay so far. The mattress had been thin and the sheets cold, the servants clearly being strangers to a warming pan. The raucous cry of a rooster had jerked him awake, and the twitter of birds combined with the chill had chased away any possibility of further sleep. The maid who had come in to clean out the ashes and start the fire had been as dull witted as the others, and her brogue was equally thick. It had taken her a great deal of time to understand his request for a pitcher of water for the washstand, and when it arrived, it had been as cold as the cup of tea he was now holding.

He saw clearly why Sir Andrew spent all his time in London — although Jack did think it cruel of the man to leave his sister marooned here. The thought of Andrew's sister was the pleasantest one he had had today, so his mind lingered on her as he forced down more bread and tea.

Her control had slipped for a few minutes yesterday afternoon, and he had rather liked watching the light flare in her eyes and her cheeks bloom with angry color — even if she was accusing him of taking advantage of her brother. Last night at the supper table she had regained her calm. She'd been nervous; he could see that in her eyes and the restless movement of her hands as she touched her glass and utensils, but she had been in command of her tongue. With a little effort on his part, she had even smiled, and seeing that had been even more enjoyable than her little spark of anger.

If Isobel's lithe form was clad in a fashionable gown and her rich blond hair done up in a more modern style, she would have ample suitors in the city. Indeed, he would not mind in the least showing her some of the amusements London had to offer . . . and other, more basic, joys as well. It was easy to envision a little dalliance with the lovely Miss Rose to enliven his time in this grim place — though, since she considered him a thorough villain, it would require his best efforts of persuasion. But he enjoyed a challenge.

Less enjoyably, his inner vision of Isobel Rose turned to her face last night, her great gray eyes filled with sadness and loss, and he felt once again a pang of remorse. What had happened to her was not his fault, but he could not but regret that he was the one who had delivered her fate to her.

At that moment, almost as if he had conjured her up, Isobel walked through the door. Jack jumped to his feet, aware of a distinct lift in his spirits. Relief, no doubt, at the prospect of company other than the glowering presence of the butler beside the door.

"Miss Rose." He managed to pull out her chair before Hamish could get there, which gave him a doubtlessly childish pleasure. "How lovely you look." Because his mind had been on it, he continued, "You should come to London with your brother. The gentlemen of the city would be at your feet."

"No doubt — as long as all the gentlemen of the city are as egregious flatterers as you," Isobel retorted, but she gave him an un-forced smile, which pleased him far more than seemed reasonable. Her smile was swift and devoid of artifice, and the small flaw of one slightly crooked eyetooth somehow only lent it even more charm.

Hamish left the room and was back almost immediately with a pot of tea — this one steaming, Jack noted — which he poured into Isobel's cup. Hamish also set down before her a silver tray containing a small pitcher of cream and a bowl of sugar.

"Hamish." Jack tapped his cup. "You may

pour me a fresh cup as well."

The old man lowered his head in a courteous nod — as if he hadn't been glaring at Jack the past ten minutes, the old charlatan — and refilled Jack's cup. This cup of tea was a far cry from the original, confirming Jack's suspicions that the servants were waging a subtle war against him.

"I see you are an early riser, Miss Rose," Jack said conversationally.

"As are you."

"Not normally." He gave her a rueful smile. "I fear I am unused to the noise in the country."

"The noise? I would have thought it just the opposite, that Baillannan would be much more peaceful."

"Mm. Until the birds began their cacophony outside my window at dawn." He was pleased to see that his wry words brought a chuckle out of Isobel this time. And since she was the only person here with whom he could converse, her smile would enliven his days.

"I am unused to greeting the dawn," he went on. "However, it will give us ample time for our tour this morning."

"You want to see Baillannan?" Her eyebrows rose. "I presumed you were merely being polite."

58

"I was. Still, it seems a wise thing to do. And since there is actually a sun in the sky this morning, I thought we should not waste the opportunity."

"Indeed not. I can see you are already learning the ways of the Highlands."

"Of course, you will wish to eat your, um, breakfast first." He cast a look down at his plate.

"Mm." Isobel followed his gaze, then said to Hamish, hovering at her elbow, "I believe I'll just have the porridge and an oatcake."

"Of course, miss." He returned quickly with a bowl of oatmeal, which appeared faintly less like gray sludge than Jack's, and a tray containing pots of preserves and pale butter.

Isobel began to eat with what seemed to Jack an astonishing lack of repulsion. He toyed with his fork, pushing the food around on his plate.

"What *is* this thing?" he asked at last, poking at the wedge of dark matter.

"It's haggis." When he lifted his brows, she explained, "It's made of bits of various meats and . . . other things. My father took his with a bit of whiskey poured over it."

"I feel sure it would improve it."

"I believe that it's an acquired taste." Her eyes danced with amusement.

59

"One wonders why one would wish to acquire it. What of this . . . sausage?"

"Blood pudding."

"That requires no explanation. And this bit of paving tile?" He lifted the hard bread.

"That's oatcake." She laughed, a bright, infectious sound that made him smile in return. "Try spreading butter and jam on it. The oatmeal is better with cream."

"Does all the food here need to be disguised?" But he did as she suggested and slathered the cake with butter and preserves. He would, he thought, need to be far hungrier to take on the porridge, even with cream and sugar added.

"We Scots are a plain folk." Isobel pulled a sober face. "We like plain food."

"Is that what you call it?"

"I will admit that the meal looks a mite . . . um . . ."

"Burned?"

"Except where it's underdone." An impish look brightened her eyes again. "I fear Cook is in a mood."

"Does she have them often? Or only when I appear?"

" 'Tis the first I've seen," Isobel admitted. "Come. Shall we start our walk? I think I am done with breakfast."

"Indeed, I was done with it ten minutes ago."

They left the house, Isobel wrapped in her cloak, though Jack left his greatcoat and hat behind. The coat was still damp from yesterday's drenching and smelled of wet wool. The hat, bought only a fortnight ago at Lock's, was a complete loss. But the sun had burned off much of the damp cold, and he scarcely felt the chill.

He could see the loch, a long, gray strip of water. One path ran down to the water and the thick growth of trees beside it. The other path went up the incline of rocky ground, and Isobel took this one.

"I hope you will not hold it against them," she said as they walked.

"Hold what against whom?"

"The unpalatable food. Hamish's glares. I know it is not pleasant, but they are good, loyal people. I would ask you to give them time to get used to the change. That you will not turn them out. Baillannan is their home as much as it is mine. I have known them since I was a child, and their resentment is all on my behalf."

"I can hardly blame them; I would choose you over a usurper, as well." He cast her a sideways grin. "In any case, I shall not be here long enough to warrant any change in staff. I cannot, however, speak for whoever buys the estate."

"No. Of course not." He could hear the disappointment in her voice, and the sound tugged at him.

Last night she had obviously hoped he would set someone to manage the place — perhaps the man with whom he had seen her talking yesterday afternoon. He wondered again what the fellow was to her. Maybe she planned to marry the man and she hoped to hold on to her home at least that much. Perhaps that was the purpose of this little jaunt, to win him over, manipulate him into doing as she wanted.

Irritated at the thought, he looked away. They had reached the crest of the ridge, and spread before them was the wide panorama of the entire loch and the rolling land beyond, the muted colors of green and blue and brown all washed in pale golden sunlight. He drew in a sharp, unconscious breath.

"It's beautiful, isn't it?" Isobel murmured.

"I am afraid I've never waxed nostalgic for the rural pleasures. Still, it does have a certain . . . stark appeal."

"It's strong and it's harsh, and there's beauty in that. But when the heather blooms and the earth is a blanket of purple, it's glorious. And sometimes, when the mist hangs over the loch and crystal drops of water are clinging to every twig and leaf, you can almost see the fey folk dancing in the glen."

"The fey folk?" he repeated skeptically.

"Aye." She cast him a twinkling glance, her voice tinged with the burr of the Highlands. " 'The ghosties and ghoulies and long-leggedy beasties.' They say at evening time, in the gloaming, if you're quiet and careful, you may see the selkies gliding out of the sea, shedding their skin, and walking abroad in the guise of mortal men."

He stared at her. "Do you mean to tell me you believe in such things?"

Isobel chuckled. "Legends are at the heart of a Scot. When you sit by the fire on a long winter evening and your aunt tells you about the red man, who comes in the winter and knocks at your door, begging you to let him in, it is hard *not* to believe."

"What happens if you do not answer the door?"

"You see? You cannot resist the tales either. The story goes, if you do not offer him hospitality, woe betide you, for he'll play wicked pranks on you. But if you do let him in, you must take care, for if you linger with him too long by the fire, listening to him talk and talk, you will never leave there."

"So you're doomed either way." He gazed down at her, enjoying the sparkle in her eyes and the smile in her voice. "Don't tell me your sweet aunt told you such tales?"

"Indeed she did. Well, many of them we heard at the knee of Andrew's nurse; Janet was . . . well, something of a woman of the forest. She knew the plants and their healing properties, and people came to her with their ailments. She also knew the old tales of selkies and kelpies and the Ghille Dhu."

"And who are all these creatures?"

"The selkies are beings who come out of the water and appear as men. Some say they're seals and shed their skin to become men. They are handsome and charming and lead many a lass astray, but at the end of the night, the selkie leaves his lover's bed and returns to the water. If a woman looks to keep him, she must find his discarded skin and hide it away. Then he cannot leave her and must become a man always." Isobel shrugged. "But others say they are spirits of the water and change their form to look human, then disappear when the morning arrives, leaving the woman not knowing who he was."

"Sounds very convenient."

64

"A kelpie, though, is an entirely different thing, for they are water horses and they do not change. They lie in the river, their heads barely above water, and if you come too close, they seize you and drag you under. They're powerful and cruel, black in color, and water streams from their bodies, their manes tangled with river weeds. Then there's the washerwoman at the ford who stands by the water's edge and washes the grave clothes of those who are about to die. She keens in sorrow for the victim, a harsh, terrible cry."

"A pleasant tale for children, I must say. I am surprised you ever went near the water."

"That may have been the point," Isobel admitted. "But there are nicer spirits as well. Ghille Dhu is a shy and gentle sort. He lives in the forests and his attire is made of moss and leaves." She paused. "Of course, I've also heard he was really a code name for the Pretender."

"To the throne? You mean James?"

Isobel nodded. "Or his son Prince Charlie. That may have been my aunt's meaning. She was always more interested in stories of people than ones of spirits. Aunt Elizabeth loved the legends of the family. She was the one who told us all about the Lady of Loch Baille, a guardian spirit who loved the first

Baillannan."

"The house?"

"No. The first laird — the heroic one who did marvelous deeds and battled fearsome creatures."

"Ah, I see — the fictitious Laird of Baillannan."

"Such cynicism." Isobel pulled a face. "There might have been . . . some slight exaggeration."

"Such as being loved by a magical spirit?"

"She was not a spirit when she fell in love with the Baillannan, just a maiden who lived by the loch and was beautiful and kind and loved by all."

"Of course."

"I can see you are not moved by romantic tales."

"No. I am not a man who believes in love. I find reality more useful than pretty pictures." He softened his words with a smile. It was a pleasure watching her face as she talked, and the way the breeze from the loch molded her clothes against her body. He did not want her to stop. "But you tell a good story. Go on."

"The Baillannan was charmed by her, too, so he stayed with her by the loch, but he had a wife, and after a time he returned to her. The maiden fell into a sadness from which she could not recover. Mad with her sorrow, she threw herself into the loch, intending to end her life, and she cried such tears that it turned the water salty, and so it has remained to this day. The earth took pity on her, and though death took her breath, she lived on in the loch, guarding and protecting it and keeping watch over Baillannan." Isobel paused, then added pragmatically, "Loch Baille is a sea loch, not a freshwater one; at its narrowest point, it connects to the North Sea."

"A far less romantic reason for its salinity."

"True," she sighed.

"Which do you believe? The romantic tale or the reality?"

She cocked her head, considering. "I know Baille is a sea loch, but I also hold the world richer for the story of the maiden's tears. A person can believe in both, can they not?"

"Perhaps." He shrugged. "I have found that fantasy usually tends to overcome reason."

"On a morning like this, it might." Isobel smiled and turned her face up to the sky, closing her eyes and soaking in the warmth. The look of sensual enjoyment stirred him, calling up a hunger to see that sensuality deepen. His hand itched to caress her cheek, to trail down her neck and onto her shoulder. He wanted, suddenly and fiercely, to kiss her.

His mouth went dry, and he turned hastily away, startled by the suddenness and intensity of longing that had run through him. He determinedly studied the loch. It was larger than he had assumed, long but rather narrow, and it curved slightly. They stood gazing down at the center of the curve, the widest stretch of water, and before them, some distance from shore, was an island, thick with trees and shrubs. Trees lined the opposite shore, and nestled in them, he caught a glimpse of a cottage, almost completely hidden by the foliage. At the far end of the loch stood a magnificent house, at least three stories high and adorned with turrets and walls, layered down the side of a hill. At the opposite end of the loch, and much closer to them, rose jagged walls of stone, some tumbled down into piles of rubble.

"What is that?"

"Duncally?" Isobel opened her eyes and saw the direction in which he was looking. "Oh. That. The ruins?"

"Yes." Something magnificent and poignant about the destroyed building pulled at him.

"That is the castle. The original Baillan-nan. That's at the sea end, you see, and they needed a fortress to repel invaders. It was abandoned long ago, after the Vikings stopped coming, and they built a more pleasant house, easier to heat and farther back from the cold winds off the sea."

Jack's mouth quirked at the notion of the cold gray-stone house being considered "more pleasant," but he said only, "It looks as if the castle succumbed to the invaders. I am surprised they let it fall into such ruin."

"The English taxes on property were based on the number of roofs." A mischievous smile flashed as she looked up at him. "So they took off the roof when they left a house."

"Ah, I see."

"Unfortunately, it makes them deteriorate more rapidly. And over the years, people have taken stones from it to build other things."

"It looks as if it might house a number of your ghosts and goblins."

She laughed. "There are ample stories of them, you can be sure." Isobel pointed toward the imposing house at the other end of the loch. "That's Duncally, the home of the Earls of Mardoun. They never live there, of course; they are in London or at their

69

English estate. The Mardoun line ended in Susanna, the Countess of Mardoun in her own right. She married an English lord, so it's her descendant who's the earl now, and more English than Scots. The present earl and his lady came one summer several years ago, but we never met them. They were not especially interested in the local society."

"Ah, that sort. I have played cards with more than a few of them." Jack grinned. "I generally win."

"I am sure you do." She turned, pointing to a spot across the loch. "That bit of rock you can see there is the top of the troth stone. The circle is just beyond it, but you cannot see them from here. Duncally looks down on it."

"The circle?"

"Yes. The standing stones."

"Like Stonehenge? There is the same sort of place here?"

Isobel nodded. "It isn't as large a circle, of course, and some of them are missing. The troth stone is smaller than the others and stands a bit apart. There is a hole in it all the way through the rock. A couple who wished to marry would go to the troth stone and stand on either side. Each would put a hand into the hole and clasp the other's hand, and they would swear to their betrothal. Not many people do it anymore, only some of the families that still cling to the old ways. We can go see it one day if you like."

"It seems we have a great many sights left to see." Jack grinned. "Perhaps we should take in that island in the loch, too. Does anyone live there?"

"No one *lives* there. Now, if you want a number of ghosts, that is the place."

"Indeed. It looks a haunted spot."

"Laugh all you want, but there are many who swear they've seen lights dancing on the island in the dead of the moon and heard strange noises — clanking and sobs and moans."

"What is the story behind the noises? Jealousy? Murder?"

"There is none I've ever heard. No one remembers anyone ever living there. Personally, I suspect it's simply someone looking for the treasure."

"Treasure?" Jack's brows shot up. "There's also a treasure?"

"Of course." Isobel's eyes twinkled. "What would a good legend be without a treasure?"

She turned and sauntered away.

4

"Wait . . . Miss Rose . . ." Jack started after Isobel.

Isobel smiled to herself. She had arisen reluctant to face a day spent in the gloom of making plans for departure, and it was a little astonishing to find herself actually enjoying the morning. Perhaps it was the unaccustomed sunshine sparkling on the loch or the beauty of the land . . . or, she had to admit, it might be the company she kept. Whatever the reason, against all logic, her spirits were suddenly floating. She swung back around to face Jack, putting on an expression of bland inquiry. "Yes?"

"You cannot leave it at that." He caught up with her. "You cannot toss out *treasure* so blithely and stop."

"I know you do not like such tales," Isobel reminded him. "I would not want you to think I am being absurd. I thought we might look at more of the estate."

"I yield, Miss Rose." His eyes were bright with amusement, and Isobel realized, a little horrified, that her manner had been perilously close to flirtatious. "You have outwitted me. Yes, by all means, let us see more of the place. But as we walk, I implore you, tell me the tale of the treasure."

"Well . . ." Isobel paused dramatically. "Many years ago, before the Battle of Culloden, Malcolm Rose — my grandfather, Aunt Elizabeth's father — was the Laird of Baillannan. He was a powerful man, with a great deal of land as well as gold and silver. He was an equal of the Earl of Mardoun, perhaps held in even higher esteem than the earl."

"No doubt — after all, Mardoun was English."

"Exactly. As you might expect, the earl took the side of the English when Prince Charlie raised the Highlanders and marched to London to take the throne for the Pretender. However, Malcolm Rose was a faithful ally to the Bonnie Prince, and he joined the Uprising. Before the prince and his troops moved south, Charles sent Malcolm to France, entrusting him with the task of obtaining money from the French king. It had been promised him, you see, but the French were slow to send the gold. Malcolm sailed to France, and there he beseeched the king every day for money for the rebellion. Finally the king realized that this man was a Scot through and through and would continue to bother him until the day he died, if need be. So he gave the laird a chest filled with gold, and Malcolm sailed for home again. But when he got back to Baillannan —"

"He found that Bonnie Prince Charlie's army had been crushed at Culloden," Kensington surmised.

"Exactly. I am impressed at your knowledge of Scottish history."

"Well, 'tis English history, too," he pointed out mildly.

"Yes, I suppose it is. So there Malcolm was: he had the money, but no one knew where the prince was or where he would go. He and his followers were in headlong flight. The story goes that Malcolm hid the gold, meaning to return for it after he had located the prince. Then he went in search of Charlie. And that is the last anyone ever saw of Malcolm Rose."

"What happened to him?"

"No one knows. Perhaps he was killed by English soldiers or taken prisoner and shipped to England to be hanged or transported to the colonies. There were men who swore they saw him in gaol in Liverpool, and others who were sure they had viewed his bloody body. Who is one to believe? None of the stories ever had any real proof. And . . ." she admitted, "there are many who say he never came back at all. That he stayed in France, hearing of the Scots' defeat, or that he took the money and sailed for America and lived a long, grand life there."

"But you don't believe those versions," he guessed.

"No. Malcolm Rose would not have run away; he would not have deserted his family or his country and prince."

"But surely someone saw him when he returned home with the fortune; they could attest to that."

"That is the problem." She sighed. "No one saw him except his daughter, and she was just a child. They dismissed her story as a child's fantasy or something she dreamed."

"His daughter . . . you mean your aunt?"

"Yes. Aunt Elizabeth." Isobel stopped and turned to face him, her face stony.

"Um . . . I like your aunt," he began cautiously. "So pray do not take my meaning wrong, but she seemed last night to be, ah, a trifle uncertain."

Isobel crossed her arms. "Aunt Elizabeth may be a 'trifle uncertain' about some things. Her memory is slipping a bit, I'll admit, and when she is upset, she is apt to forget more. But she is as sane as you or I. She does not invent stories." At his raised brows, Isobel said crossly, "Oh, yes, she told me legends and such, but those were different; they weren't real, and we all knew it. She does not *lie.* The things she forgets are recent events. She is quite clear regarding the past."

"I apologize. I meant no slur on your aunt, I assure you. She is a lovely woman, and I very much enjoyed our conversation."

Isobel unbent a little. "I apologize, too. I should not have snapped. It is just that . . . well, some people are unkind. She's *not* dottled."

"Who would say such a thing about her?"

"Her cousin, for one."

"Well, I don't know what *dottled* means exactly, but I am sure he is wrong."

Isobel smiled. It was difficult to resist Jack Kensington's charm. She uncrossed her arms and started forward again. He fell in beside her.

"Don't fly up into the boughs," he said after a moment. "I do not doubt your aunt. But why was she the only one who saw

Malcolm Rose? What about his wife? A servant?"

"I don't know. That is one of the reasons people didn't believe her. But Aunt Elizabeth was adamant that her father came into her bedroom in the middle of the night to tell her he was home. He said he was leaving again, but she must not worry; he would be back. She saw him only that once, and late as it was, there would not have been many about to see him. Perhaps my grandmother had reasons for not revealing that her husband returned. What if he had left the treasure with her? She would have needed it in those lean years after the Uprising. Even though they could not find Malcolm and hang him, the Butcher made sure the Roses were punished for their part in the rebellion."

"The butcher?" He frowned in confusion. "What does a butcher have to do with it?"

"The Duke of Cumberland."

"Ah. I see."

"Cumberland's men took the Roses' gold and burned the barn and fields, and the king gave a good chunk of their land to the Earl of Mardoun for his loyalty. Many of our men were missing — killed in battle or hanged. So Lady Cordelia, Malcolm's wife, might well have worried that the English would take the treasure, as well, if they heard of it."

"You said that people looked for the treasure. There must have been others who believed your aunt's story that Malcolm Rose returned. Why else would they be hunting for the money?"

"I think the possibility of treasure was reason enough. It has not happened often recently. My aunt said when she was young, they frequently stumbled upon people searching the caves or digging holes or poking about the old castle. They seem to particularly suspect it's on the island. No doubt that was the source of the noises and lights people have seen there."

"Why the island?"

"Because it's secluded, I suppose. Mysterious."

"Have you ever looked for the treasure?"

"I was never so mad for a treasure hunt as Andrew and Cousin Gregory; they regularly would go about searching for it." She chuckled. "I remember one summer they dug up Janet's herb garden. She was livid; I don't think either of them could sit for a week after that."

"Perhaps we should hunt for it. Just tell me where, and I shall roll up my sleeves and start digging."

"If it were that easy, I would have found it years ago. Baillannan is always cash strapped. I wouldn't know where to begin looking. The truth is, I doubt it is here."

He raised his brows in mock amazement. "Miss Rose . . . I am shocked. I thought you believed the tale."

"I do. I believe the laird returned and left again to join the prince. It's my opinion he was killed helping the prince escape. There were some, you know, who took on the prince's clothes and style and went off in other directions, casting a false scent for the soldiers. From all I've heard of Malcolm, he was the sort to do that. Whatever he did, whether he found the prince or not, I am sure he died fighting and his body simply went unidentified. But the treasure . . ." She shrugged. "If he did indeed bring gold for the prince, isn't it likely he took the money with him when he set out after Charlie? He was bringing it to him, after all. Whoever killed him took the treasure."

"True. But perhaps he wanted to prevent that very thing from happening, so he left the fortune here. A chest of gold is something of an encumbrance if one is sneaking about the countryside avoiding enemy soldiers."

Isobel looked at him askance. "Why, Mr.

79

Kensington, one would almost think you believed the story. Surely you don't give credence to such romantic tales?"

"I find that the addition of a fortune to a story heightens my interest."

"I can see you are determined to be cynical." Isobel shrugged. "You are right; my grandfather could have left the fortune behind. But surely in all the years since, someone would have stumbled upon it. There have been a great many searches in a small area."

"Perhaps someone found it and carried it off and no one knew."

"You don't know Loch Baille; nothing happens here that everyone does not know about within a day. I think it is far more likely that there never was any treasure. My aunt remembers nothing about a chest or gold, and I don't believe my grandmother did either, for she would have spent it. I imagine Malcolm wanted badly to rejoin the fight and he grew weary of the French putting him off, so he returned to Scotland without any funds."

Isobel did not add how very much she wished the story were true. If only she had Malcolm Rose's treasure, she could save her home from this Englishman. Her mood suddenly deflated. Whatever was she doing, laughing and talking with the man who was about to force her from her home? How could she even think about folktales and legends when she should be back at the house, preparing to move?

"But no doubt you have heard enough family stories." Isobel stepped back and gave him a taut smile. "Would you like to meet some of your crofters now?"

"My crofters?" He matched her shift in mood, his tone turning formal.

"The people who live on your lands."

"I see. The tenants." Jack shrugged. "There seems little point, since I have no plans to keep the estate."

"You might find that there is more to Baillannan than you assume." His casual dismissal of everything she held dear stung. "Crofters are not merely tenants. Their families have lived on their crofts as long as anyone can remember. Even though they don't own their land, they belong to it. They are clan folk, loyal and close to us."

"Not to me," Jack replied mildly.

"If you gave it a chance — if you talked to the crofters and walked over the lands — you could see the possibilities. You might find you enjoy owning an estate." She heard the desperation in her voice, but she could not hold it back.

81

"My dear Miss Rose, I am not suited for raising crops and sheep. Or for having tenants. I am not cut out to be a landowner."

"You cannot know that until you try it." He started to speak, but she went on in a rush, "You don't understand. If you sell, Baillannan will fall to someone who knows nothing of the land, cares nothing for it. The new owner will likely decide to raise sheep because they are more profitable, as so many are doing. They will clear out the crofters, turn them out of their homes. These are your people now. You have a duty, a commitment to —"

"I am not the laird." His voice was crisp and cool. "I fear you mistake me for a very different sort of man. I don't know these people or have any feudal duty regarding them. I won a house in a card game. That is what I am. That is what I do. My living lies in London, and the only people I have any affinity for are the denizens of the clubs there."

"You mean — that is how you support yourself? You are a cardsharp?"

"I am no sharp." His mouth tightened, his deep blue eyes turning wintry. "I do not ensnare flats up from the country. I don't use fulhams — indeed I don't play dice at all, for that's a fool's game unless you load them. I frequent gambling clubs, not hells, where I match my skills against aristocrats, who generally have more gold than sense. I am no gentleman. And I intend to sell this house." He stopped, pressing his lips together as if pulling himself up short.

"I see. Perhaps we should return to the house now. I have preparations to make." Without waiting for an answer, Isobel whirled and walked away. He stood for a moment, then followed, making no effort to catch up to her.

Upon arriving home, Isobel launched herself into going through her family's possessions. She went first to Sir Andrew's bedroom. It was not the master's bedroom, where her father had slept, for Andrew had been reluctant to move into it after their father's death. Opening the door, Isobel glanced around. The shelves, the chests, the bed, all were much unchanged since Andrew had been a lad.

"I wonder if there is anything from here Andrew would want, that we should ship to him in London."

She had spoken her words to Hamish, standing grimly beside the door, but it was her aunt who answered, "What do you mean? Why would you send Andy's things to London? He would prefer to have them here, I imagine."

"Yes, of course," Isobel agreed. She had done her best to persuade her aunt to stay in the sitting room with her needle-work, but Elizabeth had thwarted all her efforts and insisted on helping. "Still, we should clean out the rooms, don't you think? I am afraid I have let things accumulate sadly."

"But not Andrew's, surely. Really, Isobel, I am not sure it is at all the thing to begin spring cleaning while we have a guest stay-ing with us."

Isobel gritted her teeth. She could not tell if her aunt had forgotten they had lost their house or if she was simply ignoring the fact. Whichever it was, Isobel knew that she would be sorry afterward if she snapped at Elizabeth.

"Let's leave Andrew's room for the mo-ment, then." Isobel went across the hall to the room that had been her grandmother's.

Inside, all the furniture was laid with dust-covers, giving it an odd, almost ghostly ap-pearance. Even after all this time, it still smelled of her perfume. Isobel could not repress a little shiver. She had been in awe of her grandmother, whose small frame had held an indomitable personality.

"Isobel!" Elizabeth's voice was shocked.

"No. You cannot mean to change Mother's room."

"Aunt Elizabeth . . . it has been years since Grandmother died."

"Yes, but . . . it doesn't seem right to disturb her things." Elizabeth gazed around the room with an expression so lost it made Isobel's heart clench in her chest.

"Of course. We shall leave it the way it is." Isobel drew her aunt out of the room. "You know . . ." She was suddenly seized by inspiration. "You are right; we are being rude to Mr. Kensington. I must get to work, but it would help me a great deal if you would keep Mr. Kensington company. No doubt he is terribly bored."

Elizabeth brightened. "Are you sure? I hate to leave you with all the work. And no doubt he would rather spend time with a pretty young girl than with me."

"He enjoyed talking to you very much last night. He told me so. He is probably sick of my company, anyway; we took a long walk this morning. He might enjoy some music; you are a far better pianist than I." Music was the one thing Elizabeth seemed not to have forgotten at all, and it always soothed her to play.

"Perhaps I should go downstairs and see. Mozart improves everything."

Isobel watched her aunt leave, then returned to her inspection of the rooms. She opened door after door, wondering what she was to do with all this furniture. Most of it would simply have to be left here. She and her aunt would have little space for it wherever they went. Panic clutched at her insides, but Isobel shoved it aside. She could not allow herself to think about the uncertainty of her future. She must stick to the work at hand. Mr. Kensington —

"Hamish." She stopped and turned to her butler. "Where is Mr. Kensington's room? These are all untouched."

"Down the hall." He jerked his head toward the back of the house.

Her eyes widened. "You don't mean the old wing, do you?"

"He isna the laird. It isna right to put him in the master's room."

"Hamish!" Isobel was tempted to laugh — given Mr. Kensington's words this morning, it seemed exactly what he deserved. But she could not let Hamish ruin himself with the man. She crossed her arms and regarded him sternly. "This must stop."

"I dinna know what you mean, miss."

"Don't give me that innocent look. I saw Mr. Kensington's breakfast this morning, and the meal last night was horrid. I put it down to Cook's being upset, but I can see now that you are waging a war against him."

"He doesna belong here."

"No, he does not, but nevertheless he owns this house. You must not place yourself in opposition to him. If you continue this way, he will let you go."

"Aye, we may be tossed out, just like you." His jaw set stubbornly. "You canna think we will stand for him coming in here and throwing the laird's own daughter out of Baillannan."

"Do you think it will make me feel better knowing that all of you are homeless as well?" Tears welled in Isobel's eyes, and she hugged the old man. "You are the most loyal of people. I could not bear it if you lost your home because you are trying to defend my aunt and me."

"It isna right."

"You are a Scot, Hamish. You know as well as I that 'what is right' isn't the same as 'what is.' " She fixed him with as stern a look as she could muster for a man who had known her since infancy. "Put Mr. Kensington in the master's chamber. Tell Cook to prepare something decent to eat. And please cease whatever other little miseries you have dreamed up."

He let out a sigh, but said, "Aye, miss. I'll

do it. But only because *you* say so."

"Thank you. While you do that, I shall start on the attic. I will save my grandmother's and Andrew's rooms till last. It will be easier for Aunt Elizabeth."

"I'll send up one of the girls to help you."

"Send her up later. Right now, they need to put Mr. Kensington's room in order."

Isobel left Hamish behind, looking disgruntled but hopefully about to do as she asked, and went up to the attic. Low windows provided the only light other than the lamp in her hand, leaving pools of shadows across the huge room. Her heart sank as she surveyed the long stretch of floor, dusty and stacked with trunks, boxes, furniture, and an assortment of odds and ends left by two hundred years of the Rose family. Indeed, no doubt some of it belonged to an even earlier era and had been brought over from the old castle.

Taking a deep breath, she turned to the nearest trunk. It was filled with children's clothes, both hers and Andrew's. For a short time she allowed herself to be distracted by memories, and her progress was slow, but she soon picked up her pace, steeling her heart against nostalgia. She made her way down the central aisle, sorting things into separate piles as best she could. The attic had seemed drafty when she first came in, but she was soon perspiring, and she began to wish that she had not told Hamish to wait until later to send a servant to help her. It was with great relief that she heard the sound of footsteps on the stairs.

"Thank goodness!" She was bent over a large, hump-backed trunk, trying to retrieve a stack of letters that had fallen behind it, and she did not bother to turn around. "There are several trunks I need moved."

"Certainly. Where shall I start?"

Isobel let out a little squeak of dismay and whirled around to see Jack Kensington standing in the doorway.

5

Jack leaned against the doorjamb, looking amused. Isobel stared at him in horror, thinking of the distinctly unladylike image she must have presented, bent over the trunk. Immediately on the heels of that came the realization that she was liberally streaked with dust from her head to the hem of her skirt, one of her ruffles had caught on a nail and ripped half off, trailing behind her on the floor, and bits of her hair had come loose and straggled around her face. She must look like an absolute slattern. Her face, already pink from exertion, flooded red with humiliation.

"You!" she gasped.

"Yes. I." He smiled faintly and walked toward her.

"What are you doing here?" Isobel stepped back quickly, knocking into the wobbly stack beside the trunk and sending still more letters cascading down. "Blast!"

He chuckled and reached past her, scooping up the letters from the floor and extending them to her. "Your aunt told me where you were, and I came to apologize. I fear I was rude earlier. I spoke too harshly. It was wrong of me, especially given how kind you had been in showing me about the place."

"No. I mean . . ." Isobel grabbed the envelopes, feeling annoyingly flustered. "I should not have expected you to . . . I had no right . . . I am sorry."

"You had every right. You are a compassionate woman who was concerned for the people who have depended on you. I, on the other hand, was a coldhearted wretch." His eyes glinted at her, lightening his critical words. "Do say you will forgive me?"

"Yes, of course I forgive you." She realized, astonished, that she meant it; the resentment and anger she had felt toward him had somehow evaporated. "I was upset because I cannot help them, more than anything else."

He studied her for a long moment. "I believe you mean that."

"Of course." She looked at him oddly. "Why else would I say it?"

He smiled instead of answering and changed the subject. "Now, what is it you need moved?" He glanced around them at the multitude of boxes.

"Nothing. That is, I did not mean for you to move it. I thought you were one of the servants. Hamish was going to send someone to help me."

"I will do, I hope, until more expert help can arrive."

"Oh, well . . ." She turned and pointed down the aisle she had cleared. "That trunk needs to be moved to the door."

"Very well." He shrugged out of his jacket and hung it on a wobbly coatrack, then picked up the trunk and carried it to the spot she indicated. "You are rearranging the attic, I take it?"

Isobel realized that she was watching, fascinated, the way his muscles bulged beneath his shirt. She flushed and said firmly, "I am clearing it out. The things by the door are for the servants to take downstairs."

"I think that I shall leave that for the servants." He set down the chest and turned to her. "What next?"

"You are very kind, but surely you cannot wish to haul boxes and trunks about."

"I am not suited to be a man of leisure, I find. I am accustomed to more activity."

"Well, I can certainly provide you with plenty of that," Isobel said drily.

"I am sure you can." Something about the look in his eyes and the smile playing across his lips invested his words with an undercurrent of meaning.

Isobel was suddenly tongue-tied. She told herself that he had not intended any double entendre. Nothing in the way his mouth softened was untoward; the look in his eyes was merely amusement. Indeed, it more likely indicated something wicked in her that made her skin tingle and her insides grow strangely warm and achy. She turned away, gesturing vaguely across the aisle.

"The, um, things over there seem useful enough to be given away. And here" — she gestured to the trunk at her feet — "I am putting aside things Cousin Robert might want to have — this trunk seems to have belonged to his father, Fergus. He was Malcolm's younger brother. Fergus, I mean, not Cousin Robert . . ." She trailed off, appalled at the way she was blathering on about nothing.

"And what of the things you want to keep?" Jack stepped closer to Isobel, and she shifted uncomfortably.

"I — we cannot take much, of course. There will not be room at my cousin's or my aunt's, really."

"Isobel . . ."

She glanced up, startled by his calling her by her first name; it sounded somehow intimate on his tongue. From the faintly surprised look in his eyes, perhaps he had startled himself, as well.

"I am sorry. I have no desire to turn you out of your home."

"I know." It made her feel unsettled to look into his eyes, so she half turned away. "I do not blame you. I just —" She did not want anyone, least of all him, to know how frightened she was, how filled with pain.

"I wish everything was different." He hooked his finger beneath her chin, gently turning her face toward him. A frown pinched the space between his brows as he brushed his thumb over her cheek, catching the tear that had spilled over. "I wish . . ."

She wanted to turn away from him, but she could not. She was transfixed by the feel of his hand on her skin, caught by his eyes, so dark a blue they were bottomless pools, shadowed and dangerous. Her breath came shallowly in her throat, her heart suddenly drumming, as he bent toward her.

His lips touched hers, soft and warm, and a shiver ran through her. His warmth, his scent, the velvet feel of his mouth upon hers, drove all thoughts from her head, filling her senses. His kiss was beyond her

94

realm of experience; no man had ever given her more than a friendly peck on the cheek — save for one fellow at a dance who had had far too much whiskey. And this kiss was a far cry from that.

Jack raised his head, gazing down into her face. Isobel was too stunned to speak; indeed, she could not even think, only feel a thrumming, eager heat all through her, an urgent need to kiss him again.

"I hate to see you cry," he murmured.

She realized that while desire had shimmered through her, all he felt for her was pity. Isobel whirled away, horrified by what he might have seen in her face. That he was sorry for her was galling enough, but the knowledge that her whole body had sprung to life at the touch of his mouth humiliated her.

"What I feel doesn't concern you." She pushed the words out, harsh and hoarse.

"You're right." Jack's voice was clipped, as if her words nettled him, and heat flared across his angular cheekbones. "It doesn't. I cannot imagine why I bothered."

"You needn't have." Isobel crossed her arms, glaring back at him. The air crackled between them, and Isobel waited, a little breathless, unsure what he was about to do and strangely eager to find out.

"Oh, the devil with it!" he snapped. He pulled back, an icy reserve settling over his features and cooling his voice. "I beg your pardon for intruding on you. No doubt you will be more comfortable without my presence."

He strode away. Isobel wished he had slammed the door so that she could throw something against it. Instead she kicked the closest thing, the humpbacked trunk. Strangely, she rather welcomed the pain. It gave her something to think about other than the way her body had thrummed when Jack Kensington kissed her.

The mood that night at the supper table was strained. Her aunt's presence ensured that nothing would be said about the scene in the attic today, but every time Isobel thought of the episode, she was flooded anew with humiliation — and she was finding it amazingly difficult *not* to think about it. She did her best to avoid glancing at Jack, afraid he would see the tumult inside her.

When she and her aunt rose at the end of the meal, Kensington took a step after Isobel, saying, "Miss Rose, if I could speak to you for a moment . . ."

"Yes, of course." Isobel turned back, her stomach clenching.

"I understand that I have you to thank for my new accommodations."

"What?" His words were so far from what she had expected that it took her a moment to understand. "Oh." She shook her head. "It was nothing. Hamish should have put you into the master bedchamber from the beginning. I hope you will not —"

"Blame him," he finished for her, and a hint of a smile touched his lips. How, she wondered, could he speak to her so normally when her own nerves danced inside her just looking at him? Doubtless he had a great deal more experience in such things than she did. "You are very protective of everyone here. The servants. The tenant farmers."

"No doubt it seems quaint to you, even peculiar, but things are different here. I am a Rose of Baillannan. These are my people."

"I can see that." He studied her for a moment. "I admire loyalty even when it is at my expense. I have no intention of sacking the servants as long as the situation improves. I had a brief chat with the butler, and I believe we arrived at a truce."

"Thank you."

"I made it clear to him, and I hope it is to you as well, that my leniency is due entirely to my respect for you. I hope that you will

97

accept it as an apology for my, um, unto-ward behavior this afternoon."

"But you have already apolo— Oh." Iso-bel stopped short, and her cheeks flooded with color. "That."

"Yes, that."

"It was not your — that is, um, I have not been quite myself." She looked away.

"I wanted you to know you need not worry about a repetition of the scene. I have not been quite myself, either."

Isobel glanced up to see the gleam of warmth and humor in his dark blue eyes. She had the strangest impulse to lay her hand against his face, to glide her thumb along a high, flaring cheekbone, to see his sharply defined lips curve into a smile. She pulled her hands behind her back, interlac-ing her fingers tightly, and backed up a step. "Yes. I mean . . ." She had no idea what she meant. "Good night."

"Good night, Miss Rose."

Isobel spent the following day working in the attic, taking two of the servants with her this time. Kensington did not appear in the doorway — not, of course, that she expected him to. Certainly she was not waiting for him. Late in the afternoon, one of the maids climbed the stairs to inform her that her cousins had come to call and were waiting downstairs in the drawing room.

Sighing inwardly, Isobel left the attic. No doubt Gregory and his father had heard the news of Mr. Kensington's arrival. She had little desire to face Cousin Robert, but she could not leave her aunt alone to deal with him. She stopped first in her room to tidy her hair and clothes before she continued to the drawing room. Aunt Elizabeth was seated on the sofa with Cousin Gregory, laughing. Gregory's father, Robert, sat in the chair across from them, looking un-amused. Robert, of an age with Elizabeth and Isobel's late father, was a short, wiry man whose posture and stern demeanor bespoke his past military career. He approached life solemnly and regarded his lighthearted son with disapproval. Today, however, the chief object of his scowl seemed to be Jack Kensington. Jack lounged beside the fireplace, his elbow propped on the mantel, and gazed coolly back at Robert, a faint smile on his face, which Isobel was sure maddened her cousin beyond measure.

"Cousin Robert," she said with more pleasure than she felt. "How nice to see you. Please accept my apologies for the delay. I was in the attic." She went forward to give him her hand in greeting, then turned to his son, smiling with more heartfelt delight. "Gregory! I did not know you were home from Edinburgh. I am so glad you are here."

"I arrived in Kinclannoch last week." Gregory, a tall, slender man with strawberry-blond hair and merry blue eyes, got up and stepped forward to take Isobel's outstretched hands in his and kiss her on the cheek.

"And you are just now coming to see us? I trust Aunt Elizabeth gave you a proper scold for that." Isobel linked her arm through his as she turned to her aunt.

"You know I did not." Aunt Elizabeth waved away the suggestion. "I have never been able to be cross with Gregory. He would know I did not mean it, anyway." She beamed at the young man.

"It was not from a lack of desire to visit, I assure you. Father has been keeping me busy since my return."

"Then I suppose I must excuse you." Turning politely to Jack, Isobel said, "I am sure Aunt Elizabeth introduced my cousins to you, Mr. Kensington?"

"Yes, indeed. We were discussing the Highland weather." She saw the light of laughter in his eyes, and she was tempted to smile. She could well imagine the stilted conversation that had preceded her arrival in the drawing room.

"It is a never-ending source of conversation," she replied.

"I am sure you would like to visit with your family, Miss Rose, so pray excuse me." Kensington sketched a bow to her and bent over her aunt's hand gallantly, which made Elizabeth dimple and blush. With a cool nod to the two men, he left the room.

Robert popped out of his seat as soon as Mr. Kensington walked out. "The nerve of that man!"

"Isobel, are you all right?" Gregory asked, ignoring his father.

"I am fine. Doubtless you have heard the news."

"Of course." Gregory smiled down at her. "You know how it is; the entire glen knew within hours."

"You should have sent for me," Robert told Isobel sternly. "I would have tossed the man out."

"I don't think there was any question of tossing him out. He owns Baillannan."

"I cannot think why you dislike Mr. Kensington so, Cousin," Elizabeth said, taking up her embroidery hoop. "He is a delightful young man. It is so rare for one of Andrew's friends to come visit."

101

"You would think so, of course." Robert rolled his eyes at Elizabeth's words. "And he is not one of Andrew's friends. Honestly, Eliza, you might think once in a while."

Seeing Isobel's eyes light up pugnaciously at his father's insult, Gregory took her arm, saying, "I am sure this is all a hum."

"Of course it is," Robert declared. "The man is clearly an adventurer. He is trying to swindle you. I will talk to a solicitor for you."

"That is very kind of you, Cousin, but you need not trouble yourself," Isobel said. "I have already written to Father's solicitor about the matter. Anyway, I do not think Mr. Kensington is lying. I saw Andrew's marker; it was clearly his hand."

"You were mistaken," Robert insisted. "It is bound to be a forgery."

"I have known my brother for some years now," Isobel replied, holding on to her temper with difficulty. Her father's cousin never failed to raise her hackles. "I know Andrew's handwriting."

"Andrew would never —" Robert began, but his son interrupted him.

"No, Father. I fear it is exactly the sort of thing Andrew might do. You have not seen him when the gambling fever has him in its grip." Gregory squeezed Isobel's arm gently. "I am so sorry, Izzy."

"One cannot crumble at the first wave of attack, Gregory." Robert scowled at his son. "If it does turn out that Andrew lost the estate to him, I am quite certain that the fellow used sharp practices. The man is clearly a charlatan."

"You could tell his nature just from being introduced to him?" Isobel shot back

"One has only to look at him. He is too polished, too smooth. I seriously doubt that is really his last name, either. It is exactly the sort of thing one would make up."

"So he is a villain because he has excellent manners? Because he shares a last name with a royal palace? There *are* people named Kensington, I imagine."

"That does not make him one of them," Robert snorted. "Good gad, Isobel, are you defending the scoundrel? I have no doubt that he has cozened Elizabeth, but I thought you, at least, were too reasonable to fall under his spell."

"I have not 'fallen' under anyone's spell," Isobel said tightly. "But I know nothing to make me believe he is anything but what he appears." That was a bit of a bouncer, given that Jack had admitted to her that he was no gentleman but a man who made his living at the card tables. However, she was too irritated by her cousin's overbearing attitude to care.

"I cannot imagine why you think he is not a gentleman, Robert," Aunt Elizabeth spoke up. "Mr. Kensington is charming, and quite refined. Why, he recognized a piece I played yesterday as Mozart."

"Lord save me." Robert sent a quelling look at Elizabeth. "Just because a man makes an elegant leg or knows a bit of music does not make him respectable. Who is he? Where does he come from?"

"Why, London, Cousin, I told you," Elizabeth said, puzzled.

"One doesn't 'come from' London. Where did he grow up? What school did he attend? Who is his family?" When no one answered him, Robert went on triumphantly, "Hah! You see? You know nothing of importance about his background."

"Well, no, I do not think he has mentioned any of those things." Elizabeth turned to Isobel, her brow creased. "Has he, dear?"

"No. I did not interrogate the man."

"You should not have to. If he weren't smoky, he would have told you those things. It is what one does."

Robert was right; she didn't know anything about Mr. Kensington. She had nothing to prove he had not cheated Andrew out of the estate, only his word for it. She had believed him; she had seen the truth, she thought, in his eyes, heard it in his tone. But then, would not an accomplished liar be equally convincing?

Still, she *had* believed him, and she felt her instincts were good. There was an equal lack of proof that he had lied to her. Cousin Robert's suspicions had even less basis than her own judgment. And in any case, she was not about to admit any doubts to Robert.

Apparently Robert needed no response from her, for he heaved a deep sigh and went on, "I don't know what else one could expect from Andrew, though. He has always been a wastrel. I tried to talk some sense into him, but clearly my efforts were in vain." He turned to Elizabeth. "I told you not to spoil the boy so. It's no wonder he grew up wild."

"Andrew's mistakes are not Aunt Elizabeth's fault," Isobel protested.

"No, dear, perhaps he is right." Tears sparkled in her aunt's eyes. "I was lax with the boy; I felt sorry for him, his mother dying when he was born."

"We all did," Robert agreed. "John never paid enough attention to the boy."

"John was grief stricken when Barbara died," Elizabeth flared. It was just like her,

Isobel thought fondly, to defend her brother from their cousin's accusations, but not herself. "He loved his wife dearly; he was devastated."

"Doesn't excuse him from acting like a father." Robert waved away her words. "One has to set an example, after all. When Gregory's mother died, you did not see me falling apart. I had my command to think of. And Gregory, of course. Worse, John hired that woman to look after Andrew and even let her bring her own brood into the house. Raised them with his own children. It was disgraceful. No wonder the boy ran wild."

"Janet was an excellent nurse." Isobel set her jaw. "None of us were any the worse from being around Meg and Coll. Quite the opposite."

"Of course you would say that. She was far too close to all of you. There was talk," Robert said flatly. "The Baillannan's children growing up with the servants — it was not right. Those too are far too familiar with you even now. John should have had more care. It gave rise to gossip. There are still those who whisper —" He broke off hastily.

"What?" Isobel's eyes flashed. "That Coll and Meg are our half siblings? That is nonsense, and you know it. There was nothing between my father and Janet. It is the

106

people who whisper about it who are wicked."

"Of course it was nonsense; anyone can see Coll is the image of that feckless Alan McGee. That is not the point. There was bound to be talk. Everyone knows what the Munro women are like. The way they always have been. Living out in the woods by themselves, making Lord only knows what kind of concoctions with their plants, refusing to marry. Taking up with whatever man they choose, with no regard to morality. It's no wonder they were burned as witches two hundred years ago."

"Father —" Gregory said warningly, wrapping his hand around Isobel's arm, as if to hold her down.

"Yes, of course, you are right — it's not a fit topic for ladies' ears."

Isobel simmered with anger. She was tempted to point out that after Gregory's mother died, Robert, off with the army, had dropped his own son here at Baillannan, and Gregory had been raised by the same woman Robert so disdained. However, one look at her aunt's distraught face kept her from saying it. Instead, she turned to Gregory. "Come. Let us talk about something more pleasant. Tell us about Edinburgh, Cousin. Did you enjoy your trip?"

"Indeed." Gregory's face lit up, and he began to talk about his visit. Unlike Isobel, he had never been content in Kinclannoch, and he traveled to Edinburgh whenever he could. His enthusiasm kept the conversation on a pleasant path until it came time for him and his father to leave. As they stood up to say their good-byes, Isobel remembered the things from the attic that she had set aside for her cousins.

"Before you go, Cousin Robert — as I was cleaning out the attic, I ran across a trunk and some items that seemed to belong to your father. There was a book with *Fergus Rose* written on the inside cover and a leather case with documents also bearing his name. I thought you might want to have them." Robert looked at her blankly, and she explained, "I have to do something with the family items in the house. Elizabeth and I cannot take them with us, and Mr. Kensington will not wish to keep them."

Robert's expression hardened, but he said only, "Of course. Gregory, see to putting them in the carriage."

"I'll show you where they are," Aunt Elizabeth offered quickly, clearly wanting to escape the room.

As they left, Robert turned back to Isobel. "I am not giving up. I intend to talk to a solicitor."

"If you wish. But I fear you will find that we have lost Baillannan."

"You will live with us, of course."

"I am not sure. I must think of Aunt Elizabeth."

"What is there to think about? Where else are you to go? You haven't enough income to set up a household, just the two of you. And before long, Elizabeth will be too much for you to manage on your own."

"What do you mean 'manage'?" Isobel bristled.

"Her mind is failing her daily. You know that, even if you will not admit it. Look at what she said today about that Englishman. She has no understanding of what is happening."

"She does." At the older man's skeptical look, Isobel admitted, "Yes, very well, sometimes she is unclear about it, but she understands that we will have to leave. She just took Gregory to get the trunks."

"Because she wanted to get away from me," he snorted.

"Don't you see? That is precisely the problem — the two of you do not get along. It would not make for a happy situation."

"I am not talking about happiness. I am talking about family. You have to go somewhere, and soon. The man is a brute to toss you out, of course, but —"

"Mr. Kensington is not tossing me out. Indeed, he very kindly offered for us to stay as long as we needed. He is giving me an opportunity to decide what to do with everything."

"Why do you keep defending the man? It's not appropriate for you to stay here with a man, a young, unmarried woman such as yourself."

"My aunt is here; surely that is ample chaperonage."

"Elizabeth is hardly any sort of protection."

"I don't need protection, and even if I did, there are the servants. Mr. Kensington is not going to ravish me." Isobel thought of the kiss in the attic, and she began to blush. She looked down, hoping her cousin had not noticed.

"Isobel, really! You must not say such things. I fail to understand why you seem so determined to stay here. You and Gregory have always enjoyed each other's company. Indeed, there have been times when I have hoped . . ."

"Cousin Robert . . ." Isobel suppressed a sigh. "We discussed this before; it's impossible."

"So you think — and of course I would never urge you to do anything against your conscience — but Gregory is only your second cousin. It is not too close a blood tie."

"It isn't that. You know how I feel about Gregory. I love him, but he is like a brother to me, and I am sure he feels the same."

"You are both too young to understand how you feel. But, no —" Robert held up his hands. "I will not press you. Certainly that is not why I offer you our hospitality. It is where you and Elizabeth belong. Give it some thought, you will see that I am right."

"I will think about it. I promise."

She braced herself for more argument, but to her relief, Robert just nodded and walked to the waiting carriage. Gregory, having helped Hamish fasten the trunks on the back of the vehicle, returned to Isobel.

"Father likes to fuss," he told her. "But please don't let his manner keep you from coming to us. I promise he will not spend his time correcting you — I provide him with ample object for his criticism."

"I will think about it," Isobel promised with a smile.

Elizabeth came to stand beside Isobel, waving at the carriage as it pulled away. "Do not distress yourself over Cousin Robert, dear." She linked her arm through Isobel's. "He was always a prig, even when we were children. I cannot tell you how many times he ran with tales about John and me to our mother. Fortunately, we did not have to see him often; Mother did not care overmuch for his father. Or for Robert, either, for that matter."

"I can understand why if he was like Robert."

"Oh, no." Elizabeth shook her head. "Uncle Fergus was nothing like Robert. He was a bitter man; I don't think he ever got over losing so much in the Uprising. Not just the land and the power, but my father's disappearance as well. We all knew Papa must be dead, else he would have returned. Mother was devastated, too, but she carried on for John and me. I rather pitied Robby when we were children, even if he was a little beast. Uncle Fergus could be cutting, even cruel. No doubt that is why Robert looks on the dark side of any situation. You must not let him worry you. I am sure everything will work out well. Andrew's friend seems like a nice young man, don't you think?"

"Perhaps. But, Aunt Elizabeth, you understand that Mr. Kensington means to sell the land? We cannot live here anymore. He owns it now."

"Of course, dear. I'm not in my dotage, you know. I realize we may have to live with Robert and Gregory. You needn't fret; Robert and I will manage to get along. He is brusque, but I am used to him." Elizabeth glanced around. "And really, this house is much too large for the two of us, isn't it?"

"No doubt." Isobel swallowed against the emotion clogging her throat. She hated the quiet resignation on her aunt's face. She turned away. "I am going to see Meg."

"Didn't you go there just yesterday?" Her aunt frowned. "Or perhaps it was the day before. Have I forgotten?"

"No. I did set out for her house the other day, but I ran into Coll and never made it to the loch. But I should pick up your tonic. She said she had improved upon it."

"Of course, dear. Run along." Elizabeth smiled and patted Isobel's arm. "Say hello to Meg for me."

6

Jack rode out of the stable yard, turning Pharaoh's head toward the distant, barren hills. He had no aim, no destination. He had left the house to give Isobel and her aunt privacy in their talk with their cousins, but he found he had an itching need to get away from the great gray confines of the manor house, as well.

As he rode, his thoughts turned to Isobel. He could scarcely believe he had blurted out those damning truths about himself to her yesterday. The shock he had seen in her eyes, the disdain when she asked him if he made his living by gambling, had stung, and, perversely, he had felt impelled to throw the disreputable truth of his life at her, wielding it as if it were a weapon.

The whole thing had been most unlike him. He never let anyone's opinion nettle him; giving in to one's emotions was a quick path to losing. Nor did he reveal that he made his living by his wits, that he was not a gentleman. There was no advantage to anyone knowing him.

However much Jack despised the man who was his father, Sutton Kensington had taught his lessons well. Whether it was picking pockets or conducting a swindle or setting a fellow cardplayer at ease, the trick was to blend in. To appear to belong while staying apart. "To be anybody, you have to be nobody."

Bloody hell! Now he was thinking about that blasted man. Jack let out a growl of irritation and dug in his heels, sending Pharaoh into a gallop.

He had let Isobel Rose get under his skin. That was his mistake.

There was no reason for him to feel a pang of remorse at the thought of turning her out of her home. She was not his responsibility. It did not matter that he enjoyed the sound of her voice or that her laughter danced across his skin. It was absurd to search for a quip or a tale to tell her in order to see that smile break across her face — not broad, not flashing, but slow and secret, as if they shared something delightful, with a burst of sunshine at the end that lit up her eyes.

And the only thing more pointless than

115

pondering Isobel Rose's future was mooning about like a calfling over the thought of her smile. Obviously, she was a pretty girl — yes, admittedly, more than just pretty — and it was pleasant to pass the time by flirting with her, just as it was sweet to imagine the taste of her lips or the smoothness of her skin.

However, it would be beyond foolish to give in to those urges. Miss Rose was a lady, not some tavern wench with whom one could spend an entertaining night. Jack had no time, no interest in ladies. They had to be courted; they had to be wooed and won with sweet words and reassuring lies of love. Ladies wanted, in short, much more than he was willing to spend.

Yet when he had gone up to the attic to apologize to her, trying to smooth over his earlier mistake, he had wound up kissing her. Desire had slammed through him, shaking him with its intensity. He had wanted to pull her down right there and then to the old dusty floor of the attic, to cover her body with his and sink into her softness. It was a wonder he had retained enough sanity to rein in the need thrumming through him. Even now, his body flooded with heat as he thought of the velvet softness of her lips, the warmth of her mouth, the way she had yielded to him, her head falling back and her body melting into his.

Jack drew in a deep breath, trying to banish the image from his mind, and for the first time, he took note of his surroundings. He realized with a start that he had no idea where he was. Pulling up, he gazed all around. There was no sign of the walls of Baillannan . . . or the loch or the castle ruins or the road or, indeed, anything that was even slightly familiar.

Pharaoh had followed his own whims while Jack was lost in thought, and they were now on a path leading down a rock-strewn hillside — a *brae,* they called it here. Looking down, Jack saw a tiny thatch-roofed cottage in the valley below. As he watched, a figure emerged from the hut and peered up at him, shading his eyes.

Jack lifted his hand in greeting and urged his horse down the path. The man below continued to watch him for a moment, then turned and went back inside. As Jack reached the cottage, the fellow emerged once again. He was old, his face creased with lines and his dark, curly hair liberally streaked with gray. But his small frame was straight as an arrow and the blue eyes that peered out from beneath the bushy eyebrows were bright.

And in his hand he carried a musket, which he raised and pointed at Jack. "Gaun, noo. Get oot a' here."

"I should have known." Jack sighed and held up his hands in a peaceful gesture. "Good afternoon, sir. I intend you no harm, I assure you. My name is Jack Kensington."

"Aye, I ken who ye are. The ootlander."

"Yes." Remarkably, he was beginning to understand what these people said — at least enough to get the gist of it. "And you are . . ."

The old man regarded him suspiciously but replied, "Angus McKay."

"Well, Mr. McKay, I fear I am lost. If you could but tell me the way to Baillannan, I would —"

McKay let out a cackle. "Ye dinna ken the way to yer ain hoose?"

"No," Jack replied with some irritation. "Sadly, I do not. I am, as you said, an 'ootlander.' "

Jack's words seemed to delight the man even further, for McKay let out another hoot. "Aye, weel, maybe ye should na' be here, grabbin' other folks' land, then."

"Baillannan is *my* land now. We are standing on Baillannan land, are we not?"

"It's Rose land, aye. And *ma'* croft."

McKay glared at him belligerently, then sighed and lowered the musket. "Och . . . Just gae back up the brae and gae richt." He gestured up the hillside.

"Thank you." Jack turned Pharaoh's head and started up the path.

Behind him, the old man called, "Best if ye stay on the road, I say, and gae a' the way back to England."

"Exactly my thought," Jack said under his breath as he nudged his horse forward.

Isobel was almost to the shore when she saw Coll tying up the dinghy at the small dock. He looked up and saw her, and surprise touched his features. He glanced toward the small island in the loch before turning back to her.

"Isobel. Where are you off to, then?"

"I might ask where you are coming from." She looked past him across the loch. "Have you been to the island?"

"Aye." He shrugged nonchalantly. "I went to look about, make sure nothing needed doing there."

Isobel's eyes narrowed as she studied his innocent expression. "You're a terrible liar, Coll."

"I'm an excellent liar," he protested. "Dinna I always talk us out of trouble with your aunt?"

"Hah. You open your eyes too wide and suddenly you sound more Scottish," she retorted. "And it was Meg who talked us out of trouble, not you."

"Och, well, that's only right, as she was the one who talked us *into* trouble."

"Don't think I haven't noticed that you did not answer my question." Isobel crossed her arms and regarded him sternly.

"I know." He grinned. "Where are you off to, then?"

"To Meg's. To get Aunt Elizabeth's medicine."

"I'll take you," he offered, turning and walking with her toward the boat.

"I can row across the loch myself."

"Can you now? When you did not even remember to wear your coat? Or your gloves? You'll have blisters on your hands for certain."

"I was in a hurry." She sent him a dark look and he chuckled, shrugging out of his jacket and draping it over her shoulders.

"Here. Meg will have my hide if I let you show up without a wrap. I need to go to Meg's myself. She'll be running low on firewood."

Coll lived in the gamekeeper's cottage on Baillannan land now, rather than in his mother's cottage across the loch, where he had grown up and which now belonged to his sister, but he visited Meg frequently to take care of various tasks around the house — though both Meg and Isobel suspected that he did so more to make sure Meg was all right than because she needed his assistance.

"You'll get cold without your jacket," Isobel warned him, though she slid her arms inside the sleeves.

"Rowing will keep me warm." He handed her into the dinghy and climbed in behind her, taking up the oars. They did not talk as they crossed the narrow loch. A wind was coming down from the ocean beyond the narrow mouth of the loch, and it took Isobel's breath from her mouth. Coll seemed not to feel it, even though his sleeves were rolled up. Isobel watched the muscles bunch and relax in his arms as he rowed, and she wondered why the sight did not do the odd things to her stomach that looking at Jack Kensington had done.

When they'd tied up on the other side, they hiked into the trees, coming after a time to the small clearing where Meg's cottage lay. The trees curled around the small house, concealing it from three directions. Made from light brown stone, with ivy growing up one side onto the thatched roof and stretching around the corner to the front as well, the dwelling seemed to melt into its surroundings. In front was a small garden where Meg grew her herbs, with a larger strip to the side for vegetables.

Isobel thought of the many times she had climbed this slope to see Janet. It was a bittersweet memory, and when she glanced over at Coll, she saw on his face the same mixture of emotions.

"Sometimes when I come up this path, I almost expect to see Ma standing in the doorway," he said. "Laughing and shading her eyes against the sun, you know."

"I know. I still miss her."

"Aye." Coll looked away, and after a moment he said, "Tell Meg I'll be in later for tea. I'll cut the wood first." Coll left the path, going around the side of the house.

Isobel knocked on the door and went in without waiting for an answer. As soon as she stepped inside, the tumult inside her eased. The small cottage was just as Meg's mother had kept it, familiar and cozy and smelling of herbs. A peat fire burned in the fireplace, dispelling the chill. In one corner of the cabin, the sleeping area was separated from the rest of the room by two carved wooden screens. The remaining walls were lined with cabinets and open shelves containing bags, boxes, and jars, each filled with herbs or roots or one of Meg's curatives, all combining to create the familiar spicy aroma of the cottage.

Smiling in greeting, Meg emerged from the stillroom and kitchen that jutted off from one side of the house. Her flame-red curls were pulled back from her face and tied at her neck, and she was dressed in a plain gray wool skirt and bodice. She wore no ornamentation save for a carved pendant on a simple leather thong around her neck and small gold rings in her ears. Others would have looked ordinary, even subdued, dressed as she was, but Meg, with her large, vivid golden eyes and untamed red hair, would draw the eye of anyone.

"Isobel! I'm so happy to see you." Meg came forward, reaching out to take the jacket Isobel was wearing, then looking down at it. "Is Coll with you, then?"

"Yes, he said he needed to chop wood for you. Though I think he came more because he thought I should not row over alone."

"No doubt. He is quite certain that neither of us could manage without his help."

"I probably could not. He helps me with a great deal more than just providing the kitchen with game and keeping out the poachers. Everyone knows he will treat them fairly, and now and then he will turn a blind eye when he finds a snare, but never with any sort of favoritism. I fear that he takes more time than he should from his cabinetry in order to help me."

"Coll is a good man, but he will do as he likes. No need to worry about that. Come into the kitchen while I make tea. Coll will expect to be fed, I imagine."

"He did mention tea." Isobel followed her. Some, Isobel knew, including Cousin Robert, disapproved of her friendship with Meg Munro. In their estimation, the mistress of Baillannan did not exchange confidences with the local midwife and healer. But she and Meg had grown up together, and when they were children, they had shared every thought, every feeling. They did not see each other often anymore, for Meg had stepped into her mother's shoes when Janet succumbed to pneumonia and Isobel had gradually assumed the running of the estate over the years. Still, Meg knew her best, and she turned to Meg when she needed help or advice or just a friendly ear. "But I do worry about him."

"Coll?" Meg cast a surprised look over her shoulder. "Whatever for?"

"I cannot help but think that he may be

connected to the men who are fighting the Clearances."

"Oh." Meg turned away and busied herself with the teakettle.

"I understand why they do it, and I cannot say I disagree with their putting Mardoun's steward to a bit of trouble."

"Donald MacRae is a villain," Meg said darkly. "Did you know he set fire to the Grants' house because they couldna move out when he said? He did not even give them a day to get their belongings together."

"I know. I dislike the man as well, and I hate what the earl is doing. And if a shipment of the earl's money or supplies disappears, well, I only hope it slows down the Clearances. But Mardoun is a powerful man, and his steward is as well because he has the earl's authority. Sooner or later the men harassing MacRae are bound to get caught, and it will go badly with them. They will be jailed. Transported. Maybe even worse — I fear Mardoun's men would shoot anyone they caught."

Meg turned back to her, her eyes dark with worry. "You know Coll will follow his heart. He won't hold back for fear of what might happen."

"Then you are concerned, too."

"Aye." Meg lightened her tone. "Or I

would be if I thought Coll was involved with that band of reivers, which he is not."

"Well, if, hypothetically speaking, Coll was with them, would you speak with him?"

"Hypothetically or any other way, you know he would not listen to my worries. Or yours, either."

"But, Meg, it could affect you as well. What if they thought you were also involved? Tell me you are not."

"No. I'm not." Meg looked at her so straightforwardly that Isobel relaxed. "But I canna ask Coll to go against his beliefs."

"You are as stubborn as he is." Isobel grimaced.

"Nae." Meg laughed as she poured the boiling water over the tea leaves. "No one's that stubborn."

"I suppose not."

"But you must not worry about me," Meg went on seriously. "I've nothing to do with it and know nothing about it, and that is the truth. This cottage is mine, granted long ago to a Munro healer by the Baillannan himself. They won't toss me out. And Mac-Rae is a pest, but I don't worry about him any more than any other weasel running about the woods."

" 'MacRae is a pest'?" Isobel repeated, her brow drawing into a frown. "Are you saying that Mardoun's steward has been bothering you?"

"Nothing I cannot handle." Meg shook her head. "Now, don't go worrying about me, as well. Truth is, I think MacRae's a wee bit frightened of me." Her eyes twinkled mischievously.

"With good reason." Isobel grinned at her friend. "You haven't told Coll he's bothered you, have you?"

"Och, don't be daft. Of course I haven't. Enough of your worrying about Coll and me." She gestured toward the table. "Come. We'll drink a cup, and you can tell me what brought you here. You didna come for your aunt's tonic. Coll could have brought you that." Meg poured the tea and slid a cup over to Isobel.

"No. I wanted to talk."

"Coll told me about the Englishman." Meg's face was warm with sympathy.

Isobel took a sip of tea, letting its heat glide through her. No one else's tea tasted as good as Meg's. Isobel had long suspected that Meg must add some delicious herb to it, a mixture handed down to her from her mother (and her mother before that), for it tasted just like Janet's brew, and it never failed to revive one's spirits. "Witch's tea," she remembered her father calling it, his

127

eyes twinkling.

"What will you do?" As usual, Meg went right to the heart of the matter.

"I don't know. And it is driving me mad. Mr. Kensington is letting us stay there while I get everything in order. Packing Auntie's possessions and mine are the least of it. There's the schoolroom with all our old toys and books — I hate to throw them away, but I cannot take those things with me. There is my grandmother's room, which Elizabeth has always left just as it was. And that barely scratches the surface. The attic is stuffed with old clothes and furniture and who knows what all. No one else would want them, least of all Jack Kensington."

"There's your answer. Just spend the next few years clearing it away," Meg said, a dimple appearing in her cheek as she grinned at Isobel.

"I do not think Mr. Kensington's patience will last long enough for that." Isobel sighed and sat down again. "He plans to sell Bail-lannan."

"Ah, Izzy . . . I'm sorry."

"I suppose it makes no difference whether he leaves it in the hands of an estate agent or someone else buys it and leaves it in the hands of an estate agent. But I feel so . . . I know it will stand empty like the Mac-

128

Kenzie place, and they will bring in more and more sheep and send all the people off. And it won't be *mine* anymore." Tears brimmed in Isobel's eyes.

"I know."

Isobel knew that Meg did; if anyone understood how she loved every bit of her home — not just the house, but the rocks and the trees, the heather that blanketed the hillsides, the burns and braes, the very earth itself — it would be Meg. The land lived in Meg just as it did in Isobel, perhaps even more so; the Munro women had always been the wise women of the woods, attuned to the earth and its plants and creatures, as far back as anyone could remember.

"Is there any way I can help you?" Meg asked.

"Well, Hamish pointed out that the loch could hide a body for a long time." Isobel gave her a wry look.

"It is a time-honored Highland tradition." Meg smiled faintly. "Though I'd suggest something more subtle myself."

"I tried to take him to meet some of the crofters, hoping he'd take an interest in the farms and families. But he would not do even that. I had the mad thought that he might return to London and let me manage the estate for him, but when I broached the subject, he assumed I was suggesting that he hire a man to be the estate agent. He would not try even that, so I can imagine how well he'd receive the idea of a woman running the place."

"You have managed the estate far better than Andrew ever would have. I'd like to see any man do better! No one loves it as much as you or knows it as well."

"Yes. But he is too distrustful . . . and too little interested in Baillannan. His decisions are based on nothing but logic and self-interest." Isobel sighed. "I should do the same, no doubt. I must decide where Aunt Elizabeth and I will go."

"You are welcome to come here, though I fear it would be a trifle small for three people."

"Yes, I think so." Isobel smiled at Meg. "But you are kind to offer."

"Go live with Andrew. 'Tis he who put you in this situation."

"The three of us in his bachelor apartment in London? I think not. He could not support us all in any case. He has lost the thing that provided the bulk of his income. I cannot imagine him living on what he has in the Funds — if he even has it still. Lord only knows, he may have gambled that away as well. Aunt Elizabeth and I could make do on a small income, but neither of us has that. I have dreamed up wild plans to take her to Edinburgh and open a millinery or a school for young ladies. But either of them would require an investment of money, and neither of us has that. Besides, I haven't any idea of hats — or how to turn out young ladies, either, if it comes to that. I could perhaps earn my keep as a governess, but I could not take Aunt Elizabeth with me there, and I cannot abandon her. It makes me quite despair; I fear we shall have to throw ourselves on the mercy of our family."

"Your cousins? Gregory and his father?"

"It's either them or my mother's sister in Edinburgh. Aunt Adelaide is . . ." Isobel sighed. "She is generous, really; she would welcome us, and her house is very pleasant. It's only — I know I must sound the most ungrateful person, but she chatters so, and her conversation is always of the most trivial things you can imagine. I could not impose on her and then ignore her, so I should have to spend all my time listening to her talk about parties and clothes and gossip. Accompanying her on calls and running errands and all the things a poor relative must do because they have nowhere else to go. 'Tis horridly selfish of me, but I cannot but dread the thought."

"It isn't only you who would hate it. Aunt Elizabeth would be miserable, as well. Everyone has trouble with things changing as they get older."

"Not just older people." Isobel gave Meg a wry smile. "I do as well."

"Of course you do. We all do. But it is worse for your aunt. You have seen how a sudden change upsets her. It rattles her, and she gets even more vague, which only makes her lose her certainty in her own thinking even more."

"I know." Tears welled in Isobel's throat. "I don't know what she would do if we moved to Aunt Adelaide's. It will be hard enough for Auntie to leave Baillannan, but to stay in a city the size of Edinburgh, so far from everything she knows, in a house that is completely unfamiliar to her — well, it doesn't bear thinking of."

"I can give her a tincture of oats to help her nerves, and hops tea would help as well, but I cannot if you are so far away. Or her tonic, either. I have added periwinkle to it this time, and I think you will see some improvement. But if the tonic does help her, it makes taking your aunt to Edinburgh a poor choice."

"I know. Which leaves only Cousin Robert." Isobel grimaced.

"At least your aunt would be able to remain in Kinclannoch, and she knows Mr. Rose and Gregory. Mr. Rose is somewhat, well . . ." Meg hesitated.

"You needn't search for a polite way to term it. Cousin Robert is overbearing and priggish and an utter martinet. I sometimes wonder how Gregory could be his son. They came to call on us this afternoon, and I realized how horrid it would be to have to depend on his charity. Everything he says raises my hackles — I even found myself defending Mr. Kensington to him! — but I could not disagree or do aught but obey him if he is being so generous as to support us. It would be even worse for Aunt Elizabeth. The two of them cannot be around each other without bickering; Cousin Robert finds her frivolous and impractical."

"Mm. I can imagine how he feels about her love of legends and heroic tales."

"Indeed, he hates that. Now that she has become . . . confused sometimes, he is impatient and out of sorts with her. He acts as if she does it simply to annoy him, and he has no sympathy at all. A few weeks ago, he caused her to burst into tears, and that irritated him even more."

"It does not sound like a good solution,

either." Meg frowned. "There must be something else you could do."

"I am quite willing to take any suggestions."

"You could marry."

"Marry!" Isobel let out a bark of laughter. "I like that — the woman who told me she would never marry is advising me to do so?"

"I did not say that *no* woman should ever marry. You know we Munro women are not the marrying sort. I have no need for a husband and no wish to have a man tell me what to do. I own my cottage, and I can make my own way. People will always want my potions and poultices. Nor do I have an aunt to look after."

"And what about love? You have no need for that?"

"Ah, well . . ." Meg cast her long lashes down demurely. "I did not say I would not ever love a man. I just will not marry one."

Isobel rolled her eyes. "Bold words for someone who has not even let any man court her."

"I may be brazen, as people say, but that doesn't mean I am not particular."

Isobel laughed, but shook her head. "I cannot marry a man to get a roof over my head."

"It is what most women do, wealthy or poor."

"And you think I should as well?"

"I don't think you *should*. But you may have to. There are not many choices left."

"Aside from the fact that no one has shown the slightest interest in marrying me —"

"They may not have been brave enough to approach you, but I assure you, you have no dearth of admirers. All you would have to do is give them the slightest bit of encouragement."

"And who should I choose for this honor? Maybe Dougall MacKenzie; he still has some of his teeth and I hear he's looking for a new wife since his died after thirty years. Or perhaps the parson; he might enjoy guiding a wife along the narrow path of righteousness. Or maybe Donald Mac-Rae."

"The earl's steward?" Meg made a sign as if warding off evil. "You might as well choose the devil. But I hear Mardoun himself is now a widower."

"Speaking of the devil," Isobel snorted inelegantly. "Anyway, the earl hasn't visited Duncally in twenty years. I don't even know what he looks like."

"Nor I. But still, he would probably be

preferable to Dougall MacKenzie." Meg laughed.

"It is no use." Isobel shook her head. "There are no eligible men but my cousin and your brother. That is the hope Cousin Robert cherishes, that Gregory and I will marry, which is another thing that makes the thought of living on his charity so unappealing. Robert would press me about the matter constantly, I know."

"Coll would marry you, you know that."

"Perhaps, to rescue me from sleeping under the hedges. But I would never ask him to sacrifice his life like that."

"I don't think he would consider it a sacrifice."

"But it would be. Coll deserves a woman who loves him passionately, not someone he grew up with like a sister."

"And he would say you should not marry beneath you," Meg admitted.

"Coll is not 'beneath' me or anyone else."

"I agree. But Coll would not stand for anything that would set tongues wagging about you." Meg shrugged. "So, clearly, we must find some other way. Perhaps you *should* visit your aunt in Edinburgh. You would be much more likely to meet eligible men there. You could go alone so you would not have to be looking after Auntie all the time. She can stay here, if not with your cousins, then with me. She knows me, and she would be in a familiar place. I think the two of us could get on fairly well, and if you did find a husband, she could move in with you."

"That is very good of you." Isobel reached out and took her friend's hand. "But I could not ask you to take on such a burden. Besides, I fear Coll may soon need your hospitality as well. I doubt that Mr. Kensington will keep on a gamekeeper. Anyway, I would feel wicked to try to lure some man into marrying me, to pretend that I care when all I want is a house."

"Then I see nothing for it but to convince Mr. Kensington to keep Baillannan and allow you to remain there."

"And how am I to do that?"

"So you think you could not talk to him? Is he disagreeable? Unpleasant?"

"Oh, no." Isobel shook her head. "Quite the opposite. He is charming. Agreeable. I have enjoyed his company." She thought of how enjoyable she had found the kiss he had given her yesterday — but that was something better not thought of. "It is just that he was so adamant about selling the house. He has made up his mind, and I don't know how to change him."

137

"You said he listened to logic and self-interest. Appeal to that."

"I don't know. Perhaps . . ." An idea struck Isobel, so absurd that she immediately dismissed it. However, her thoughts kept coming back to the matter even after Coll came inside and they sat down to tea. Isobel contributed little to the conversation, her thoughts churning, and she was quiet throughout the ride home across the loch.

Back at Baillannan, she walked slowly through her house, studying the faded, old tapestries and the familiar portraits of her ancestors that lined the long hallway. Halfway up the stairs, she turned and looked down at the entryway — the thick, carved wooden door, the stone floors, the fan of swords that decorated the wall. Her life was bound up in this house; she could not bear to think of leaving it. But did she have the strength to hold on to Baillannan? To save herself and her aunt as well?

At the top of the stairs, she paused under the portrait of Malcolm Rose. The grandfather she had never known gazed out at the world, confident, even arrogant, wrapped in his tartan, one hand resting on the hilt of his claymore. A dirk was thrust into a scabbard on the other side of his wide leather belt, its curved hilt engraved with the rose pattern that was the emblem of their family. A brooch with the same design fastened the tartan at his shoulder.

The Laird of Baillannan.

Isobel stared into his face for a long moment. She shared his coloring, the thick, dark blond hair and gray eyes. Once, when she was young, her grandmother had found Isobel staring at the huge painting, and Lady Cordelia had said, her voice threaded with sorrow, "Malcolm was iron at the core. There'll not be his like again."

Isobel turned, her decision made, and marched back down the stairs. She found Jack Kensington, sitting in the office, *her* office, the accounts book open on the desk before him.

He looked up when she came in and rose smoothly to his feet. "Miss Rose. You have arrived in time to save me from a vast array of numbers. I must confess that I am unaccustomed to studying accounts."

"If you wish, I can go over the figures with you and explain them."

"Ah, then you do understand them?"

"I entered them, so, yes, I do. I have been running Baillannan for my brother for many years now."

"I see." His brows rose a little. "I will be happy to take you up on your offer. But no

139

doubt something else brought you here. Did you wish to speak to me?"

"I did." Isobel squared her shoulders. "I have come to offer you a proposition."

"Indeed? Intriguing. What is your proposition?"

"That you marry me."

7

Kensington stared at her for a long moment before saying lightly, "Miss Rose, this is so sudden."

"Allow me to explain."

"Please do." He gestured toward the chair in front of his desk. "I believe this is a conversation best held sitting down."

"Of course." Isobel clutched her skirt in her hands to hide their tremor. Her stomach was like ice. But she could not back down now. She sat on the edge of the chair, back straight, hands clasped primly together, resting on her knees, and fixed an unwavering gaze on him. "You said the other day that you were not married and that you were not 'romantically inclined.' You told me that you did not believe in love."

"And this made you decide I would wish to marry you?"

"No, of course not." Annoyance flared in Isobel and somehow that steadied her. "It made me decide that you might be amenable to a marriage based on business considerations."

"Ah. A marriage of convenience."

"Yes."

"I can see that it would be convenient for you to remain in your home," Kensington replied affably. "But where exactly is the convenience for me?"

The tension inside Isobel eased a bit. At least he had not dismissed the notion out of hand. "You could return to London and resume the life you prefer while I manage Baillannan and send you the income."

"*You* will run the estate?" His brows rose in disbelief. "Or an estate manager whom you choose? Perhaps that fellow Munro?"

"Coll?" Isobel was surprised that Kensington knew his name. He had seemed to have no interest in those who worked here. "No. Coll is the gamekeeper. He helps me now and then, but I run Baillannan and have done so for many years."

Kensington studied her for a moment, idly toying with a letter opener. "That is most admirable, I am sure, but as we discussed before, I intend to sell the land, which will bring me a good deal more money than whatever its income is."

"Immediately, yes, but not over the course

142

of many years. If you like, I can show you the account books. The income is ample to live on; you may have seen that Andrew has lived well enough off it. If one was not foolish with money, it would be more than enough, and the rest could be invested. The important thing is that you would still have the land, which, as you know, is valuable."

"I could accomplish the same thing if I had an estate agent."

"You would have to *pay* him, and you told me you were reluctant to take that path because you did not know if you could trust an agent. I would hope you would feel more inclined to trust your wife."

"An estate agent might be more trustworthy than some wives." Amusement lifted the corner of his mouth.

"You are joking, I presume." It irritated Isobel that he always seemed to be amused at her expense. Did he think she was simple? "I assure you that you may rely upon my character. You have only to ask anyone around here."

"My dear Miss Rose, who am I, a mere gambler, to question your character? I am quite certain that it is of the most sterling quality."

"In any case," she added pragmatically, "you will have the figures from the past years; it would be apparent if I held more back from you. And since I would be your wife, even if I did steal from you, my money would still be yours, so what would be the point in it?"

"There is that."

"No manager whom you could hire would do as well as I. Not only am I competent, but I am a Rose of Baillannan. The people here are loyal to me."

"That sounds precariously close to a threat, Miss Rose."

"I do not mean it to be. It is simply the truth. The crofters trust me; they deal honestly with me. An estate manager will always be an outsider. *You* will always be an outsider."

"Unless, of course, I married you."

"You would still be an outsider." Isobel's expression softened into a smile as she went on in a Scottish burr, "But you wouldna be so far an ootsider."

"Appealing as it is to be only somewhat despised by all, it does not seem worth shackling oneself for life."

"But you would not be shackling yourself to me." Isobel's hope rose more and more the longer they talked. He seemed to actually be considering the idea. "You will live in London and I, here. You could have all

144

the freedom you would have if you were not married. I would not know what you did, nor care. You would not have to endure any of the normal ties. And since you have no affinity for the married state, there would be no chance of later regretting the decision because you wish to marry someone else."

"No, there is little chance of that." He studied her for a moment, tapping his forefinger against his lips. "So you would be a complaisant wife? It would not matter if I kept a mistress?"

"It would not matter to me if you kept ten mistresses."

"That might prove to be a trifle tiring." His smile was slow and intimate, and the meaning of his words sent heat flooding up into Isobel's face.

But she refused to let him divert her from her purpose. She leaned forward, her voice crisp. "Mr. Kensington, I will not mince words. We both know you are not a gentleman. But since you make your living gambling with wealthy young aristocrats, it is useful to present yourself as such. One of the *ton*. Someone who belongs. Think how much more believable your pretense would be if you owned an estate."

"You do not mince words, indeed." His

eyes, laughing before, were cool and flat now.

"I do not have the time for courtesy; my situation calls for immediate action. In the future, as you sit around the card table with Lord This and the Duke of That, you could casually mention your land in Scotland. Or you might bring a group of your 'friends' back to your country house for a few weeks of card play and shooting grouse."

"I do not need a wife for that."

"But you do need me as your wife for you to say, 'Baillannan has been in the family for generations.' Marrying me lends you immediate respectability. It gives you importance and a family. I know you do not care what the people here think of you. But it *is* important what the sheep you shear in London think of you. More than that, I think you have an ambition to *be* the gentleman they think you are." A flicker in his usually unreadable eyes told her she had guessed successfully.

"You think I should be other than who I am?" His voice was silkily dangerous.

"It does not matter what I think." Isobel stood up, her face lit with triumph. "The fact is that you wish it. Why else would you try so hard to seem a gentleman? It may make it easier to gather your prey, but the

146

truth is that you could fleece foolish young men in any gambling den in London without adopting their manners or speech. Why did you accept my brother's offer of his house as a bet? And why did you ride all the way up here in the rain to look at Baillannan? You want something more than the price of it."

"And you believe that something is you?" He rose to face her.

"I believe that I am a means to the end you seek."

"What am I a means to?" He leaned forward, bracing his hands on the desk. "Are you so desperate for a roof over your head that allying yourself to someone like me is worth it?"

"Baillannan is worth it."

He stared at her narrowly for a moment, then dropped back into his chair, the careless, faintly ironic manner once again in place. "When shall we announce our impending nuptials?"

"What?" The blood rushed from her head, and Isobel's knees gave way. She grabbed for the corner of the desk, and in an instant he was beside her, his hand under her arm, propelling her back into her chair.

"That is the first time I have made a maiden swoon," he said as he put his hand on the back of her neck, lightly pushing her head toward her knees. "Lean over. Not as ladylike as smelling salts, but effective, I've found."

The touch of his fingers against the sensitive skin of her neck sent a shiver through her. She lifted her head, embarrassed. "I am sorry. I'm fine. Really. I was just . . . surprised."

"Why? Did you think I was so dense I would pass up such an opportunity?" He settled on the edge of the desk, watching her.

"It seemed to me you disapproved of the idea."

"You are, as you said, a Rose of Baillannan." He shrugged. "I am merely Jack Kensington. If you are willing to sacrifice yourself for these people and this pile of stones, who am I to turn down the chance to perfect my disguise as a gentleman?"

She had prepared herself for the worst, the humiliation of his rejection, the pain of losing her only chance at her home. But she had not prepared herself for achieving her goal. Isobel pressed her fingers to her mouth, afraid she might suddenly start to cry.

"Here, now." His voice was surprisingly gentle as he tipped up her chin to look at

148

her. "Don't tell me you are already regretting your proposal. It wouldn't be the thing to cry off, you know."

"No. Of course not. I am . . . a trifle stunned, I think."

"Your hands are like ice." He took her hands in his, warming them. He was so close it was unsettling, and she could not help but remember the afternoon in the attic when he had pulled her to him and kissed her, his warmth and strength enveloping her, his scent filling her nostrils, the taste of him on her lips.

She tried to tug her hands from his, glancing toward the door. He chuckled, holding on a moment longer before letting her go. " 'Tis acceptable now, you know, to be caught like this; we are betrothed."

Isobel felt herself blushing, and inwardly she cursed her fair skin. She stood up, ignoring his comment. "I must tell Aunt Elizabeth."

"She will not object. Against all reason, she seems to like me."

"Her mind is slipping," Isobel retorted, then let out a little gasp, her hand flying to her lips.

To her surprise, Jack laughed. "Well, that should put me in my place."

"I don't know what is the matter with me.

Truly, that was rude, and I apologize. I am most grateful."

"Don't be," he said shortly. "I don't want your gratitude." She looked at him, surprised, and he gave a careless shrug. "It is an arrangement suitable to each of us. There is no need for thanks or tears or worrying that you may tread upon my sensitive feelings. Anyone would tell you that I have few of them, sensitive or otherwise. The last thing I want is for you to hide your sense of humor. It is as much a part of you as your blond hair." Smiling, he reached out to brush back a lock of hair from her forehead. "Or your bonny gray eyes." He brushed his knuckles along her cheekbone. "I have that right, don't I? *Bonny?*"

"*Bonny?*" Isobel was a little surprised she could get out the word, for her throat had gone dry and her brain blank. The promise in his eyes, the timbre of his voice, the feel of his skin against hers, stirred a heat deep inside her. "Aye. *Bonny* is 'pretty.' "

"Then it definitely suits you." He took her hand in his and raised it to his lips.

She could not disguise the shiver that ran through her at the touch of his lips upon her flesh, soft and velvety, and she snatched her hand away, backing up a step. "Mr. Kensington! I think you mistake. Ours is

150

not that sort of marriage."

"And what sort is that?" His smile was slow and teasing.

"You know what I mean." Color lit her cheeks, and she clasped her hands tightly together, as though to pull herself back into order. "An ordinary marriage, a —"

"Oh, I agree. Our marriage is anything but ordinary, but that is part of its appeal, surely?"

She was certain he was laughing at her, which rattled her even more. He did not mean he wanted a real marriage; it just amused him to see her lack of sophistication. She glared at him. "I mean that ours is a marriage of convenience, as you said. It is nothing but business."

"Ah, but business can be a pleasure as well."

"No. That is not what we agreed to. You cannot pretend that you want to . . . to . . ." Her cheeks burned even more hotly.

"To what?" He moved nearer, not touching her, but holding her captive somehow with his gaze, his closeness, as though his body were a magnet from which she could not pull away. "To have you in my bed? I would think that is the sweetness of wedding."

"Our marriage will not be sweet," she shot

151

back, though she knew the effect was marred by the shakiness in her voice.

He laughed, light sparkling in his dark blue eyes. "I find that tartness is even more to my taste." Taking her chin between his thumb and fingers, he bent and touched his lips to hers. Though his kiss was as light as a butterfly's touch, it set up a raging storm inside her. "But do not fear. I would never force you to do aught you did not want." He released her chin and moved back, adding with a flash of grin, "But perhaps I can persuade you to change your mind."

8

"Now, my dear Miss Ro — I believe it would be quite proper to call you Isobel since we are engaged, don't you agree?" Jack went on conversationally, as if nothing untoward had just happened. "Shall we announce the happy news to your aunt?"

He held out his arm and Isobel took it, too distracted to refuse. She had wanted to tell Aunt Elizabeth by herself, unsure how her aunt would take the information, but she could hardly exclude him now, so they went together to break the news of their engagement. To Isobel's surprise, Elizabeth's face lit up.

"That is wonderful!" She jumped to her feet and came forward to kiss Isobel on the cheek. "I have been hoping for this." She took Jack's hand in hers, saying playfully, "As soon as I saw you, I thought you were exactly the man for my Isobel. Who could be a better match than one of John's friends?" She paused, frowning. "Did I say John? How silly of me. I meant . . . um, Isobel's brother."

Isobel started to step in with her brother's name, for obviously it escaped Elizabeth at the moment. But Jack smiled down at Elizabeth as if he had noticed nothing odd about her response and said smoothly, "Yes, Andrew is the Rose I know. But who is John? Have I met him? If so, I must apologize, for I have quite forgotten his name."

Elizabeth beamed back at him. "No, you would not have met John. He was Isobel's and Andrew's father. My dear brother. He passed on several years ago — such a good man; it is a shame that he is not here to see this day. You would have liked him, I am sure, and he, you. There are so few left in our family anymore. Just the children — well, and my cousin." She disposed of Cousin Robert with a little wave of her hand. "No doubt *he* shall have something disagreeable to say about your engagement. I hope you will not be offended. It is his nature; I think he cannot help it. One simply has to ignore what he says. Come, sit down. Ring for Hamish, Isobel dear, we should have a little toast on this happy occasion."

Isobel did as her aunt requested, and as she joined her aunt on the sofa, she flashed a quick smile of gratitude at Kensington. He quirked an eyebrow at her in response and continued his light banter with Aunt Elizabeth. Isobel looked at her aunt. The sparkle that had been more and more missing from Elizabeth's face had returned. It occurred to Isobel that her aunt seemed to have actually improved since Jack Kensington had arrived. Perhaps the bargain Isobel had struck with him would prove to help Elizabeth more than Isobel had imagined. Surely that would make up for the annoyance of his teasing.

"When do you plan the nuptials?" Elizabeth asked, turning to Isobel, and Isobel could only stare blankly back at her.

"We would like to wed as soon as possible," Jack answered for Isobel, and turned to gaze at her with apparent devotion, mischief lurking in his eyes. "Isobel and I are eager to be together. Aren't we, my dear?"

"Yes, of course." Isobel shot him a quelling look. "Mr. Kensington must return shortly to his obligations in London, so the date has to be soon."

He grinned at Isobel, acknowledging her returning shot. "I am sorry to say that is true."

"That is too bad," Elizabeth sympathized.

"But you would want to hasten anyway; it will soon be May and you do not want to marry then, of course." Seeing the puzzlement on Jack's face, she added, "May is an unlucky month for marriage."

"Ah. I was not aware."

Isobel nodded.

"The banns can be read this Sunday, so that will mean we have two weeks to plan for the wedding. Oh, goodness, Isobel, there is such a lot to do. It will have to be small, of course. It is too bad that Andrew will not be here. Do you think if we wrote him today, he could make it here in time?"

"No." Isobel smiled at her aunt to soften her flat response. "It will be some time before the letter would reach him, and then he would have to travel all this way. I will have Cousin Robert or Gregory give me away." She could well imagine how her brother would receive the news of her betrothal to the man who had taken his home from him, and she had no desire to add any fireworks to the situation. "I shall write Andrew a note later, explaining."

"What about your family, Mr. Kensington?" Elizabeth turned to him. "You would wish your parents to come, I imagine. Brothers or sisters — I am sorry, I realize I don't know whether you have siblings."

"No, pray do not worry yourself about that," Jack told her with a charming smile. "You have a great deal to do without adding extra guests. And, as Isobel said, London is too far away. I would not want to delay our wedding day. I am sure you understand."

"Oh, indeed." Aunt Elizabeth chattered on lightly about Isobel's wedding dress, the feast, the guest list. "You can wear my mother's pearls," she told Isobel, then frowned a little and cast an inquiring glance at Jack. "I just realized — a wedding ring?"

"I don't have one," he confessed. "Our engagement was rather . . . unexpected."

"If you do not mind, there is Isobel's mother's ring. The one John gave her — Oh!" Elizabeth's eyes widened.

"What is it? Is something wrong?"

"No. No, dear. I just had a thought." The older woman jumped to her feet. "Wait. I shall be back in a tick."

Isobel and Jack glanced at each other, equally baffled. A few minutes later, Elizabeth bustled back into the room, a silver object in her hand. "I realized that I had the perfect thing for you, Mr. Kensington."

She held out her hand, and Isobel saw a pocket watch and chain. The cover was ornate, with raised figures in a sylvan setting. Taking Jack's hand, Elizabeth laid the watch in his palm. "This was my father's watch."

He glanced at her, startled. "But, ma'am . . . you cannot wish to give this away."

"Please, I want you to have it. I should have given it to my brother, but I could not bear to let it go."

"But surely it should go to someone in your family. Sir Andrew . . ."

"But you are in our family now." Elizabeth smiled, closing his fingers over the watch, and gave his hand a little pat. "It should be yours. I am certain of it."

He sat back, looking bemused.

"I never knew you had Sir Malcolm's watch," Isobel said, leaning over to look at it. Jack opened his hand, holding it out. An odd, almost wary look was in his eyes. Isobel traced her forefinger over the embossing. "It's beautifully done."

"Yes, and it's engraved on the inside with the Rose emblem." Elizabeth smiled in the sad, fond way she did whenever she spoke of her father. "I remember he once said that emblem was on everything he owned. Papa gave this watch to me that night when he came home from France."

"Really?" Isobel turned to her aunt, intrigued.

Elizabeth nodded. "I remember it clearly. I woke up when he came into my room. He was standing beside my bed, looking down on me. He sat down on the side of my bed. I was so happy to see him. He hugged me and laughed — he had such a wonderful laugh — and he said that he had told me he would come back. How could I not believe him? But he had to go away again to help the prince. I knew Prince Charlie needed help; I had heard my mother and Uncle Fergus worrying about what would happen. But I told Papa someone else could help the prince; I wanted Papa to stay with us." She smiled, tears of memory welling in her eyes.

Isobel took her hand, squeezing it, and Elizabeth sent her a grateful smile.

"Of course, he did not stay. But he promised that he would return as soon as he could. And he gave me his pocket watch. He kept the winding key, though, and he said he was stopping time until he came back to me. It was his pledge to return." Elizabeth let out a little sigh. "He never did."

"But this is proof that my grandfather returned from France!"

159

"Yes, dear, I told you that many times."

"Yes, but . . . you said that the others didn't believe you. How could they not when you had his watch?"

"I didn't tell them. I should have, I know." Elizabeth sighed. "I was afraid that if I showed it to them, they would take it away. I was just a child, and I thought they would not let me keep so valuable an object. Besides, Papa had given it to me and told me it was our secret, his pledge that he would return. In my child's mind, I feared that if I told anyone, he would never return. If I held it close to me and kept it safe, he could still come back." She shrugged. "Foolish, I know, but children think differently."

"No, not foolish," Isobel assured her. "I understand."

"After I was older . . . well, it always made Mother sad to talk about him. She said she had not seen him that night. I thought, What if he really hadn't gone to see her? Or if he slipped into her room to see her as he did with me, but she had not awakened. I thought she would feel worse, knowing she had missed the chance to see him again. Besides, I wasn't about to give people the satisfaction of trying to prove my words. Let Uncle Fergus and the others think what they liked. I knew the truth."

"Look." Jack, who had been examining the watch, held it out to Isobel, opened to reveal the works beneath the face. "There is its trademark beside the number: *Le Roy.* And at the bottom: *Paris.*"

"Did he purchase it while he was in France?" Isobel's voice rose in excitement.

"I don't know." Elizabeth frowned. "I cannot remember whether he had always worn it or not. Perhaps he did buy it there. It would make sense." She gazed off into the distance, then shrugged. "But that is all past. Now is what is important. What do you think — is there time to make you a new dress? David Grant's wife is very quick with a needle, but have we any material suitable?"

"I am sure one of my dresses will do fine."

"Oh, but we must! A bride must have a dress made for the occasion — though you must not see it until you put it on, of course, but we can fit it from one of your other dresses. I am sure Mr. Kensington would want to see his bride in something lovelier than 'fine.' "

"He will not care," Isobel put in, which earned her a quizzical look from her future spouse.

"Miss Rose," he said smoothly, "you are quite right. Isobel deserves the most elegant

161

of frocks. However, I would hate to delay the wedding for the dress. My eagerness to make Isobel my own outpaces my desire to see her clothed as she deserves. Besides" — he looked toward Isobel with the lazily teasing smile to which she was growing increasingly accustomed — "I know that Isobel will be beautiful whatever she wears."

"Very prettily put," Isobel retorted with some asperity.

"Yes, it is." Her aunt beamed at Jack. "But we will manage it, never fear. Mrs. Grant and I shall put our heads together."

Isobel's eyes drifted over to Jack, who had returned to studying her grandfather's pocket watch, absently rubbing his thumb over the raised figures. He was not, she thought, as immune to emotion as he chose to believe.

If her aunt had not reacted to the engagement in the way Isobel had expected, there were certainly no surprises in Cousin Robert's reception of the news. The day after the banns were posted, she saw Robert's carriage lumbering up the road to the house.

"Cousin Robert is here," she announced to her aunt, who was happily embroidering the neckline of a lawn nightgown.

"Bother!" Elizabeth poked her needle into

162

the material and set the hoop aside. "I knew that man would make a fuss."

"I suppose we might as well go down. 'Tis pointless to put him off."

They had reached the foot of the stairs just as Robert handed his hat and gloves to Hamish. "Isobel!" he barked, striding over to her. "What can you be thinking! Posting banns! To marry that English usurper!"

"You should be thankful, Cousin," Isobel told him lightly. "After all, now you will not have to worry about my reputation, sleeping under the same roof as an unmarried man."

"Do you dare to make light of this — this travesty of a marriage? Your father must be turning in his grave."

Isobel's face hardened, but she said only, "I suggest we take our conversation into the drawing room — unless, of course, you relish airing our family quarrels to the world."

Robert scowled, but swung around and strode down the hall to the drawing-room door, belatedly stopping and stepping aside to allow Elizabeth to enter the room before him. Isobel hung back to take Gregory's arm and strolled more slowly down the hallway.

"I am sorry," Gregory told her ruefully. "I tried to stop him, but you know how he gets when he is convinced he's right."

"I'm sure you did your best." Since Gregory's father was always sure he was right, Isobel could not imagine how he acted otherwise.

"Isobel . . ."

She glanced up at Gregory and saw that her cousin's usually cheerful face was creased in a frown. "Oh, Gregory, not you, too!"

"Is this really what you want to do?" he went on in a rush, his voice low and urgent. "I cannot think that you care for this man. He is a stranger."

"Don't be absurd. Of course I don't care for him. But most people do not marry for love."

"Perhaps not. But you! I hate to think that you must. It is not right that you should be placed in such a position." He set his jaw manfully, his expression one of preparing to take his medicine. "Isobel, you know that . . . that you have only to say the word. That is, I would be most honored if you would agree to . . . to become my wife."

Isobel let out a gurgle of laughter. "I can see that you have 'screwed your courage to the sticking place.' But there is no need for such a sacrifice."

" 'Tis no sacrifice," her cousin protested. "You know that I have always loved you."

"Yes, of course. Just as I love you. We both know that it is not in the way of a husband and wife."

"No, of course not, but — hang it, you need not do this to put a roof over your head. My father is not the easiest of men, but he would welcome you into our home."

"It is not the solution, as you are well aware. Cheer up." She gave his arm a squeeze as they stepped inside the drawing room. "It isn't as if I am going to the guillotine."

Robert, who had been striding impatiently up and down the room, wheeled around and glared at her. "How could you do this?" He turned to pin Elizabeth with the same scowl. "How could you let her?"

"I think it is a wonderful idea," Elizabeth retorted. When he snorted, she added, "It's time we had some new blood around here."

"New blood! That's what you call joining one of the oldest, proudest names in the Highlands to some English rabble? You have no idea who his family is or what sort of gutter he crawled out of."

"I know who he is," Isobel shot back, her eyes flashing. "He is the man who is about to become my husband, and I will not allow you to speak ill of him under his own roof!"

Robert blinked, taken aback, but he was

not silent long. "Have you written Andrew about this?"

"No. Why should I?"

"Why?" He gaped at her. "He is your brother. The Laird of Baillannan."

"Not any longer. He lost Baillannan — tossed it away like an old shoe. It is his fault we are in this position. He hadn't the sense to even hold on to his inheritance; I certainly don't intend to seek his advice. And I do not need his permission to marry. He is not my keeper."

"You need a keeper if this is the kind of decision you make."

"I am doing what is best for me and my aunt, as well as what is best for this land and the people on it. You have nothing to say about the matter. Nor does Andrew. He is my brother, and I love him, but he does not rule me — nor Baillannan, come to that."

"She is right." A voice came from behind them, and Isobel swung around to see Jack Kensington standing in the doorway, his face as hard as granite. "*I* am the owner of Baillannan. And if you have objections to me or to our marriage, then you had best say them to me."

166

"I will not have you upsetting Miss Rose," Jack said, crossing the room to Robert.

Robert's eyes bulged, his color rising dangerously, and he spluttered, "Why . . . why . . . how dare you! She is my niece, and I will speak to her as I please."

"No. You will not. Isobel is my wife." He slanted a glance at her and a smile touched his lips. "Or as near to it as matters." His gaze returned to the other man, and nothing of a smile was left on his face. "If you berate her again, I will tell the servants to toss you out on your ear. Have I made myself clear?"

The older man gaped at Kensington, and there was utter silence in the room. Isobel came up beside Jack, saying, "I believe you've made it amply clear." She laid a hand on his arm and turned to her cousin. "I suggest we all sit down. Aunt Elizabeth, why don't you ring for tea."

167

"Of course, dear. Mr. Kensington, do come sit here by me." Elizabeth gave the bellpull a tug and came over to link her arm through Jack's, steering him toward the sofa. "I have been intending to show you Barbara's ring."

"Barbara's ring?" Robert grumbled, taking a seat at some distance from Jack. "What are you on about now?"

"It is the wedding ring John gave Isobel's mother," Elizabeth explained, pulling it off her finger. She twinkled up at Jack as she handed it over to him. "I put it on this morning so I would not forget it again."

"It is lovely." Kensington took it and studied it. "I am honored, ma'am."

"The man cannot even provide his own wedding band?" Robert turned his glare on Isobel. "There! You see? I told you he was an adventurer. What kind of man asks a woman to marry him and then tells her she must provide the ring?"

"The kind who came to Scotland not knowing he would find his future wife there," Jack responded before Isobel could say anything. "I do not casually carry about family heirlooms on my person, Mr. Rose," Jack said disdainfully. "I will, of course, send for the *contessa*'s ring; it is worn by all the Kensington brides. But in the meantime, I

168

fear I must borrow from Aunt Elizabeth."

"The *contessa*! Hah! As if you were heir to an earldom."

"Oh, no, not the heir," Jack demurred modestly. "The *contessa*'s title was Italian, in any case. She brought the ring with her as part of her dowry."

"The *contessa*," Aunt Elizabeth said, enraptured. "How romantic. You see, Robert?" She shot her cousin a triumphant look. "I told you your worries were nonsensical. You are far too suspicious."

Seeing Robert's face flush beet red, Isobel jumped into the conversation before he could find his tongue. "Speaking of keepsakes — I have a few more things from the attic, if you would like to have any of them, Cousin Robert."

"What?" He blinked at her, caught off guard. "Do you mean you are still tossing out the family's possessions?"

"It isn't as if I am throwing away heirlooms." Isobel kept her voice mild. "However, the attic could use some clearing out. I have found a great deal there that does not need to be kept. Perhaps you might want to help sort through things."

"Yes, of course, I shall," he replied, glowering.

Isobel suspected Robert was not likely to

come help in such a dusty and mundane task, but her words had accomplished her goal of getting him off the subject. "Cousin Robert . . . I meant to ask you if you remembered anything about Sir Malcolm's watch?"

"What? Sir Malcolm's watch? What are you talking about?"

"The one he gave Aunt Elizabeth the night he came back to Baillannan. She showed it to us the other day." Isobel related the story her aunt had told them, ending, "I think that proves that Sir Malcolm did return from France."

"Then there really was a treasure?" Gregory's eyes lit up. "Remember how we used to hunt for that treasure every summer?" He grinned at Isobel.

"I remember how you and Andrew used to look for it every summer."

"I like that!" Gregory laughed. "Don't pretend you and Meg and Coll didn't come with us."

"Someone had to look after you younger ones," Isobel retorted primly, then laughed.

"You're daft, the lot of you." Robert shook his head. "There is no treasure. Sir Malcolm never came back."

"He did. I saw him," Elizabeth contested

hotly. "Mr. Kensington, show him the watch."

Jack pulled the watch from an inner pocket of his jacket, walking over to where Robert sat, and dangled it in front of the other man.

"What are *you* doing with Uncle Malcolm's watch?" Robert narrowed his eyes.

"I gave it to him," Elizabeth explained. "As a wedding present."

"You gave Sir Malcolm's watch to this foreigner?" Robert glared at his cousin. "Have you no sense of family? Andrew should have it. Or Gregory."

"It is mine; he gave it to me," Elizabeth retorted. "I can do what I please with it, and I think it's fitting that Jack should have it. He is the master of Baillannan now."

"So you are giving him everything else of the family's as well?"

Isobel sighed. It seemed to be a losing battle to try to keep her aunt and her cousin from bickering, but she made another attempt to pull the subject back to a civil topic. "Do you remember the watch, Cousin Robert?"

"No." He continued to glower at Elizabeth. "I never saw it before. I don't recall Sir Malcolm wearing that watch."

"Of course you do not. You were only a

171

baby," Elizabeth said in exasperation.

"And you claim you do?" Robert's brows rose. "You were scarcely older than I."

"I was almost six," Elizabeth protested. "And I didn't say I remembered seeing him wear it. I remember him giving it to me the night he returned."

"Pah!" Robert shook his head in disgust.

"We think he may have bought it in France." Jack opened the watch to show the trademark of the French watchmaker on the works.

"That doesn't mean he got it on that trip. He might have gone to France years before that. He might have bought it from someone else. Or perhaps he ordered it from Paris."

"Possibly so. But it was still his watch, no matter when he bought it. And he gave it to me," Elizabeth insisted.

"That doesn't prove anything. If, in fact, he gave it to you, 'tis more likely he did it before he left for France. You got the two times mixed up."

"*If* he gave it to me! Are you saying I lied?"

"No, of course not. But you know how you have been the past year. You get confused. You remember things wrong or don't remember them at all. What's to say that you don't also remember things that did not happen? Or you dreamed it, and after a while you thought it was real. Maybe it was a nice story you made up, like all those other tales you were always on about — the First Baillannan and the ghost of Annie MacAuley and whatnot — and you told the story so many times, you decided it was real."

"It was Annie MacLeod, not MacAuley, and it's not the same at all. That was an old tale. This is the truth."

"Well, it is the first time I have heard about it. If it really happened, why did you not tell us before?"

"Robert Douglas Rose!" Elizabeth surged to her feet, bright red spots of anger glowing on her cheeks. "I cannot imagine why you think I would tell you anything! You were a disagreeable little boy, and you are a disagreeable man."

"Elizabeth . . ." Robert rolled his eyes. "For pity's sake, do not be this way."

"I *saw* Papa that night. He told me he had come back from France. He gave me this watch and told me to keep it for him till he came back. It was our secret, and I kept it. Papa gave me the watch and he winked in that way of his, then he kissed my forehead and told me to go back to sleep. I could not, of course, so I followed him. I watched him walk down the hall to the sitting room, and he went into the fireplace, and he was gone."

She stopped, suddenly aware of what she had said. The room around her was frozen in silence. Elizabeth blinked, her eyes suddenly uncertain, and she seemed to shrink before them. "I saw him," she repeated softly, then whipped around and hurried from the room.

"Why are you looking at me?" Robert asked, throwing up his hands as the others turned to him accusingly. "I'm not the one who is losing his mind."

"You are the one who keeps jabbing at her," Isobel retorted hotly. "And she is *not* losing her mind!"

"Och. I'm beginning to think you are as mad as she is. Why will you not admit she is slipping?"

"She is better when we are alone. And Meg's tonic has helped her."

"Pffft. Magic potions."

"It is medicine, not magic."

"Father," Gregory said wearily. "I think it's time we left."

"Yes." Robert pushed to his feet. "Isobel, I wish you luck. Good afternoon." He gave her a brisk nod and favored Kensington with a sour look before walking out of the room.

Gregory let out a sigh. "Cousin, I wish you great happiness." He bowed over Isobel's hand. "Congratulations, Mr. Kensington. I am sure you realize how well loved Miss Rose is by everyone in Kinclannoch."

"Indeed." Neither man offered to shake hands. Jack watched Gregory leave, then swung back to Isobel. "You are, it seems, watched over by all."

"Including you!" Isobel grimaced at him. "There was no need for you to get into an argument with Cousin Robert. I would have handled it. I have been dealing with him all my life."

"I can hardly allow someone to annoy my wife. After all, that is a husband's prerogative." Jack smiled.

"We are not wed yet."

"We will be soon enough. I think I can enjoy some of a husband's pleasures." He moved closer to her, and Isobel's eyes flew to his face warily.

"I don't know what you mean."

"Don't you?" He reached out, idly twining one of her curls around his finger.

Isobel glanced away. It was disconcerting to feel as she did, so aware of her own body, so sensitive to every sensation. She felt the touch of the air on her skin, the pulse of blood through her veins, the rush of breath in her throat. He was tall and solid beside her, and it would be easy to lean against him, to rest her cheek upon his chest. She imagined his arms curving around her as they had the other day when he kissed her, encircling her with his warmth.

She stepped back quickly, drawing a shaky breath. He made no move to stop her, his hand sliding from her hair, and Isobel was aware of a strange sense of disappointment. It would be weak, she reminded herself, to lean on him. Jack would soon be gone. Relying on him would only lead to disappointment, and it would be even more foolish to allow herself to feel anything for him.

She turned away, crossing her arms as if suddenly cold. "Why did you tell Cousin Robert that story? 'The *contessa*'s ring' — really, Jack . . ."

"You think that was doing it too brown? It may have been," he mused. "But in my defense, I hadn't any time to prepare."

"It isn't funny."

"Isn't it?"

"No. You act as if everything is so light . . . so comical, as if life is just an amusement for you."

"I find it's preferable to living in gloom."

"But some things are serious. Not everything can be reduced to a jest."

"Perhaps not everything." He shrugged. "But your cousin Robert, now . . ."

"Yes, all right, he is pompous and rude and he thinks it is his duty to favor everyone from the butcher to the dustman with advice on how to live their lives. But he was not the only one to whom you told that bouncer. My aunt was there, too, and she will believe it, however suspicious Robert may be. She already has enough uncertainty about what is real and what is not. It is cruel to lead her to believe a lie."

He raised his brows. "I assure you, I had no intention of deceiving your aunt."

"Perhaps not. But now she will tell everyone about your ancestor the Italian *contessa,* and people will think her even more foolish." Isobel's shoulders sagged, her irritation draining out of her. "Oh, Jack, what if Cousin Robert is right? I feel disloyal to even wonder. But what Auntie said tonight, about her father walking into the fireplace, did not make any sense. Maybe it *was* just a dream."

"What does it matter whether she remembers it correctly?" Jack took Isobel's hands in his. "Whether your grandfather came here or not is of little import today. You do not believe there is a treasure hidden here?"

"No."

"In any case, hunting for buried treasure is a child's game. A bit of fun and adventure, but the odds of finding it are astronomical. Trust me, I deal in calculating the odds."

"I don't care about the treasure. It matters because I do not want her to be wrong!" Isobel's voice ended in almost a cry, and tears sprang into her eyes. "I love her, and I fear she is slipping away. Not in body but in mind . . . and spirit . . . in the things that make Aunt Elizabeth herself."

"She has her moments." His voice hardened slightly as he went on, "But she does not lie."

"Of course not." Isobel bristled.

"She does not live in a constant fog. And she is here with you."

"Yes. I should count myself lucky. It is just — she was always so intelligent. She loves a good story, and she could tell them in a way that had us round-eyed with suspense. But she also had a boundless curiosity about things. Janet taught us about the plants and trees, the flowers; we used to roam the braes and burns with her. But it was Aunt Elizabeth who taught us how things worked, how things lived and died, what our past was. You have seen the library downstairs."

"Yes, and it is an impressive one. That is where I have spent my hours while you have been laboring in the attic."

"You are interested in books?"

He laughed, widening his eyes in gentle mockery. "You needn't look so stunned. I do not spend my entire life in gambling dens. I have never been a great reader, I admit. But I am curious."

"It is no wonder, then, that Aunt Elizabeth likes you. You are two of a kind."

"I doubt that." He smiled faintly. "Your aunt has a gentle soul. I simply want to understand things. She is a wealth of information. We have talked many an afternoon, and she has directed me to books on various subjects."

"She bought most of the books in the library — or, rather, persuaded my father to buy them. But she does not read so much anymore."

"People get old. It is a hard fact. I doubt that she walks as fast as she used to or climbs the stairs as easily. It is not any more unusual, surely, for her brain to slow down, as well."

"No, you are right." Isobel smiled. "Thank you."

"I have done nothing but tell you what you already know."

"Still, it helps to hear it." She paused, then went on a little stiffly, "I think that you have

179

helped my aunt as well."

He raised his eyebrows slightly. "Hard, I know, to believe."

"Harder still to say so."

"No doubt. I have detected a mite of stubbornness in the Scots' nature."

Isobel let out a soft laugh. "You could be right. But 'tis hard to admit that a stranger helped her where her kin cannot."

"Kin, I find, are more likely to make things worse."

"What a thing to say! Surely you do not believe that."

"Don't I? Look at the effect her cousin has upon Miss Rose."

"Cousin Robert has a bad effect on a number of people, kin or not," Isobel retorted. "Come now. You must have family upon whom you rely. A father. A brother. A cousin."

"I rely on myself," he replied shortly, his face closing down. "I would think your experience with your brother would have taught you the same thing."

Isobel blinked, rebuffed by the change in his manner. She felt vaguely embarrassed, as if she had overstepped the boundaries of their relationship. "Yes, no doubt it should have. Pray excuse me. I should go see to my aunt. Good afternoon, Mr. Kensington."

As she walked out, she heard him let out a soft curse and take a step after her, but she continued without pause, and he did not follow.

Jack gazed out his bedroom window into the night. There was little to see; the pale wash of moonlight barely outlined the darker clumps of trees and the edges of outbuildings, and in the distance the loch was boundlessly black. He had been amazed at the absolute darkness of the night here, accustomed as he was to the city.

He thought of going downstairs and taking a turn about the yard, perhaps smoke a cigar. He wasn't sure why; it was not the sort of thing he did, and he could not imagine that it would be pleasant to be out in the cold and misty air. He supposed it was the same strange kind of impulse that had motivated him to search the library for books on the flora and fauna of the Highlands and accounts of its bloody history. He had even taken up a book about farming methods that he'd found on the desk in the study. While it was true that he liked knowledge and enjoyed acquiring it, as he had told Isobel this afternoon, he had never before strayed so far from his interests. No doubt it was simply that this place was so different, so unknown, that it roused his curiosity.

A flicker of light on the loch drew his attention, but it vanished immediately in the strands of fog drifting over the water. He remembered Isobel's tales of mysterious lights and noises on the island in the loch, and he smiled to himself. Perhaps the ghosts were busy tonight.

The idea of taking a walk tugged at him more insistently. He could stroll toward the dock he had seen the other day, when he had caught sight of Isobel returning with Coll. Now, as then, the incident pricked his curiosity. Where had the two of them been? His thoughts had flown immediately to the idea that they had sneaked away for a tryst. It was the second time he had seen the two of them together in a way that bespoke great familiarity.

Jack had made a point of meeting Coll Munro after the first time he saw him with Isobel, and he had taken an instant dislike to the man. Though the Scotsman had said nothing overtly insulting, Munro had spoken the fewest words necessary to answer Jack's questions, his demeanor surly, even antagonistic. It was, of course, the attitude of most of the people Jack had had the misfortune to meet at Baillannan — though at least since his engagement to Isobel, the servants had settled into a carefully neutral pose rather than one of complete hostility. But in Coll Munro, the attitude bothered him more. The reason was not hard to figure out, if he was being honest. He disliked the man because Isobel favored him.

Thinking of Isobel, he grimaced. He had taken a misstep there. She had been warm, even friendly — until he had recoiled from her mention of his family. He never talked about them — least of all to her — but he should have deflected the subject with humor, as he usually did. He had been clumsy.

People were his area of expertise, the knowledge he used — their tics and oddities, weaknesses and vulnerabilities, the mannerisms and tones and expressions that would tell him how to win their money. He knew how to charm, how to smooth the way, what to say, what to do, to achieve his purpose. But since arriving at Baillannan, he found himself thrown off-kilter. Isobel intrigued him and caught him off guard. All too often he responded impulsively.

Not that it mattered what Isobel thought of him. He would be gone before long and would rarely, if ever, see her again. He had accepted her offer of marriage because it made sense — and if that marriage involved a few weeks of pleasure with an attractive woman, that had sweetened the pot. Yes, he found his thoughts straying to her lissome form and imagining how it would feel to have those long legs wrapped around him, and sometimes he daydreamed about taking down her neatly pinned blond hair and letting it flow through his fingers, as thick and rich as the dark honey its color resembled. But the low tickle of desire he felt whenever she entered a room had not been his reason for agreeing to marry her.

If she piqued his interest, if he found her intriguing for the odd mixture of qualities she possessed — the courtesy coupled with the forthrightness of her proposal, the practicality of proposing their marriage that contradicted her love of fantastical stories, the strength that underlay her pliable nature — well, that merely made it more agreeable to pass the time until he returned to London.

Jack was accustomed to making quick decisions that seemed instinctive, even impulsive, but which were firmly based on logic and observation. He had done the same thing here. Isobel's arguments had made sense: He would have an asset as well as income, all without effort on his part if

Isobel's claim of running the estate success-fully was true. It would make it far easier to establish a rapport with the gentlemen of the *ton* if he could casually refer to his "house in Scotland."

And, yes, he would admit, as she had surmised, he would find some satisfaction in being a man of property, with an aristo-cratic wife waiting for him in the country. A man, moreover, whose heirs would carry his blood, mingled with that of a family who could trace its lineage back hundreds of years. His mind lingered for a moment on the thought of Isobel carrying his child, and the image was strangely pleasing.

None of that depended on her viewing him with favor. She would still marry him. And he suspected that when it came down to it, she would not deny him access to her bed, despite her protest the other day. She was the sort of woman who did her duty. So it did not matter that Isobel had pulled away from him at his curt reply.

Still, it bothered him that he had mis-played his hand. Isobel was the one thing that made staying in this cold, unfriendly spot bearable. Nor was he a man who desired to bed a woman who did not want him. The next few weeks would be slow and tedious if Isobel retreated behind a wall of remote courtesy. Clearly he had to win her over.

Turning from the window, he picked up his jacket from the back of the chair and shrugged it on, not bothering with the sartorial niceties of a cravat or waistcoat. A spot of brisk evening air might be just the thing for thinking.

Jack started toward the door, but he stopped abruptly at the muffled but distinct sound of a metallic screech coming from almost directly beneath him. He returned to the window and looked out. The wisps of fog had grown thicker and more numerous, creeping in from the loch, but the yard directly below him was clear enough that he could see a dark form beneath his window.

He shoved up the window, barking, "Who's there! What are —"

The dark figure below jumped as if shot and took off into the night. With a shout, Jack whirled and ran after him.

10

Isobel awoke with a start. She sat up, vaguely aware that a noise had disturbed her sleep. Pushing the heavy fall of her hair back from her face, she slid out of bed and stepped into her slippers. As she was lighting a candle, she heard Jack's shout, and an instant later, a door down the hall slammed back against the wall.

She ran to her own door and stuck her head out just in time to see Jack disappearing down the stairs. Without thinking, she followed the thunder of his footsteps, shielding the flickering light of her candle with one hand. Sconces burned low along the stone corridor, making it easier to see her way, and she broke into a trot. She could not see Jack, but just before she reached the library, she heard the long, piercing shriek that she recognized instantly as the scrape of the side door against the stone floor as it opened. She turned down the short side hall and saw that the outside door stood ajar.

She slipped through the narrow space of the open door into the side garden and saw Jack disappearing down the garden path into the fingers of fog. There was no sign of whatever he was chasing. Isobel, more familiar with the area than he, stopped to light the twin globes beside the door, casting light onto the path, before she started after him.

"Jack!" He stood at the end of the path where the walled garden gave way to the open yard, fog eerily creeping across his feet and calves.

He turned, startled, and walked back toward her. "Isobel! What are you doing out here? Did you hear it as well?"

"I heard you pounding down the hall like a madman. What happened?"

"I heard a noise below my window — that door, as it turned out." Jack gestured toward the side door.

He stopped a few feet from her, and his eyes drifted down her, the lines of his face shifting subtly. Isobel's heart began to thump in her chest; it occurred to her that she had not thrown on her dressing gown over her nightdress before she pursued Jack down the stairs. In the next instant, she realized that the light burning in the lamps behind her must shine right through her white cotton nightgown, illuminating the curves of her body.

A shiver ran through her, though she was not sure whether it was caused by the chill of the night air or the look on Jack's face. He moved closer, his eyes drawn to her nipples, prickling in the cold and pressing against the cloth of her nightgown. Isobel drew in a shaky breath, her mind a jumble. A strangely pleasurable ache started between her legs, and she was suddenly aware of the soft touch of the nightgown against her skin, the brush of mist upon her cheek. She wanted to turn and run; she wanted to go to him; she wanted, shockingly, to feel his mouth on hers and his arms closing around her, pulling her into his body.

Jack stopped only inches from her. Isobel could feel the heat of his body, see the heat in his eyes. He reached out and put his hands on her arms, sliding his fingers up and awakening every nerve in her body. She trembled, waiting, certain that he was about to kiss her.

"You're cold." His voice was low and hoarse. He pulled off his jacket.

Disappointment shot through her, and Isobel struggled to keep it from showing in her face as he draped the jacket around her shoulders. Gripping the lapels, he drew his hands slowly downward, pulling the sides together. She could feel his fingers through the cloth, his knuckles grazing her breasts and making her nipples tighten even more. Her eyes flew up to his, and he smiled, the movement slow and evocative of languid pleasure.

"My dear Isobel, you are a most tantalizing woman."

Isobel was lost for words, aware of nothing but his nearness and her raging pulse. Her mouth was dry as dust, and unconsciously she wet her lips. His eyes leapt with light and his fingers clenched the cloth of his coat, pulling her infinitesimally forward.

"You — you should not," Isobel stammered. "Your jacket — I mean, surely you will be cold without your jacket."

"I think I am quite warm enough. And it is, after all, a husband's right, is it not, to see to his wife's comfort?"

He bent his head toward her, and Isobel raised her hands between them, with some vague thought of warding off his embrace, but then her hands spread out on his chest, his heat pouring through the thin lawn of his shirt and into her flesh. She could feel the contour of his muscles, imagine the texture of his skin. His face came nearer, and her eyes fluttered closed.

"What happened?" a voice called, accompanied by the crunch of footsteps on the gravel.

Isobel sprang backward, and Jack let out a low curse. They turned to see Coll Munro striding toward them out of the fog, lit by the yellow glow of the lantern he carried.

"Oh!" Coll stopped, his brows shooting up. "Isobel. I . . . I did not see you."

"Hello, Coll." Isobel hoped her voice did not come out as shaky as she felt.

"Is something wrong?" Coll started forward again, his brows drawing together. "Isobel?"

"No. I mean, I don't know. Jack — that is, Mr. Kensington — heard something."

"Heard something?" The faintest trace of skepticism was in Coll's voice as he joined them.

"Yes." Jack returned Munro's gaze coolly. "I heard the side door opening."

"This late at night?" Coll's eyes flickered from Kensington's shirtsleeves to Isobel in her nightgown, Kensington's jacket wrapped around her.

"I was asleep," Isobel explained, shifting beneath Coll's stare. She could feel a blush rising in her cheeks. "I heard Jack shout, and I, um, came out to see what had happened."

Jack moved to stand beside Isobel, curling an arm around her shoulders. "In my experience, intruders rarely break in during the day."

"No doubt you would know more about that," Coll replied. "But how do you know it was an intruder? We don't have many of those here. Dinna you think it was just the wind slamming the door shut?"

"The wind?" Jack cast an expressive glance at a nearby bush, its leaves unmoving. "And that door?"

Isobel could not deny that Jack's arm about her was warm and even pleasantly protective, but she was uncomfortable under Coll's gaze. She turned away and pointed back toward the side door. "It's the door that catches on the floor, Coll. No doubt that's why he heard it."

"I know it was an intruder," Jack said with some impatience. "I looked out my window, and I saw a man."

"A man." Coll straightened. "Who?"

"I would scarcely know him," Jack retorted caustically. "Anyway, I could not see his face. It was dark, and I saw only a hat and coat. When I shouted at him, he ran away. I went after him, but I lost him in the fog."

He gestured toward the end of the garden. Isobel, following his gaze, saw that the fog, though thick in some areas, was now beginning to feather out nearer the loch. A light moved on the island, disappearing into the mist.

Isobel cast a sharp glance at Coll. The whole incident had confused her until this moment. She was unsure why someone had opened the side door of their house, but now she uneasily suspected it had something to do with the light on the island — and, in all probability, the men who had been fighting the Clearances of the Earl of Mardoun's lands. And that, she feared, meant Coll might be involved.

Jack glanced over, following her gaze, and Isobel quickly put a hand on his arm to bring his attention back to her, sliding over a step so that he had to turn his back to the island to face her. "Are you sure it was a man?"

Jack's eyes went to her hand, then up to her face. Isobel hastily dropped her hand from his arm. "I don't know. I just assumed . . ." He paused, considering the idea. "I think so. It seemed rather large for a woman. And why would a woman be trying to break into the house?"

"Why would a man do so?" Isobel countered. "Perhaps it was someone leaving the house, not entering."

"Who? Do you think Hamish decided to prowl about at midnight?"

"No. I have no idea why anyone would. There is nothing to do."

"Are you *certain* there was someone there?" Coll asked bluntly.

Jack narrowed his eyes at the other man. "You think I made this up?" Jack's voice was calm and quiet but was all the more dangerous for it.

"I think things can look different in the Highland mist, especially to a city dweller."

"London has been known to have a bit of fog itself, so I am not entirely unfamiliar with it. I have never known it to shove open doors or to make it appear that a man is running down a path."

"No, of course not." Isobel sent a warning glance at Coll. "I am sure Coll did not mean to imply anything. It is just so odd, one doesn't know what to make of it."

"I'm going to take a look around," Jack decided.

"But you cannot hope to find anyone," Isobel protested. "Not at this time of the night and in the fog."

"I'll take a lantern like Munro." He nodded toward Coll. "I am sure there's one in the house."

"Nay, I'll go. I am already about and fully dressed." Coll cast a pointed glance at Jack's shirt. "You should take Miss Rose back inside 'fore she catches her death of cold."

Jack bristled, and Isobel slipped her hand through his arm, curling her fingers securely around it. "Yes, please do, Jack. I *am* rather chilled. And Coll is more familiar with the place, anyway."

Jack gave Isobel a long, considering look. She could feel his muscles tighten beneath her hand, and for a moment she feared he would refuse. But then he inclined his head slightly. "Of course. It would be my pleasure." He turned his cool, assessing gaze on Coll. "You will give me a report tomorrow."

Coll stared back for a long moment, then gave Jack a nod, tugging at his cap in a way that should have been respectful but came out mocking. Isobel glared at her friend. Jack had clearly taken an immediate and unreasonable dislike to Coll, but Coll was not helping matters.

She gave a small but insistent tug on Jack's arm, and to her relief he turned away from Coll and started with her back toward the house. Coll walked in the other direction, and after a moment his figure was swallowed in the fog.

"Surly sort," Jack commented.

"Not usually." Isobel looked up to find him watching her.

"Mm. No doubt he is different with you." As they walked on, Jack continued in a casual way, "Odd, don't you think, that Munro was out at this hour?"

The nerves in Isobel's stomach tightened. She wondered if Jack had seen the lights on the island, too. He would not know anything about the recent incidents or the men involved in them, but he might well suspect Coll of being the intruder he had chased away. She could not imagine why Coll would have come secretly into the house, but if he had done so, she knew he had a good reason for it. Jack, however, would assume Coll had been there to steal something.

"The gamekeeper's cottage is quite near," she explained. "Perhaps Coll was taking a walk before bed."

"Yes, that's a possibility."

"Or he might have been looking for poachers," she went on, struck by inspiration. "No doubt they lay traps and come to take their catch in the dark of the night."

"No doubt." Jack opened the door, and they stepped into the house. As they walked down the hall, he went on in the same neutral voice, "Rather familiar for a servant."

"Coll's not a servant." Isobel stopped and faced Jack.

"Yes, I know; you've explained, he's the gamekeeper. Still, he is an employee."

"He's a friend."

Jack arched one eyebrow in a way she found particularly annoying. "And do you always greet friends thus attired?" He swept an encompassing glance down at the nightgown she wore beneath his jacket.

"No!" Isobel blushed, which made her doubly irritated. "Of course not. I did not set out to greet anyone. I heard you shout, so I thought you might be in trouble. I ran out to *help* you."

"Or to warn someone," he murmured.

"What?" Isobel stared at him. "Have you gone mad? You think I would be party to breaking into my own home?"

"What I think is that you had best have a care." Jack came closer, his voice low but threaded with danger. "Ours may not be a love match, but do not think that I am so complaisant a husband that I will turn my head while my wife dallies with another man."

Isobel gaped at him, outrage slamming through her. "You think Coll was coming

197

here to meet me? That we were — that we had a tryst?"

"What else should I think?" Jack retorted. "The fellow is always hanging about you."

"That's nonsense."

"Is it? You ran to him straightaway the day I arrived at Baillannan. And I've seen you with him since."

"Are you spying on me?" Isobel bridled.

"Of course not. But I can scarcely look out the window without seeing him. The man is everywhere. Tonight someone tries to get into the house, and when I go down to investigate, who should appear out of nowhere but your 'friend' Munro? And there you are, clad in nothing but your night rail, your hair down about your shoulders." His voice thickened slightly as his eyes went to the thick fall of her honey-gold hair.

"You are being ridiculous." Isobel pushed back her hair, shifting under his gaze.

"Am I? The lady of the manor is not usually 'friends' with the gamekeeper. Munro is insolent and far too familiar with you. I will not have my wife —"

"Stop saying your *wife* as if I were your property!" Isobel stabbed her forefinger into his chest. It felt so satisfying, she did it again. "You may own everything else here at Baillannan, but you do not own me."

198

"I don't care to own you, believe me, for I am sure you are far more trouble than you are worth, like everything else in this benighted place. But I have no intention of marrying you to provide you the cover of respectability while you settle down here with your lover."

Isobel drew in an enraged breath and swung her hand to slap him, but Jack caught her by the wrist. She tried to jerk her hand from his grasp, but his grip was too tight. The light in his eyes made her think Jack was enjoying their confrontation, even anticipating whatever fire came next.

Suddenly the air around her was so hot and stifling that Isobel could barely breathe. She was afraid that she might swoon, thoroughly humiliating herself — and, worse, that Jack might catch her, his arms sliding around her to keep her upright, her head settling against his hard chest.

The jacket was causing her to be so warm, she told herself, and she started to shrug out of it, but stopped, remembering the way the soft cotton of the nightgown had revealed the curves of her body, barely shading the dark circles of her nipples. Jack's eyes were already sliding down to the rise and fall of her bosom; it would be pure folly to remove the covering of his jacket. Isobel self-consciously grasped the lapels and pulled them together. He smiled faintly, and the heat in his eyes only deepened at her action. He leaned forward slightly.

Isobel jerked her arm from his grasp. "What a charming opinion you have of your future wife. I can only wonder that you would consent to marry a woman you consider a trollop. Clearly the idea of our marriage was a mistake."

She whirled and started toward the stairs, but Jack grabbed her wrist and spun her back around. Her heart jolted as he seized her arms, his hands clamping firmly around them. "No. I don't think it was a mistake at all." Jack pulled her flush against his body, and his mouth came down on hers.

He pinned her against the wall with his weight, bracing his forearms on either side of her head as he drank her in. She was trapped by his strength, permeated with his heat. And she had never felt so eager, so fierce, so consumed by need.

Making a low animal noise she did not even recognize, she thrust her body up against him and wrapped her arms around his neck, taking his mouth as fervently as he took hers. Her breasts were pressed into his chest, blossoming with a sweet, harsh ache. She twisted a little against him, delighting in the friction of the cloth across her sensitive nipples, and wishing in a primitive, incoherent way that his jacket were not around her, blocking even closer contact.

As if Jack had sensed her thoughts, he slipped his hands under the jacket, fingers spreading out over her waist. They moved slowly up her body, coming up at last to cup her breasts and send her heart into a frenzied beat. His mouth left hers and he kissed the curve of her jaw, moving down onto her neck. She would have protested the loss of his lips on hers had they not been igniting bright frissons of pleasure all through her body.

He murmured her name against her skin, the touch of his breath, his lips, his tongue, all arousing her in a way she had never dreamed possible. His hands slid down over her hips and his fingers clenched in the cloth of her gown, gathering the material and dragging it upward. Air kissed her bare legs, and she shuddered, aware of an ache deep within her, growing, swelling into a hunger so profound and insistent it frightened her. In another moment, she thought, she would be lost, drowning and consumed.

With a soft cry, she broke away. For an instant she stared at him. His face was flushed, the flesh drawn tautly across his sharp, high cheekbones. He radiated a power barely held in check, his eyes bright and fierce. He held her with his gaze, as tangible as a touch. She wanted to throw herself back into his arms.

Instead, she turned and fled up the stairs to her room.

11

Isobel awoke the next morning with a pounding headache and a deep realization that she had behaved in an appalling manner. After Jack had all but accused her of being a wanton, she had melted in his arms, no doubt confirming his suspicions. She could not imagine what had come over her. Isobel covered her face with her hands, letting out a groan, as she thought about facing Jack again. It would be humiliating. Worse than humiliating.

How had everything veered so badly from her plan? She had not expected her engagement or marriage to be smooth, but she had imagined an entirely different set of hardships — giving up the hope of falling in love, letting go of the desire to have children, settling herself to the knowledge that she would grow old alone. It had not occurred to her that Jack would infuriate her as he had last night, that he would think such base and untrue things about her, or that she would let him kiss her and fondle her and, well, treat her like the doxy he presumed her to be. Far worse than that, she had *enjoyed* it. It made her blush to recall how passionately she had kissed him, how her flesh had quivered beneath his caresses.

Jack would have realized how she had been consumed with lust; he had to, an experienced man such as he. He had been fully aware of how much he tempted and aroused her. And that was the most lowering thought of all.

She could not bring herself to go down to breakfast and make polite conversation with Jack in front of the servants and her aunt. But she knew she had to deal with the matter. Midmorning, after she had taken her breakfast of tea and toast in her room, she picked up Jack's jacket, folding it carefully over her arm, and went downstairs in search of him.

Unfortunately she found him in the library with her aunt. Isobel paused at the doorway, tempted to beat a cowardly retreat, but Elizabeth caught sight of her.

"Isobel! How are you, dear? I was afraid you might have taken ill when we did not see you at breakfast this morning."

"I am fine. I was just . . . I woke rather

late." Isobel steeled herself to look at Jack.

"Good morning, Isobel," he said, rising and coming forward. "I trust you had a restful night." He smiled down at her, his eyes glinting.

"Yes. I slept quite well." She set her jaw.

"I cannot see how you could," Aunt Elizabeth put in. "The spirits were putting on a show last night."

"Excuse me?" Isobel looked at her aunt.

Elizabeth chuckled. "The lights on the island, dear."

"Your aunt and I were discussing the unfortunate souls doomed to a restless afterlife on the island in the loch," Jack put in.

"There were noises, as well," Elizabeth added. "I distinctly heard voices."

"Surely not." Isobel struggled for a light tone. "The island is some distance."

"The voices were much closer than that. I was telling Mr. Kensington that the house has its share of ghosts. The laird who built it, you know, was said to have strangled his mistress and walled her up in the cellars as the house was being constructed."

"Aunt Elizabeth, you will have Mr. Kensington thinking we are a dastardly lot."

"On the contrary. I find the Roses fascinating. Especially the women of the family."

205

Isobel avoided looking at him, carefully picking an infinitesimal bit of lint from the dark blue jacket over her arm. It occurred to her that the coat was much the color of Jack's eyes, which was a perfectly idiotic thing to be thinking about.

"I am sure your ancestors were equally interesting, Mr. Kensington," Elizabeth continued pleasantly.

"I fear I haven't the knowledge of my ancestors that you display, ma'am," Jack responded politely.

"Oh. Well, then, we must look into them sometime." Elizabeth brightened, obviously intrigued by the idea. "We can start with what you do know, your parents and grandparents and so forth, and work backward. Local histories are often quite helpful. Where is your family's home?"

"That sounds like an excellent plan," Jack replied. "I will look forward to it. Perhaps after the wedding. I know you are much too busy now with preparations for the ceremony."

Isobel noticed that he had not answered her aunt's question, which was annoyingly typical of the man. But now was not the time to press him about the matter; she had more important things to discuss. "I am sorry to interrupt," she said politely, turn-

206

ing to Jack, "but I wondered if I might have a word with you, Mr. Kensington."

"Of course. Run along." Aunt Elizabeth beamed at them. "I am sure you two have many things to discuss."

No doubt her aunt imagined them exchanging sweet words and loving looks. Elizabeth would have been shocked down to her toes if she had witnessed the scene between them last night.

"I have not yet seen the ruined castle up close," Kensington said conversationally as he offered Isobel his arm. "Perhaps we could take a walk there."

"Now?" Isobel glanced at him in surprise. She could not imagine why he would want to set out on a long excursion to conduct what would surely be a brief conversation.

"It seems an excellent time to me."

"Yes, dear, do take him to the castle," Aunt Elizabeth chimed in from behind them. "I was showing Mr. Kensington the map of it just the other day. He was quite interested in its history."

"He was?" Isobel cast a doubtful glance at Jack.

"Indeed." Jack smiled blandly. "Though I fear I am not as excellent a pupil as Miss Rose is a teacher." He turned his smile toward Aunt Elizabeth, who, predictably, beamed back at him.

"Very well, the castle it is." It occurred to Isobel that perhaps he preferred to hold this conversation outdoors, away from the curious ears of servants and her aunt, something she would prefer, as well.

As they walked to the front door, she held out his jacket, saying awkwardly, "You will want this back. I — uh, thank you for lending it to me."

"Perhaps you should wear it on our walk. I am sure it is chilly outside." He bent his head to her, murmuring, "I thought it looked quite fetching on you."

"My cloak will be adequate." It was most annoying that the mere sound of his voice made her insides begin to melt. She shoved the jacket at him, leaving him little choice but to take it, which he did, albeit with a quirk of his lips that told her he knew he had ruffled her.

Isobel set a brisk pace toward the castle, considering how best to broach the subject of the evening before. Jack strode along easily beside her, looking around at the landscape, not offering any conversation of his own. She envied him his lack of nerves.

When their path emerged from the trees, revealing the barren slope crowned by the castle ruins, Isobel stopped and turned to

Jack, squaring her shoulders. "I am sure you realize why I wished to speak with you."

"Then I fear I must disappoint you." Jack's voice was relaxed and maddeningly devoid of the emotion that threaded through hers. "I haven't any idea. Though I am, of course, quite looking forward to hearing what you have to say."

"Our engagement." Was the man trying to be obtuse? "I am sure you must regret our agreement."

"Must I?" His brows rose quizzically.

"Do you have to make things so difficult?" Isobel snapped.

"Apparently I do. I haven't the slightest notion what you're talking about."

"I am talking about last night," she burst out. "You cannot still wish to marry me."

He took a step closer to her, his hand curving around her nape. He ran his thumb along the cord of her neck. "My dear girl, last night only made the arrangement more appealing."

Her eyes widened slightly as she took in his meaning, and she jerked away from him. "I did not mean that! Dallying is not marriage."

"No doubt you're right about that. Still, it seems to me that dallying sweetens the bargain."

"Why are you being so frivolous? You cannot want to marry someone whom you hold in such . . . such low regard." To her chagrin, her voice broke on the words, and she whirled, stalking away from him.

"Low regard!" Jack followed her, taking her arm and planting himself in front of her so that she had to look at him. "I do not hold you in low regard. Quite the opposite. I have the utmost respect for you — your intelligence, your spirit, your love for your aunt, even your mad conviction that you have a duty to save Baillannan and its people." At her startled expression, he went on, "Are you surprised I realize you aren't marrying me just for your own survival? That you want to save the estate from being sold to some greedy soul who would toss your crofters off the land?"

"I — well, yes, I am surprised."

"I am not entirely unthinking; you know I have ridden about the estate. I have even spoken to people and sometimes, amazingly, understood the gist of what they said in reply, despite their best efforts to be unintelligible. I know what the crofters think of you. And what they think of the earl and his steward . . . and of me," he added wryly.

"Oh. Well." She raised her chin. "Still, I cannot imagine that you would want a wife whom you considered a wanton."

"What? I have never —"

"You accused me of having an affair with Coll! Clearly you did not think me virtuous."

"I did not think about your virtue at all," he shot back. "What I *thought* was that I do not want you in another man's bed." He stopped, looking a little startled at his own words. He turned aside, moving restlessly a few steps toward the ruins, then back. "Isobel . . . I spoke in haste, and I based my words not on any lack of esteem for you, but on the circumstances. Appearances. However, you made it clear that my suspicions were not true."

"You believe me?"

"Yes. One thing I have acquired over the years is an ability to sniff out a liar, and you are not a liar." He smiled faintly. "Or, at least, not a very good one. You were hiding something from me last night; I am fairly certain of that. But now I am inclined to believe your deceit had more to do with your aunt's mysterious lights on the island than with any rendezvous with Munro."

Isobel stiffened, alarmed. "I am sure the lights were merely —"

"No. Please." He raised a hand. "There is no need for you to rack your imagination for an explanation. I suspect that it is better if I remain blissfully ignorant of whatever happens on that island. What I know, and what I want you to know, is that I do not hold — and never have held — you in 'low regard.' "

"Oh." Everything she had expected had been turned upside down, and she was equally relieved and unsettled. Little as she had wanted to face a broken engagement, with all the public embarrassment and personal hardship it would cause, she should not be so elated at Jack Kensington's words. What he thought of her should not matter, surely. "Then you, ah . . ." She cleared her throat, pulling her gaze from his, and took a step back. "You are still agreeable to our, um, arrangement?"

"Yes." He followed her, reaching down to take her hand in his. "I am still . . . most . . . agreeable." He brought her hand up to his lips, punctuating each word with a soft kiss upon her fingers, her palm, the tender skin inside her wrists. "Unless you have changed your mind, of course."

"What?" Isobel looked at him distractedly. She knew he must feel the leap of her pulse beneath his mouth. "No. No, I have not changed my mind."

"Good." He moved even closer, his hands

sliding beneath her cloak and onto her waist. He bent so that his mouth was only inches from her ear as he murmured, "For I am looking forward to the wedding with great anticipation."

His thumbs circled over her waist in a hypnotic fashion, soothing and stirring, and he pulled her hips slowly forward until she was flush against his lower body. Isobel's eyes widened and she drew in a sharp breath. He rubbed his cheek against her hair, and his sigh drifted over her ear, prickling her skin.

Isobel felt herself warming, opening, that strange ache forming between her legs. She remembered the touch of his lips, the taste of his mouth, the warm, faintly musky scent of male and cologne, and her knees turned embarrassingly wobbly. His arms went around her, and he bent toward her.

12

"No!" Isobel stepped back from him, wrapping her cloak tightly around her though she was not cold, and held it that way, arms clasped at her waist. "It's — it's not that sort of marriage."

"All marriages are that sort." His voice was husky, yet tinged with the hint of amusement that seemed always to cling to him. He reached out and ran his thumb along the line of her jaw. "I think you'll find that is a great deal of what makes a marriage bearable."

"Bearable!" She stepped to the side, avoiding his hand. "You have an odd notion of marriage, I must say. I can only wonder that you would agree to marrying at all."

"Well, you made an appealing offer — near five hundred miles between us. Distinct and separate lives. Solitude. No tears or recriminations, no arguments, no pleading or justifications. No anger."

"I would think one could have all that simply by *not* marrying."

"True, but then one would not have the other benefits you offered. You do remember those, don't you?"

"Of course I do. But they did not include . . ." She rolled her hand vaguely, searching for some polite way to phrase it.

He leaned forward a bit, as if sharing a secret. "The marital bed?"

"Yes." How had he managed to get so close to her again? How had she not noticed? "I mean, no. They did not include that."

"Pity." He played with one of her curls. "You seemed to enjoy it last night." He smiled slowly, a light flaring in his eyes.

"I — you — surprised me."

His smile widened. "Is that what you do when you are surprised? I shall have to startle you more often."

Isobel let out a low noise of exasperation, then whipped around and started toward the ruins again, striding swiftly, as though she could outrun the turmoil inside her. Jack fell in beside her without comment, easily keeping up with her. She wished he would go away; she wished she could run from him. Indeed, she wished quite heartily that he was back in London instead of here, igniting all these dangerous feelings.

Isobel stopped at the edge of the ruins, out of breath. She was not sure whether it was from the brisk uphill walk or her own thoughts. She gestured toward the line of stones sunk into the earth before them.

"This was the outer wall, obviously. It's been picked clean for building materials. It ran in an arc around the castle." She swept her hand, indicated the curve of the line toward the edge where the land dropped away abruptly. "There was no outer wall on those two sides, as it's a sheer cliff down to the loch on one side or the sea on the other."

She started forward, showing him around the partial walls and tumbled heaps of stones, pointing out where the gates had been and where the various outbuildings had lain. They climbed a few stone steps to a wide ledge, gaining a better perspective of the area.

"This was the front door, and that was the great hall." Isobel pointed in front of them.

"Not as large as I would have thought."

"No. It was built for war, not comfort. There are none of your grand southern castles here, I'm afraid. We Highlanders tend to be a practical lot, and this was a fortress to guard the entrance to the loch."

"Was there so much war?"

"Och, you need to be reading more histories in Baillannan's library if you can ask that question. The Norse raided the coast." She pointed toward the horizon. "And of course behind us, there were all the other Scots. We did not have the border raids that went on between the Lowlands and the English, but there were ample reasons for protection here, too. Blood feuds between clans; reivers after one's cattle; or maybe just someone who envied your lands."

"What's that?" He pointed at the area on their left, where a haphazard jumble of stones led toward a wide hole in the ground, with a partial wall beyond it. A frayed and sagging rope marked it off from the rest of the ruins.

"It's not safe. You must not go beyond that old rope. You can see where the floor fell into the cellars below, and it can crumble around the edges. Over here though, it's solid rock beneath. We can walk out to the side along the sea." She turned to go back down the steps.

"Here. It's shorter this way, surely." He pointed to the short drop below the steps to the ground.

"Yes, but rather a long step," Isobel retorted.

He jumped lithely down and turned to her. "Come. I'll catch you."

Isobel hesitated, but his hands were already at her waist, lifting her down, and she had little choice but to go with him. She put her hands on his shoulders to steady herself, and when he set her on her feet, she was mere inches away from him. His hands lingered for an instant, then slid down to her hips as he released her.

Jack turned and strolled toward the seaward side of the ruins, maddeningly calm and unconcerned. How could the mere brush of his fingers through layers of clothing make her feel so jittery and uncertain? And how could it not cause him any bother at all?

She remembered the feel of Jack's body against hers a few minutes earlier, the sudden surge of heat in his skin, the quickened breath. He had felt something. She suspected that she could make him change in those ways again. Perhaps she could even wipe the smug calm from his face. Last night when she pulled away from him, his face had been stark and taut, the sharp ridges of his cheekbones lined with red. How would he look if she went into his arms right now? If she touched him? Kissed him?

Isobel shook her head, irritated with herself, and started after him. When she reached him, he was standing on the grass beyond the outside wall of the house. A few feet from him, the land dropped down to the gray expanse of the North Sea. Below them the ocean surged and foamed around the rocks.

"You are right. It was certainly inaccessible by sea." He glanced at her. "It's a bleak place."

"The tide is in now. But when it is out, there is a sandy beach below us. It is sheer right here, but there is a path that takes one down to the shore. We used to play there as children. Climb the rocks and explore the caves — though we knew better than to go far. You can get trapped by the tide if you are not careful."

"You and Sir Andrew?"

"Yes, he and Gregory came with us when they were a little older. Before that, it was just Meg and Coll and I." She turned to face him. "My mother died giving birth to Andrew. Janet Munro was Andrew's nurse, and she moved into Baillannan with her children, Meg and Coll. They were raised with us. We did everything together. My governess taught them as well, and outside of the schoolroom, we were always in each other's company."

"I see." Jack studied her. "And that is why you are . . . unusually close to Munro."

"Yes. I know it may appear odd to an outsider. Cousin Robert thought it was deplorable and used to lecture my father on the inappropriateness of our growing up with the Munro children. Not, of course, that that stopped him from leaving his wife and child with us while he was off in the military. My father did not stand on formalities as many do. Janet was a healer, and my father respected that, just as he accepted the fact that the Munro women have always been a law unto themselves. Aunt Elizabeth did, too." Isobel smiled faintly. "A number of people will tell you that the Roses are a mite odd."

"I would say more that they are charming."

"And you are very adept at compliments," Isobel retorted. "I thought you should know why I speak as I do to Coll. I am fond of him, just as I am fond of Meg. But Coll is like a brother to me. Indeed, I know him better than my own brother. I dearly love Andrew, but he is five years younger. And since he went off to school as the boys in our family do, I actually spent more time with the Munros than with Andrew. Coll enjoys reading, as I do, and we talk about books. He carves lovely things out of wood — furniture and figures and such — and we talk about that. About the estate." She shrugged. "We are friends."

"You may have a sisterly feeling toward Munro. That doesn't mean his feelings for you are the same."

"You think Coll is romantically inclined?" Isobel laughed. "He is more likely to scold me like a big brother than wax lover-like. The day you came, he had heard about your arrival, and he was worried you were taking advantage of me. The other day I happened to run into him when I was going to Meg's for my aunt's remedy. He was going there, too, to do some chores for his sister, so he rowed me across the loch. That is why we were walking up from the dinghy together. I assure you, it was neither planned nor illicit."

"And I am sorry to have misjudged you." Jack took her hand in his. "I hope you will forgive me. Remember, I am only a blundering Sassenach."

Isobel chuckled at his mangling of the word. "Then I suppose I shall have to." She tried to pull her hand from his grasp, but he retained his hold on it, his thumb stroking lightly over the back of her hand.

"Are books the way to your heart, then?" he asked, moving closer, his voice warm and rich. It seemed to wrap around her, holding her as surely as his hand.

"I do not know why you would care about the way to my heart." She hoped she sounded tart but uneasily suspected that she sounded more flirtatious than anything else. She went on in a brisker tone, "There is no need to woo me. We have already agreed to marry. I have assured you I will not besmirch your name when you leave. What more do you need?"

"Oh, I need a good deal more." His lips curved in a slow, seductive way, and Isobel was shocked to realize that she wanted to trace her finger over them.

"Stop." Isobel jerked away.

"Why?" He followed her, still moving in that lazy fashion that seemed casual and unthreatening but gave her no room to think or gather her resolve. His fingers drifted lightly down her arm. "I enjoy touching you. I think you do as well." His other hand slipped between the sides of her cloak again and moved across her collarbone, slowly pushing the garment back until it fell behind her.

Jack pressed his lips to the crook of her neck. She sucked in her breath at the velvet-soft touch of his mouth on her skin. He followed the path his fingers had taken along the bony ridge to her shoulder, moving with infinite slowness, setting her flesh afire. When he teased his tongue along her collarbone, she shuddered, bright shards of pleasure shooting through her.

Straightening, Jack gazed down at her, his eyes heavy-lidded with desire. He trailed his forefinger down her chest, following its movement with his eyes. When he reached the neckline of her dress, he traced along it.

"Jack, please," she whispered, unable to articulate her rapidly scattering thoughts.

"That is what I am trying to do." He leaned down until his forehead rested against hers. "Please you." He hooked two fingers inside the neckline, smoothing them across the soft swell of her breasts. "If I am not, you must tell me what you want me to do." He pressed his lips softly to her forehead as his fingers inched downward.

"Stop." Her breath caught as a bright frisson of pleasure shot through her, and she sank her teeth into her lower lip to steady herself.

"Ah, that I cannot do." His finger reached her nipple and dragged across it. "But if you mislike this, I can move." He pulled his teasing fingers out of her dress and cupped her breast through the material. "Perhaps this would suit you more." His thumb stroked across her breast, finding the button of her nipple through the cloth and circling it. "Or this." He took the bud between his thumb and forefinger and gently squeezed.

"Jack," Isobel murmured, her eyes drifting closed. Her abdomen was bathed in heat, an aching emptiness between her legs.

"Mayhap you prefer I went in a different direction." He slid his hand down her body and between her legs, pressing upon the very spot that ached, and she knew then that the need that pulsed there, the piece that had been missing, was him.

A small, choked noise escaped her, and Isobel felt her knees buckle. His other arm went around her securely, and it was suddenly so easy to lean against him, her head resting on his chest.

"Yes, I think that is it." His voice was rich with self-satisfaction as he stroked his fingers between her legs.

The friction ignited her desire. Her breasts were ripe and aching, the nipples contracting tightly, and she knew she wanted to feel his hands there, as well. She wanted his hands all over her. Isobel turned her face into his coat, embarrassed at her thoughts.

Moist heat blossomed between her legs, and she instinctively opened them to the rhythmic insistence of his hand. His fingers probed delicately, pressing and releasing, and she felt the liquid desire pooling there. She wondered if, humiliatingly, he could feel the moisture through her garments, tangible proof that she could not control her lust.

He bent to nuzzle her neck, and his teeth nipped lightly at the cord of her throat. He moved his mouth up her neck, discovering her with lips and teeth and tongue. Finally his lips claimed hers. Isobel dug her hands into his coat, holding on as the taste and feel of him rocked her. She felt herself sliding down into the deep, dark well of pleasure.

With a low cry, Isobel broke away from him, and whirling, she ran away home.

It was best, Isobel decided, to spend as little time as possible in Jack's company until the wedding. Once they were married, he would go back to London, and everything would return to normal. Until then, she could avoid scenes like today's by simply avoiding Jack Kensington.

She had to see him, of course, at supper and in the drawing room, but her aunt was there as a buffer, and Isobel kept the conversation running along the well-worn path of social niceties, maneuvering so as not to be seated beside him. Now and then she saw a glint in his eye that told her he knew exactly what she was doing and was amused by it.

During the day, she escaped to the attic. It was not, she supposed, any longer necessary to sort through the piles of old possessions, but cleaning it gave her something to do away from Jack, which was reason enough at the moment.

It occurred to her that Jack might follow her to the attic, as he had once before, so she took one of the maids with her to ensure she would not be alone. There was no sign of him, however, at least the first few days. When he did climb up to the attic one morning, Isobel was so accustomed to being undisturbed that she let out a yelp and whirled around when he spoke to her from the doorway.

"Sorry. I did not mean to startle you."

"My mind was elsewhere." Isobel got to her feet, feeling foolish and very aware of the maid watching them with unabashed interest. It took a conscious effort not to brush at her skirts or smooth her hair into place.

"No doubt you are busy." *He,* of course,

226

looked impeccable. Even more irritating, he looked well rested. Obviously he did not spend his nights twisting and turning, his imagination running rampant.

"Indeed." She made a vague gesture around the huge room. "May I help you with something?"

"No. Pray do not let me disturb you. I had meant to tell you at breakfast, but I did not see you."

"Yes. Um, I — I was not hungry."

"You must look to your health while I am gone. I should hate to return to a bride who is a mere shadow of herself."

"While you are gone?" Isobel's eyes widened, alarm suddenly zinging along her nerves.

"Yes, I came to bid you adieu."

Isobel's heart sank. "You are leaving?"

13

Isobel realized that she had sounded far too disappointed. She recovered hastily, saying, "You are returning to London, then?"

"No." He smiled in a teasing way as he walked over to her. "You will be relieved to know that you will not have to postpone the wedding. I am going only as far as Inverness."

"I see. But why?"

"There are a few matters I must attend to. Nothing important."

"You are very adept at answering without actually saying anything."

"Well, there are some things a man must keep to himself, aren't there?" He leaned in, giving her a wicked grin. "Tell me, my dear fiancée, will you miss me?"

"I have quite enough work to keep me busy," she retorted.

"Well, that put me in my place." His eyes glinted at her. He reached out, and Isobel tightened, sure he was about to touch her. Instead, he only touched the bow that decorated the high waistline of her dress, taking one long streamer of it between his fingers and slowly sliding them down the satin ribbon. "Have you any parting words for me?"

His gesture sent a frisson of lust through her, as urgent and eager, she thought, as if he had actually touched her. She swallowed, hoping her face had not betrayed what she felt, and said calmly, "I wish you Godspeed."

"Thank you." His face was wry as he released the ribbon. "I will not ask if you wish me a safe return."

"I would think that is understood. After all, I will lose Baillannan altogether if we do not marry."

He let out a little crack of laughter. "At least I need never wonder if you offer me blandishments and lies." He bowed to her. "I shall take my leave of you, then. Is there any errand you wish from me? Something I could bring you from the town? Your aunt has already entrusted me with the purchase of various ribbons, laces, and buttons, though I suspect she harbors little hope of my returning with the proper items."

"Oh. No. I —" Her head was buzzing; the

last thing she could think of right now was errands or purchases. "No."

He nodded and walked away. Isobel watched him go, then turned back to her task. But she was too restless to work, and she drifted aimlessly down the aisle until finally she wound up sitting on one of the trunks and staring into space, lost in her thoughts. Why was he traveling to Inverness? Why now? And why was he being so mysterious about it all? Did he really intend to return for the wedding? Or was he, in fact, just running away?

The sound of steps on the stairs sometime later broke her reverie, and Isobel turned, rising. Perhaps Jack had returned. Or decided not to go. He would take her into his confidence and explain what was taking him to Inverness. Maybe he would even ask her to accompany him.

Cousin Robert came through the doorway.

Isobel sighed. "Cousin Robert. I am surprised to see you."

"I can't think why. I told you I would help you sort out the attic."

"Yes, but, well . . ." She could hardly tell him she had not believed him. "I did not expect you so soon."

"Might as well get to it." He cast a disparaging look around the dusty, dimly lit room.

"Did no one ever toss anything out?"

"I wondered that, as well."

"Elizabeth tells me the Englishman has run off."

"He has gone on a trip to Inverness," Isobel replied stiffly. "That is not what I would call running away."

Robert shrugged. "If he comes back."

It was exactly what she feared, but Robert's saying so irritated her. "I see no reason not to believe him." She picked up the basket of items she had accumulated and carried it to the door.

"I suppose at this point we have to hope he will," her cousin replied darkly. "If he jilts you, it will be a terrible embarrassment for us all."

"Somewhat worse for me, I would think," Isobel said drily.

"And it would mean we lose all hope of Baillannan."

"We, Cousin?" She faced him, hand on hip. "I believe *I* am the only one marrying Mr. Kensington."

"You know what I mean." Robert grimaced. "The Rose family. At least your children and their descendants will continue to rule Baillannan, even if it does mean that the bloodline's been tainted by a common Englishman."

"I am surprised to hear that you are now in favor of the marriage." Isobel's stomach clenched at his mention of children. "Since only the other day you were storming about telling me I was disgracing the family by marrying him."

"It is still a disgrace. But I realized you were right," he admitted grimly. " 'Tis the only way a Rose can hold Baillannan. In the end, that is what's important. The family. All we can do is hope that the Englishman has some sense of honor."

"He has a name, Cousin — Jack Kensington. Since he is about to be your relative, I think it would behoove you to use it."

"Yes, of course, of course." The older man waved aside her words. "Enough of that. Let us get to work."

Robert's version of work, apparently, was not to lift, stack, unpack, or organize, but to putter about, poking into this trunk and that corner until he found something he thought might have belonged to his father and then to order the maid to carry it out to his carriage. All the while, he favored Isobel with advice on a number of topics ranging from her attitude, which he sadly felt sometimes bordered on the disrespectful, to the Rose family's lost position of power, to hints on how to run the estate much more efficiently.

Isobel grew thoroughly tired of his presence and wished he would leave, but he clearly enjoyed having a captive audience, and even after he ceased working at all, he sat down on a nearby trunk and continued to lecture her. Finally her aunt stuck her head into the attic to tell them it was time for tea.

Silently blessing her aunt, with great relief Isobel rose and brushed the dust from her hands. "Thank you for coming today, Cousin Robert. It was most generous of you. We accomplished so much, I think I am finished with the attic now." She hoped that would ward off any more "helpful" visits from the man.

"I thought you would find it a wearying task," her cousin replied with a patronizing smile that made Isobel grind her teeth. He continued as they descended the stairs, "I trust you have decided to leave your grandmother's room as it is?"

"There is no hurry, but eventually I shall pack up her personal items and store them away. That room has the loveliest view in the house. It would make an excellent chamber for guests."

"You are going to move Mother's things?" A furrow formed on Elizabeth's forehead, and Isobel mentally chastised herself for letting Robert's condescending tone goad her into mentioning the task in front of her aunt.

"Really, Isobel, don't you think you are taking this a bit too far?" Robert harrumphed.

"I'm not getting rid of any of her things, Aunt Elizabeth. But it has been years since Grandmother's been gone. I am sure she would like for the room to be brightened up and used instead of staying dark and shrouded in dustcovers."

"Perhaps . . . though Mother was not very fond of brightening things up." Elizabeth's frown eased a little.

"Why don't you help me, Auntie?" Isobel suggested, seeing that she had made a little headway with her aunt. "You can decide what should be packed away. You might want to keep some of her things with you. We could start after the wedding."

As Elizabeth wavered, Robert said, "I shall be happy to take Aunt Cordelia's keepsakes off your hands, Isobel, since you seem so anxious to move them out."

"You?" Elizabeth gave him a scornful look. "I cannot imagine why you would want Mother's things."

"I was very fond of Aunt Cordelia," he said frostily.

"Don't be nonsensical, Robby. You were scared of her. Don't you remember the time you ran and hid in the root cellar because you broke her favorite vase?"

Robert flushed. "I was eight at the time. As I grew older, I came to value her character and wisdom."

Elizabeth snorted. "What a plumper!"

Isobel hid a smile. Inadvertently, Cousin Robert had probably just secured her aunt's approval for clearing the bedroom simply by setting himself against it. Unsurprisingly, Robert refused Aunt Elizabeth's invitation to take tea with them, bidding them a stiff adieu and stalking off to his carriage.

"Well. The nerve of that man." Elizabeth turned to Isobel, her eyes sparkling. "Fond of my mother, indeed! He just wants to pick through her things in the hopes of finding something valuable."

"He did think there were a number of items he should take home, including an elegant snuffbox and the first Robert Rose's claymore."

"I hope you did not let him take that!" Elizabeth looked at her in alarm. "Your father would never let him have it. He told Robby that sharing a name with the laird did not entitle him to the man's possessions. Papa always hung the old laird's claymore

235

in a place of honor. Mother stuck it up in the attic only because she feared the British might seize it."

"No. I told him Papa would not have let it leave Baillannan and I could not possibly go against Papa's wishes. He could scarcely argue with that since he is so wedded to tradition."

"Clever girl." Elizabeth linked her arm through Isobel's. "Now, let us talk about things that are far more important than Cousin Robert. Did you mean it when you said you were finished in the attic? For we have a number of tasks — far more pleasant ones, I might add. They will soon start bringing in food for the wedding, and the barn, of course, must be made presentable for the feast afterwards."

"I am happy to help." Isobel glanced over at her aunt as they took their places before the tea tray. In a carefully casual voice she went on, "I was rather surprised when Mr. Kensington came to take his leave earlier. Did you know beforehand that he intended to visit Inverness?"

"No. I knew nothing about it until this morning." Elizabeth began to pour the tea. "He asked me what nearby town was larger than Kinclannoch, so I told him there was nothing but Wick to the north and Brora to the south, but neither of them are nearly the size of Inverness. I think he was a bit surprised that he had to go so far."

"So it was a spur-of-the-moment decision?"

"That was the impression I had."

"Did he tell you why?" Isobel took the cup from her aunt, but did not drink from it.

"Only that he had a few things he needed to purchase. I did not want to pry. You know how men are; no doubt he felt the need to . . . well, be on his own for a while . . . spread his wings a bit." Pink tinged her cheeks. "After all, he *is* giving up the bachelor life soon."

It dawned on Isobel what her aunt was trying to say, and she set down her cup and saucer with a clatter. "You mean he was going to — to visit a bawdy house?"

"Isobel! You should not even know of such places. I am not certain that is what he intends. But when he did not explain further, I assumed his purpose was one that it was better we not know."

"Better for men, doubtless." Isobel scowled. Jack might have kept silent about his trip for no reason other than to tease her, but he would not have done so to Elizabeth. Clearly he was embarked on something improper — and her aunt's assumption seemed the likeliest possibility. No wonder he had been so mysterious about the purpose of his trip. "That wretch!"

"I'm sorry, dear, but, well . . ." Her aunt looked at her a little quizzically. "It is not as if it is a love match."

Her aunt's words pulled Isobel up short. "No, of course. You are right. It isn't as if I am jealous. I don't expect Jack to be a faithful husband. I assumed he would seek out the . . . the company of women when he returns to London. But here, so close to home, it seems insulting, don't you think?"

"I suppose," Elizabeth said doubtfully. "But if you are concerned about gossip, Inverness is quite some distance, and it is unlikely anyone in Kinclannoch would ever learn. Mr. Kensington would be discreet."

"Jack is always most discreet. Secretive, one might say." Isobel wondered why she had not realized the truth earlier. She had heard that men were apt to react to the prospect of marriage by engaging in a round of their wildest behavior.

Isobel thought of their hot, urgent kisses, remembering the way Jack's skin had surged with heat and his mouth had consumed hers. Clearly Jack had a highly sensual nature — and he had none of the loving attachment to her that another man might feel for his future wife. It was easy to imagine that Jack might have gone in search of a woman more willing to satisfy his desires, more attuned to his needs — especially since she had assured him she had no interest in being his wife in anything but name only.

It was a bit lowering to think that any other woman would satisfy his hunger as well as she, but it was better this way. If his desires had been taken care of, he would cease importuning her. They would be able to coexist easily, at least for the few days until their wedding, and after that he would leave for London. She was glad that he would find what he wanted in another woman's bed.

Really, she was.

14

The week following Jack's departure dragged by. Aunt Elizabeth was happily immersed in preparations for the upcoming wedding, but Isobel could not seem to settle down to anything. Finally she was forced to admit to herself that she was bored. She missed the lively conversations at the dinner table. The house was excessively quiet without the sound of Jack's voice or laugh. All too often she caught herself waiting for the sound of his footsteps in the hall. There was no sense of anticipation each morning when she awoke nor any of the little spark she felt when she entered a room and saw Jack standing there.

It was most annoying.

She tried throwing herself wholeheartedly into her aunt's plans, but all too often her mind drifted to thoughts of Jack and what he was doing in Inverness. Was he spending his days in debauchery? At this moment, while she stitched flowers on the ruffle of a lawn nightgown, was he lying in bed with some other woman? Did he smile at her — in Isobel's mind a voluptuous brunette with a stunningly beautiful face — and wind her curls around his finger? Did his heart hammer and his breath catch when he pulled her to his chest?

Isobel tried to wrench her mind from such pictures. It should not matter what he did. Theirs was a sham of an engagement, just as it would be a sham of a marriage. She did not herself want his attentions. The bitter burn that hovered in her chest was not jealousy. It was . . . it was resentment at his secretiveness. Yes, that was it. He had hidden it from her, deceived her.

Jack might, of course, have had some other, better reason to suddenly decide he must go to Inverness for a few days. Something that did not involve a woman. He could not have gone to visit a friend, for he was as much a stranger to Inverness as he was to Kinclannoch. He might have missed the city life he was used to — though Inverness would be a poor substitute for the lights of London. Maybe he missed gambling or needed money, so he had gone in search of a few nights of gaming. That was not unreasonable. But then she thought

241

about the smoky public room of a tavern in Inverness, the tables of men drinking and playing cards. She did not have any experience of those, but from the remarks she had overheard of Andrew and his friends, that sort of place also had buxom wenches serving ale to the customers. And were not women of easy virtue also involved?

Isobel tore her mind from such thoughts and tried to concentrate on the preparations for her wedding feast. She envisioned the songs and dancing, the merriment. She thought of taking the floor with Jack, laughing, flushed with excitement, fizzing with the happiness of the celebration. But such thoughts always came thudding back to earth.

What would happen after the dancing? Would she simply go to her room and sleep alone in her bed? Would he come to her? Try to seduce her? Demand his marital rights? She could not believe Jack would be harsh or abusive. He would not try to force himself upon her. But seduction . . . that was more his style. Sweet words and sweeter kisses, that glinting look from beneath his lashes, the teasing smile and enticing caresses.

She would not give in to his blandishments. She could not. After all, pleasurable as his kisses might be, she knew that Jack would soon return to London. And she would stay here. For the first time she could remember, the thought of staying at Bail-lannan left her empty.

Even worse, what if he did not come back to Baillannan at all? What if her cousin was right and Jack had simply fled from their marriage? She told herself that he would not abandon her. He had promised he would return. But in the cold, dark hours of the night, when she lay tossing and turning in her bed, she had to face the fact that she had no reason to believe him.

Jack had admitted that he was no gentleman though he found it useful to pretend so. He was charming and pleasant, always ready with a smile or a quip. It was easy to like him, even to trust him. But those qualities, she knew, were his stock-in-trade, the passage he used to enter the world of the wealthy from whom he won money. Was that his true nature . . . or just a façade?

The fact was that he revealed little of himself. Whatever emotions bubbled beneath his surface rarely spilled out. He turned aside any talk about his past, just as he had avoided telling her why he was going to Inverness. When her aunt asked him where he was from, he had sidestepped the question and had done so again when Elizabeth asked whether his family would come to the wedding. Isobel remembered how easily the lie about his "ancestor" the *contessa* and her fictitious ring had sprung to his lips the other day.

The truth was, she knew nothing about the man. Had she made a terrible mistake?

Four days went by, then five and six, and still Jack had not returned. Isobel knew that others noticed his long absence and were concluding that he had jilted her. She saw the sidelong glances and heard the whispers as the local women gathered to prepare for the wedding feast. The servants had begun to look at her with pity, mingled with apprehension as they realized what it would mean for them if Isobel did not marry Jack.

Sleep became more and more elusive. With only two days left before the wedding, she climbed into bed, dreading the night of tossing and turning that she knew lay in front of her. Then she heard someone call out in the courtyard. She froze, listening. More voices. A whinny.

Isobel popped out of bed and shoved the drapes apart. There below her, a tall, dark figure was dismounting and handing the reins of his horse to a groom.

"Jack!" Isobel whirled and ran down the

stairs.

The village of Kinclannoch lay in darkness as Jack passed through it. The half-moon provided little light, clouds drifting over it intermittently. He would be lucky if his horse did not step in a hole on the rough road. But he pressed on, keeping the pace slow and hoping that his horse could see the way better than he. He was not about to stop when he was this close to home.

He had already spent far longer than he had intended. Who would have thought it would be so difficult to find an adequate ring in Inverness? After an afternoon of frustration, it had become clear that the only solution was to take the stones from his cuff links and have them reset in the best of the wedding bands the jeweler possessed. The result had been surprisingly good, but he had been forced to idle away two days longer in the town than he had expected.

And a dreary two days it had been. The town offered little in the way of entertainment. He had found a game or two, but the stakes were too low to make it worth his while. The tavern at the inn was small and smoky, and though the wench who served his ale gave every indication she would welcome his advances, he discovered to his surprise that he had no desire to make any. After the past few days with Isobel, his body was thrumming, and he should have welcomed the chance to slake his desire with the wench. Instead, when she bent over the table to place his drink, offering a clear view of her lush breasts, his thoughts went to Isobel and the feel of her soft breast cupped in his hand, the nipple hardening provocatively beneath his touch. The come-hither glances the girl shot him held none of the allure of wide, grave gray eyes suddenly lighting with laughter or sparkling with heat. Her skin was white and soft, but it had none of the creamy texture that made his fingers itch to caress Isobel's skin. The girl's face did not glow as if lit from within when she smiled. And when she walked past him, hips swaying seductively, he compared her voluptuous figure to Isobel's willowy form and found the barmaid too obvious and overblown.

However much hunger he might feel, it was only for that odd, unpredictable, unconsciously sensual woman who waited for him at Baillannan. The woman who in a few days would be his. Anticipation coiled within him. The marital bed had always sounded deadly dull to him, ordinary and orderly, with none of the lure of secrecy and the forbidden. Instead, he was beginning to think married sex might be the most enticing of all.

He had no doubt that he would eventually lure Isobel into that grand monstrosity of a bed he slept in — he had felt the passion simmering below that cool, controlled surface — and the thought stirred him in a way he had never before experienced. There would be no obstacle of time or deceit or fear between them, only the limitless freedom to follow their pleasure. She would be his in a way no other woman had ever been, bearing his name, even, someday, his child. She would come to him untouched and unschooled, and he would be the one to awaken her to desire. No other man would share her bed, none would hear her cries of passion or feel the sharp pleasure of her fingers digging into his back. Just thinking of it turned him hard and impatient.

That hunger had sent him from the tavern without even a backward glance at the willing serving wench. It was what drove him now. He wanted to be home. He wanted to seduce and cajole and tease Isobel. Damnit, he wanted to see her again.

He was so lost in thought that he had no hint of danger. His horse followed the road as it curved around a large outcropping of rock, then suddenly the animal stopped, whickering, and pricked its ears. Before Jack could move, a man stepped out in front of him and raised the front shield from his lantern, spilling a half circle of light over the road.

Jack's mount stepped back, snorting and shaking its head, and Jack tightened his hand on the reins, reaching toward his inside pocket with the other.

"Nay, dinna," growled a voice above him, and Jack glanced up to see a figure standing on the rock, pointing a musket down at him. Even the poorest of shots could not miss him at such close range.

"The devil take it," Jack muttered, and let his hand fall. It would be folly to try for the little gun he carried in the inner pocket of his jacket, and anyway it would be useless against the group of men before him. At least four of them were on the road, as well as the man aiming the musket at his head, and he could see vague shapes behind the others.

"It's na him," one of the men in the road said, turning to speak to one of the men beside the road.

"Nae, it's the bonny lad frae the sooth."

"The English," another one added darkly. The lantern at their feet cast only a dim light, still shielded on three sides, casting all its glow toward Jack. The men wore hats pulled low and mufflers wound around the bottoms of their faces, making it impossible to identify them — though Jack suspected that it would not be prudent to do so, anyway.

"Shall I shoot him, then?" asked the man on the rock.

"Nae," came a low voice from the side of the road. "Dinna be daft. Are ye wantin' to swing for it?"

Out of the corner of his eye Jack watched the man standing away from the others. His face was hidden by darkness, and Jack could see only the outline of his bulk against the darker rocks behind him. He could tell little about the man other than that he was tall and that his voice had a note of authority, which was confirmed by the way the others turned toward him when he spoke.

"Aye." The man beside the lantern nodded sharply. "Just empty yer pockets then and ye can be on your way."

"Slowly," added their leader.

"Of course." Jack lifted his hands, holding them up to show he held nothing, then reached down to pull out a small pouch of coins and toss it down in front of the lantern.

"And that one." The man nodded his head toward the pocket on the other side of Jack's coat.

"No." Jack set his jaw, thinking of the things he had purchased in Inverness. "Take the money and go. I'll say nothing. But you will not have aught else."

"You forget; we hae the gun." The man in front of him planted his hands on his hips.

"And as your friend pointed out, you will swing for it if you shoot me. A landowner. English. Think on that for a moment." Jack turned and stared intently at the large man standing in the darkness. "If I die today, Miss Rose will lose Baillannan."

A long, tight silence stretched between them. Then the other man stepped back, jerking his head toward the others. "Let him pass."

Reluctantly the men moved aside, and Jack rode through them. The spot between his shoulder blades tingled all the while, but he kept his gaze leveled in front of him. He would not give them the satisfaction of casting an uneasy glance back. He rode on at an unhurried pace, turning his face toward home.

Isobel was almost to the bottom of the stairs, her heart pounding in excitement, when the front door opened and Jack stepped inside. "Jack!"

He glanced up, and a smile flashed across his face. "Isobel."

He strode forward, and in that instant Isobel launched herself down the last few steps and into his arms. He caught her, laughing, and his mouth found hers.

She was lost in him, in the kiss, surrounded by his warmth and solidity, enclosed by his strength. His greatcoat was rough against the tender, bare skin of her arms, and her nostrils were filled with the scent of horse, damp wool, tobacco, and him. The taste of him, too, was familiar and yet excitingly new. He kissed her as if he could not get enough of her, and she matched his eagerness, overwhelmed by the sensations slamming through her.

When at last their lips parted, she buried her face in his chest, her fingers clenched in his coat, struggling for some bit of composure. "You're home," she said, her voice muffled by his coat.

"I am." Amusement tinged his voice.

A shoe scraped on the stone floor behind them, and a man cleared his throat. Isobel sprang out of Jack's arms as if she'd been stung and turned to see Hamish standing a few feet down the hall.

"Hello, Hamish," Jack said drily, turning toward the servant and shrugging out of his coat.

"Welcome back, sir." The butler's voice was starchy with disapproval despite his polite words. "We dinna know if something happened to you." He reached down to swoop up Jack's hat, which had been knocked to the floor by Isobel's impetuous greeting.

Isobel took another step backward, the heat of embarrassment flooding her cheeks. She had behaved like a complete romp. Jack would think her forward behavior sprang from delight at seeing him again, that she could not wait to kiss him and hold him, which was not at all true. Merely relief that the wedding would go through had sent her flying down the stairs to greet him.

"I am surprised to hear that I caused you such worry. I do apologize," Jack told the butler, his eyes dancing with amusement. He turned to Isobel, catching her hand, and said in a softer tone, "I am sorry indeed if I have caused you concern."

"Nonsense," Isobel replied in an airy tone meant to convey how little she cared that he had not been there for a week. "I was quite sure you were not hurt."

"I intended to return earlier, but I ran into

a delay."

Isobel frowned. It was on the tip of her tongue to ask whether the delay had been a blonde or a brunette, but she stopped herself. It was beneath her dignity.

She tried to tug her hand from his grasp, but Jack stubbornly held on. He started up the stairs, and she had no choice but to go with him if she did not wish to tussle with him over possession of her fingers.

"I hope you will forgive me," he went on.

"There is nothing to forgive." Isobel held on to her light, remote tone. "Of course, one could not help but imagine that you had decided to return to London. That would have been a trifle awkward."

"You thought I had cried off?" he asked in surprise. "Do you think I am such a poor-spirited fellow as that?"

"I am sure I don't know what sort of fellow you are." She turned to him with a determinedly expressionless face. "You are virtually a stranger, after all."

He let out a laugh, pulling her to a stop on the stairs, and leaned closer, murmuring, "And you kissed a stranger thus? Isobel, I am shocked."

Isobel glared at him. "I was . . . I was carried away." It occurred to her that that did not sound as she wished. "I mean . . ."

253

"I like it when you are carried away." He lowered his forehead to hers, and his thumb traced a lazy circle on the back of her hand. "I hope you will be carried away more often."

She had forgotten how dark a blue his eyes were and how his voice could slide inside her, making her melt. She had told herself that her memory had made him more handsome than he was, that his flaring cheekbones did not stir her in some indefinable, illogical way, that the cut of his upper lip did not make her own lips long to press against his. But she knew now that she had been lying to herself.

"Come, Isobel." He kissed her lower lip, then the upper. "Do not deny us both." He moved on, pressing the same light, teasing kisses on her cheeks, her chin, the tip of her nose. "Did you miss me?"

"Of course not." Her words came out too breathlessly to be believable.

He chuckled. "I think you are telling me a clanker." He nuzzled her neck.

"Jack!" she hissed, glancing behind them down the stairs. "Someone will see."

"Then come." He trotted up the last few steps, pulling her with him, and at the top he turned to take her in his arms and kiss her. He slid his hands around her waist and

254

down over her buttocks, pulling her into him. "I think you can tell that I missed you."

She could feel the hard length of him pressing into her, and she was horrified to realize that she wanted to rub herself against him in response. Struggling to pull together the tattered pieces of her dignity, she turned away from him. "My aunt could come out at any moment."

He grinned down at her. "My room is right here." He nodded his head toward his door. "There's ample privacy in it."

Isobel let out a noise of exasperation and stalked down the hall to her bedroom. To her surprise, Jack followed her and closed the door behind him. She whirled around. "Jack!"

"I like my name in your mouth." He smiled and linked his hands behind her waist, holding her loosely. "You are right. It is much better in here."

"I did not mean —"

He ignored her, dropping kisses across her face. "Is this proper enough? Secluded enough?" His voice thickened. "May I kiss my wife now?"

"I am not your wife," she replied shakily.

"You will be soon enough." But he left off kissing her, seemingly content for the moment just to gaze at her, his eyes taking her in from the top of her head to her feet in a slow sweep. "I like your hair like this. Loose and tumbled." He combed his fingers through it. "Your attire." His hand drifted down, skimming her shoulder and breast, the featherlight touch bringing her nipples to hardness. "You have a deplorable habit of running out in your nightdress." A sensual smile tugged at the corner of his mouth. "I rather enjoy it."

He ran a finger lazily around the circle of her nipple, watching with heated eyes as it tightened at his touch, pressing against the thin material of her gown. Isobel felt as if she were turning to liquid inside, the ache between her legs growing.

"I will like it even more," he went on huskily, "when there is naught between us." He hooked his finger into the neck of her gown, and the touch of his skin on her bare breast sent a quiver through her body. "I thought about you all the while I was gone."

His words touched upon a nerve in her, rubbed raw by a week of anxiety. Isobel let out a wordless noise of disbelief and turned away. "Words come very easily from you."

Jack quirked a brow. "Would you rather I were more inarticulate? I can bumble about with the best of them, if you wish."

"No, of course not," she snapped. "All I

want from you is the truth!"

He went still. "I have not lied to you."

"You don't need to since you tell me nothing."

"Don't be absurd."

"I'm not. At first I could not understand why you were so secretive about your trip, but then I realized: you are secretive about everything. I know nothing about you."

"And what is it that you would like to learn?" He folded his arms and gazed at her indulgently. "Come; ask your questions. What are these vital facts you need to know?"

"Well . . ." Now that she was put on the spot, her mind went annoyingly blank. "Where are you from?"

"London, but surely you are already aware of that."

"No, I mean, where were you born? Where did you grow up?"

"All over." He shrugged. "London, Liverpool, Bath. We moved whenever the mood struck us. Or perhaps I should say, whenever the constable was at our door. Really, Isobel, doesn't this strike you as a foolish argument? What does it matter where I lived as a child? You are aware that I am not a gentleman. I did not attend Eton or Oxford."

"Yet you told my aunt you did."

"When — Oh." His face cleared. "That was the day I arrived. I scarcely knew either of you then. It meant nothing."

"Then why did you say it? No doubt your tale about the *contessa* meant nothing, either, yet you told Cousin Robert that Banbury story."

"Are you still holding *that* against me?" He stared. "Your cousin is a pompous —"

"This is not about him. It is about you. The fact that you do not like someone or that they are strangers to you does not make a lie into the truth."

"It was still inconsequential. I cannot understand why you are in such a dudgeon about it."

"It isn't just that you lied a time or two about unimportant things. The fact is, you keep everything about you a secret."

"Very well," he said, tight-lipped. "I am a gambler; I make my living by my wits. I did not have tutors or dance instructors; nor did I tour the Continent. I have no lineage, or at least none it's advisable to know. I suspect more than one of my ancestors met his end swinging from the gallows. But you were aware of my lowly station when you suggested that we marry. If you want a man of high station, you should —"

"That is not what I meant! I don't care about your name, and you know it. You are twisting my words about. That is what you do when you cannot glide out of a question. You hide your real self from the world. From me. You are a man of wonderful manners, eternally glib, difficult to dislike. But I have no idea who you really are, what you really feel. Where is the person in you?"

Jack stiffened and his eyes took on a frosty glitter. "I fear that what you see is who I am. No doubt it will become clear to you soon that I am not a man with depths."

"I did not mean —" Isobel felt a stab of remorse; clearly her words had wounded him.

"Did you not?" He took a step closer, his eyes trained on hers. "You believe I have fashioned a man from whole cloth, made him up to play the role of gentleman. And you are right, of course. I carefully constructed me — the clothes, the air, the words, the manners. And that is all I am. I do not reveal what dwells inside because there is nothing there. I am surprised you have not realized it by now. Why else would I agree to this marriage?"

Stung, Isobel lifted her chin. "Exactly. There is no need for you to try to beguile me. No reason for sweet words or kisses.

Why pretend that our marriage is anything but a sham?"

"Why indeed?" He sketched a bow, as rigid and correct as an automaton. "Good night, Miss Rose. I will see you at the ceremony."

15

The atmosphere the next few days was strained. Isobel regretted the words between them. She wanted to explain that her words had come out wrong, that she did not think him a shell of a man. Then he would smile at her in that devilish way and turn her apologies aside with a quip, and everything would be easy between them again. But something in the impassive lines of his face, in his careful, impersonal courtesies, made her timid and uncertain.

The night before her wedding, Isobel climbed the stairs to her chamber, tired but certain that sleep would elude her tonight, as it had for so many days. She had barely stepped inside her room when an arm snaked around her waist and a voice whispered close to her ear, "I've come to abduct you."

"Meg!" Isobel whipped around, startled laughter bubbling up out of her. "Whatever are you doing here?"

Meg chuckled at Isobel's reaction. "I've come to whisk you out of the house. You did not have a *réiteach,* but surely you dinna think I would let you spend the night before your wedding alone, did you?"

Meg reached out to take Isobel's arm, but Isobel pulled back, saying suspiciously, "You'll not be washing my feet." That custom usually involved more blackening than washing, from the tales she had heard from the village.

"Nae." Meg laughed again. "I know you fine folk are different. We are just going over to the cottage to spend the night. You must have at least a little fun, and it's been an age since we've had an all-night gossip and giggle." Meg picked up Isobel's cloak and held it out to her. "Come. We'll row across."

"But my wedding dress —" Isobel hesitated.

"Your aunt will send it round bright and early to the cottage, and I'll help you dress. Coll will walk with you to the road to meet your cousins. He wanted to do that since it is Gregory's and Mr. Rose's place to take you to the kirk. I shall come back here so your aunt and I can escort Mr. Kensington. It will give her a chance to spread your wedding dress out to work on it without worrying you might catch sight of it."

Isobel rolled her eyes. "I am surprised she let me out of her sight lest I slip and bring bad luck down on my head."

Meg chuckled. "She trusts me because of my mother. She asked me what I saw ahead for you. I told her I did not have the *sicht*. None of us have since my grandma, and I'm not sure I believe she did, either."

"Just tell Aunt Elizabeth you saw a good omen. Tell her I put my right shoe on before my left."

"You will; I'll see to that. We can count on there being a bird singing outside the window; they're always about. Now if only the day dawns sunny, we will do fine."

Isobel laughed and looped her arm through Meg's as they started down the stairs. "I don't know why Auntie has become absolutely mad about all the superstitions."

"She wants very much for you to be happy."

"Ah, well. I will be happy to be at Baillannan."

Isobel felt her friend's eyes on her, but Meg did not say anything as they left the house and moved quickly to the small dock, where Meg's dory was waiting. They rowed across the water, taking turns, in the way they had done many times before. Pulling the boat up onto the opposite shore, they turned it over and walked up the hill to the cottage. The darkness closed around them beneath the trees, shutting out even the partial moon, but Meg moved as swiftly and surely as a cat along the familiar path.

Meg had always been an outdoor creature, and the brae was as much her home as the cottage in which she lived. She had followed her mother from the time she was a baby, and by the time they came to live at Baillannan, Meg already knew the glen in a way Isobel never could. Baillannan might be hers, but the loch and all around it were Meg's.

Inside the house, Meg lit a lamp and added another block of peat to the fire. Isobel sat down on the hearth, and Meg joined her, holding out a bottle of golden-brown whiskey, much the same shade as Meg's eyes.

"Now, as it's the eve of your wedding, it's only fitting that we have a wee dram, don't you think?"

"Of whiskey? Meg, you'll have me reeling down the aisle."

Meg laughed. "Nae. 'Tis MacKenzie's best, smooth as silk; he gave it to me for helping his wife with the birthing. The wee babe was the wrong way around, you ken, and I had to turn it. But the bairn came out with a lusty yell. A bonny thing, she was." Meg handed Isobel a cup and began to pour. "We'll have just a few sips. Remember when Coll slipped us that whiskey?"

"Indeed." Isobel grinned as she took a drink. The liquid slid down her throat like fire and burst in her stomach. "I remember your mother boxed our ears."

"Aye, well, Coll got the worst of it. He could not sit for three days afterwards." Meg laughed, then sighed. "Everything is changing, isn't it? So many people gone. Tomorrow you'll be Mrs. Kensington."

"I will still be the same."

"You'll be a married woman."

"It's not a real marriage."

"It's in the kirk." Meg gave her an odd look. "That seems real enough to me. It isn't a handfasting."

"No, it will be legal. I just meant . . ." Isobel shrugged. "We won't really be husband and wife."

"Oh." Meg's eyes widened as she took in Isobel's meaning. "Does Mr. Kensington know that?"

Isobel laughed. "Yes. I made it clear. We have a . . . a practical arrangement. I will run Baillannan as I always have. And he will return to London and spend the money."

"I see." Meg studied the whiskey in her glass, swirling it around. "Still . . . it does not seem to me most men would be content with that."

"I don't know if *content* is the word. But he is not the sort of man who would" — a blush stained Isobel's cheeks and she glanced away — "who would force me." She took another drink, grimacing as the fire rolled down her throat.

Meg poured again. The whiskey was going down more easily with each sip. Isobel was beginning to feel warm and peaceful, the twanging nerves that had plagued her for a week easing.

"Of course, that does not mean Jack will not try to persuade me," Isobel added. Her eyes widened, and she let out a little giggle as she realized what had slipped out of her mouth.

"Aye, well, he is a man. The question is, do you want to be persuaded?"

"No." Isobel's voice was firm despite the wistful look in her eyes. "But he is very good at persuasion."

Meg laughed.

Isobel joined her and raised her hands to her heated cheeks. "I think I am a wicked woman deep down. I scarcely know the man. I dinna even know if I like him." Her voice slipped deeper into the Highlands accent as her inhibitions loosened. "I mean, I *do* like him, but I am not sure if the man I like is who he really is. He is handsome and clever and kind. And, *oh,* I like his laugh. I truly do. He doesn't look like anyone I know; his eyes are such an odd blue, and when he is teasing me, this light comes into them . . ." She shook her head. "I think I could never tire of looking at him. But I know that looks are scarcely the measure of a man. Neither is a silver tongue, which he has aplenty. I don't know what he really thinks. What he feels. Do you know, he's never said a word about his family?"

"I would not think his family is so important. You'll likely not see them, will you?" Meg dimpled. "And you never cared that Coll and I are not fine folk."

"I don't care about his lineage, and you are right, I'll not see them, anyway. But it is odd, don't you think? He never mentions his parents. He does not talk about his friends or where he has lived or — or anything like that. I don't even know if he has a brother or sister. He's — he's closed, like a sheep cote. He makes his living playing cards with young gentlemen, outwitting them."

"That would not be difficult, judging by

Andrew's friends."

"No." Isobel laughed. "Do you remember that boy named Stickham, the one who turned brick red whenever you came around?"

"The one with eyes like a sheep? Oh, yes. But he was not as bad as the blond lad who kept trying to pull me behind a door and kiss me."

"Jeremy Latham? No! Did he really?"

"Oh, aye, more than once, until I jabbed one of your aunt's knitting needles into his arm."

"I didn't know that! Why didn't you tell me? He never tried anything with me." Isobel tilted her head consideringly. "Should I be offended, do you think?"

"Och, he was English." Meg dismissed him with a snort. "I wasn't blue-blooded, so he dinna think he had to be polite." She waved her hand. "That does not matter. Why does Kensington's playing cards matter?"

"It doesn't really. But Andrew and the other young gentlemen play cards with him because Jack draws them in by appearing to be one of them, 'bang up to the mark.' When you look at his face, you don't know what he thinks. I don't know what he truly feels. He never gets angry."

"That sounds like a pleasant difference in a man." Meg grinned.

"Well, yes, but it's not natural, is it? He cannot be so even tempered. I think he keeps it all hidden inside him. Hamish was dreadful when Jack arrived; they all were. Cold food, a room in the old wing, no warming pan for his bed, accents so thick even I could hardly understand them. You would think he would have raged, wouldn't you? Yet he turned it all aside with a quip."

"You want him to storm about?"

"No, of course not."

"I don't know — I like a bit of temper in a man, I think," Meg mused.

"Well, he's angry with me now, but it's all cold. As if he drew farther back into himself." Isobel shrugged. "I probably needn't worry about him trying to entice me into his bed, as remote as he has been the last few days."

"Dead polite is the worst. I hate it when Coll freezes up; it's easier if he yells." Meg paused. "Why is he angry? Because he hasn't been able to 'persuade' you into his bed?"

"No, it's not that. Well, mayhap it started like that. But then, well, I was unkind. I think — I think perhaps I wounded him. But he would not say so." She sighed. "It is just as well he'll be leaving soon."

"Then everything can go back to the way it was."

Isobel nodded. It was absurd that the thought should make her throat ache. "It's just that — Oh, Meg, when he touches me, it is so sweet I can hardly bear it. He kisses me and —" She blushed and looked down at her skirt, picking at a nonexistent flaw. "Have you — have you ever — you know?"

"No, I haven't, no matter what people say about the Munro women."

"I've never even been kissed before. When Jack kissed me, it was . . . it's like this whiskey. It sweeps through me, so fiery and fast." Isobel's blush grew and she concentrated even harder on the spot on her skirt. "It's like nothing I've known. It makes me want — well, I'm not sure what. It makes me want to do whatever he wants."

"Would it be so bad a thing, then?" Meg asked gently. "You will be married, after all."

"It would be legal, yes. I would not have to fear the gossip. Even the kirk approves — though, I must say, it feels much too good, I think, not to be a sin. But it's not those things that hold me back." Isobel raised her head and looked at Meg, her eyes stark. "In a few days, Jack will go back to London. And I will be left here at Baillannan. I will not do that, Meg. I cannot."

Jack stared balefully out the window. The sky was beginning to lighten, though the sun had not yet broken above the horizon. His wedding day was dawning.

He drew in a sharp breath and turned away. He had slept in fitful starts throughout the night; no doubt any further efforts in that regard would prove equally futile. However, it was too early for breakfast, even here. He picked up his watch from the top of the dresser and opened it, then set it down with a sigh. Turning to the wardrobe, he pulled out the jacket he would wear to the church later and slid his hand into the inside pocket to check that the ring he had purchased in Inverness was still there. So too were the other small boxes he had brought back from Inverness. He rubbed his thumb over them idly, a now familiar prickle of unease teasing at his chest.

After another glance at his pocket watch, he began to roam restlessly around the room. The fourth time he checked the time, he let out an oath and swung away to pull on trousers and a shirt. Not bothering to tuck in his shirt or put on a neckcloth or jacket, he crammed his feet into his boots and left the house.

He stood for a moment on the front steps, pulling in a deep lungful of air. It was easier to breathe out here. The morning mist was lifting and that odd, indefinable scent that was Baillannan hung in the air. He turned and started toward the loch. As he neared the water, he glimpsed a form on the dock, half-hidden by the fog. With a few more steps, the figure resolved into a small man with a fishing rod in his hand. The man turned at the sound of his approach and Jack took in the weathered face and the burst of graying hair.

"You!" Jack stared.

"Aye." The old fellow lifted his chin pugnaciously. "Me."

"Angus McKay." A smile touched the corner of Jack's mouth. "I believe it is you who are intruding on my place now."

"Loch Baille belongs to no man," McKay retorted.

"Ah, but the dock is mine," Jack tossed back. "And you are occupied in what is usually termed poaching."

"Miss Isobel disnae mind."

"No. She would not. And since *I* am not carrying a firearm, you are safe from me as well."

The old man's only answer was a snort. He eyed Jack up and down. "Ye dinna look ready for the kirk. Is it running that's on your mind, then?"

"Running?" Jack stiffened. "From the wedding? Of course not."

"Guid." The old man nodded. "Folks widnae take to that. They're richt fond of Miss Isobel here."

"So I've noticed," Jack said drily. He joined the other man on the dock and gazed out across the water.

"Fog's lifting," McKay said after a moment, and Jack glanced at him, surprised. Was the belligerent old man actually offering a pleasantry? "Guid day for the wedding."

"Miss Elizabeth will be pleased," Jack agreed. "She has been watching for omens."

"Aye."

"Will you be attending?" Jack asked after a moment.

"At the kirk?" McKay lifted his brows skeptically. "Nae. But afterward, aye." He jerked his head back toward Baillannan. "Why else am I oot here? I hae to bring something to the party, now, don't I?' "

"So you are poaching fish from our lake to bring as a present to our wedding celebration?" Jack let out a laugh.

"Och, I told ye, lad, Loch Baille belongs to no man. Least of all a Sassenach," he

273

added darkly.

"I thought the Lady of Loch Baille gave it to the first laird," Jack countered.

"The Lady of the Loch!" Angus cast a startled look at him. "What do ye ken of the lady?"

"Very little," Jack admitted.

The old man let out an odd, strangled sound, and it took Jack a moment to realize that Angus McKay was laughing. "Ye'll get over the nerves."

"Nerves? I beg your pardon." Jack glanced at him. "I am not nervous."

"Oh, aye. Must be something else sends ye oot to the loch at dawn on your wedding day, then."

"Yes, well . . . it isn't nerves. Precisely." Jack crossed his arms. "I have wagered thousands of pounds on the play of a card and never turned a hair. Ask anyone; they'll tell you."

"Ice water in your veins, eh?"

"Exactly. 'Twas the one thing my father admired in me."

"It's just the lassie, then, that makes ye jittery?"

"Of course not. I'm not jittery. It's just — what am I doing?" Jack burst out. "I have no idea why I even came to this place. Now I am marrying someone I don't know. I

274

should have given her the wedding present I got her in Inverness, but I could not seem to find the right time or place or the words to do it. Me! Why is it so bloody difficult to talk to her?"

"Och, weel. Women . . ."

"You don't understand. I am a man who can talk to women. To anyone. I am glib; she is right in accusing me of that. But with her — I've been tiptoeing around her for days now, unable to explain. To set it right."

"Set what richt?"

"I don't know! That's just it." Jack turned to McKay. He knew it was ludicrous to be pouring out his thoughts like this to a man whom he had not even met until a few weeks ago — a man, moreover, who had greeted him with a musket. But he could not seem to stop. The words rushed up out of him, like water gushing from a breached dam. "What does it matter if I have brothers or sisters? Or if I told her about my mother and father? Why should she care where I lived? What use is it to talk about everything I've ever done?"

"Och, weel. Women . . ." McKay said again, shaking his head.

"I thought she was glad to see me when I returned. I *know* she was glad. Then she changed. Turned to frost in an instant. And she called me —" He stopped abruptly, clamping his lips together.

"A sharp?" McKay offered. "An ivory-turner? A rum 'un?"

"No!" Jack glared at him, and the old man shrugged, turning back to his task. "I am *not* a sharp." He let out a long breath. "She accused me of being a sham. She said there was nothing inside me."

"Whisht . . ." McKay let out one of the odd noises Scots seemed so fond of. "Ye look real enough to me. Are ye nae standing richt here? Same insides as the rest of us, I'd guess."

Jack let out a chuckle, his muscles relaxing. "True enough."

"The lasses'll drive ye mad. Best not to marry, I say." McKay cast a measuring look at Jack. "But I wager you'll gang your own gate. Lads always do." He shrugged, then nodded at him sharply. "Now, I'd say ye'd best get back and make yourself respectable. Ye canna marry Miss Isobel looking like ye just fell oot of bed."

"Yes. No doubt you're right." Jack sketched a bow to the old man. "Good day, Mr. McKay. I shall see you later at the feast."

"Aye." As Jack started away, McKay added, "Ye could coom up to the hoose sometime. When ye need to get awa'. We'll go doon to the river to fish. Calms the nerves, fishing."

Jack smiled faintly. "I'm afraid I don't know how."

"Och, weel, I can teach ye, now, can't I?"

"Yes, I suppose you can, at that. Very well. I shall take you up on your offer."

Oddly, Jack felt more settled after his talk with Angus McKay. However, his stomach was still too jangling with nerves to face one of the cook's heavy breakfasts, so he took only a cup of tea and went to his room to get ready for his trip to the church.

An hour later, washed, clean-shaven, and dressed in his finest suit, he was standing in the drawing room, staring out the window and once again waiting for the minutes to crawl by. The sound of a woman's voice at the door pulled him from his reverie. "Mr. Kensington?" A woman he had never before seen stood in the doorway, studying him. Her hair was a cloud of dark red curls, and her wide-set eyes were a startling gold. Small and curvaceous, she did not possess the aristocratic beauty of Isobel, but something about her was vibrant — a look, a stance, a quality that set her apart. She was the sort of woman whom it was impossible not to notice.

"Yes?"

"I am Meg Munro. Coll's sister." She came forward. He noticed she did not extend her hand, but continued to observe him in the same grave way. He had the distinct feeling he was being measured.

"I see. How do you do?" He gave her a polite bow. This, then, was the girl who Isobel had said grew up with her. She was certainly a far cry from the towering, blond Coll, but Jack suspected that she was as little prepared to like him as her brother.

"Miss Rose and I are going to lead you to the kirk."

"Lead me?"

" 'Tis the custom." Meg shrugged. "Isobel's cousins and Coll will take her there from my home. Her aunt and I will take you from here. That way you will not see each other until the wedding."

"Everyone seems at great pains to avoid that."

"Aye." A grin tugged at the corners of her mouth. "Aunt Elizabeth is determined to follow the rules. She wants the best for Isobel." Meg paused, the humor falling away. "As we all do."

Jack quirked his eyebrow. "Miss Rose is most beloved."

"She is. Especially by me." Meg came

278

closer, and the steel in her eyes took him aback. "Take good care of Isobel, Mr. Kensington. She deserves more than a farce of a marriage."

"Miss Rose is under no duress to marry me."

"If you call saving her home and her people no duress, then I suppose not. But dinna hurt her, or you will regret it." Meg regarded him steadily. "Ask anyone around Baillannan, and they will tell you, I am not a woman to cross."

Jack returned her gaze, torn between amusement and amazement. "I believe you, Miss Munro. And I assure you, I have no interest in harming Miss Rose in any way. She will have exactly what she wants."

"I am glad." Meg gave him a merry smile. "Well, then, we'd best be going to the kirk now, shouldn't we?"

Elizabeth met them at the door, her cheeks pink with excitement, and they rode to the church. There the two women led him down the aisle to the front pew, where Isobel sat with her cousins. Her head was slightly bowed, revealing the vulnerable curve of her white neck. She raised her head and turned as Jack and his escorts reached the pew. She was pale, her gray eyes huge in her face. She stood up to face him, slim and lovely in the pale blue dress, her expression a mix of pride, uncertainty, and determination.

In that moment, the knot in his chest dissolved, the uncertainty and unease melted away, and Jack reached out to take Isobel's hand.

16

Isobel's stomach had been churning all morning. She would have liked to blame the unaccustomed drinks of whiskey she had imbibed the night before, but the truth, she knew, was simply that she was terrified. But when Jack smiled at her and took her hand, his warmth engulfing her icy fingers, her insides finally began to settle. It seemed peculiar that his presence should give her strength, given that so many of her worries revolved around him. But though he gave nothing of himself away, that very implacability had a rock steadiness.

Isobel said her vows with a steady voice, keeping her eyes on Jack's face. She glanced down as he slid the ring on her finger and was surprised to see that the jeweled band was not the ring Elizabeth had given him. She looked up at him questioningly, but the minister was speaking again, and Jack kissed her, sealing their vows.

The courtyard of Baillannan was already filling with wagons and carts of all sizes when Jack and Isobel arrived at the house. Inside the barn, now scrubbed clean, food had been set up on long tables at one end, with the center left empty for dancing. Most people were grouped near the entrance, and they swarmed to Isobel and Jack as soon as they stepped inside.

Isobel found herself stumbling over the words as she introduced her husband to the guests. It was, she thought, entirely strange to refer to Jack that way. But at least the lack of ease between Jack and her seemed to have disappeared with the wedding, and she was grateful to once more be able to talk and laugh with him. The rumble of her stomach reminded her that she had been too nervous to eat today, and she cast a longing glance toward the tables of food at the back. There was no hope of eating, though, pinned in as they were by well-wishers.

In the background Isobel could hear the pipes tuning up, and after a long wail that made Jack start and swing around, the pipers began to play. Isobel laughed as she watched Jack regarding the men in astonishment. He glanced back at her and joined in her laughter. "I had heard tales, but I had not imagined such a caterwauling."

"You will get used to it soon enough," she retorted unfeelingly. "There will be dancing all night."

"One is expected to dance to this?"

"Well, not this song. It is a lament. But to others, yes." Her eyes twinkled mischievously. "Just wait. Soon enough they'll drag you out onto the floor."

"Making a fool of the Englishman?" He grinned. "I studied all the graces, my dear, including dancing."

"Not dances like these." Isobel laughed.

Jack leaned in, his eyes warm. "Will you give me the first waltz?"

Isobel ignored the flutter his closeness caused and put on a wide-eyed look of shock. "Goodness, no, we have no waltzes here in Kinclannoch. 'Tis far too scandalous. Why, since Andrew told Mrs. Grant that he had waltzed in London, she is convinced that he is going straight to hell. I have never waltzed."

Jack curled his arm around her waist, pulling her against his side, and murmured into her ear, "I shall be happy to teach you, my dear. I think you will find it most enjoyable."

The look in his eyes suggested that he was thinking of teaching her something other than a dance. Isobel felt suddenly a little breathless. She was saved from having to respond by her aunt and Meg, who swept them out onto the floor to join the set in the first reel. Afterward, her hand was claimed by first her cousins, then Coll, and Jack turned to partnering Aunt Elizabeth, Meg, and seemingly every other woman in the building.

He did well enough in the first reel or two, which were typical country dances, but as the songs and the dances grew more Scottish, his performance provided everyone with much hilarity. Isobel was relieved to see that Jack was laughing as much as anyone else. He was going a long way, she thought, toward making himself liked by the locals. Though she told herself she had no reason to care one way or the other, she could not help but be pleased and proud.

Her first time off the dance floor, she was surrounded by a number of the crofter wives, all of whom apparently had bits of wisdom to impart to the bride. Isobel gave a fleeting wistful thought to the feast at the other end of the room, then settled in to listen with good humor. She was surprised a few minutes later when a hand slipped in between her and Mrs. Grant, handing Isobel a plate piled high with food. Her eyes widened and she half turned, looking up, and met Jack's twinkling gaze.

"Och, now there's a lad worth keeping," one of the women said.

"A husband must provide, must he not?" Jack tossed back, giving them all the full extent of his smile.

"Thank you," Isobel said in a heartfelt way. "How did you know?"

He laughed. "By the emptiness of my own stomach. I thought you might have been as little able to eat as I was." From the whiff of alcohol on his breath, Isobel suspected that he had located the barrel of whiskey as well as the table of food.

Mrs. Grant laughed. "I remember my own wedding day; I dinna eat a thing, you ken? I nearly fell doon at the altar, I was that weak. Davie had to grip my arm to keep me upright."

The other women hastened to add remembrances of their own wedding days and the nerves that had afflicted them, each seemingly more horrifying than the last. Jack listened to each one gravely, shaking his head in amazement. But when he turned to Isobel and winked, bending over to kiss her cheek, she could not control the little flip of her heart. He smiled at the other women. "Dear ladies, I must leave, for I can see Miss Munro heading this way, and I must escape before she inveigles me into embarrassing myself on the dance floor once again."

As soon as he left, the women immediately began to catalog Jack's favorable characteristics, some of them so frank they turned Isobel's cheeks scarlet, which set them all off into laughter. Isobel was grateful that Meg rescued her, pulling her away from the cluster on the pretext of an important task and leading her out into the yard.

"Thank you!" Isobel exclaimed. It was edging toward evening, the sun hanging so low behind the hills that only a glow of light was along the horizon. The evening breeze cooled her flushed cheeks, and she sank down on a stone bench beside the barn wall, letting out a sigh.

"I thought you might like a bit of peace." Meg sat down beside her and stretched her legs out in front of her.

"Yes — and a chance to eat." Isobel laughed and dug into the food.

"Everyone wants to talk to the bride. I noticed Mr. Kensington brought you your bite. That was good of him."

Isobel nodded, and not looking at Meg,

she said carefully, "What did you think of him?"

"Kensington?" Meg tilted her head consideringly. "I can see why you are tempted."

"Meg . . . I'm serious."

"As am I. He is a fine figure of a man, and he has a way about him. If he were not your man, I wouldn't mind a bit of a flirt with him."

"Just a flirt? Nothing more?"

"Nae." Meg shook her head and looked a trifle wistful. "Cam Frasier told me I have a heart of stone. He may be right." She shrugged. "But I think a number of women would take him up on something more."

"No doubt they have," Isobel said tersely, and poked at the potato on her plate.

Meg glanced at her, frowning. "Do you mean he's been sneaking about with some other woman?"

"Not here. Not sneaking either, really. But he went to Inverness."

"Ah, I see. You think he found some doxy there." Meg shrugged. "Did you ask him why he went there?"

"No! I could not!" Isobel turned a shocked face to her. "He would not tell me, anyway. He was very evasive about it when he bid me good-bye, which is why I feel so certain that was his reason for going. Besides, to ask him would make it seem that I care whether he was dallying with some light-skirts. And I don't. I mean, I shouldn't. We agreed that we would have separate lives."

Meg studied her friend for a long moment, her eyes warm with concern. "Isobel . . ."

"No." Isobel set her jaw. "I will not have you feeling sorry for me. I will be fine. I have made my bed and I'll lie in it."

"Or not." Meg sent her a sideways glance, the corner of her mouth quirking up.

Isobel relaxed and chuckled. "Or not."

"Ladies!" They looked up to see Cousin Gregory walking toward them across the yard. "What are you doing out here? Hiding from all your admirers?"

"Just taking a wee rest. And giving Isobel a chance to eat."

"I can see why you sneaked out. It's a crush in there. Isobel, you are too popular by half. I have been able to get only one dance with the bride. You would think a cousin would get more consideration."

"I like that!" Meg joked. "You want another dance with Isobel and you have not asked me to dance a single time."

"Ah, you have had an unaccountable antipathy for me ever since I dipped your braid in the inkwell." He sighed theatrically.

"I know my hopes are doomed with you."

Meg rolled her eyes and stood up. "Hah! Just for that, I'll prove you wrong and dance a reel with you. Isobel?"

"Yes, I'm coming." Isobel set her plate aside and followed them into the barn, bracing herself for another round of socializing.

But when she stepped inside, she saw far worse than a gaggle of curious and talkative women. Jack and Coll were standing in the opposite corner of the room, and their rigid postures and tight faces told more clearly than words that they were in the midst of an argument.

17

Isobel hurried across the room toward the two men. As she neared them, she heard Jack say, his voice hard and clipped, "I'll thank you to remember that Isobel is *my* wife. If she needs a defender, *I* shall be the one to do it. Your protection is neither necessary nor wanted."

A dull red flush rose up Coll's neck, and he balled his fists at his sides, but before he could retort, Isobel reached them, sliding one hand around Jack's arm and placing the other on Coll's.

"Gentlemen!" She smiled fiercely, pinning first Coll, then Jack, with her gaze. She went on, her voice low and hard despite the determinedly pleasant expression on her face, "What in the name of all that's holy do you two think you are doing? I will not have my wedding ruined by a brawl."

Isobel felt Jack's arm tighten beneath her hand, and the look he sent Coll would have made most men take a step back. For an instant, Isobel feared that Jack would pay no attention to her words, but then he relaxed, visibly smoothing out his expression, and turned to sketch a bow to Isobel. "Of course, my dear. I would not presume to mar this happy occasion."

Isobel looked toward Coll, and he gave a short nod. "Of course. I beg your pardon, Isobel." A fulminating glance toward Jack made it clear that Coll's apology did not include him.

As Coll strode away, Isobel hooked her arm through Jack's and did her best to look as if they were on a casual stroll as she steered him toward the outer doors. His walk was steady, but the scent of whiskey clung to him like perfume. She peered up at him, her eyes narrowed suspiciously. "You are drunk, aren't you?"

"Nonsense."

"You smell like a distillery."

"Of course I do. How could I not when every time I turn around someone is shoving a 'wee dram' on me? But I am not bosky." He cast a disdainful look down at her.

"Of course not," she agreed drily as they stepped out into the cool air of the yard. "That is no doubt why you were about to get into fisticuffs with Coll."

"I was about to get into fisticuffs with Coll because he is a smug, meddling, self-righteous —." Jack stopped abruptly and turned to her, flinging his arms out to the sides. "What exactly is it that everyone here thinks I am about to do to you? Your friend Munro is the third person today to tell me that I had best not hurt you or I will have to answer to him."

"Oh, dear." Isobel pressed her lips together to hide a smile. "That many?"

"Yes. But the day is not over yet, so I suspect there will be many more."

He looked, she thought, somehow charming this way, his hair mussed, a boyishly put-upon expression on his face. It made her want to laugh, and it made her want to throw her arms around his neck and kiss him until he gave way and laughed with her.

"Before Coll," Jack went on in an aggrieved tone, "while I was fetching a plate of food for you, your cousin Gregory accosted me with dire warnings of my fate should you be unhappy. The first threat today was from your friend Meg." He paused, then added judiciously, "I must say, I believe hers was the most frightening of them all."

Isobel chuckled, and he reached out, curling his arm around her shoulders and pulling her into him. "Ah, Isobel, you are a bonny, bonny lass."

"Och, you canna say it right," Isobel retorted, but she could not disguise her shiver as his hands slid down her back and over her buttocks, pressing her firmly against him.

"I don't need to speak to tell you what I feel for you." He nuzzled his face into her hair.

"No, I think that's clear enough." She strove for a tart tone but was dismayed to find her words came out breathless instead.

"I have been thinking about this night for a long, long time. . . ." He pressed a kiss against her temple. "Wanting you."

"You're only saying this because you've been drinking."

"No." She could feel his smile against her skin. "Drink may have loosened my tongue. But the desire has always been there."

"Jack, I don't want to —" Isobel broke off with a little gasp as he took her earlobe between his teeth, sending a sudden flood of heat all through her.

"Don't you?" He raised his head and grinned down at her. "You are the one who asked me to marry you. What's a man to think at such a proposal?"

"Tease all you want, but you know that I . . . I . . ." Looking into the depths of his eyes, she lost her train of thought.

"I know you tremble when I touch you." He kissed the corner of her mouth. "I know your mouth is sweeter than honey, and when I kiss you, you kiss me back." His lips went to the other side of her mouth. "I know that when I returned home, you threw yourself into my arms, and it felt like heaven."

His mouth settled on hers, all teasing done. She felt his body surge with heat against her, and his arms tightened, crushing her into him. In that moment, all thought was lost to her, and she knew only the pleasure shimmering through her, the ache swelling deep inside.

"There's the lucky couple!" a slurred voice sounded from the open doorway of the barn.

Jack cursed under his breath, letting go of Isobel, and they turned to face the group of men who had just emerged from the barn.

"Aye, and we're just in time to see them off to their wedding night, from the looks of it." A chorus of suggestive laughter followed this quip, and one of the men turned to call to the festive crowd inside the barn.

"Another Highland custom?" Jack gave

Isobel a quizzical look. "Do not tell me they plan to accompany us to the bedroom?"

"Weddings have been known to get a trifle rowdy," Isobel allowed. "But, no, I think they want only to see us safely across the threshold."

The partygoers trickled out of the barn, gathering around the couple and sweeping them, amid laughter and jests, across the courtyard to the front door. Isobel turned to Jack as the door was flung open, saying, "You have to —"

"I know." He bent to sweep her up into his arms. "I have been well instructed by your aunt."

Carefully stepping over the threshold and thus avoiding whatever ill luck happened to those unfortunate enough to tread on it, Jack set Isobel down in the entry. As the others spilled after them into the house, Jack took her hand, drawing her up the staircase to the whoops and cheers of the crowd below. As they passed from the view of those below, he darted up the last few steps and whisked Isobel into his room, closing the door after him and turning the key.

"I am taking no chances with that group," he said, and Isobel laughed.

She turned away, her laughter dying in her throat as she looked around her, the reality of the situation sinking in. The massive, old bed, long a symbol of the laird's position and authority, towered against the wall between the windows. With thick, square posts and topped by a tester of dark green brocade, it dominated the room. The room was suddenly airless, and Isobel didn't know where to look.

Jack came up behind her, putting his hands on either side of her waist, and she jumped, startled.

"Shh, now." He slid his hands around her, encircling her lightly, and rested his cheek against her head. "There's no need for that. I have no intention of forcing you into my bed tonight. I am not the beast everyone seems to believe."

"I know." She did not think it was wise to add that it was not the possibility of his *forcing* her that caused her tension. "It is just, the day has been . . . difficult."

He let out a little laugh, his breath stirring her hair. "You have the right of it there. But it would not do, would it, for someone to see you leaving my room only a moment after you entered it?"

"No. You are right."

"Come." He pressed a light kiss into the crook of her neck and released her, walking away. "We'll sit down and gather our breath.

I think a bit of brandy will help."

"I am not sure I want any liquor." She put a hand to her stomach. "I already had 'a bit' of whiskey with Meg last night."

"Isobel!" He pulled a face of mock horror. "You got foxed on the eve of your wedding." He began to laugh. "And to think you were ringing a peal over my head about my slight condition of inebriation."

"I was not foxed!" Isobel retorted, though she had to laugh, too. "I had only two, well, perhaps it was three little drams."

" 'Three little drams.' " He grinned as he walked over to a cabinet and picked up the decanter of brandy. "I have seen tonight what a dram is — apparently a glass of whatever size you make it."

"They were wee!"

"Not to mention the fact that your whiskey is like to take the top of one's head off."

"You do not like our whiskey?"

"I didn't say that." He strolled back to her, carrying two glasses of brandy, and handed her one. "Here. This will take away whatever ill effects you still have. I have it on good authority that brandy cures all."

He took her hand and led her over to the fireplace, sitting down in the large wingback chair and pulling her into his lap.

"Jack!" she protested. "You said you had

no designs on me."

"I didn't say that." His eyes twinkled. "I said I had no intention of forcing you." He looped his arm across her legs, his hand settling at her waist, and leaned back, stretching his legs out in front of him.

Isobel sat primly on his lap, her hands folded around her glass, unsure what to do. It seemed much too familiar to sit like this, his legs pressing into her, only the thin material of their clothes between her skin and his. However, there was no other chair, and it would be silly to stand. She carefully refrained from looking at him, though she was intensely aware of his gaze on her. She took a nervous gulp of her drink, then coughed as it seared through her.

He moved his thumb in small circles against her waist. "It is all right, you know; you may relax. We are married now. And there is no one here to see."

Perhaps he was right. Isobel felt her muscles loosening under the warmth of the brandy. She took another, more careful sip and allowed herself to lean back a little against him. Taking another drink, she moved about a bit, trying to settle herself more comfortably. He made an odd, muffled little noise, and taking her glass from her hand, he set it on the small table beside them, then laid his palm on her shoulder and gently pressed her back against him, his other arm curving around her back.

Isobel let out a little sigh and gave way, leaning her head on his shoulder and curling her legs up, letting his body support her. It was amazing how well her head fit into the curve of his shoulder, how easy it was to lie against him. His hand slid slowly, rhythmically, up and down her arm. The steady beat of his heart beneath her ear, the warmth of his body, soothed her. She realized how utterly weary she was. Her eyes fluttered closed, and in another moment she was asleep in his arms.

Isobel woke up and lay for a moment, disoriented. A thick, dark curtain lay to one side of her, and above her was an equally dark canopy. She turned her head and looked out the opened hangings on the other side of the bed. The room was still dark, though the faintly lighter sky outside the window indicated that dawn was not far off. Jack was silhouetted against the window, gazing down at something below. The trappings of a gentleman were gone; his feet and legs below his breeches were bare, and his shirt hung open, revealing his chest.

She remembered now where she was. In

Jack's bed. She had, astonishingly, curled up in his lap and fallen asleep. Vaguely she remembered opening her eyes for a moment and finding herself in his arms as he carried her across the room. He had laid her down on the bed, and she had instantly gone back to sleep. In sudden alarm, she looked down at her body. A sheet and blanket covered her modestly. Her dress was gone, as well as her shoes, but she breathed a sigh of relief to see that she still wore all her undergarments.

Jack must have heard some noise from her, for he turned his head. "I'm sorry. Did I wake you?"

"No. I don't know." She was glad for the cover of darkness, which made the situation somewhat less embarrassing. "What are you doing?"

"I was watching the revelers. I must say, your countrymen celebrate with great enthusiasm." He strolled over and sat on the other side of the bed.

"I fell asleep. I'm sorry."

"You had a tiring day."

"And you carried me to bed. Thank you."

"I did, and you are welcome. It seemed the least I could do. As pleasant as it was to hold you, I thought it would prove awkward for the entire night."

"I . . . my dress . . ." Her hand went to the covers over her, as if to hold them in place.

His grin flashed. "Yes. I removed your shoes and dress. It seemed a mite uncomfortable to sleep in them."

"Oh."

He leaned closer, bracing his hand on the bed. "I confess, I enjoyed every lascivious moment of it. But I stopped there." He reached out and hooked his forefinger in the sheet, tugging it down to reveal the top of her chemise. "I would rather discover your body with you awake."

"Um." She cleared her throat, heat rising in her cheeks. "Is it morning? Have you not slept?"

"I lay down, but" — he shrugged — "I had trouble sleeping." He ran his finger along the neckline of her chemise. "I found my promise to you rather more difficult to keep than I realized."

"I should leave."

"No. Don't go." He leaned over her, bracing himself with a hand on the edge of the bed, effectively trapping her.

"Jack." She shifted uneasily.

"Don't worry. I have no intention of breaking my word to you. I shall do nothing you do not want. Lying in bed with you is a form of torture, but it is one I enjoy."

Isobel could find no place to set her gaze. His face never failed to stir her, but it was no safer to drop her eyes to his chest, a large swath of it laid bare by his open shirt. The sight of the hard center line of his chest, the hair black against his skin, made her mouth go dry. She could see the play of muscles across his stomach as he shifted position and the ridges of his ribs. Her fingers tingled with the desire to touch him, to learn the texture of his skin and hair, to discover the map of his bone and muscle. She had never imagined how fascinating the male body might be, how tempted she could be to explore it.

As if he knew her thoughts, Jack took her hand and brought it to his chest, holding her palm against him. Isobel drew in a shaky breath. She should pull her hand away. She should turn aside and leave his room. Leave his bed.

Instead she slid her fingertips down him, intrigued by the smoothness of his skin, the tickling brush of his hair, the firm padding of muscle beneath his flesh. His skin was hot, and it flared into even greater heat as she touched him. Her fingers moved onto the hard ridges of his ribs, gliding around toward his side. Isobel looked up into Jack's face, and her breath caught in her throat at the stark stamp of desire she saw there — his eyes dark as a storm, skin stretched tightly across his bones, mouth softening.

She snatched her hand away and started to push herself up from the bed. "I'm sorry. I should not —"

"No. You should. You very much should." The blanket and sheet had slid down at her movement, and he edged them lower. "Stay. Just a moment. Let me show you how it feels."

Isobel let her head fall back to her pillow, the humming anticipation of her body over-riding all sense of caution. She wanted, she hungered, to know the things he offered. His smile was slow and sensual as his hand drifted over her, soft and light as falling snow. Every inch of her flesh was suddenly alive with nerves, so that the merest brush of his fingers, even through the cloth of her chemise, inflamed her skin. She trembled beneath his touch, amazed by the flood of sensation. She was filled with a yearning so fierce and commanding that it shook her to the core.

Closing her eyes, as if to hide from the embarrassment of her desire, she gave herself up to the moment. What she felt was delightful, yet it was not enough. She

303

wanted to have his fingers upon her skin without the barriers of her clothes, a desire so strong that she had to bite her lip to keep from asking him to remove the thin cotton shift. Again, he seemed to sense what she wanted, for he undid the bow of ribbon at the top of her chemise, loosening the neck and sliding his fingers beneath it, roaming down over her breasts and coming to rest on the hardened center of her nipple. Stroking and teasing, his fingertips glided farther, moving across the soft plateau of her stomach and downward until he was stopped by the waistband of her petticoat.

Isobel let out a little noise of frustration. She heard his low, smugly satisfied chuckle, and he grabbed the hem of her chemise, pulling it up and over her head. The cool air on her bare breasts was another touch all its own, and her flesh prickled in response. She opened her eyes to find him watching her, his hot, hungry gaze moving over her bare flesh like the stroke of his fingers. Shocked, she realized that mingled with her embarrassment, pushing it aside, was a profound satisfaction, even pride. There was, she realized, an eagerness to arouse him, a pleasure in being naked before him.

"Isobel," he murmured, and bent to press

his lips upon the soft flesh of her breast. "Beautiful Isobel." Bracing himself on his forearms, he roamed across her with his mouth, planting soft, lingering kisses. "I have been dreaming about this night for days. Weeks."

The low timbre of his voice, the caress of his breath against her sensitive skin, stirred Isobel almost as much as the velvet touch of his lips, and the ache between her legs grew.

"Lying awake at night, thinking about you in your bed only a few steps down the hall. Remembering how you looked when you ran downstairs in your night rail, the light behind you outlining every sweet curve of your body." He kissed one rosy tip, then the other. "I wanted you like a madman that night." He hooked a finger in the waistband of her petticoat, tugging it down to expose her navel. "And every night since." He placed his lips against her quivering flesh, his tongue stealing into the shallow depression.

Isobel sucked in her breath in surprise and her hands moved involuntarily, her fingers clenching the sleeves of his shirt. He did not seem to mind that her fingertips dug into his arms, for he gave a breathy, little laugh, shoving the covers off her. As his mouth explored her upper half, his hand roved down over her petticoats, smoothing up and down her legs. Her petticoats grew shorter with every slide of his hands.

"I tortured myself wondering exactly how long those elegant legs were. All that kept me sane was knowing soon I could measure them with my hands. Learn each curve and line. Feel them wrap around my back." He slipped his hand beneath the thin petticoats and up her leg, skimming over the stockings and garter and onto the bare flesh of her thigh.

Isobel started at the unaccustomed touch, and his name fell from her mouth in a soft moan. "Jack . . ."

His skin flared with heat. He gazed down at her, his eyes fierce and consuming, watching the play of emotions on her face as he slowly glided over her skin, setting every nerve tingling in response. "Say it again. I have been waiting to hear you call out to me in just that way. Say my name."

His hand crept higher, his fingers tracing lazy circles on her flesh.

"Jack." Her whisper caught as a shiver took her. "Oh, Jack . . ."

He moved over her, taking her mouth in a long, hard kiss. His body was heavy on hers, pressing her into the soft bed, but Isobel relished the weight. She wrapped her arms tightly around him, her mouth as eager, as hungry, as his. The ache between her legs throbbed and she was seized by a mad desire to wrap her legs around him as he had described.

He broke their kiss, rearing up on his knees to yank off his shirt and toss it onto the floor. He fumbled at the drawstring at her waist and Isobel shoved his hand aside, expertly unknotting the ribbons. Light flared higher in his eyes, and he slid out of bed, skinning out of his breeches as she shoved down her undergarments and kicked them aside. Isobel turned to him and went still as she took in her first sight of a fully aroused nude male.

Then he was kissing her again, his hands and mouth awakening her every sense, and she lost all thought, all hesitation, knowing only that she wanted him more than she had ever dreamed of wanting anything. His hand went between her legs, finding the moisture there, and he let out a half laugh, half groan, as if lost somewhere between pleasure and pain. He took her breast in his mouth, sucking gently, as his fingers opened and stroked her, and the combined pleasure coursed through her with such heat and urgency that she dug her hands into the sheets, unable to silence the soft moans that slipped through her lips.

He mumbled against her skin, low, incoherent words, but her body was well attuned to their meaning. His fingers slipped down and inside her, opening and stretching her, and Isobel lifted her hips against his hand, seeking the satisfaction that her body craved though she hardly knew what she sought. He slid between her legs, and instinctively she opened them wider to receive him. And this, she knew at last, this was what she longed for, the single thing that would satisfy her hunger and fill the aching void.

Bracing himself on his forearms, Jack loomed above her. His face was dark, almost gaunt, all courtesy and polish stripped away, and Isobel thought, with a little spurt of triumph, that this at last was *him.*

"I meant to go slowly with you," he told her, the unevenness of his breath betraying the urgency pouring through him. "To beguile and tease and teach. But I fear I cannot wait."

His hands slipped under her buttocks, lifting her, and Isobel felt the full, hard length of him probing and entering, and for an instant she tightened all over, her fingers digging into his arm. Then, with a flash of pain, he was inside her, filling her in a way that made her groan with pleasure. He began to move, stroking in and out, and a delightful friction built in her, rushing ever faster toward that elusive, beckoning end.

Her world exploded, and she cried out, shaken to the core. Isobel felt him strain against her, shuddering, muffling an explosive cry against her neck. She went limp, clinging to him as if to hold that ecstasy forever. Slowly, sweetly, the world righted itself again.

18

Isobel jerked awake, pulled up from some hot, urgent dream. Her breasts were swollen and sensitive, and her skin tingled all over. Deep inside her, she felt malleable and warm, aching slightly but in a pleasurable way. She realized, with great surprise and a newfound awareness, that she was aroused.

The reason for that state was stretched out beside her, his arm flung across her and his hand curved around her buttocks. If he moved that hand just a few inches, his fingers would slide between her legs from behind, seeking out all the supremely sensitive and pleasurable spots residing there. Isobel blushed a little at her wayward thoughts. Whatever had happened to her?

She had set out yesterday full of trepidation, certain that she would not consummate this pretense of a marriage, yet here she was, no longer a maiden, replete with satisfaction, and utterly in the thrall of this man and the heart-stopping pleasure he brought to her. It was deplorable, and she was undeniably weak and licentious.

And she would like very much to explore every inch of Jack's bare skin. A smile crept across her lips.

"I like that smile," a voice rumbled not far from her ear.

Startled, Isobel jerked upright. The covers slid down to her waist, exposing her bare chest, and she grabbed them to cover herself, but Jack laid a stilling hand on hers.

"Don't." He grinned. "I like that even more."

He lay propped up against the pillows, his face rough with stubble and his eyes languid with sleep. His broad shoulders and bared chest were as enticing in the clear light of morning as they had been last night. Isobel did not know where to look, what to say, and she turned her head aside in confusion. How could it be that her insides melted under the heat of his smile?

She had never thought of herself as a woman of loose morals, but she was too honest not to admit that she was brimming with lustful thoughts about a man who, while he might be her lawful husband, was not a man she loved or even knew well — though, she thought with a tightening deep in her abdomen, she had to admit she did know him now in a basic way.

Unable to contain her curiosity, she sneaked a peek at him from the corner of her eye. Arms folded behind his head, he was continuing to study her in a leisurely manner, his face softening with desire. Reaching out a hand, he cupped her breast, eliciting a sharp indrawn breath from Isobel as his thumb rubbed gently over her nipple.

"You are a beautiful sight first thing in the morning." His eyes went to hers and he smiled. "I think I could get used to waking up this way."

"I . . . um."

"You are even more charming when you're flustered. Come here." He took her arm and pulled her down to him. "Let's rest a moment longer. What is it you say? *Bide a wee?*"

"Yes." Her voice came out shakily as she nestled against him. His skin was warm beneath her face, and the scent of him filled her senses — sweat and sex and the lingering bit of whiskey. If she turned her head a little, she could press her lips against his chest, and the thought tempted her. She laid her hand on his arm instead — and found that his smooth skin stretched over the pad of muscle was arousing, too. The wicked pulse between her legs, already ignited by her lustful dream, picked up heat.

Jack smoothed her hair back from her face, his fingers gliding over the thick mass, lifting it, then letting it cascade back over his chest. Isobel drifted her fingers down his arm and back up, enjoying the tickle of the hair on his arm. She traced the tendons and bones of his hand, intrigued by the contrast of textures. She closed her eyes, imagining how it would be to run her hand down his legs or to touch the soft skin of his stomach.

"I heard you this morning, before you woke." He ran his thumbnail up her arm from wrist to shoulder, sending a tendril of pleasure rippling through her.

"Oh." Embarrassment heated her skin. "I'm sorry."

"Don't apologize. It was a pleasant way to wake up." He ran his thumb down her side in the same fashion. Kissing the top of her head, he went on in a husky voice, "What were you dreaming? What brought such delicious little moans from your lips?"

Now her skin was hot as fire and she turned her face into his chest to hide it. It seemed the height of humiliation that he had heard her, had realized what sort of thing she was dreaming. He chuckled and lifted her hair to kiss his way down the back of her neck. Isobel trembled, desire flooding through her, overwhelming her embarrassment.

With one hand, he flipped back the covers, exposing her completely to his gaze. Starting at her shoulders, he moved his hand unhurriedly down her, curving over her breast and across the slats of her ribs, up over the swell of her hips, then slipping back to roam over her stomach and down until his fingers tangled in the wiry hair at the apex of her legs.

Isobel stiffened, stifling a noise in her throat, and squeezed her legs together, but his fingers crept insistently between them, seeking and finding the hot, wet heat, the quivering, tender flesh.

"Jack," she choked out as his fingers stroked her slowly and rhythmically. She felt as if she were melting beneath his hands, dissolving into a mindless pulse of desire. "No — what are you doing?"

"Pleasing you, I hope." His voice was husky and a little unsteady. He pressed his lips into her hair. "Does it? Please you?"

She could not hold back a low groan. "Yes, but, oh —" She broke off with a shudder as the undertow of desire caught her. His clever fingers were slow, then fast, stoking the fire blossoming between her legs. She dug her heels into the bed, opening herself to him, and he responded by driving her deeper and deeper into a sultry maelstrom of passion. Her hips moved instinctively, urging him on, and her breath rasped in her throat as she raced, desperate and eager, toward the shimmering goal that waited just beyond her grasp.

Then it crashed over her, dragging her down into the dark, mindless depths, and she moaned, arching up against his hand. He buried his face in her hair, holding her as she collapsed against him, trembling.

Isobel lay, limp and replete, blissfully naked in Jack's arms and beyond all sense of shame. She stretched to her fullest extent, pulling her arms back above her head and arching her back. She felt as boneless, elegant, and smug as a cat stretching in the sun. Jack's skin was searing, and she was aware of his manhood, engorged and prodding against her hip.

"But, Jack . . . aren't you . . ." She twisted and raised herself onto her elbow to look up at him. One look at his face, heavy with desire, answered her question. "Why did you not — I mean, did you not need to, um, want to . . ." Isobel stumbled to a halt.

"Yes, I need . . . I want." He reached out

to toy with a strand of her hair. "But I thought it might be too soon, that you would not be ready." He smiled faintly. "I have little experience with virgins, I fear."

"Really? You have never taken a maiden to your bed?"

"Not since my first time, and truth is, I was as green as she was, and we were both afraid of her father, who had the devil's own temper." He grinned, giving her a glimpse, she thought, of how that green lad had looked. "But hot blood usually wins out over fear, I've found." He sobered, running his thumb and forefinger down the strand of her hair. "I did not want to cause you pain."

"Oh." She looked at him for a long moment. "I don't care. All I want is to feel you inside me again."

His eyes lit with heat, and something very much like a growl rumbled in his throat. He pulled her beneath him. Isobel wrapped her arms around him as he pushed up into her, expanding and filling her in a way that took her breath from her. Jack thrust into her in long, powerful strokes, and to her astonishment, the heat burgeoned in her again, until finally he drove into her with a hoarse cry, sending them both tumbling over into the shattering chasm.

■ ■ ■ ■

When Isobel awoke the next time, sunlight streamed through the window. She glanced around, disappointed to find herself alone. Stretching, she lay back against the pillows, contemplating the night before. She giggled and rolled over, burying her face in the pillow. Her wedding night had been nothing like what she'd expected. She knew that she had opened herself up to a wealth of pain in the future, but right now she could not make herself think of that. Indeed, she could not make herself think of the next few days ahead. The only thing she wanted was to revel in the moment.

At a noise from the door, she turned as Jack entered, still unshaven and wearing only his shirt and breeches. He carried a large tray with a jumble of foodstuffs piled on.

"Good, you're awake. You looked so peaceful I hadn't the heart to wake you when I left." He set the tray down on the bed and leaned over to kiss her, a simple kiss of greeting. But as soon as he started to step back, he changed his mind and came back to kiss her more deeply. Isobel rose up on her knees, the covers sliding down, and wrapped her arms around his neck.

Finally, letting out a half-mocking groan, he set his hands on her hips and held her aside, pulling back from their kiss. "Ah, Isobel, you break my will the instant I see you." He turned to the wardrobe behind him and pulled out his dressing gown. "Here. Little as I like to cover up that view, I must or I fear we shall starve."

Isobel took the robe and wrapped it around her, rolling up the sleeves until her hands were free. She settled down beside the tray, examining the hodgepodge of dishes. Various meats and cheeses and rolls were piled on plates, along with a bowl of almost solidified porridge, a pot of cream, and another dish of soft, pale butter. Two cups were with a pot of tea, which, she found to her delight, was warm to the touch.

As she poured out the tea, Jack picked up a long roll and tore it in two, sending a shower of hard crumbs over the bed. He handed Isobel half of it and stretched out on the other side of the tray, propping himself up on one elbow.

"Cook took pity on me and made the tea. Apparently she has finally accepted me — no doubt she realizes I am now under your complete dominion, an utter slave to your lust."

"No doubt." Isobel rolled her eyes and handed him a cup of tea.

"I told her I was like to waste away to nothing trying to satisfy your carnal demands."

"Jack!" Isobel choked and glared at him.

He laughed, stuffing another chunk of bread in his mouth, and she reached over to slap his arm. He simply laughed more and dodged her next blow. He caught her wrist and brought her clenched fist to his lips to kiss, saying, "No, have mercy, you savage Highlander. I did not say it."

"You are very merry this morning." Isobel pulled back, trying to achieve an aggrieved tone, but she spoiled it with a smile.

"Indeed, I am. I am discovering that being a husband is a very pleasant thing. I should have tried it earlier."

"Humph. You just have not received a scolding yet. I am sure I can be a veritable fishwife."

"Ah, but I know how to wheedle you out of it." He gave her so smug a smile, she had to laugh. "At any rate, I was persuasive enough that Cook pulled out a few bits and pieces left over from the feast. Though she foisted that bowl of oatmeal on me, as well." He watched as Isobel tentatively poked a spoon at the gelatinous glob. "I will gladly offer it all to you."

In response, Isobel slathered a bit of bread with butter and jam and popped it into his mouth. "Oh, no, Husband, I would not dream of taking even a spoonful of what Cook obviously intended for you."

"You are too kind." He tore open another roll and picked up a dark, round slice, tucking it into the bread. "I shall not ask you what this substance is. It tastes delicious, and I'd rather not spoil my enjoyment with knowledge."

"I think you are wise." Isobel watched him, a faint smile playing at her lips. She had rarely seen Jack aught but even tempered, but neither had she witnessed him in this unguarded, almost buoyant mood, the ironic, even cynical, edges of his humor softened. He appeared younger, almost boyish, and she realized, with a pang, how much she wanted to keep that lighthearted expression on his face. "What is the state of affairs downstairs? Are the revelers still at it?"

"Happily, no. Most of our guests have departed." He chuckled. "Though there are a number of them asleep on the barn floor. Several of the maids are moving about, trying to tidy the place. I saw your cousin Robert in the library, but I was able to avoid crossing his path. Your aunt is closed up in her room, more, I suspect, to avoid running into your cousin than from having gotten foxed last night — which *is* the reason I presume your cousin Gregory has not made an appearance."

Isobel drank the last sip of her tea and looked down at the tray, now half emptied of food. She glanced around the room, realizing she had no reason to stay here any longer. "Well . . . I . . . I should get back to my room."

"I told the maids to bring up a bath for you. I thought you might like one."

"Oh, yes." Her face brightened.

"They are bringing it here." His eyes were on her face. "And some of your clothes as well." He paused. "Unless you would not like that?"

"No. I mean, yes, that is fine." She was suddenly flustered and shy. "If you wish it, that is."

"Yes. I wish it." His eyes darkened, and Isobel felt the response of her body to that small action. She wondered if he was about to kiss her. She was certain she would like him to.

Jack started to move, and at that moment a timid knock came on the door and one of the maids entered. A second girl followed her, carrying the long, narrow tub between them. Their eyes were large and bright with curiosity, and they glanced around, particularly at Isobel, while trying to look as if they were not. Isobel could imagine what they were thinking, and her cheeks pinkened. Another maid followed with pails of water, and for the next few minutes maids passed in and out the door, carrying pails of water to fill the tub, then kettles of water to warm it.

Isobel avoided their eyes, embarrassed at being the object of their attention. She knew that later in the servants' hall they would dissect every little detail of the room, from the mussed bed to the clothes tossed on the floor to her tangled hair and his dressing gown wrapped around her. When at last the servants left, closing the door behind them, the room was oppressively silent. Isobel sneaked a glance at Jack, her former ease in his presence broken.

"I . . . um . . . I'm going to bathe now. Are you —" She cleared her throat. "Do you plan to . . ." She made a vague motion toward the door.

"Leave?" He pushed away from the bedpost where he had been leaning. His smile was sensual, his eyes dark and somnolent. "No, I think I'll stay." He trailed his knuckles down her cheek. "In fact, I believe I shall take that bath with you."

"Jack!" Her eyes widened, and heat flooded through her. "But how . . ."

"You'll see." He bent to kiss her.

19

Taking a bath with Jack, Isobel discovered, was not only a pleasurable experience but time-consuming, and it seemed to take an equally long time to get dressed afterward — especially with the re-dressing. As she stood before the mirror, putting the last pins in her hair, Jack came up beside her, picking up a watch and chain from the dresser.

"You are wearing Malcolm's watch," Isobel said, surprised and pleased. "My aunt will be happy."

"It seemed too kind a gift not to wear it so I bought a key for it while —" He stopped abruptly. "Blast! I meant to give you this last night." He turned and went to his jacket, pulling a square, flat box from an inner pocket.

"What is this?" Isobel asked in surprise as he held the box out to her.

"Open it and see." She reached out tentatively, and he laughed. "Go on. It is something you will like — or, at least, I hope you will."

Isobel opened the hinged lid and drew in a sharp breath. Inside, nestled on black velvet, lay two pearl earrings and a necklace of gold beads and pearls, centered by a single large creamy pearl pendant. "Jack! It's beautiful." She looked up at him, her eyes glowing.

"If a few pearls get me that expression, I can only wish I had bought you diamonds."

"Silly." She laughed and studied the pendant again, smoothing a finger over its slick surface. "Diamonds could not have been lovelier. But why? How? I did not expect anything like this."

"I think a bridal gift is customary from a groom, is it not?"

"Yes, I suppose — though I don't know how things are done in London. But surely you don't go jaunting about the countryside with jewelry in your pocket in case you should decide to marry."

"No. But I did go to Inverness, if you remember."

"Inverness!" She stared at him. "Is that why you went to Inverness?"

"Yes." He looked at her oddly. "Well, I had to buy a few things from the haberdashery and order some clothes; I did not come prepared for a long stay. And there was the watch key. But I needed the gift immediately, and I knew there would be nothing suitable in the village. Unfortunately, the selection was not terribly impressive, either." He paused, frowning. "I seem to have shocked you."

"No. I mean, well, yes, a bit; it was just that I thought —" Isobel broke off, suddenly realizing that she might just have stepped into a quagmire.

"Thought what?" Jack took the box and set it down on the dresser. "Isobel . . . why did you think I went to Inverness?"

"I thought . . . well, that you had gone to visit a . . . a place where . . . that you intended to, you know . . ."

"No, I don't know." He stopped, struck. "Did you think I had gone looking for a bordello?" He began to laugh.

"It is the sort of thing men do," Isobel retorted defensively. "You were about to be married."

"Is that a Scots wedding custom?" He laughed harder. "A week of debauchery before the ceremony?"

"No, of course not. But Aunt Elizabeth said —"

"I am *positive* I did not tell your aunt I was going to Inverness to visit a light-skirts."

His laughter had died, but his eyes were still merry.

"You did not tell anyone why you were going, so how was I supposed to know?"

"You did not ask."

"I presumed if you had wanted me to know, you would have told me. When Aunt Elizabeth said that it was probably the sort of thing one did not tell a lady, I realized that you must have gone there to, to satisfy your needs. . . ." She shrugged and looked away. "It does not matter, really."

"I can see that it does not." He crooked his finger beneath her chin to tip up her face. "Jealous, my dear?"

"No, of course not."

"I don't think I believe you." His eyes smiled down into hers. "It's all right. I find I like a little jealousy in a woman." He kissed her lightly. "I did not seek out a woman in Inverness. I admit I do have needs — and they seem to have grown more urgent since I reached Baillannan." He slid his hands slowly up and down her back. "But the only one who can satisfy them is you."

"Oh." Isobel leaned against him, hiding the happy relief on her face. "I did not like to think that you had done what we did with another woman."

"I'm not entirely sure that I have ever done exactly what we did." He pressed his lips against the top of her head. "Is that why you were so annoyed with me the night I returned?"

Isobel sighed and nodded. "Yes," she admitted miserably. "I am sorry for what I said. I did not mean —"

"That you did not know me? But you were right; you did not," he said lightly.

Isobel raised her head, her eyes glinting mischievously. "I believe I know you somewhat better now."

"Indeed." He kissed her again, more deeply. "Now, turn around and let us see how the bauble looks on you."

She faced the mirror obediently, and Jack fastened the necklace around her throat. Sliding his arms around her waist, he pulled her back against him as he studied her image in the mirror.

"It looks just as I thought it would."

"It is beautiful. Thank you." She raised her hand to stroke the lustrous pearl again, then frowned. "This looks —" She turned to study him. He had dressed for dinner, and the usual snow-white cravat was in place around his neck, but it was centered by a plain gold pin. "Where is your tiepin? The pearl."

"You know my tiepins by sight?" He raised his brows. "I am flattered."

"Is this it? You took it from your pin to make the necklace?"

"Yes. None of the necklaces they had were adequate, and neither were the jewels they had in stock. But I thought the pearl ear-drops were pretty enough, and this chain as well if we added a little something to it. I'm sorry," he added somewhat stiffly. "I had nothing else to hand. I can find you a much better piece in London."

"No! Oh, no!" Isobel covered the pendant protectively with her hand, as if he might snatch it from her neck. "I love it. I do not want another. It only makes it more special that you gave up something of yours for it." She took his hand impulsively and went up on tiptoe to kiss him.

He grinned down at her. "Then I should tell you that the stones of your ring came from my cuff links."

Isobel laughed and went back into his arms.

In the days that followed, Isobel encountered none of the problems of married life that she had envisioned. Indeed the only thing she wrestled with was a question of marital etiquette: What were the rules regarding where she slept? It seemed too bold to simply take up her place in his bed without his asking her. On the other hand, if she went to her bedroom instead and waited for him to come to her, might he not assume she did not want to be with him that night? And where was she to change clothes?

Fortunately, each night Jack began kissing her and pulled her into his room as soon as they reached the top of the stairs, so she had yet to face that decision. Every morning, Isobel slipped down the hallway to her room to dress, feeling vaguely guilty and illicit, hoping she would not have to face the embarrassment of running into one of the servants.

Gradually Jack's room began to change. First a second chair appeared before the fireplace. A few days later, a vanity table with a delicate chair had been added. At the sight of it, a sweet warmth bubbled up in Isobel's chest. Her silver-backed brush and comb lay in their mirrored tray on one side of the vanity. Her dish of hairpins sat beside it, and in front of her mirror were lined up her various pots and bottles of perfume and lotion.

"It looked rather awkward for you, standing in front of the dresser to put up your hair," Jack explained stiffly.

"That was very thoughtful of you." Isobel turned to him.

"Yes, well . . . it seemed more . . ." He looked around vaguely and adjusted a cuff.

"Practical," Isobel finished for him, faintly amused by his sudden awkwardness.

"Exactly." He hesitated. "I hope I did not presume too much in having them bring your things as well." He gestured toward the vanity top, then turned to the dresser, where he seemed extraordinarily interested in straightening his own brush and comb into precise lines. "Of course, if you wish it, you have only to take them back. I . . . uh, it seems inconvenient . . . going to your room each morning to change. There is ample space in this room; my wardrobe is rather limited. Even after my things arrive from Inverness, there will be many vacant drawers. And the wardrobe is quite empty. I thought you might like, that it would be easier, if you were to put some of your clothes in here." He stopped and finally turned back to her.

"Jack . . . are you asking me to share your bedroom?" Isobel smiled, her voice faintly teasing.

"Well, yes, I suppose I am. Of course, if you dislike the idea, there is no need —"

"No, I don't dislike the idea," Isobel interrupted, soft laughter bubbling up, and started across the room toward him. "I think it is a very good idea."

"Well, then, that's settled." He grinned and swooped her up in his arms to carry her to bed.

It was, Isobel reflected, how their conversations often seemed to end. That, she found, was perhaps the best surprise in being married.

"And how is the bride?" Isobel looked up to see Meg lounging in the doorway of the study.

"Meg!" Isobel bounced up from her chair and went to hug her friend. "I am so happy to see you."

"I brought Cook some herbs, so I thought I would stop in and see you as well." Meg paused, smiling. "I was going to ask how you were doing since the wedding, but I can see from looking at you that everything is well."

"Very well." A broad smile stretched across Isobel's face. "Oh, Meg, it is so well that it's a little frightening."

"Somehow I think that you did not stick to your intentions of a celibate marriage." Meg's eyes danced.

"No." Pink tinged Isobel's cheeks. "As it turned out, Jack convinced me to stray with very little effort. It is no doubt brazen of me, but I am excessively glad he did. I never dreamed what it would be like. I must seem quite mutton-headed, I know, as if I cannot hold to my convictions."

"Nonsense. If you are happy, that is all that's important. How can it be foolish to enjoy one's marriage?"

"It will no doubt seem very foolish to me when he leaves for London."

"Perhaps he will decide to stay. Maybe he is happy as well."

"He seems to be." Isobel gave a hopeful smile. "But this is new and entertaining right now. After a while, he will grow accustomed to it. Bored. People do. They always say that men enjoy the hunt, and once it is over they grow dissatisfied."

"And who are these 'they'? I am convinced not all men are like that. Why should he become bored?"

"Because he is used to life in the city. People, excitement, entertainment. There is little for him to do here. We have walked along the beach and to the castle. We even rode over to the standing stones. But there is little else to hold his attention." Isobel paused, frowning. "Jack has started riding out every day. I worry that he is already growing bored. He has even taken to talking to the crofters, I hear."

"Just because he likes to ride or admires the view doesn't mean he is bored. There is nothing wrong with his being interested in the land or the people. Indeed, I would think it is just the opposite."

"I would like to think so." Isobel smiled and shrugged. "If not, well, I made my choice knowingly. I will have to accept it."

"Are you worried about being left with a babe? There are ways —"

"No. Oh, no," Isobel said hastily. "Indeed, just the opposite." She laid a hand upon her stomach. "I always wondered a bit, you know, what made women so enamored of the idea of a baby when it caused such pain. But now . . . I think about a little boy that looks like Jack running about, and it makes my heart swell with joy."

"Then I wish very much that you will have it." Meg reached out to take Isobel's hand and squeeze it gently.

"Enough of me." Isobel smiled, waving Meg to a seat. "Come, sit down and tell me all the gossip of the village. We had been a world apart here the last two weeks."

They settled down for a cozy chat. When Meg left an hour later, Isobel could not interest herself in the accounts again. Talking to Meg about the possibility of Jack's leaving Baillannan had left her feeling restless, and she prowled about the study. When she heard the screech of the side door closing and Jack's footsteps in the hall, her heart lifted, and she went out to meet him, smiling.

"Isobel, my love." He bent to kiss her. "I have been thinking of doing that all the way home."

"You must have had a very dull ride."

"Quite the contrary." He hooked his arm around her shoulders and strolled with her toward the stairs. "It was most entertaining." He cast a devilish look down at her. "I shall endeavor to show you tonight just how intriguing my thoughts were. In fact . . ." He looked thoughtful. "Perhaps you should come upstairs while I clean up and dress for dinner, and I can show you right now."

Isobel gave him an admonitory little pinch, but she went with him willingly. They were halfway up the stairs when Elizabeth appeared at the top. "Isobel! Did you see the carriage? Who is it, do you suppose?"

"What carriage?" Isobel looked at her aunt blankly.

"The one coming up the drive," Elizabeth explained patiently, coming down the steps to join them. "I saw it just now out the window."

Isobel let out a little groan. "Cousin Robert?"

"No, it isn't Robby's carriage. It's a post chaise; it must be guests."

"But who in the world would be coming here?" Isobel remembered the last conversation like this between them, when Jack arrived. It seemed an age ago.

"Perhaps it is a friend of yours, Mr. Kensington." Aunt Elizabeth turned toward Jack.

"I cannot imagine who."

The three of them turned toward the door. Hamish, who had obviously also spotted the vehicle, was hustling down the corridor, but before he could reach the front door, it swung open, and a tall, fair-haired man stepped inside.

"Andrew!" Isobel sucked in her breath sharply, and the man turned to look up at her.

"Hallo, Izzy," he said cheerfully.

Isobel broke from her stunned immobility and started down the stairs to him, followed by her aunt and, somewhat more slowly, Jack. Andrew laughed as Isobel flung her arms around him, then hugged his aunt, who was pink with happiness.

Isobel's brother turned to look past the women. "Jack."

"Andrew." Kensington gave the other man a nod. "This is a surprise."

"Indeed." Isobel smiled broadly. "Why did you not write to tell us you were coming? If that isn't just like you . . ."

"I wanted to surprise you." Andrew grinned. "And I brought a guest with me."

His eyes trained on Jack's face, Andrew swept his arm wide in a grand gesture, ushering in a plump, middle-aged woman in a black carriage dress and a bonnet much bedecked with ribbons and bows. She paused, smiling tentatively at the group before her.

"Hello."

Jack's voice was grim. "Mother."

20

Isobel managed to keep her jaw from dropping as she watched Jack step forward to bow over his mother's hand, and she looked at the woman with a good deal more interest. Jack's mother was pleasantly plump, with a faded prettiness. Her carriage dress, like her bonnet, was liberally adorned with ruffles and bows. Little about her looked like Jack. Her eyes were a much paler shade of blue, and the hair that showed beneath her hat was a light brown liberally streaked with gray. Her sweetly rounded face held no hint of the high, distinctive cheekbones that gave her son's face such a distinctive stamp.

"This is indeed a surprise." Jack sent an unreadable glance at Andrew, who gazed back at him with a spark of challenge in his eyes. "I assume I must thank you for this visit, Andrew."

"Oh, yes," the woman chirped, letting out a giggle and bobbing her head. "Sir Andrew was so kind to look me up and offer to bring me with him. Of course I had your letter, Jack dear, telling me about your marriage, and I did so regret I missed the occasion."

"Indeed. Pray, allow me to introduce you to my wife, Isobel," Jack said politely, turning toward Isobel. "My dear, this is my mother, Millicent Kensington."

"How do you do, Mrs. Kensington? Welcome to Baillannan."

"La, such a lovely name. Baillannan." The woman let out another titter. "I cannot say it properly, I fear, though I do so love to hear Sir Andrew talk about his home. Don't they speak in such a wonderful way, Jack?"

"Indeed," Jack said drily, then introduced Aunt Elizabeth.

"I must apologize that you find us so ill prepared, ma'am," Isobel told her. "Please, come in and I shall have tea brought. You must be tired after your long journey."

"Yes, indeed, such a long way. But a wonderful trip, of course. Such a lovely country." Mrs. Kensington continued to chatter as Elizabeth led her into the drawing room, Jack and Andrew following them.

Isobel turned to Hamish, who stood watching the proceedings with great interest. She grabbed his arm and tugged him aside, saying, "Bring us tea and cakes, and

339

for pity's sake, send the maids up posthaste to ready a room for Mrs. Kensington."

Isobel wished now that she had gone back to cleaning out her grandmother's room after the wedding, as she had intended. It would have made the perfect bedchamber for Jack's mother, large and commodious, with the sort of old-fashioned elegance that befitted the owner's mother.

"Put her in the green chamber," Isobel instructed, adding darkly, "Andrew's room can wait; he deserves to sleep on a cold, bare bed for springing this on us without a word of warning."

"Yes, miss. Master Andrew was always one for making a grand entrance."

She would have called it something worse than that, Isobel thought as she went to join the others. Jack was obviously less than pleased that Andrew had turned up so suddenly with Jack's mother. She suspected that her brother was well aware of that. Andrew had always had a knack for stirring the pot.

It was a mystery to Isobel, though, why Jack disliked his mother's arrival. All her doubts before their wedding came flooding back in. Had he purposely kept his past hidden from her? And why would he do so?

When she slipped into the drawing room,

she found the others seated on the sofa and chairs in a conversational grouping, except for Jack, who stood apart, leaning against the mantel, observing the others. He glanced over at her as she entered, his face guarded. Isobel paused for an instant, wanting to go to him, but she realized it would look odd for her to stand by the mantel as well, so she took a seat in the armchair at right angles to the sofa.

The talk had clearly centered on the trip up here, with all its attendant beauties and trials. As Isobel sat down, Jack said in a casual voice, "What of Mrs. Wheeler? Did she accompany you, as well?"

Mrs. Wheeler? Was there another member of his family he had kept secret? Jack's mother sent him a nervous glance and cleared her throat. Strange as it seemed, she appeared a little frightened of him.

"Well, um, no."

"No room in the post chaise, you know," Andrew put in languidly. "I told Mrs. Kensington I was sure one of the girls here would be happy to act as her personal maid."

"Mrs. Wheeler is more a companion than a maid, surely." Jack's voice was flat.

"But she can be a bit of a bore sometimes." Mrs. Kensington did not look at Jack

341

as she went on in a rush, "And in a post chaise, it would be impossible to get away from her chatter. I did not need a companion with Sir Andrew along to handle everything for me. So kind of him." Mrs. Kensington beamed at Isobel's brother before sending Isobel an anxious look. "I hope you will not think badly of me for showing up like this. I know it is most inconvenient, but as Sir Andrew pointed out to me, we would be here by the time a letter reached you."

"It's no inconvenience at all," Isobel assured her smoothly. "You are always welcome here. I am very happy to have the opportunity to meet you."

Mrs. Kensington brightened. "I confess, I could not wait to see you until Jack brought you to London. I was so amazed. I had begun to think that Jack would never marry and give me grandchildren."

Hamish brought in a tray of tea and cakes, and they settled down to the polite ritual of tea. It was a welcome distraction from the odd and awkward conversation, though the air still hummed with tension. When Hamish returned to remove the remains of the light meal a few minutes later, he gave Isobel a significant nod, and Isobel was quick to bring the occasion to a close.

"I believe your rooms are ready now. No

doubt you would like to go up and rest from your journey." Isobel stood up, setting the exodus in motion.

Jack offered his arm to his mother, and Aunt Elizabeth accompanied them, but Isobel hooked her brother's arm and held him back after the others left. "What are you doing, Andrew? Why are you here?"

"Why, Izzy, are you not happy to see me?"

"Don't try that innocent face with me; I have known you since you could crawl, and it is clear that you are up to some sort of mischief. How did you even know I had married?"

"I certainly didn't hear it from you, though one would think you would inform your only brother of your impending wedding."

"It was Cousin Robert, wasn't it? That interfering old —"

"Of course he is, but, really, Iz." Andrew dropped his lofty tone and reverted to an aggrieved manner with which she was much more familiar. "It's the outside of enough, you marrying that jumped-up cardsharp Kensington. The man who took Baillannan from me."

"You mean, the man to whom you *gave* Baillannan. Did you give even a thought to me or Aunt Elizabeth or what we would do

343

when you lost our home?"

"I didn't plan on losing it!" he retorted indignantly. "I was sure my luck was about to turn. I was wearing Papa's ring on my left hand, you see, and I realized that the week before, when I won that gold boy from Harchester, it had been on my right hand, so I switched it."

"Andrew!" Isobel stared at him. "Surely you realize how absurd that is."

"You don't understand," he said sulkily. "You don't know what it's like. I couldn't just stop because I'd dropped a bit of brass. I would have looked purse-pinched."

"Because you were!"

"Harchester was there and Silas Brandon, as well. Silas lost ten thousand last week and never turned a hair."

"And because he is a fool, you have to be one, too?"

"He is not a fool. He's bang up to the mark; lots of chaps would give their right arm to be one of his set. It's not about money."

"You certainly spend a lot of it for it to be so unimportant."

"There. I knew it. I knew you would blame me." He looked suddenly so young and unhappy, much as he had when he was a little boy and had broken a kite or lost his favorite toy, that a sharp pang of love and regret pierced Isobel.

"Oh, Andrew . . ." She sagged, the anger slipping out of her.

"I know." She saw the glint of tears in his eyes as he stepped forward and wrapped his arms around her, letting his head sink down to rest against hers. "I have made a proper mull of everything. I'm sorry, Iz. I didn't know where else to go."

"Of course you should come here. You can always come home."

He hugged her tightly for an instant, then turned away, walking over to the window to look out. "Only it isn't my home anymore."

"It is mine, and so it is yours, too."

He flashed a sad smile at her, reaching up to shove his hair back from his face in a dearly familiar gesture. "I understand why you married him. Whatever I said, I know you had to marry him to keep Baillannan. I just wish . . . I hate it that you had to lower yourself. To take that bastard's name."

"Andy. Jack is my husband. I will not allow you to speak of him like that."

"Very well. No doubt you're right. Have to be respectful of a man in his own house." His voice had an edge of bitterness, but he gave her a determined smile. "Let me wash off the dust of the road and take a lie down,

and then you'll see, I'll be polite as damn-
all."

Isobel took his arm and walked with him
up the stairs, giving him a kiss on the cheek
when they parted in the hallway. "It's good
to have you home, Andrew."

She found Jack in their bedroom, as she had
expected. He was standing at the fireplace,
one arm braced on the mantel, staring down
at the coals he was shoving about with the
poker. His riding jacket was flung in a
crumpled wad on the floor at the foot of
the bed, and his boots lay on their sides
halfway across the room from each other. It
did not take a great deal of imagination to
envision that he had yanked off each item
and hurled it at something. He straightened
and turned at the sound of her entrance.
His posture was stiff, his face remote, and if
there had been anger there earlier, it was
gone, replaced by a cool courtesy — and
something else, she wasn't sure what, perhaps wariness.

"Well, now you have met my family." His
tone was light, but no spark of humor was
in his eyes.

"Yes. I'm glad. Your mother is very nice."
Isobel crossed the floor toward him, a host
of questions bubbling up inside her. "But

why did you not tell me about her?"

"I am sorry that you were caught unprepared," he said formally. "I would have told you if I had realized that she might take it into her head to visit — or that your brother might put it there." Now the bite of anger was in his voice. He faced her, resting the tip of the poker on the hearth, though his hand still gripped the handle as if it might run away from him. "I never thought you would meet her, given the sort of marriage we have."

Isobel was brought up short. Of course. The sort of marriage that was not really a marriage. An experience so fleeting, of so little importance to him, that it did not warrant even telling her about his family. She had thought him guarded, but apparently he was simply uninterested. Her happiness of the past two weeks had been a fool's dream. She blushed to think of her silly prattling to Meg this afternoon. The only intimacy she and Jack shared was physical.

"I see," she said, pleased that she managed to sound as calm and detached as he. "Is there anyone else who may have slipped your mind? A father? A brother? Some mad uncle hidden away in an attic somewhere?"

"No." His voice iced over. "I will have no more inconvenient relatives popping out of

347

the woodwork, I assure you. I will remain the primary embarrassment to your reputation."

"Don't." Fury swept up in Isobel. "Do not act as if I am the one being unreasonable. As if I have treated you or your mother with contempt. It was you who hid his past. You are the one who has lied — and do *not* say it was trivial or that you simply 'forgot' you had a mother or that an omission of the truth is not a lie. You *chose* not to tell me about her — or anything else in your life. You did not want me to know. I am your wife, and you have treated me as if I were a casual acquaintance — or worse, someone who cannot be trusted, even with the merest facts of your existence."

"Blast it!" He slammed the poker back in its stand with such force that it all went clattering to the floor. "Why do you care? Why is my history so important to you? Will you not rest until you have peered into every nook and cranny of my soul? You know me here and now. Isn't that enough?"

"No!" Isobel was startled at her own vehemence. She realized that her fists were clenched by her sides, her body rigid, and she willed herself to relax. She took a step backward, saying in a tone devoid of feeling, "It's not enough. Clearly our marriage was a mistake. All that binds us is that." She pointed at the bed. "I am nothing but a doxy to you, and Baillannan is the coin in which you pay me." She whirled and started for the door.

"Isobel . . ."

She paused, but did not turn around. "No. I shall see you at supper."

Isobel continued through the door.

21

Either Cook was thrilled to have Andrew home or she wanted to make sure Jack's mother would not find her skill wanting, for at supper she laid out an array of food such as Isobel rarely saw. If her intent was to impress Mrs. Kensington, she succeeded, for the woman responded rapturously to each course. It was, Isobel was beginning to realize, Millicent Kensington's response to most things. The trip had been "delightful," the view "magnificent," the loch "breathtaking," Baillannan a "castle."

"I am pleased you like it here," Isobel told her, hoping her tone did not reflect the icy emptiness she felt inside. She and Jack had not spoken to one another except for a formal nod and greeting when they had gathered in the anteroom for a drink before supper. If he was distressed by that fact, it was impossible to tell.

"I adore it," Millicent assured her.

"Mother adores a great many things," Jack put in.

"Oh, you." His mother patted his arm, beaming at him. "Jack has always been such a levelheaded boy. He thinks me fanciful, I'm afraid."

"Then you will enjoy it here. We are quite fanciful in Kinclannoch." Andrew smiled. "Ah, I see your glass is almost empty. Hamish, pour Mrs. Kensington some more wine." Jack stirred in his seat at the head of the table, and Andrew glanced at him. "I'm sorry," he said sheepishly. "I spoke out of place — force of habit, I'm afraid."

"No offense, I assure you," Jack replied silkily. "However, I suspect that my mother has had her fill of wine."

"Yes, indeed," Millicent Kensington agreed, nodding so that her multitude of curls bobbed. "Jack knows I am not accustomed to alcohol. Though this is so good, perhaps I shall just have a little bit more. We were never allowed to drink it in our home; Father was such a strict man. Not like my dear Sutton at all." She sighed wistfully, then added in explanation, "Jack's father, you know."

"Oh. Yes," Isobel responded. Of course, she did *not* know. She refrained from glancing at Jack.

"I don't believe I know Sutton." Sir Andrew took up the conversational slack.

"He is gone," Jack said flatly.

"Yes. For many years now." Mrs. Kensington's voice was threaded with tears, and she dabbed at the corners of her eyes. "Poor Sutton. Not a day has gone by that I have not felt the loss. I try to take comfort in the fact that he saved that poor child's life — he snatched him right out from beneath the wheels of the wagon, you see."

"Oh, my!" Elizabeth exclaimed.

Millicent Kensington nodded. "Yes. But he was not lucky enough to escape himself. His last words, they said, were for me and Jack, but, alas, I was not there to hear them."

"I am so sorry," Aunt Elizabeth put in feelingly. "I had no idea."

"No. Jack does not like to speak of it, naturally. He was barely more than a lad when his father was taken from us."

Isobel sneaked a glance at Jack. He seemed to be inordinately interested in straightening the chain of his watch.

"It must have been very hard on you, raising a child on your own," Elizabeth sympathized.

"It was. Indeed it was. But Jack was a tower of strength for me. He always has been." Mrs. Kensington turned adoring eyes on her son. "He is so like his father. You have only to look at Jack to see Sutton. So tall, so handsome."

A muscle jumped in Jack's jaw. "Mother, please."

"He does not like me to compliment him." Mrs. Kensington chuckled. "I shall say no more. Except to tell you, Isobel." She turned toward her in a confiding way. "You doubtless know exactly how I felt the moment I first set eyes on my Sutton." She heaved a sigh, putting one hand over her heart. "When I saw him on that stage, I knew."

"The stage?" Andrew asked, his voice amused. "Jack's father was an actor?"

"One of the greatest that ever trod the boards." Millicent beamed. "Such a voice. And so elegant. They were performing *Hamlet* when we met. He was Laertes, and I remember thinking that he should have played Hamlet, for he was much better suited to be a prince. We were in the box to the right of the stage, and when he walked over to our side, he looked out right into my eyes. I knew — right then and there, I was certain that he was the man I would marry. My father was against it, of course."

"Astonishing," Andrew murmured, and Isobel shot him a quelling look.

"There was nothing for it but to run away."

"Naturally," Andrew agreed.

"My father was set on my marrying one of his clerks. Papa was a solicitor, you see; Arthur Benning was reading for the law under him and he was terribly bright. Papa wanted to make sure I was secure, he said, but all Mr. Benning could talk about was the law and the weather, and I could not love him. When I met Sutton, I knew he was the man I should marry."

"Just like Weeping Annie," Aunt Elizabeth said.

"Who?" Andrew looked confused. Jack was stone-faced.

"Weeping Annie," Isobel repeated. "You remember, Andrew. The tale Auntie used to tell us about the mill."

"Yes." Elizabeth nodded. "It was one of Aunt Agnes's stories, and it could fair gar your grue, I'll tell you. Annie's father wanted her to marry the laird, but he was a wicked man, so she ran off with the miller's son, who was her true love. But it ended badly; the wicked laird cut off the lad's head and Annie drowned herself there at the mill."

"Oh, my," Millicent said, her eyes wide. "She became a ghost, then?"

"Yes, indeed. She walks along the bank at night looking for the poor lad's head and keening. If you get too close to the wheel, even in daylight, she will pull you into the water and keep you there with her."

"I suspect, Mother," Jack commented drily, "that you will enjoy a good many of Miss Rose's Highland tales."

"I will! I love a romantic story, even when they end sadly. Well, they so often do."

"I always thought you told that story just to keep Gregory and me from hanging about the waterwheel," Andrew said.

Elizabeth's eyes twinkled. "It is a useful tale, as well."

"On that note, ladies, I believe it is time we left the gentlemen to their port, don't you?" Isobel said, not waiting for any replies before she stood.

There was the polite shuffle to stand and pull back the women's chairs. Isobel cast a perfunctory smile toward her brother and Jack to acknowledge their bows before linking her arm through Mrs. Kensington's and strolling toward the door. Out of the corner of her eye, she saw Jack make a movement, and she thought he was about to come forward or speak to her, but he did not. Little as she wanted to face him, that he had not tried added to the spot of soreness deep within her chest.

Jack balefully watched the women exit the room. He wanted to stop Isobel, to pull her back and talk to her, to break through that chilly reserve. But that was impossible with all these people around them. It was impossible, anyway, to put things back the way they were before his mother and Andrew had come blundering in. He had known it would be as soon as his mother stepped into the house. He had just not counted on the ruination happening so quickly.

Like a fool, he had mishandled the situation, as he seemed to do so often with Isobel. His usual poise and ease in talking — what Isobel called his glibness — had vanished. He hadn't known what to say to her. It had been all he could do to hold his anger at her brother in check, to appear normal and unruffled despite the disaster he knew was coming.

Looking back on it, he supposed it did not matter what he said. Isobel's fury was not something he could vanquish with a smile and a kiss. The look on her face had frozen him; her words pierced him through. Why was the woman so bloody determined to know every grimy detail of his life?

Jack swung back around to face the root

of his troubles. Andrew was lounging in his chair, pushed back from the table, his legs stretched out comfortably in front of him, at ease in the house where he belonged. Jack waited for the twitch of irritation to subside before he spoke; the heat of anger usually resulted in mistakes.

The silence apparently worked on Andrew, for after a moment he shifted in his chair and offered, "No doubt you are wondering why I came here."

"Oh, I understand exactly why you are here. I have little doubt that the river Tick was lapping at your door. One can, however, only wonder why you saw fit to drag a middle-aged woman along with you."

Andrew's eyes danced. "I could hardly come without bringing a wedding gift, now could I? I knew you must be eager for your mother to meet your new wife . . . and vice versa."

"You might have shown your sister more consideration by giving her notice of your arrival so that she could have the rooms prepared."

"I knew Isobel would handle it." Andrew dismissed the matter with a flick of his wrist. "She is well accustomed to my fits and starts. Besides, she never allows this house to fall out of order. Isobel loves Baillannan

357

above all else — as I am sure you have discovered."

"Indeed. It is fortunate someone valued it." Jack gave his words a sardonic inflection, his eyes steady on the other man's face.

A faint flush rose in Andrew's cheeks, and he broke their gaze. "I was certain I was going to win that night."

"Ah. The gambler's motto."

Andrew's eyes lit with anger, but what he would have replied was lost as Hamish came bustling in with the tray of port. The butler set the tray down on the table, positioning it vaguely between the two men. "There you are, Master Andrew. Good to have you home again."

The young man grinned. "It's good to be here. Nothing like the Highland air, is there?"

"No, sir, there is not." The dour butler beamed at him.

"Tell your Nan hello for me."

"I will indeed." He turned to Jack with a polite nod. "Sir?"

"Thank you, Hamish. That will be all."

As the man left, closing the door behind him, Jack said, "Has the man ever breathed aught but Highland air?"

Andrew chuckled. "No. I doubt he's traveled as far as Inverness. But any Highlander knows that anything here is better than everything anywhere else."

Jack poured a generous glass of port for each of them, seizing the brief moment of geniality. "I do not want my wife upset. I know she loves you dearly, and for her sake, I suggest that we call a truce."

"A truce? I did not know we were at war." Andrew took a sip of his drink, relaxing in his chair.

"Then a treaty, shall we say? I do not know you well, so I am unsure what your aim was in bringing my mother to this house — though I must say that the initiative you showed in finding her raised you somewhat in my estimation."

"Are you saying you kept her hidden?"

Jack leaned forward, quelling the urge to plant his fist in the young man's smirking face. "What I am saying is that I own Baillannan, and I would suggest that you remember that fact. If I wish it, you will be out on your ear. No amount of childish pranks or verbal barbs will change that fact. You remain here solely out of my respect for Isobel, and that position will change if you push me too far. Am I clear?"

"Perfectly." Andrew's face took on a petulant look. "You needn't threaten me. I would not hurt Isobel."

Jack responded with only a raised eyebrow. He took another swig of his port. "Drink up. It's time we joined the ladies."

Jack found little comfort there, however, for as soon as he stepped into the drawing room, he saw that Isobel was not there. She had, his mother explained, already retired, and Mrs. Kensington went on to worry at some length about the dear girl's health. Though Elizabeth hastened to reassure her that Isobel was rarely ill, Mrs. Kensington could not help but recall numerous acquaintances and relatives or friends of acquaintances and relatives who had fallen ill suddenly. In all these instances, apparently, the result had been an untimely (and often unsightly) death.

Jack stood up abruptly. "Mother, you have convinced me I should look in on Isobel. Pray excuse me. Ladies. Sir Andrew." He nodded toward them and strode out of the room. His first instinct was to go straight upstairs to talk to Isobel, but he paused at the foot of the stairs. Plunging ill prepared into another conversation with his wife was undoubtedly the worst thing he could do. He had proved on more than one occasion that he was all too likely to make a mull of things with Isobel if he spoke in the heat of the moment. He needed to remove himself, take some time to think things through, prepare his campaign to woo her back.

Turning, Jack walked out the front door and started around the house, the rough path familiar to him now. The cool night carried the familiar scent of trees and earth, threaded through with a trace of peat smoke, a far cry from London's thick miasma from coal fires and sewage. He would miss the smell when he returned, he thought. The nighttime strolls as well. And Isobel.

Jack stopped, jamming his hands into his pockets and staring sightlessly in front of him. What the devil was the matter with him? He had never felt this confused, this torn, this eager to get back into a woman's good graces. He lived his life as he wished, without worry or regret, and had to please no one. It was a selfish life, he freely admitted that; it was also exactly the way he liked it. And he could return to it this very moment, if he chose.

Yet here he was, suddenly, seemingly surrounded by people — he had a wife and in-laws and an odd assortment of people who were important in some way to Isobel, and beyond that this whole collection of crofters who Isobel insisted were dependent on him. All because by chance he had won a house.

And the house had brought him a wife.

He turned and gazed up at the long, gray line of the manor. He had come around to the opposite side and was standing now at the end of the walkway down which he had chased the intruder weeks ago. Looking up, he could see the window of his bedroom, light glowing behind the drapes. Isobel was still up. He could go to her, kiss her and caress her until she forgot all the wrongs she held against him and dissolved into pleasure in his arms. His loins tightened in anticipation at the thought.

He wanted to be there with her, to be lost in the sensations, the heat, driving deep within her until the climax shattered him. It was ridiculous to be standing out here instead, sorry and stupid and cold. . . . But he had barely taken a step when the light in the window disappeared. She had gone to bed without him.

It brought him up short, but a moment's reflection reminded him that she could not be asleep yet, and even if she was, he could wake her in a most pleasurable way. It would be easier in the dark; it was always easier in the dark.

He went in the side entrance, turning to squeeze through in the now-familiar way to avoid the screech of the door on the tile.

His pulse picked up in anticipation as he climbed the stairs and eased into his room. He walked softly to the bed, dimly visible in the pale moonlight. And there he stopped, unable for a moment to take in what he saw.

The bed was empty. He turned and glanced around, but there was no sign of Isobel. Frowning, he lit the lamp. Had she gone back downstairs? He turned and his eyes fell on the vanity table. Her brushes and bottles were gone. Jack's heart began to pound, and he crossed to the dresser, opening first one drawer and then another. Empty. All empty. He went to the wardrobe, but he knew before he opened it that her clothes would not be there. She had taken her things and moved back into her bedroom. Isobel had left him.

22

Isobel opened her eyes, disoriented and aware of a heavy ache in her chest. In the next instant she remembered the day before — Mrs. Kensington's arrival, the bitter words Isobel had exchanged with Jack, and the cold, lonely minutes alone in Jack's room when she had decided to move her things back into her old bedroom. She lay in her own bed, but now she felt like a stranger here.

She turned over, burying her head in her pillow. She had heard Jack come up to his room not long after she'd moved out the last of her clothes. For a few minutes, she had stood still, waiting, her heart knocking in her chest, wondering if he would come to her door, if he would try to talk her out of her decision or even demand that she come back. But he had not, which she told herself had been a relief, and after a time she had gone to bed. And cried herself to sleep.

Sighing, she sat up and jackknifed her legs, wrapping her arms around her knees and resting her head atop them. Yesterday morning at this hour, she had been lying in bed with Jack, replete with satisfaction and desultorily talking about nothing in particular. Now she was alone and her heart felt swollen and bruised within her chest. How could everything have gone so wrong in one day's time?

She did not know if she had made the right decision last night. Perhaps she had merely widened the gulf between them, and Jack would make no move to narrow it. But she had realized that she could not bear to sit there waiting for him to come back, much less sleep with him, live her life with him, all the while knowing how little of himself he was willing to share with her. How deeply he resented her questions, viewing them as intrusions on him.

With a sigh, she shoved her gloomy thoughts aside. She had guests to see to, tasks that needed doing. She could not give in to her dark worries; she had a life to live regardless of the problems between her and Jack. Dressing and doing up her hair in a tidy coiled braid, she went downstairs. She found everyone, even her usually late-rising brother, there before her. Jack rose politely, and she nodded to him with equal formality. He was once again a stranger to her.

"Jack was just telling us he will be riding out after breakfast," Aunt Elizabeth said.

"I can scarce believe how rural he has become." Millicent smiled, leaning over to pat his hand. "Jack has always been one to like the city. More activity there."

"Yes. I fear he must find it a trifle dull here." The words tasted like ashes in Isobel's mouth, but she strove to keep her tone light.

"Never dull," Jack countered. "Angus McKay has promised to teach me to fish."

"Angus McKay?" Isobel stopped, her cup of tea halfway to her mouth.

"Old Angus, down Corby Brae?" Andrew asked.

"Yes. Is that so odd? I got thoroughly lost one day and wound up at his cottage."

"And he did not send you packing?"

"Of course he did. But only once. I think the old chap rather likes me."

"Will wonders never cease?" Elizabeth laughed. "Old Angus likes no one that I have ever seen."

Jack left soon after breakfast, and Andrew declared his intention of going to see Cousin Gregory. Isobel retired to the sitting room with her aunt and Mrs. Kensington, where she was soon awash in boredom as the other two women happily discussed needlework, which, it seemed, Jack's mother enjoyed almost as much as Aunt Elizabeth did.

The days that followed fell into the same pattern. Jack spent most of his days out of the house, riding or walking or something — Isobel wasn't sure what, for he and she barely spoke except in company with the others, and then it was in stilted, impersonal sentences. Isobel spent her days in a dreary monotony, tired and heavy-lidded from another night of sleeplessness.

She missed Jack, more than she had ever dreamed she could. Indeed, she ached for him, not only in her heart but in the depths of her body as well. All her life she had lived without a man's touch, and she had not felt the lack. But now — now it seemed as though she could think of nothing, dream of nothing, be satisfied by nothing, but Jack's touch, Jack's mouth, Jack's long, muscular body wrapped around her, plunging deep inside her.

Her mind drifted constantly to memories of their lovemaking, and she would feel the heat blossom between her legs, her breasts swelling and aching for his touch, even at the most inappropriate times. At night she would come awake with a start, her skin searing and bedewed by sweat, an insistent throbbing deep within her. She would lie there, hoping that Jack would come to her and take her into his arms, would somehow break through this barrier between them.

But he did not. Though many times she felt so desperate, so lonely, so yearning, she started to go to him, each time her nerve failed her. She could not bear it if she knocked on his door only to face the same aloof gaze with which he greeted her each day at the breakfast table. Even if he let her in, if he took her in his arms and satisfied the hunger in her, it would change nothing. The desire might lessen, but she would still feel empty inside.

Andrew stayed at Gregory's for a few days, for which Isobel was grateful. She was sure the atmosphere would have been even more uneasy if Andrew had been there, making quips and barbs. Andrew had always had a ready tongue, but Isobel did not remember his humor being quite so biting in the past. She thought it must have grown more acidic in London — or perhaps she had simply overlooked it when he was younger. He now displayed several traits that it seemed she had not noticed.

In less than a week, however, Andrew returned to Baillannan, having had his fill of Cousin Robert's lectures. Isobel tried to keep from looking dismayed at his arrival. At least Gregory had come with her brother, happy to escape his father's strictures as well, and Gregory's friendly good humor would do much to ease the air; Isobel could always count on him to provide a bit of conversation if things turned grim.

With the young men there to keep Millicent and Elizabeth entertained, Isobel decided once more to start clearing out her grandmother's room. If nothing else, it might take her mind off the soreness encircling her heart.

Isobel stepped into the dim room and shoved the heavy drapes aside to let in the sun, then turned to survey the room. Oddly, the dustcover on the dresser was hiked up on one side, and when she went closer, she saw that its corner had caught in one of the drawers. Isobel frowned, faintly uneasy. She pulled the cloth out from the drawer and peeled it off the mahogany top, tossing it onto the bed. Another of the drawers was open a fraction, a garment hanging out an inch, preventing it from closing.

Isobel opened the drawer and straightened the jumbled clothes. When she had worked in this room a few weeks ago, everything in the drawers had been tidily arranged. Feeling uneasy, she opened one drawer after another. None of them were in neatly folded order. Now that she looked at the dresser more closely, she saw that one side of the heavy piece of furniture stood out farther from the wall than the other end.

She opened the wardrobe, and a hat tumbled from the top shelf onto the floor. The shoes, before in neat rows, were haphazard, some of them turned on their sides. The jars and boxes on the vanity were shoved up against one side. Nothing seemed damaged, and the place was still chock-full of items. But someone had clearly been here, pawing through her grandmother's possessions.

Isobel put her hands on her hips and turned in a full circle, scanning the room. It was absurd to think that anyone had searched this old bedchamber — and to what purpose? But she could not ignore the evidence before her eyes. Removing the dustcovers, she started a more careful search. It was difficult to tell whether anything was missing, for she could not remember the exact contents of the drawers. But the certainty grew on her that someone had been searching the place, and it gave her a distinctly uneasy feeling.

At the sound of footsteps, she rose and went to the door to look out just as Jack appeared at the top of the stairs. Isobel was swept with relief. "Jack!"

He looked up and saw her. "Isobel. What is wrong?" He reached her in a few quick strides, his hand going to her arm, and for an instant it was as if nothing had changed between them. "What is it? What's happened?"

"I'm not sure." Isobel was tempted to lean into him, to rest her head upon his chest. But she stiffened and the brief moment was gone.

Jack stepped back, his face falling into aloof lines. "You looked — I thought perhaps something was amiss."

"I started cleaning out my grandmother's room. I regretted not having it done in time for your mother's visit."

"I am sure she is happy where she is."

"I hope so. But that is not the problem. It looks as if someone has been in her room."

"A maid?" he hazarded. "I'm not sure what is wrong."

"No, just the opposite. It is messy, not clean. There were drawers open and clothes pushed awry. As though he searched her things."

"He?" Jack frowned. "Who is 'he'?"

"I don't know. It could have been a woman as easily as a man, I suppose. But why would anyone have been looking through Lady Cordelia's things?"

"Perhaps your aunt was in her mother's room, looking for something."

"I suppose. But it would not be like Aunt Elizabeth to leave it looking messy. Here, come look." Instinctively Isobel reached out to take his arm, then realized what she was doing and let her hand fall back to her side. She turned, embarrassed, and walked back into Lady Cordelia's room. "You see?" Isobel made a sweeping gesture encompassing the room. "Elizabeth's is neat as a pin and she's always seemed in awe of her mother; I would think she would make sure everything was just so."

He looked around, his frown deepening. "Is this how it looked when you came in?"

"No. The dustcovers were on but" — she opened the door to the wardrobe to reveal the tumbled shoes — "it looked like this." She pulled out several other drawers to show him the jumbled contents. "I know everything was perfectly in order the last time I was in here, and no one comes in here, not even to dust. That is why everything's covered."

"Do you think it was a thief?"

"But that's absurd, isn't it? I don't think there's anything valuable here. Her good jewels would have been locked up in the strongbox downstairs long ago. I suppose there could be something or other missing; Auntie might know." Isobel looked doubtful.

"If something was stolen, who was the thief? One of the servants?"

"That seems likeliest. There is someone about the house all the time. It would be hard for anyone else to sneak in without being seen. But I would have sworn all the servants are honest and loyal."

"I cannot help but think of that night I heard the side door open." Jack's familiar wicked grin flashed across his face. "The time you came out so enticingly clad in your night rail. Remember? I thought someone was breaking in. Mayhap they were leaving, having already searched your grandmother's room."

"No," Isobel said quickly, turning her head so he would not see the flush that rose to her cheeks at his words. "I have been in here since that night, and it was still perfectly neat."

"When were you here last?"

Isobel considered. "I was still working in it a few days before the wedding."

"There were a large number of people here the night of our wedding feast. The house was deserted most of the time, and I doubt anyone would have noticed if someone slipped away from the party for a bit. Haste would explain the sloppy search." His eyes gleamed. "But why would they disturb only this room?"

"I have no idea. Most thieves would go after something obvious, like the silver or the strongbox, I would think."

"They must have been looking for something specific." At Isobel's nod, he went on, "However, if the whole room was searched, they must not have found it easily."

"If at all."

"Perhaps we can." He grinned. "Shall we take a look?"

"Of course." Isobel would have done almost anything to keep that look upon his face, even if she had not been intrigued, too. She swept her eyes around the room. "Here is her jewelry box. It seems a likely place to start. Grandmother was very fond of it."

The rectangular box was a miniature chest of drawers. Isobel pulled out the small drawers one by one, each containing necklaces or bracelets. "These were her everyday things. I have seen her wear them many times, but I don't think they are valuable. Some jet, some onyx. An ivory cameo."

"I think it must be more hidden or else they would not have continued to search." Jack picked up the box, feeling carefully all around its sides and even under the bottom, his fingers gliding over it with care.

"What are you doing?"

"Looking for some mechanism — a spring, a pin, an indentation, something that would open a hidden treasure trove. Alas, I cannot find one." He set down the box. "Let's try the chest."

He knelt before the trunk that stood at the foot of the bed and tried to lift the lid, but it would not open. "Locked." He turned to Isobel. "That seems promising."

"Yes, except I haven't any idea where the key is." She looked helplessly around the room. "I don't remember seeing one anywhere."

"Never fear." Jack plucked a pin from Isobel's hair and knelt by the chest. Inserting the pin and moving it carefully around, he bent his head close to the lock, listening. When the lock popped, he grinned at her shocked face and opened the lid.

Unfortunately, it held nothing but blankets, smelling redolently of herbs.

They moved through the room, pulling out drawers and feeling under, above, and behind them, knocking to find the sound of a hollow space. Jack even slipped the poker behind and below the pieces of furniture and stood on a stool to check the top of the tall wardrobe. Stepping down, he cast an assessing look around the bedroom.

"Those books." He nodded toward a low bookcase next to the rocking chair in the corner. Squatting down beside it, he began to take out the volumes one by one, flipping through the pages and checking the bindings.

"I find it somewhat alarming that you know so many places to look." Isobel sat down in the chair beside him and picked up a book. She hoped this fragile peace between them would not soon end. If she was careful, it might even blossom into something more.

"I know where people like to hide things." He gave her a sidelong glance. "Especially money." When she opened her mouth, he added, "And, no, you don't want to know how I learned them."

"Jack! Do you mean to tell me that you are a thief?"

"Not in many and many a year," he replied equably. "But as you saw, I can still pick a lock if I have to." He flexed his fingers.

"You needn't seem so proud of it." Isobel laughed.

By the time they finished the books, Isobel's shoulders ached and her stomach was beginning to rumble. She leaned back in the chair, sighing. "I fear we are no more knowledgeable than we were. Though far more dusty."

"Mm." Jack wandered over to the small table beside the bed and reached down to pick up a large book bound in supple brown leather. "Lady Cordelia's Bible?"

"Yes." Isobel's interest was once again piqued as he began to investigate the binding.

"A Bible is something people tend to keep close to them." But after a moment, Jack shook his head regretfully and set it down. Opening the drawer beneath the table, he began to poke about in it.

Isobel stiffened. "But that wasn't the one she read." He turned his head to look at her. "She had a smaller one. I don't think it was a Bible, exactly. She had a smaller missal, the *Book of Common Order*. That is what she would read each night."

"Do you know where it is?"

"Yes, of course. She left it to me."

She hurried back to her room, and Jack followed her. As she went to the wardrobe, she glanced back at Jack. He was looking about the room, and suddenly she realized how peculiar this situation felt — to be standing in the bedroom where she had grown up, the room that she had left his bedroom to live in, with Jack beside her. He turned to her, the aloof look back in his eyes, and she knew that he had felt the same sensation.

Suppressing a sigh, she opened the wardrobe and went up on tiptoe to take down a tin box. "This was an old candy tin of Grandmother's." Isobel pried off the lid. "She kept buttons and such in it, and she used to let me play with them as a child. I thought it was magical." She stirred the collection of buttons and odds and ends with her forefinger, smiling to herself. "When she died, I kept the tin because of those memories, and I put the prayer book she left me inside."

Isobel held the small book out to Jack. It was covered in fine leather the color of dark red wine, and the print on the front was in gold, worn half away by frequent use. Jack took it carefully, turning it over in his hands and opening the cover, running his forefinger lightly along the stitching. He went to the inside of the back, doing the same thing. Suddenly he went still.

"What? What did you find?"

"I'm not sure. There's something about

378

the stitching." He walked over to the window to peer at it in the sunlight. "This stitching is not as even, and I think the thread is a little different." He picked at the thread, and Isobel went to her vanity, returning with a set of tweezers. Jack pulled out stitches until he could spread the leather binding apart to peer inside. His eyebrows lifted. "There *is* something here."

"What?" Isobel moved closer as he returned to removing more of the thread. "What is it?"

"I'm not sure. Paper, I think." Prizing the cover open with one hand, he reached in with the silver tweezers and with great care pulled out a folded and yellowed piece of paper.

Jack laid the square of paper down on the dresser, delicately opening it to reveal that the sheet was also folded the opposite way, with a blob of wax crossing the fold, dried and no longer attached on one side.

"The Rose seal," Isobel said excitedly, and pointed to the red wax, which was stamped with the shape of a flower. "That rose emblem is ours. You've seen it on plasterwork all about the house. On the hilt of the dirk in Malcolm's portrait. It's carved into the bedposts in our room."

"And the sides of the fireplace," Jack

added, unfolding the paper with great care. It was fragile and creased, yellowed by age and splotched with mildew. A few lines of faded ink crossed the page.

"Oh, my God." Isobel sucked in a breath, staring at the bold *M* at the bottom of the page. "It's a letter from Malcolm."

23

"Lady Cordelia's husband?" Jack asked. "The one with the treasure?"

"Yes. Elizabeth's father." Isobel bent over the page, squinting to make out the scrawled words. " 'Dearest love,' it begins." She glanced up at Jack. "A love letter. No wonder she kept it always." Isobel returned to reading. " 'Be careful. Lobsters about' — that's the British soldiers. Lobsterbacks, they called them. He goes on, 'I dare not' — I'm not sure, oh, I see, 'come to you.' 'I dare not come to you. I must leave again. Duty demands it. But I cannot go without seeing you just once more.' I can't read this next bit; there's mildew, then something like 'to you,' or maybe that's 'for you.' Then it says, 'Come to me; you know where. I will be there. My heart is yours, always. M.' Oh, Jack." Isobel turned her face up to his, tears glittering in her eyes. "This must be his last letter to her."

Jack reached up and brushed his knuckles down her cheek, his eyes warm on hers. "He loved her." He leaned closer, and for an instant Isobel thought he was about to kiss her. Her heart began to pound and she stiffened, uncertain. His face changed subtly and he dropped his hand, stepping back. "It certainly sounds as if he did return from France, as your aunt maintains."

"Yes." Isobel drew in a shaky breath, unsure whether she was relieved or disappointed. "The reference to the soldiers would place it after Culloden. He had to go find Prince Charlie; that's the duty he must do, I'm sure. Apparently he couldn't come to the house; perhaps the soldiers were watching it."

"So he sent her a cryptic note to meet him somewhere that only she would know."

"I wonder if she found him," Isobel mused. "If she saw him again. It would be so sad if she did not."

"We should show it to Elizabeth; this vindicates her story. Her father did come home. Though . . ." He paused, frowning. "If your aunt's memory is accurate, Malcolm came here to the house."

"Perhaps my grandmother could not get to this place he spoke of, wherever it is, and Malcolm felt driven to come to the house

382

despite the danger."

"Or even though Elizabeth is right in saying he returned to Scotland, her memory is a little smudged," Jack added. "Maybe her father gave the watch to Lady Cordelia and she gave it to your aunt, and over time the story became . . . embellished in her mind."

"That could be," Isobel admitted with a sigh. "She also said she remembered him walking into the fireplace, so I don't know how much her memory can be trusted. Grandmother could have told her a bedtime story about it, to comfort her, and over time Aunt Elizabeth came to believe it was her own memory. But at least it proves she was right. Malcolm didn't flee to the colonies at the news of Culloden. He returned to Scotland."

"True." Jack nodded. "What I wonder is, does this mean there really was a treasure?"

The answer to that was a hearty yes, at least in the minds of the people gathered at the dinner table, in particular Andrew and Gregory. When Isobel announced she had proof that Malcolm had returned from France, they all stared at her in a stunned silence. With a triumphant smile, she spread the letter out on the table before Elizabeth, and her aunt's eyes widened.

"Isobel, where did you find this?" Elizabeth's eyes filled with tears. "That is Papa's hand."

"It was in Grandmother's old prayer book," Isobel explained, glossing over the impetus for their search. "The binding, um, came loose, and this was inside it. He wrote her after he returned to Kinclannoch."

Andrew and Gregory immediately crowded around Elizabeth's chair, craning their necks to read the missive. Andrew's jaw dropped. "Is this really our grandfather's letter? He *did* return from France?"

"I've always told you so, Andrew," his aunt reminded him.

"Yes, but this means —"

"Treasure!" Gregory let out a whoop. "It means there really was a treasure hidden here. I knew it! Remember how we used to search for it, Andy?"

"Of course." Andrew lost his usual air of sangfroid, his eyes sparkling like a boy's. "We should go exploring."

"I remember your explorations, too," Isobel said warningly, "and you had best not dig holes all about again."

Gregory laughed. "We would be much more scientific about it now, wouldn't we?"

"The letter won't help you find it," Isobel pointed out. "In fact, it doesn't even prove

384

there is a treasure. It says nothing about that."

"Well, of course he wouldn't be blabbing about that in a note to your grandmother," Gregory replied scornfully. "But he went to France to get money, so odds are he had it with him when he returned."

"I don't understand," Jack's mother put in, her eyes round with interest. "What treasure?"

Gregory was happy to tell the story of the Laird of Baillannan and his lost treasure, spinning it out dramatically. Mrs. Kensington's response was all he could wish for, as she gasped and exclaimed and put her hand to her chest.

"My! And the laird actually came into your room, Elizabeth?" Millicent turned to Isobel's aunt.

"He did, and he gave me his watch, just as Gregory said. Show your mother, Jack."

Obediently, Jack unfastened his watch from its chain and handed it to Millicent.

"Aunt Elizabeth!" Andrew stared at her. "I never knew you had Grandfather's watch."

"Oh, yes." Elizabeth nodded.

"Why did you not tell us?" Andrew turned to Isobel, frowning. "Is it only I who does not know? Apparently Greg knew all about it."

"No, none of us knew until recently, Andy," Isobel hastened to assure him, seeing the suddenly mulish set of his jaw. "Auntie told us just a few weeks ago."

"But why does *he* have it?" Andrew looked toward Jack.

"Your aunt gave it to me." Jack gazed back at him levelly.

"Yes. It was a wedding present," Aunt Elizabeth explained.

"And such a lovely one," Millicent put in, smiling at Elizabeth. "You are so thoughtful."

"Yes, isn't she," Andrew bit out.

"Andrew," Isobel said, hastening to change the course of the conversation, "do you and Gregory truly mean to hunt for lost treasure?"

She thought he was about to ignore her diversion, but then her brother smiled tightly. "Yes, why not? Or is our grandfather's gold Jack's, as well?"

"I would guess our grandfather's gold was long since spent," Isobel replied lightly, shooting her brother a warning look. "If there ever was any."

"Don't be a spoilsport, Izzy," Gregory took up Isobel's conversational gambit.

"How can you believe there is no treasure?"

"I don't *know* that there isn't. I just think it's unlikely. In that letter he said he was going to do what duty demanded, and I would assume that meant he went to find the prince. Surely he took the money to him. But if he left it here, he would have put it in Grandmother's keeping, and she would have spent it in the lean years following the Uprising."

"A mystery!" Millicent clasped her hands together, starry-eyed. "How exciting! I know exactly what your father would have done, Jack." She nodded at her son. "He would have been out there hunting for it."

"No doubt," Jack retorted drily. "I believe that I shall refrain. Baillannan's a rather large piece of land to search."

"We shan't scattershot as we did when we were little," Gregory said. "When you think about it, how likely is it that he just dug a hole randomly on his land and buried it? It's clear from this note that he was hiding out somewhere, and that is likely where the treasure is. It probably isn't even on Baillannan. My first guess would be the caves. Or maybe the old castle."

"Gregory . . ." Isobel looked alarmed. "Promise me you two won't go poking about in the ruins. You know how unstable

387

they are. You could injure yourselves."

"Always the big sister." Gregory grinned. "Very well. We'll steer clear of the ruins, so you need not worry. My money is on the caves near the sea, anyway. That would have been where he landed, and what better place to hide from the soldiers?"

"Careful, Gregory, or she will be warning us not to get lost in the caves," Andrew joked, putting aside his flash of ill humor, though the smile he gave Isobel was a little strained.

True to their words, the next day Gregory and Andrew plunged into a treasure hunt. They determined that it would be easier to start from Baillannan, so Gregory moved into the house, taking the old room next door to Andrew's that had been Gregory's as a child. The two of them set out each morning, returning at teatime to regale the ladies with stories of their adventures.

Isobel, well acquainted with them, took their tales with more than a grain of salt, but Millicent and Elizabeth were a much better audience, appropriately impressed with the distance they had gone into the caves or the depth of a pit they came upon there or the risk of getting trapped by high tide.

Isobel busied herself with the task of setting Lady Cordelia's room to rights. She was working her way through the wardrobe one afternoon when she heard her aunt cry out, followed an instant later by Millicent's voice rising in alarm: "Jack, what happened to you? Why are you bleeding?"

Isobel shot to her feet and ran out of the room and down the stairs. Jack stood in the entry, facing his mother and Elizabeth. His hair and clothing were covered in dust, as well as a few twigs and leaves. A large tear went down the front of his shirt, revealing a long scratch. One cheek was marred by a vivid spot of red, raw skin, and his hair was matted with blood.

"Jack! Are you all right? What happened?" Isobel took his chin in her hand and went on tiptoe to inspect his face.

He shook his head. "It's naught, really. It looks much worse than it is. Head wounds always bleed like mad."

"But how — what —"

"I got caught in a rockslide. I was riding down the path when I heard a tremendous clatter, and I looked up to see a great rock tumbling down the hillside."

Isobel sucked in her breath, her hand clutching his arm. "Jack, you could have been killed!"

His mother let out a high-pitched moan and swayed. Elizabeth took the woman's arm and supported her to a seat on a nearby bench. Isobel had no eyes for anyone but Jack.

"Mm," he responded mildly. "Fortunately, my horse's reactions are swifter than mine, and at the first sound, Pharaoh bolted down the path. Rather less fortunately, he slammed me into a tree and I went tumbling." Jack looked down at his left leg, and Isobel saw a slash across one leg of his breeches, as well as a large scrape on the side of his elegant riding boot. Ruefully he went on, "I fear my best pair of Hoby's is ruined."

"For pity's sake," Isobel said, fear and relief making her voice tart, "who cares about your boot? You are lucky to have escaped. Here." She slid her arm around his waist and led him toward the stairs. "Let's get you cleaned up and put something on those cuts. You shouldn't have gone riding alone. Take a groom with you next time," she scolded him as they climbed the steps to his room. "I didn't think to warn you about the rocks. Sometimes they fall, especially when it has been raining a great deal."

"Which would be always, I assume."

"Don't be pert. I am serious." She steered

him to the bed. "Take off your coat." She reached up and gingerly began to pull the coat from his shoulders.

"You need not be so careful. Nothing is broken."

"Yes, it's a good thing it was only your head. Now, hush. Sit down." She pushed him back onto the bed and knelt to remove his boots. When she looked up, she found him studying her as he untied his cravat, his eyes dark. He looked, she realized, as he did sometimes when he lounged in his chair, watching her, and those occasions almost invariably ended with his whisking her to bed.

Heat flooded her face, and she realized that for the past few minutes they had been just as they were before Mrs. Kensington came, the constraint of the past few days forgotten in Isobel's concern for him. Suddenly she was very aware of the sexual undertones of their positions. She stood up abruptly, breaking the moment, and went to the washstand to wet a rag.

Cupping his chin in one hand, she washed the blood and dirt from his face, dabbing carefully at the matted blood near his hairline. "It isn't as bad as it looked."

"I told you. Head wounds bleed all out of proportion." He winced. "Ow. Have a care."

"I have to clean it. You deserve worse for being so careless." She stopped, looking into his eyes. "Promise me you will be more careful."

"I shall be the most timid creature alive. Like a rabbit, I will pop up my head and look in all directions."

"Don't joke." She scowled. "You could have been killed."

His eyes were suddenly hot and intent upon hers. "Would you have cared?"

"What?" Isobel stepped back. "Of course I would care. How can you ask such a thing?"

" 'Tis a little hard to tell these days." Jack stood up and began to unbutton his shirt. "You'd best go now," he said dismissively as he turned away. "I am about to undress, and I wouldn't want to offend you."

"You think that is the reason I left your bed? Because I cared so little?"

"What other reason is there?" His voice was cold as frost. "You realized what I am and what you were doing — sullying the Rose name. The daughter of the laird should not climb in bed with a peasant."

"You are a fool!" Isobel slammed the rag back into the washbowl and stalked to the door. She turned back, her body rigid, fury shooting from her like sparks. "I did not go because I didn't care. I left because I cared too much!"

"Isobel —" He took a step toward her.

"No!" Isobel raised her hand. "Stop. Stay away from me."

"I don't even know what you want from me," he ground out, his face a study in frustration.

"I know." Suddenly her anger drained, leaving a bitter sorrow in its wake. "And that is what breaks my heart."

She turned and walked out the door.

Isobel was late going down to supper that evening. She dreaded the thought of facing Jack after the scene that afternoon. But when she stepped into the anteroom where the others had gathered, she saw that Jack was not there. The atmosphere was convivial, with Gregory holding forth and Mrs. Kensington tittering and blushing at his overblown compliments while Elizabeth and Andrew looked on, smiling. Isobel joined in as best she could, though she could not keep her mind on their frivolities.

"Jack, love!" Millicent cried. "There you are. I feared you were hurt too badly to join us."

Isobel turned, her heart racing, doing her best to keep her face from showing any of the turbulent emotions inside her.

"I am fine." Jack shrugged. He did not look at Isobel as he entered. "It was a trifling wound . . . nothing more. I hope I did not worry you overmuch."

"Of course, I was worried sick. That's how it is with mothers." Millicent patted the seat beside her. "Come, sit down, love. Mr. Rose has been telling us the most amusing stories."

"Gregory, ma'am," Isobel's cousin said. "You must call me Gregory. After all, we are related now, aren't we?" He paused, looking thoughtful. "Though to save me, I could not tell you exactly what that relation is called. Cousin-in-law, perhaps? But to what degree?"

"Don't ask me, young man. I have never had a head for figures. No doubt Jack could tell us. He was always so sharp with numbers. His father used to say he was the cleverest of anyone when it came to numbers. He could remember every card —"

"Mother, please, you will make me blush," Jack interrupted coolly.

"Mrs. Kensington, I see your glass is empty. Shall I get you another sherry?" Andrew said politely, starting to rise from his chair.

"Such a thoughtful young man." Mrs.

Kensington beamed at him. "You know, perhaps a spot more would be nice. I have become quite parched, I've talked so much."

Jack swooped up the glass before Andrew reached his feet. "No need, Sir Andrew. I'll take care of it."

"Of course." Andrew settled back in his chair with an easy smile.

Isobel could not help but notice the interplay between the two men — nor how Jack, though he picked up the sherry glass, made no move to refill it. She stole a peek at her brother. She had been glad the past few days that Andrew and Gregory's quest had kept Andrew out of the house, else he might have let his tongue get away from him.

He was upset, she knew, about their father's watch. Isobel could not blame him; she had at the time been surprised that Elizabeth had chosen a stranger to receive it rather than her nephew. Andrew's resentment was not reasonable — he himself had, after all, gambled away his inheritance, and Elizabeth was free to give her possessions as she chose — but Isobel could not help but feel for her brother. But she dreaded being caught between her husband and her brother if their uneasy relationship exploded into an argument. She wished that Andrew would return to London, which made her feel guilty, as well.

"Jack." Millicent turned to her son, frowning. "My throat is quite parched." Her querulous tone surprised Isobel, for however talkative and even silly Mrs. Kensington might be, she had never before seemed anything but adoring of Jack.

Jack hesitated, looking down at her. "We will be repairing to the dining room in just a moment, I'm sure."

"That will scarcely help me now."

"Of course. Pardon me." He acquiesced, bowing to her and crossing the room to pour a small amount of sherry in her glass. He had barely returned when Hamish entered the room to announce dinner. "Ah, there we are." Jack set the glass down on the table beside Millicent and offered her his hand to rise.

His mother picked up the glass and knocked back the drink in one quick gulp. "Ah, that is much better." She rose and took Jack's arm, smiling at him. "Such a dear boy. So like your father."

Millicent clung tightly to Jack's arm as they took the brief trip down the corridor to the dining room. Jack's mother, Isobel realized, was a trifle tipsy. Isobel looked down to hide a tiny smile. Millicent must be unused to alcohol, indeed, if those two little glasses of sherry had made her wobbly.

Her amusement soon faded, however, as Millicent drank down the glass of wine beside her plate before the first course was even done. Isobel saw that Hamish was starting toward Mrs. Kensington, no doubt to refill her glass. A trifle alarmed that the woman, in her inexperience with alcohol, might embarrass herself or even make herself ill, Isobel stopped the butler with a look. However, after a few minutes, Millicent began to look around impatiently, finally twisting in her seat and motioning to Hamish, then tapping the top of her wineglass. He glanced at Isobel, but she could do little without embarrassing Millicent, so Isobel merely smiled at him, and he poured the wine.

As the supper progressed, Millicent continued to drink. She laughed too loudly and too long at Gregory's witticisms, and she talked at length, now and then losing the thread of what she was saying. Sneaking a glance at Jack's rigid face, Isobel realized that the problem was not that Millicent was a novice at drinking alcohol, but exactly the opposite.

A murmured direction to Hamish kept the

meal moving at a faster pace than normal, so much so that Andrew protested, "Wait, man, I have not finished. Are we in a race?"

"Don't be absurd, Andrew." Isobel laughed. "You were ever the slowest at the dinner table."

Andrew began to deny it, but Gregory joined Isobel, saying, "It's the truth, Andy. You cannot convince anyone otherwise."

"Jack never was." Millicent spoke up, slurring her words a little. "Always in a hurry, that was my Jack. Just like his father, rush, rush, rush, all the time." She lifted her glass, then set it down again as tears welled in her eyes. "I do miss him. Don't you miss him, Jackie?" she appealed to her son.

Jack's face was like stone. "I think often of his absence, yes."

"There. I knew it. You cannot fool your mother, no matter what you say." She turned to Isobel. "He was a wonderful man, you know. I wish, I just wish you could have met him. You would have liked him, too."

"I am sure I would have."

"A brave man, too. He died too young, but I knew . . ." Millicent's breath hitched, and the tears swimming in her eyes spilled over. "I knew he died just as he would have wished. If it had not been for him, she would have died in the fire."

"Fire?" Elizabeth repeated, and Isobel saw the same confusion she felt reflected on her aunt's face.

"My life has been filled with far too much sorrow." Millicent dabbed at her eyes with her napkin. "First Sutton was taken from me, and then my lamb."

"Mother." Jack's voice was short. "You are upsetting yourself. Let us talk of something else."

"He doesn't like for me to talk about her, you see," Millicent told Isobel. "My Dolly." She turned to Jack, her eyes accusing. "You always try to hush me. I cannot bear it. I simply cannot bear it."

"Mrs. Kensington . . ." Impulsively Isobel reached out and laid her hand on the other woman's arm. "Please, don't be distressed. I am sure Jack just hates to see you unhappy; that is all."

"Him." The older woman shot Jack a look so venomous it made Isobel's eyes widen in surprise. "That's not it. He thinks I'm to blame." Millicent's eyes flashed, and she whipped back to Isobel. "He hates me; you ask him. He thinks I'm to blame." Millicent's face crumpled, and she began to cry. "And he's right. I am. I am."

For an instant, Isobel simply froze. Down the table she could see her aunt staring, horrified, and Gregory, looking as if he wished he were anywhere but here. Jack, of course, looked as cold and distant as a marble statue, and Andrew . . . disdain was on his face but Isobel saw a flicker of satisfaction in his eyes, as well.

Anger surged through Isobel, releasing her from her inaction, and she jumped to her feet, going around the corner of the table to Jack's mother. "Please, you will make yourself unwell," she told Millicent gently, putting her hand under the woman's arm and tugging her up. "Let me help you to your bed. You should lie down and rest a bit."

"I don't want to rest!" Millicent snapped, then immediately clapped her hand over her mouth. "Oh! I am so sorry, dear. I didn't say that — I mean, I mean I should not have. You are a dear, dear girl." She reached out and folded Isobel into her boozy embrace. "I'm so sorry. I'm so glad he found you. So glad. I was terrible to say" — Millicent stepped back, scrubbing her tears from her cheeks like a child — "whatever I said."

"Let me help you."

"No, no." Mrs. Kensington reeled away from Isobel. "I'll go. I'll go myself." She bumped into the high back of her chair, and Isobel reached to steady her.

"Here. I have her." Jack had reached

them, and he put an arm firmly around his mother's waist. "Come, Mother. I'll take you upstairs."

"Dear boy." Millicent looked up at him with a watery smile. "I'm sorry." Her tears began to flow again, and she leaned her head against his chest, crying into it. "I am a terrible mother. I know. Please forgive me. I've ruined it. Ruined it. I didn't mean to."

"No, of course you didn't." His voice was weary, but not unkind.

"You don't hate me, do you? Please say you don't hate me."

"No, I don't hate you." He steered her out the door, bracing himself to steady her. Isobel could hear his voice, low and indistinct, as they moved down the hall.

24

Isobel turned back to the table, stunned and empty.

"Oh, dear," Aunt Elizabeth said. "Poor woman."

"I'm sorry, Iz," Gregory said. "I wish we had not brought her back that blackberry cordial from Meg's. She must have had a tipple before she came to supper. I didn't know . . ."

"Oh, I think Andrew did." Isobel stared levelly at her brother. "Didn't you, Andrew? You brought her that cordial on purpose."

Andrew lifted a shoulder negligently. "Can I help it if the old girl cannot hold her liquor?"

"Andrew, how could you! Is that why you came here? Why you brought her? To retaliate against Jack? To embarrass him?"

"I came here because I had no place else to go!" Andrew lashed out, rising to face her. "Am I to blame that Kensington hides away his raddled, old sot of a mum? That he hires a keeper for her? What did I do that was so horrid? It isn't as if I killed someone. I gave her a bottle of cordial. I brought you your new mother-in-law so you could see just what you'd married into."

"Then it was me you wanted to pay back for marrying Jack?" Isobel raised her brows.

"Don't be nonsensical." He dropped back into his chair and crossed his arms, muttering, "I didn't pour it down her throat."

"You knew what would happen. Oh, Andrew." Isobel sighed and sat down, too. The heat had gone from her voice. "I understand that you are angry with Jack and even that you feel I've betrayed you by marrying him."

"No, Isobel," Gregory put in. "Andy knows you did it to save Baillannan. We all do. No one blames you. And Kensington doesn't seem too bad a sort, really."

"She did not have to *like* him," Andrew shot back. Gregory snorted, and Isobel rolled her eyes.

"You are being childish, Andrew, and you know it. I realize that you love to play pranks, and I know that men have some very peculiar ideas about what is funny. But this is not merely a trick on Jack. You have humiliated that poor woman in front of her new family."

"I'd say she humiliated herself. Why are you flying up in the boughs about it? Everyone has a few relatives that are drunk as a wheelbarrow half the time."

"That's true," Gregory said encouragingly. "Just think of my uncle Murdoch."

"It's different. They aren't ladies."

"Well, neither is Mill—"

"Andrew!" Isobel's eyes flashed. "Have a care what you say."

Her brother subsided. Elizabeth glanced worriedly from Andrew to Isobel in the uncomfortable silence that followed. Finally she said, "I fear I got a trifle lost. Didn't Millicent say the other day that her husband was killed in a carriage accident?"

"Yes. Apparently the manner of his death changes from time to time." Andrew shot his sister a challenging look.

"I don't know how he died, Aunt Elizabeth. I would not put much faith in anything Jack's mother said tonight."

"Perhaps I should go look in on her." Elizabeth's brows knitted worriedly.

"That's very kind of you. But I am going up there now, so I will check on her. Perhaps you might look in on her before you retire."

"Of course, dear."

Isobel rose and left the table, not looking back at her brother. She went first to Jack's room, but it was empty. A peek into his mother's room showed he was not there, either, just Mrs. Kensington, fast asleep on the bed.

Isobel went back to her room and prowled about restlessly. She longed to go to Jack and hold him, to do what she could to ease his pain. She understood now why his mother's arrival had upset him, even why he had been reluctant to talk about the matter, though it made her heart hurt that he would not entrust her with his innermost feelings. Obviously he was engaged on his usual solitary path, unwilling, perhaps unable, to seek any comfort from her. That hurt most of all.

She turned out her lamp so that she could see better into the dark of the night outside, and she was standing at the window, hoping to catch a glimpse of him, when the door opened behind her. She whirled to see Jack standing in the doorway. His face was etched with pain, his usual composure vanished. Her throat closed up with emotion, and she could not speak.

"Isobel." His voice was low and hoarse. He took another step forward, then stopped. "Please do not turn me away. I . . . I need you."

Tears sprang into her eyes and she rushed

forward, throwing her arms around him. His arms clamped around her like iron, and he buried his face in her hair, murmuring her name over and over. He kissed her until she was dizzy from it, and she clung to him, not wanting the kiss to end. His mouth was hard and greedy, his whole body aflame. He lifted her from the floor and carried her to the bed.

There was no gentleness in him, no finesse or teasing or tenderness, only a raw, driving hunger. His hands tore at the fastenings of her clothes, careless of ties snapped or buttons popped as he exposed her breasts to his eager mouth. His lovemaking was fierce and desperate, unlike any other time they had come together, and it touched a match to the tinder of Isobel's own desire.

She dug her fingers into his back, frustrated by the cloth of his shirt. He reared up, tearing off his shirt and flinging it aside, then returned to her. Isobel wrapped her arms around him, digging into his back with her nails as the ache swelled within her, hot and wet and trembling. Jack reached down and shoved her skirts up to her waist, hooking his hand in the last flimsy barrier between him and what he desired, and he ripped the cotton pantalets down. He groaned as his fingers found the center of her, pooling with moisture.

He fumbled impatiently at his own breeches, and then he was sliding into her. Isobel could not hold back a soft gasp as he filled her, satisfying her as nothing else did. He began to thrust within her, and Isobel locked her arms and legs around him, binding him to her. Mindlessly she rode the storm of his passion until it swept her up and over the edge, and they tumbled down into the deep, dark well of pleasure.

They lay together afterward, exhausted and replete. And finally, there in the dark, Jack began to talk.

"That is my mother. She drinks, and she lies, and she cares for no one but the blackguard she married and her own deluded self."

"I'm sorry. I know it pains you."

"No," he said shortly, his bitter voice belying his words. "Not for many years. I removed myself from her sphere when I was sixteen. She went back to my father again after he had abandoned us, and I washed my hands of her. Her lying, her tears, her rages and accusations."

Isobel did not know what to say, so she only held him closer.

"Her sorrow over my father is real enough.

Though he did not die — least of all in some honorable way. Those are only the tales my mother dreams up to make her life more dramatic. More pleasing to her. Between drinking and lying, I wonder sometimes if she even knows the truth anymore."

"Then he's still alive?" Isobel asked, startled. "Do you see him? Is he —"

"No, you needn't worry that *he* is going to pop up here one day as well. He is long gone. He left her; he left her frequently, left all of us whenever it suited him. Another woman, another opportunity, more excitement." Jack shrugged. "The last time was for good; he sailed for America with a new benefactress. I had not seen him for years at the time; Mother, naturally, was crushed. She always took him back, certain that this time he would stay. Her liquor comforted her when he was gone, but that didn't match her joy when he reappeared. She loved him above all else. Still does, though she has not seen him in nigh fifteen years. He was a —" Jack paused, then bit out his words in neat, precise cuts. "My father was a liar. A cheat. A swindler. His every thought was for himself and how he could wrangle some bit of gold out of any situation. I despise the fact that I look like him. That I am like him."

"No, I don't believe that."

"No doubt you would not." Jack smiled wryly. "But I deal in hard truths. I learned it all from him. He taught me how to play the part — the speech, the dress, the manners. Sutton Kensington *was* a talented actor — though I suspect that his name, my name, is a fabrication, as well. He trained me for far more than my role as a gentleman. He showed me how to work an audience, though they were only gathered for a game of chance. How to dress and play the beggar when he needed it. Or the poor lost child if that profited him. He taught me how to use my hands." Jack held up his hands, wiggling his fingers. "I saw your face when I wrestled open the lock on that chest with your hairpin. You knew what that skill meant.

"I have a delicate touch. Even as a child my hands were quick and my legs even swifter. I was the best little cutpurse you ever saw. No one paid much attention when I loitered about while Sutton was playing cards. Mother was right; I was always good with numbers. I could lean against his shoulder as if I doted on him and whisper the cards that had been played all around the table. Nobody could catch me palming a card or switching a fulham for a good die in the midst of the play. And, God help me, I loved it when he praised me for my aptitude. Even more than I hated it when he boxed my ears for being clumsy."

"A child is not a sinner for doing what his father commanded him," Isobel countered.

Jack shrugged. "I did it on my own as well. I gave it up when I grew older, after I'd seen that I could make my living dealing honestly. I valued my neck too much to continue on that road."

"Whatever you say, you have a good heart. I know it. Despite how you feel, despite what happened, you have taken care of your mother."

He snorted. "I gave her money to ensure she left me alone. She came to me after he left her the last time, full of regret and promises. . . . I gave it to her every time she reappeared with her pockets to let and nowhere to go. I knew it was hopeless, and once I had enough blunt, I set her up in a house and I hired someone, ostensibly a companion, but in reality a guard. Mrs. Wheeler makes sure that she does not drink, and on the occasions when Mother outwits her and finds some liquor, Mrs. Wheeler keeps her from going out and doing some mad thing. She listens to her stories and puts her to bed and sits up with her to make sure she does not drown in —" He stopped abruptly. "But that is nothing fit for your ears."

"I am sure you did everything you could."

"Don't paint me as a good son," he rasped. "I pay for her; that is all. She bore me and she did not beat me, and for that I will continue to pay for her care. But I rarely visit; after an hour I am itching to be gone. I make no effort to pretend to believe her stories or placate her. I cannot love her. And I bloody well wish I could escape her altogether."

"Oh, Jack . . ." Tears filled Isobel's eyes at the anguish that lurked behind his harsh voice.

He blew out a breath, his muscles relaxing against her. "Ah, Isobel, forgive me. I did not mean to make you cry. Trust me, Millicent Kensington is not worth your tears."

"I am not crying for her." Isobel's voice was clogged with emotion, and she dashed away her tears from her cheeks. "I am crying for you."

"Isobel." His arms tightened around her, and he kissed her hair, murmuring her name, his voice soft and tender.

They made love, not in the mad rush of earlier, pulsing with hunger and passion, but gently, lingering over sweet, slow kisses and tantalizing caresses. They joined together in a long, leisurely prelude, letting their hunger build and strengthen until finally passion broke over them in deep waves of pleasure and they slid gently over the edge into joy.

Isobel was not surprised to find that she, Jack, and Aunt Elizabeth were the only people at the breakfast table the next morning. Her brother and Gregory were never early risers, and she was sure Andrew had little desire to come face-to-face with Jack right now. She suspected that it would be some hours before Jack's mother felt well enough to put in an appearance. Isobel was glad, for she wanted no shadow to cloud her happiness this morning.

She supposed she should feel a trifle guilty for feeling this way, given the unhappy events of the night before, but Jack, too, was relaxed and smiling now that the storm had passed. When he left on his morning ride, he pulled Isobel to him and kissed her even though they stood at the bottom of the stairs where anyone in the house could see them.

Shortly after Jack's departure, Gregory trotted down the steps, confirming Isobel's suspicion that he had been loitering upstairs waiting for Jack to leave. "Hallo, Cousin."

"You're in a cheerful mood," Isobel remarked, following him into the dining room.

"You know me; I find it far more satisfying to be happy than to mope."

"As opposed to my brother?"

Gregory shrugged a shoulder as he sat down at the table. "Andrew will be fine soon enough." He grinned. "Once we find our fortune."

"Do you really believe that?" Isobel asked, pouring them both a cup of tea.

"Of course. I also find it's more fun to anticipate good fortune." He took a swig of tea. "However, I have decided we need a change of direction. I am returning to Kinclannoch after I eat. Andrew, too." He grinned. "No doubt that will come as a relief to you."

"I won't deny that life will run more smoothly here if Andrew and Jack do not have to be in the same room together. Thank you for that."

"It's no farther to the caves from town, anyway. Indeed, I imagine it is closer to some. Besides, little as I am given to organization, we need to move forward in a less slapdash manner. Map out the caves and explore them in an orderly way. We can pick my father's brain a bit as well. I'll warrant he may have a better idea what Malcolm might have done and where he went. For all we know, Malcolm could have hid out with my grandfather. It was after Culloden, so Fergus might very well have been here as well. They were brothers, after all; they probably banded together."

"True enough." Isobel saw no reason to point out her doubts that Cousin Robert, being three or four years old at the time, would have known anything of his uncle's whereabouts — or remembered it. "I have never heard when Great-Uncle Fergus returned."

"Everyone was hiding from the British then."

Their conversation was interrupted by the arrival of Hamish with a tray loaded with food, and Gregory tucked into the meal with gusto.

"Are you leaving as soon as you've eaten, then?" Isobel asked once his eating slowed.

"I am. Andrew was barely up when I looked in on him. And you know how he is. I have no desire to sit about cooling my heels all morning while he arranges his neckcloth to his satisfaction. He'll ride over later."

Andrew, however, was apparently more eager to leave Baillannan than his cousin realized, for Gregory had not been gone even an hour when Andrew appeared at the door to the sitting room. "I've come to take my leave," he said, then spoiled his air of hauteur by adding petulantly, "No doubt you will be glad to see the back of me. I can return to London straight from Gregory's house, if that is your desire."

"Don't be a goose, Andy," Isobel said, and her aunt erupted in a series of denials, getting up and going over to embrace Andrew. "Of course I don't want you to turn around and rush back to London. Baillannan is your home, and you're always welcome here."

"I'm not sure your husband would say that." Andrew relaxed into a more normal expression, returning Aunt Elizabeth's hug and patting her on the back. "Now, come, come, Auntie, I'm not going away forever. I'm just going to stay with Greg and his father for a few days. Until your memories of my bad behavior have had a chance to fade." He cast a sheepish glance toward Isobel. "I am sorry, Izzy. You were right; I should not have done that. Will you forgive me?"

"Of course. But perhaps it is Mrs. Kensington to whom you should apologize. And Jack."

"Good gad." His eyebrows flew up in an expression of such alarm that Isobel had to cover a smile. "I mean, well, of course. When I return from Kinclannoch. Right now would be, well . . . and I feel sure Mrs. Kensington would be embarrassed by a discussion of last night, don't you? I need to go, actually; Gregory will be wondering what happened to me."

"But, dear, surely you must have something to eat," Aunt Elizabeth protested.

"No, must run. Cook will let me grab a bit of sausage and bread, I warrant." Hastily he made his good-byes and left the room.

Isobel watched him go, sadness lurking in her heart. She could not help but wonder if Andrew would ever change.

"I do worry about our boy," Elizabeth said, surprising Isobel by echoing her thoughts. Picking up her needlework, Elizabeth sat down again. "Ah, well, much as I love those boys, it will be nice to have the house quiet again."

Isobel smiled and agreed and sat down at the secretary by the window to catch up on her correspondence while her aunt began to ply her needle. The morning passed in this quiet, comfortable manner until shortly before luncheon when Millicent made her way downstairs. Millicent paused in the doorway, looking pale and subdued.

"Mrs. Kensington." Isobel rose and went to her. "I hope you are feeling better."

"Yes, indeed." Millicent reached up to give her curls a nervous pat. "I — I must apologize. I do not know what came over me last night." She could not meet Isobel's gaze, looking from her to Elizabeth briefly, then heading toward the sofa, where she sat down with an air of relief, as if having reached safe harbor. "I, um, felt quite faint, you know. I feared I was coming down with a fever, but I am better now."

"I cannot help but wonder," Isobel said carefully, "if there might have been something amiss with that cordial Andrew brought back from Meg's."

"Why, yes!" Millicent seized on the excuse with enthusiasm. "No doubt you are right. I am not accustomed to liquor, you know; my father was so strict."

"But, Isobel, what could be wrong with Meg's —" Elizabeth broke off abruptly. "Oh, yes, that is probably true."

"I'll just tell the maid to pour the rest of it out," Isobel went on smoothly.

"Oh, well . . . I don't know if that is necessary." Millicent's brow wrinkled.

"No, I insist. We dare not risk you getting ill again."

"I would not want to offend Sir Andrew. Such a courteous young gentleman."

"He will understand perfectly," Isobel assured her. "You need not worry."

"Of course. Yes. Well. Thank you," Millicent said faintly. She sat for a moment, twisting her handkerchief in her fingers. "Jack must be quite cross with me."

"I know he understands."

"Perhaps." Millicent's tone was doubtful. "Where is he?" She glanced around vaguely.

"He is out riding, but I am sure he will be back before long. 'Tis almost time for luncheon."

"Oh. Yes, I do remember he was always fond of horses." Millicent paused, looking down at the handkerchief she was worrying in her hands. "I . . . I think sometimes that I was not, well, not a very good mother."

Her words left Isobel at a loss for something to say, so she was grateful that Elizabeth quickly responded, "I am sure that is not so, Millicent. Sometimes I feel exactly the same about Andrew. Boys are so difficult to raise, don't you think?"

"Yes." Millicent brightened. "That's true. Especially without his father."

"Indeed."

With Millicent ensconced with Elizabeth, Isobel seized the opportunity to leave, pleading the necessity of seeing to the accounts. She went first to the butler's pantry, where she found Hamish and one of the maids polishing the silver, a never-ending task.

"Edith, run upstairs to Mrs. Kensington's chamber and dispose of the bottle of cordial there. She has decided it does not agree with her. And any other spirits that might be there," Isobel added as the girl started out the door. Isobel turned back to Hamish. "For the time being, I have decided to stop serving wine with the meals, Hamish."

"Yes, miss." If Hamish saw anything odd with her request, he did not show it. "Shall I put the whiskey and brandy decanters in the smoking-room cabinet?"

"Excellent idea. Just give the key to the cabinet to Mr. Kensington when he returns."

Isobel could not be rude to Millicent and could not help but feel sorry for her. However, Isobel was determined not to allow the woman to put Jack through any more scenes such as last night's. Her plan, she hoped, would enable her to do that without embarrassing Millicent. Satisfied that it had been put into effect, Isobel went down the hall to the study.

In truth, she had no work to do on the accounts but was glad of the chance to be alone. She finished up her correspondence, pausing only a few times to think about Jack. When she went into the dining room later, she was disappointed he had not returned for luncheon.

When another hour, then two, passed without his return, she began to grow concerned. By the time tea came and went without him, her stomach was dancing with nerves. She did her best to keep a calm demeanor when Millicent began to ask about Jack, reassuring her that he had undoubtedly stopped to talk to someone. But as soon as she could, Isobel fled outside to the stables to question the groom. Jack had apparently given no indication that he might stay out longer than usual or where he intended to go or when he might return. She walked back to the house thoroughly dissatisfied.

She was being foolish, she told herself. Jack was a grown man. There was no reason why he shouldn't stay out all day if he chose. It wasn't as if he had told her he would return at a certain time. She was being overly nervous because he had gotten caught in the rockslide yesterday. To think that he would get caught in another was absurd. Still, she could not help but consider that if something had happened to him, if he had fallen, say, and hurt his leg or had gotten ill or been thrown from his horse or any of a host of things that could happen, he could be lying out there somewhere, unable to walk back. And she would not know.

As she neared the house, she heard the whinny of a horse, and she whirled around, her heart lifting. A man was walking up the path toward the house, leading a horse. She started to smile, but in the next instant she realized the tall figure had light hair that glinted in the sun. In another heartbeat, she saw that the horse was indeed Jack's. And a man's form lay slumped against the horse's neck.

25

"Jack!" Isobel lifted her skirts and ran toward the horse. She could see now that it was Coll who led the horse, and though she could not see the face of the man on the horse, she knew it was her husband. "Coll! What happened?" She stumbled to a halt, ice gripping her heart, her breath coming in sharp, harsh pants. "Oh, God. Jack. Is he all right? What happened?"

She went to the horse, which danced to the side.

"There, there, now, lad," Coll said soothingly, turning to the animal and stroking his hand down his neck. "He's scared and skittish, Iz, don't rush at him."

Isobel nodded, still as a statue, her hands clasped in front of her chest. "What happened? Is he . . . is he . . ." She could not choke out the words.

"He's alive, aye." Coll's voice was too grim for Isobel to feel much reassured. He cast her an assessing glance. "I found him lying on the ground. He's been shot."

Isobel simply stared at him. A buzzing started in her ears, and her vision began to darken.

"Izzy! Don't you go fainting on me, lass. I canna carry the both of you." Coll reached out and grabbed her arm.

"No." Isobel let herself lean into the strength of his arm for an instant as she sucked in a long breath, then straightened. "No. I won't faint. What happened? How —"

"I don't know. But that's not important now. Find someone to help get him off this horse."

Isobel nodded, not wasting her breath with more questions. She ran to the kitchen, calling for Hamish. Within minutes, Hamish and Coll had lifted Jack down from the horse and given him to the footmen to carry upstairs.

Isobel started after the men, then swung back. "Coll —"

"Aye, I know. I'm going for Meg right now." He took off toward the dock, and Isobel whirled and ran after the others.

The servants were halfway up the stairs when she caught up with them. The sight of Jack's body in their hands, limp and pale, a dark red stain across his shoulder, made her heart stutter. She paused, gripping the stair rail. She had to be calm. She had to be strong. It would not help Jack in any way for her to shatter and fly apart. Taking a steadying breath, she continued up the stairs.

"Isobel?" Elizabeth appeared at the door of the sitting room. "What's happening? Was that Jack —"

"Jack!" came Millicent's alarmed voice from behind Elizabeth, and an instant later, Millicent popped her head into the hall as well. "Is something the matter with Jack?"

"He . . . I . . . he was injured on his ride, apparently. Coll just brought him in."

His mother let out a shriek and sagged back against the doorjamb, covering her mouth with her hand.

"Please, don't worry," Isobel said quickly. "I am going in to look at him right now."

"I should go to him." Millicent pushed away from the door and started determinedly toward her.

Isobel cast a pleading glance at her aunt.

"Millicent." Elizabeth took the cue and caught up with the other woman, taking her by the hand. "No. Come. Don't upset yourself. Isobel will handle it. I promise you."

"But I must. He's my son."

Isobel turned and went into the bedroom, leaving the two women behind her. Someone else would have to deal with it if Millicent insisted on coming in to see her son. Isobel's only concern was Jack.

Hamish and the footmen had laid Jack out on top of the bed and were wrestling his boots off him now. Jack's eyes were closed and his face was so pale that he looked horrifyingly like a corpse. Only the slight rise and fall of his chest reassured Isobel that he was alive. The stain across one side of his chest was a dark reddish brown, the material already stiffening with the dried blood. Isobel swallowed hard and clasped her hands together to stop their trembling.

Behind her she heard the sound of footsteps, then Millicent's gasp before Elizabeth led her out of the room, murmuring comfortingly. Isobel straightened her shoulders and reached down to take Jack's hands in both hers.

"Jack?" Her voice trembled, and she cleared her throat. "Jack, it's Isobel. Can you hear me?"

His eyes drifted open, their dark, vivid blue momentarily hazy. "Isobel." His voice was barely a whisper, and Isobel leaned closer.

"Yes. I am here. You're home. We're going to take care of you."

His tongue touched his dry lips. "Thirsty."

"Yes. I'll get you some water." She looked at Hamish, and he gestured to one of the maids, sending her running to fetch a glass. "Hamish, bring the bowl and pitcher over here. And a rag." Isobel nodded toward the small table beside the bed.

Hamish set the things she requested on the table. "Best get his jacket off, miss." He reached out and grasped the lapel, starting to peel it carefully from his shoulder.

Jack let out a gasp and a sharp oath.

"Don't. It's stuck to the wound," Isobel said quickly. "I'll soak it first."

Isobel laid the cloth against Jack's dried lips, then washed his face, her movements light and careful. Wetting the cloth again, she laid it over his wound, letting the water sink in and loosen the dried material.

"Get me some scissors and clean cloths and bandages. Meg will be here before long, but best fetch my medicine basket in case she needs it." As Hamish started toward the door, she added, "And a bottle of brandy."

"Isobel . . ."

"Yes, I'm still here. I have your water now." She took the cup from the maid's hand and held it to his lips, sliding her other hand behind Jack's head to lift it. He made a move as if to sit up, but winced and managed only to raise his head a little. She gave him a few tiny sips and eased his head back down to the pillow. "Coll went to get Meg, so she should be here soon."

"Meg?" He looked confused. "The girl with the potions?"

"Yes, but she does a great deal more than that. Trust me; you will be in better hands with her than with any doctor. Besides, there is no doctor in Kinclannoch. It would take hours to get one here to see you." She took his hand again and squeezed it. "I trust Meg.

"In the meantime, I'm going to take this jacket off you." The footman who had been hovering in the background stepped forward at her words, but she waved the man back. "No. I'll just cut it. Jenny, fetch my sewing scissors."

Jack made a noise of protest when Isobel took the scissors to the sleeve of his coat, murmuring, "It's new."

"I think that great hole in the front has already rendered it unwearable," she told him tartly. "Now, hush."

She carefully cut up the sleeve and across the shoulder, then eased the jacket back from the wound. It was slow work, for even damp, the material still stuck a little to the wound. Jack let out a low groan.

"I'm sorry, love." Isobel looked at him. Jack was paler than ever, and his eyes wavered. Her eyes filled with tears. "Stay with me. I am almost done."

After she peeled back the jacket, she had to remove his waistcoat and the lawn shirt beneath. It made her stomach lurch to reveal the white shirt, now soaked with red, and it was even worse when she cut it away, exposing his chest and the raw, red wound with the black center just beneath his shoulder. She swallowed hard and glanced up at his face. His eyes were closed. They flew open, however, when she began to clean around the wound.

"Bloody hell!" he bit out through clenched teeth.

"I'm sorry. I am trying not to hurt you."

"You're not . . . succeeding."

"I know." Her voice wobbled at how faint and slurred his words were. How long could it take Coll to get to Meg's? She looked to the clock on the mantel and was astonished to see how little time had elapsed. "Here is Hamish with the brandy."

Hamish helped lift Jack's head so she could give him sips of brandy, and she thought the spirits put a bit of color in his face. She stood up to set down the glass, and Jack clenched his fingers in her skirts.

Her throat closed with tears, and she moved back, taking his hand. "I'm here, love. I won't go anywhere. Hold on."

After what seemed an eternity, the sound of quick, light footsteps came in the hall, and Meg hurried into the room.

"Thank God you are here." Isobel squeezed Jack's hand and released it, and she started to step back.

Jack made a noise and his eyes opened. "Where —"

"Meg's here now, love. Let her see to you. I'll be right over here."

"Hello." Meg's voice was calm, even cheerful, as she stepped to Jack's side. "It looks as if you landed yourself in a mess, didn't you?" She bent over, looking intently into his eyes, then pressing her fingers to his neck. "I'm going to look at your wound now."

He gave her the faintest of smiles. "Do your worst, then."

"Well, I will try to do my best, but you may be cursing my name." Coll had come in after Meg and set a small wicker chest on the dresser. Meg went to it and took out a small bottle, dousing a rag with the liquid. She took up her place at the bed again, saying, "Coll?"

"Aye. I'm here." Her brother went to the other side of the bed and leaned over Jack, putting one hand on Jack's chest and the other on his unhurt arm. Meg bent over him, washing away the blood to examine the wound.

Jack choked back a curse, digging in his heels, but Coll's firm grip kept him flat on the bed. Isobel's stomach lurched and she looked away, clenching her fists, fighting down the cries that tried to shove their way up her throat.

"There, now," she heard Meg say. "That's it for a bit. I think some brandy would do you well right now. Coll . . ."

Meg took Isobel's arm and pulled her away. "He has lost a lot of blood; you can see that. But I don't think the ball pierced his lungs; there's no sound of his lungs filling. The thing is, the ball is still in him, just below his collarbone. I have to pull it out; we cannot leave it there to fester."

Isobel paled, but nodded. "I understand."

"Coll will help me, and Hamish if I need him, but you might want to leave the room."

"No. I won't leave him." Isobel shook her head firmly.

"I thought as much." Meg smiled faintly and put her arm around Isobel's shoulder.

430

"I will try to hurt him as little as possible."

"I know."

"Promise me you won't spring up and try to stop me."

"I promise." Isobel faced Meg, taking her hand. "Please save him, Meg. I don't . . . I can't bear it if he . . ."

"I'll do everything I can." Meg squeezed Isobel's hand. "Now, go help Coll pour that brandy down Kensington's throat while I get my things."

Meg went to the small chest, and Isobel walked over to the bed. Coll had Jack halfway sitting up and was trying to get him to drink from the cup.

"Blast." Coll turned to Isobel. "I got some down him but now he will not open his mouth. I can't tell if he's unconscious or half-drunk already."

"Jack. You need to drink this."

"Don't want it," he mumbled. "Don't like."

"It's the best brandy, and you know you like it. Here." She took the cup from Coll and raised it to Jack's lips.

Jack took a sip. "Him," he said, a bit more distinctly. "Don't like him." He sent the ghost of a scowl toward Coll.

Coll chuckled. "That's good, Sassenach, as I don't like you."

"Well, I am sure you are both quite happy with that, then," Isobel said crisply, even though all she wanted to do was lean her head against Jack's and burst into tears. "But you will take another drink for me, won't you? It will help it not hurt so much."

In this way, she managed to get several more swallows down Jack.

"Why's *he* here?" Jack asked, his voice slurring. "Wanna sleep."

"I know you do. And so you shall. Just take one more sip for me." She tilted the cup up again, then stepped back and took away the pillows as Coll eased Jack back down flat on the bed.

"You shoot me?" Jack asked Coll.

"Nae, I did not. I stumbled upon you lying in the road, and I thought Isobel would not like me to leave you lying there."

As Coll turned away, Jack said quietly, "Thank you."

Isobel retreated to the corner of the room, unable to look and equally unable to move farther away. She could not leave him, no matter how hard it was to hear the muffled groans Jack made as Meg worked on him. But Isobel was thankful that Coll's broad back blocked her vision of what Meg was doing to him.

After a few minutes and a particularly

loud groan from Jack, Isobel heard Meg say, "Thank goodness. He passed out."

At the sound of metal rattling in a dish, Isobel knew that Meg must finally have pulled the ball from Jack's shoulder and discarded it. Isobel sagged against the wall, unsure her shaking legs would hold her up any longer. She heard the relief she felt echoed in Meg's voice: "I got the wee beastie."

Isobel sank down on the chair at her vanity and propped her elbows on the table, leaning her head in her hands. Behind her she could hear Meg and Coll still working, their voices hushed. But at last Meg stepped back and went to wash her hands.

Isobel hastened to the bed. Jack lay still and white as death, the dark hair framing his face in stark contrast. Meg had thrown a colorful knitted blanket across his lower half to keep him warm, but his chest was bare, exposing the bulky white bandage across his shoulder. Traces of blood still clung to his chest and stomach.

Turning from the washbowl, drying her hands, Meg told Isobel, "I imagine he will sleep for a while. That's the best thing for him. Do you have any laudanum?" At Isobel's nod, Meg went on, "Good. Give him a spoonful if the pain gets too bad. He will bleed still, I think, so be sure to change the bandage frequently. Get broth down him whenever you can; he needs to rebuild the blood he's lost. I'm going down to your stillroom and make up a few things to leave with you. A paste to spread on his wound when you change the bandage, and a tincture for the fever; I imagine he will get feverish."

Isobel nodded. "Is he . . . do you think . . ."

"He survived my getting the ball out and the loss of blood, which makes me hopeful. He is young and healthy, and I know he'll get good care." Meg paused, looking straight into her friend's eyes. "The biggest enemy now is infection. I washed the wound out and treated it, and the paste will help, too. But if it looks swollen and inflamed or starts to ooze pus, send for me. I'll look in on him again before I leave. And I'll come tomorrow."

"Thank you." Isobel threw her arms around her friend and hugged her tightly. "Thank you with all my heart."

"Take care. And get some sleep yourself when you can. You'll need your strength."

Meg packed up her chest and carried it from the room. Coll turned to follow his sister, but Isobel stopped him at the door, laying her hand upon his arm.

"Coll. Tell me what happened."

"I don't know, Izzy. I found him like that. He was on the burnside path just up from the Fraser croft. I don't know how long he'd been there. A while, I guessed, by the amount of blood. Sorry," he added as he saw her wince. "He came to when I hauled him up, but he was weak. He did not say much. And I was thinking only about getting him on that horse and back here."

"I know, and I am grateful for that."

"Isobel, there's no need for thanking me."

"*I* need to say it." Her fingers tightened on his arm. "But, Coll, I want you to tell me. Who would have done this to him?"

Coll shook his head. "I've no idea. But we cannot be certain it was on purpose. It could have been a poacher."

"Who mistook Jack for a deer? I think not."

"An accident, then. A gun went off, and the lad ran when he saw who he'd shot."

"Jack did not tell me, but I know he was stopped on the road when he came back from Inverness."

"How did you hear that? No, I know." Coll heaved a disgusted sigh. "Gossip. A man sneezes in a tavern, and the next day every woman in Kinclannoch knows it."

"I heard the men were unhappy with Jack because he refused to give them something."

"Aye, but they would not have killed him for it," Coll protested. "Izzy, you canna think one of — one of them shot him!"

"You're right; I can't. But who, then? He is a landowner and an Englishman. I know there's resentment." She fixed him with a fierce gaze. "He is my husband, Coll. Who hurts him, hurts me. If he dies, I'll not rest till I have found the one who did it. I may not be a man, but I am a Rose of Baillannan."

"I know you are." Coll smiled faintly. "There's no man on this land who wants to earn your ill will."

"Good. I want to make sure everyone knows it."

"They will. I promise."

"Will you listen about? Will you tell me if you hear anything?"

"You know I will. A fellow makes an enemy of you, he's an enemy of the Munros, as well." He grinned. "They may not be scared of me, but only a fool doesn't fear Red Meg Munro."

Isobel smiled. "Thank you. Will you do something else for me, then?"

"Tell me."

"This is the second time Jack has been

almost killed."

"Are you talking about that rockslide?" Coll's brows went up. "Surely that was an accident. Rocks fall."

"I was sure it was an accident, too. Until this happened. Coll, in only two days Jack has almost died twice."

Coll frowned. "I will look at it tomorrow morning. And the place where I found him. If there is something to be found, I'll get it." He took her hand in his and patted it. "Don't worry. Just rest and look after him."

Isobel nodded and walked back to the bed. She slipped her hand into Jack's and once again smoothed her fingers across his forehead. Panic rose in her throat, but she forced it down. Pulling a chair over to the side of the bed, she sat down to wait.

Afterward, Isobel would remember that afternoon and evening only as something of a blur. Hours dragged by in a strange blend of tedium and anxiety, broken now and then by laying her hand on his forehead to check for fever or to follow Meg's instructions about changing his bandage. All the while, Jack lay still. Now and then he would shift in the bed, a movement that was invariably followed by a groan.

Isobel had the servants bring in a cot for her to sleep on, but she could find little rest on it throughout the night. She must have fallen asleep, however, for suddenly she jerked awake, disoriented. She heard Jack's voice, and everything came rushing back to her. She ran to the bed. Jack's head was moving restlessly on the pillow, his hair sticking damply to his forehead. In the morning light, his face was flushed, and even as she placed her hand across his forehead, she knew what she would feel: Jack's forehead was blazing hot with fever.

26

The fever raged throughout the day and into the night. More than once Jack awoke and looked at Isobel without the least sign of recognition. Then, minutes later, as she walked across the room to pick up the bottle of tincture Meg had left for his fever, he barked, "Isobel! No. Watch out. The water. You're stepping in the water."

She turned her head to see him pointing at the perfectly dry floor in front of her feet, his face creased in a frown. "But there's no —"

"You don't know how deep it is. You don't know. Be careful." He struggled to push himself up on his elbow, wincing at the pain.

"I'll step around it," she said hastily, edging along the dresser.

He relaxed back onto the pillow.

When she returned with the medicine, diluted with water, and raised it to his lips to drink, he looked at her as if she were a stranger bent on poisoning him and knocked her hand away, spilling the cup all over the blanket. With grim determination, Isobel called in Hamish to hold Jack while she forced the liquid into his mouth.

She spent the long day at his bedside, repeatedly wiping his face and chest with a cool wet rag in an attempt to bring down his fever, until she felt as if her back would break from bending over the bed. Her aunt came in frequently, usually accompanied by Millicent, who stood a few feet away, wringing her hands and crying softly. Her aunt offered to take over Isobel's nursing duties for a while, but Isobel shook her head. No matter how exhausted she was, she could not bring herself to leave Jack.

As the evening wore on toward midnight, Jack became more agitated, and to Isobel's alarm, his fever flared even higher. His face flamed with color, and he carried on a fragmented conversation with someone only he could see. Isobel continued her ministrations throughout the night, smoothing a cool wet rag over his face time after time, but she feared it could not counteract that heat pouring from his body.

Hating to drag Hamish from his sleep to help her give Jack a dose of medicine, she woke her aunt and Jack's mother to help her. When they were finished, Elizabeth once again offered to relieve Isobel for a few hours.

"No," Millicent said. "Let me." She put her hand on Isobel's arm and looked into her eyes. "You can sleep on the cot, and I will call you if he needs you."

Isobel cast an uncertain look back at Jack. She was not sure that she could sleep, but her brain was foggy and her back ached. It would help to at least lie down a bit.

"Please, dear," Millicent urged her. "I know I'm — I've never been the mother Jack should have had. But I can do this. I want to. And you know that I would cry for help at the first sign of trouble." She gave a wry flicker of a smile, and for just an instant Isobel could see a flash of Jack in her.

Isobel nodded. "Thank you."

Isobel managed to doze, floating in and out of consciousness, troubled by vague, restless dreams. It was almost a relief when Jack's mother woke her.

"I think he needs more medicine," Millicent told her, her brow creased with worry. "He was better at first, but now he's very hot and restless again."

Isobel nodded and made the mixture. He did not, she thought, seem quite as agitated as earlier, and they were able to get the medicine down him between the two of them. Isobel persuaded him to take a few sips of water as well. Millicent left, looking relieved, and Isobel settled down beside Jack's bed to begin once more the routine of ceaseless waiting.

She leaned her head against the mattress, trying to fight the despair that threatened to overwhelm her. Meg had told her to be patient, but here, in the darkest hours of the night, Isobel found it hard to hold on to hope.

"Isobel?" Something touched her head, and Isobel jerked awake. The room was light and she realized she must have fallen asleep. Her neck felt permanently crooked.

"Isobel," came the faint voice again.

"Jack!" She shot upright and stared at him, stunned.

His skin was not flushed, and his eyes were weary, but clear. "Isobel? Why are you sitting there?" His tone was vaguely puzzled. "I don't feel well."

"Oh, Jack!" Isobel began to laugh, then her slightly manic laughter turned into tears. She leaned her head upon the mattress again and wept.

" 'S all right." Jack patted her head weakly. "Don't cry, Izzy."

She took his hand in hers and raised it to

her lips.

" 'S all right," he mumbled, and when she lifted her head again, she saw that his eyes were drifting closed.

Isobel sat for a moment, watching him, as she wiped the tears from her cheeks. Still holding his hand, she laid her head down again and slept.

"Blast!" Jack, when he awoke a few hours later, was not only clearer of head, but also louder of voice.

Isobel, who had been soaking in the sunlight at the window, turned and smiled. "Good day to you, too."

"What the devil happened?" Jack raised his head and started to push himself up, then grimaced and muttered an oath. His head dropped back to the pillow. "I feel as if someone shoved a red-hot poker through my chest."

"Do you not remember?" Isobel came back to him, reaching down to feel his forehead. It was far cooler than it had been, though still warmer than she would have liked. "You were shot."

"Shot!" His brows rose and he looked away, thinking. "I was riding home. I remember — something slammed into my shoulder, and I dropped the reins. Pharaoh reared — yes, there was a bang — I went flying." He paused. "It's . . . very vague after that." Jack ran his hand over her face and back into his hair. "I'm weak as a kitten."

"That's no surprise. You lost a great deal of blood. I didn't know if you —" Her voice caught. "You must have been lying there for hours."

"Isobel . . ." He reached out to take her hand. "You're not going to cry again, are you?"

"No. Of course not." She smiled determinedly. "I was . . . tired before."

He rubbed his thumb across her knuckles. "You have been taking care of me. I — I remember a little." He looked a little fretfully toward the carpet. "Was there water on the floor?"

"No." She chuckled and sat down on the side of the bed, keeping her hand curved in his. "Though you apparently thought there was. You were delirious with fever."

"Everything seemed . . . a bit mad." He frowned.

"What else do you remember?"

"About getting shot? Nothing, really. I woke up now and again. The sun was in my eyes. I think — yes, I tried to walk, but I fell. Was Coll Munro there?"

"He found you and brought you home."

"I remember being on a horse; my shoulder hurt like hell every step he took." He frowned. "That redhead — Meg Munro was here. Did she take the ball out of me?" His voice rose in astonishment.

"Yes. And a very good job she did, too. She made the medicine as well." Isobel went on carefully, "Did you see anyone? When you were shot, I mean."

"You mean the chap who shot me?" Jack shook his head. "Unless it was Coll."

Isobel made a face. "I do hope you won't accuse him again. Coll did not shoot you. He brought you home; he saved your life. Would he have done that if he had just shot you?"

Jack grunted softly. "I suppose not."

"Coll thinks it may have been a poacher. An accident."

"Perhaps."

"You're tired. You should sleep." Isobel stood up, leaning over to kiss his cheek. "I'll ring for some broth."

At the door, she paused and swung back around. "I told your mother and Aunt Elizabeth that you had awakened and were better. They were very happy to hear it. Your mother sat with you while I slept last night. I know she would like very much to come in and see you."

He looked at Isobel for a long moment, then sighed. "Very well. Send her in."

When Isobel left the room, Jack lay, looking up at the tester high above him. He felt like a turtle on its back. An empty and weak turtle. He tried to squirm higher on his pillow and discovered that any movement set off the fire in his chest and shoulder. Clearly he could do nothing on his own. The thought galled him. It was bad enough that he had been carried back to the house by Coll Munro, but it shamed him even more to think of Isobel seeing him in such a state.

When his mother tiptoed hesitantly into his room, he was swept with relief. At least he would not have to ask Isobel to help him sit up now; his mother could do that. "Thank God."

Millicent blinked at his unusually enthusiastic greeting, but hurried over to his bedside. "Oh, Jack, I have been so worried. I thought you would die, hating me, and I could not bear it." Her eyes welled with tears.

"Yes, I know. For pity's sake, don't cry about it. I don't hate you, and in any case I didn't die."

"You are always so cold."

"Mother, please. I need your help."

She gaped at him.

"I cannot sit up by myself."

Her face cleared. "Ah . . . you don't want to have to ask Isobel." She stepped forward with a little chuckle and slid her hands beneath his head and chest. "You see? Sometimes having a mother about is not so bad."

With her help, and enough pain to leave him white-faced, Jack managed to sit up, and Millicent plumped up the pillows behind his back.

"There now." She patted his leg and sat down in the chair beside him, then launched into a description of her emotional reaction to his arrival, half-dead, at the house.

"I am glad I provided you with some drama." Jack's wry smile took the sting out of his words.

"Oh, you." Millicent gave an airy wave of her hand.

"What about everyone else?" he asked casually, straightening out a wrinkle in the sheet.

"We were all amazed! Isobel had been worrying. I could see that. You know I notice little things that —"

"Was she . . . surprised?"

"Of course she was! Everyone was."

"What about her brother? Was Andrew there?"

She furrowed her brow, thinking. "No, I don't believe so. You know, I don't think he has even been by to see how you are, which is most unlike him. He is usually so courteous." She narrowed her eyes. "Jack, these are very peculiar questions. What are you thinking?"

"Cui bono."

"What? You know I don't like it when you use those legal words. There are times when you are very like my father."

"Who benefits," he explained.

"Who ben—" She stared at him. "You think it was someone here who shot at you? Somebody in this house? No. Don't be silly. It was a poacher, that's all. An accident."

"That seems to be the popular explanation."

"You cannot suspect Isobel!"

"No, no, of course not." His mind skittered away from the thought.

"She has been at your side the whole time. She's barely slept or eaten. She wouldn't even let me in the room at first, and I am your mother." Millicent added with a touch of resentment, "I must say, Isobel is a bit of a martinet, though you would not think it to look at her. Do you know, she had a maid

448

pour out that little bottle of my cordial, which was a gift, you know, from Sir Andrew, and purely medicinal, besides. She doesn't serve wine at the table now, either, which seems a bit rude when one thinks about it."

"Did she really?" Jack's mouth quirked up on one side. "She is something of a manager."

"I suppose it's the money. Well, you know how the Scots are."

Jack laughed. "No, Mother, I have found I don't know how the Scots are at all."

"But I don't think they would try to *murder* you. It's clear that Isobel loves you madly."

"Is it? You see romances everywhere, Mother."

"That is because I look instead of ignoring them. You might try it sometime."

"What about Andrew? Where was he?"

"I don't know, dear. He was not with me, but then a young man is not likely to be sitting about with two old ladies, is he? Oh! I believe that was the day he went to stay with Gregory, so you see, it couldn't have been him."

"Yes, I see."

"I cannot imagine Sir Andrew would try to harm you. He is a gentleman through and through — such address, such courtesy."

"It would be rather impolite to shoot one's host."

"It's the fever." Millicent nodded. "I am sure that is why you are thinking such morbid thoughts. But don't worry. I won't let on that you suspected Isobel and Andrew."

That, Jack thought with an inward groan, undoubtedly ensured that she would tell everyone.

Millicent leaned in toward him. "This is so nice, isn't it? Talking together like this. It is just as it used to be. Remember when you were little? I could talk to you about anything."

"Yes, I remember."

"You were a wonderful little boy. Such a support to me during all the bad times. You took good care of my Dolly. You loved her so."

"I did."

"Don't be sad, dearest." Millicent patted Jack's arm consolingly. "She is in a better place, I'm sure."

"Yes, I am sure she is."

"Ah, there, I've made you tired. I can see it in your face. Isobel will be quite out of humor with me. I told her I would not stay long. You should sleep." She stood up and bent to kiss his cheek. "Shall I help you lie back down?"

"No. I prefer this." He watched her leave, letting his head sink back into the pillows. He felt weary to the center of his bones. She was right; he should sleep. But though he closed his eyes, he could not stop the thoughts drifting through his head.

Isobel would not have tried to kill him. But . . . if he died, she would have her beloved Baillannan back. He had made a new will leaving the estate to her; that was another of the tasks he had performed in Inverness. Jack thought of Isobel's eyes, her smile, her mouth soft on his. It could not be her. Much more likely her brother. Andrew could not get his estate back, but he would be able to live on Isobel's largesse. Was he one of the young gentlemen who visited Manton's shooting club? It was possible, and killing someone from a distance would suit his nature.

Or Coll — though he seemed more the sort to attack close up and straight on. Jack was sure it was Coll who had spared his life that night with the highwaymen. And Coll had also brought Jack back to the house. But perhaps Coll was certain Jack would soon die and thought to make himself look more innocent by pretending to save him. Love could drive a man to do strange things. Despite Isobel's protestations, Jack found it hard to believe that the man didn't harbor a desire for her. How could he not?

Or perhaps it was one of the crofters who had decided to relieve Isobel of the burden of Jack. One of the other highwaymen might have decided on his own to rid the world of another landlord.

But not Isobel. It could not be Isobel.

27

Jack slept for most of the first day or two of his convalescence, but Isobel soon discovered that he was not the easiest of patients. He grumbled at the broth she put before him and even more so at the oatmeal porridge. He was restless and hated lying in bed all the time, yet he perversely disdained her efforts to help him sit up or get out of bed, so that she hovered at his side, terrified he was about to topple over. At times Isobel was positive he wished her gone, yet if she was absent for more than twenty minutes, he grew fretful.

He wanted to sit up, leave his sickbed, walk about, even dress himself although he could not raise one arm. The sling she fashioned for his arm was uncomfortable. His beard itched but he would not allow her or a servant to attempt to shave him, insisting on standing in front of the washstand to do it himself.

She tried to keep him occupied by reading to him or playing games with him, but he declared her so poor a cardplayer it was not any fun to win a game from her. Finally, one afternoon, in the midst of an especially exasperating argument over which of three books he wished her to read to him, Isobel snapped, "You are the most irksome man alive. 'Tis no wonder someone shot you!"

Her eyes flew wide in horror as she realized what she had said, but Jack burst into laughter and reached up, clenching his fingers in the front of her dress and pulling her down to kiss her. "I am sorry, love. I know I'm a perfect bear."

"You are," she retorted. "But I did not mean that. You know I did not mean that."

"Yes, I know." He kissed her again lightly. "You would have bashed me over the head twice already today if you were the sort to murder someone."

"More times than that." She smiled as she reached out to stroke her hand across his hair.

"I am bored to tears, and I hate that it taxes my strength to walk across the floor and sit by the window."

"But you are already stronger than you were two days ago."

"I want to get out of the house. I'm tired

of looking out that same window."

"Then tomorrow, we'll go to the sitting room and visit with Aunt Elizabeth and your mother."

"Now I am certain you're trying to kill me."

"Jack, don't even joke about that."

"I miss looking at . . . the land." He started to shrug, then winced. "Truth is, I think I miss talking to your crofters."

"Many of them have come to ask about you." Isobel was unable to completely mask the surprise in her voice. "I think they are perhaps more *your* crofters than you realize."

"My dear girl, I am not the Rose of Baillannan."

"But you are no longer the 'damned Sassenach.' "

"I suppose that is progress." Jack trailed his fingers along her arm. "You know, there is something else that would relieve my boredom more than anything." He looked up at her, his eyes glinting.

"What?" Isobel drew her head back suspiciously.

He slid his fingers higher up her arm, slipping them beneath the short sleeve of her dress. "Climb into bed and I'll show you."

He tugged her down onto the bed beside him.

"Jack! You can't mean it?"

"I can." He roamed up her front, cupping her breast in his hand. "I do. I am shot, not dead." He caressed her languidly, his thumb teasing at her nipple. "In fact, I can feel my strength returning as we speak."

Isobel laughed a little breathlessly. "Are you certain that is your strength we're talking about?"

He grinned, curving his hand around the back of her neck and pulling her down to kiss her with a thoroughness that left no doubt of his intentions. "You are the best restorative, my love. If you but take off that dress, I can show you how much health I've regained."

Isobel kissed his forehead, luxuriating in the touch of his hand upon her. "But your shoulder, Jack . . . you could not."

"I could . . . as long as you did all the work." His hand crept up her leg, finding the hot center of her. "Ah, there you are." He took her mouth again as his fingers stroked her, sending desire flooding between her legs. "Hot." He kissed her in brief, hungry bites between his words. "And wet. And ready for me."

Isobel let out a soft moan and cupped his

456

face in her hands, holding him in place for a long, deep kiss. At last she lifted her head, peering deep into his eyes. "Are you sure?"

"What do you think?" he asked hoarsely, taking her hand and pulling it beneath the sheets.

"Ah. I see." Isobel's lips curved up in a provocative smile as she began to take the pins from her hair. "I might be able to provide you with a bit of . . . entertainment."

"I am sure you can." He curved his uninjured arm behind his head, settling in to watch Isobel as she shook out her hair, combing her fingers through it and letting it flow like liquid gold over her shoulders and down her breasts.

Reaching up to the top button of her dress, Isobel unfastened it slowly, moving without haste to the one below. Jack's eyes darkened as they followed the achingly languid movement of her fingers.

"You're taking a damnably long time about this," he murmured.

"I'm sorry." Isobel widened her eyes innocently. "Am I doing it wrong? Perhaps I should stop."

He let out a breathy little laugh. "Don't you dare."

"If you're sure . . ." She undid another

457

button, and now only the sash of her gown held the bodice together. The two sides gaped open, revealing a V-shaped swath of the feminine material beneath. With a tug, she pulled the wide scoop neckline of her dress down over her shoulders.

Jack's eyes were fastened avidly on the material as it continued to sag farther down her arms, his breath coming in short, sharp pulls. Isobel smiled a trifle smugly as she grasped the ribbon fastening her chemise and slowly pulled one end until the bow popped undone and the chemise sagged open, exposing the inner curves of her breasts. Taking the sides in her fingers, she started to pull them apart, but stopped.

"No, wait. Perhaps I should not." Isobel studied him with a considering pout of her lips. "You look much too feverish. And I believe you're panting." She leaned over him, laying her palm upon his forehead. "Yes, you are very warm."

"Isobel . . ." he grated out. "You're being a bloody tease."

"I know." She laughed, her eyes dancing. "But you did say you were bored."

"Not anymore," he growled, and grabbed the end of her sash.

"No, no, now. You mustn't exert yourself." Isobel straightened up. "You must let me do all the work for you." Her eyes were intent on his as she stepped backward, letting her momentum pull against the sash, so that it untied slowly in his hand and slipped from her dress. Her gown opened, and she shrugged it off. "You just think of how it would feel if it were *your* hands undressing me."

"I am." Jack's voice was uneven.

"Imagine your fingers sliding through my hair." She fitted her actions to her words, sinking her fingers into the thick amber mass and letting it slip through them. "I believe that is something you like to do."

"I do." The light in his eyes could have sparked tinder into a flame.

Isobel continued to undress, reaching down and drawing her petticoats up to her knees, showing her shapely calves. "Your hands sliding beneath my underskirts . . . to pull off my garters, first one, then the other." She eased off the garters and tossed them onto the bed.

Jack grabbed the lacy bands in midair, crushing them in his hand as he asked hoarsely, "Then what would I do?"

"This, I think." Isobel perched on the end of the bed, beyond his reach, and removed her slippers. She hooked her thumbs in her stockings, working them down her legs.

"You'd slide down my stockings, moving over my skin in a long, slow caress."

"I would. Your skin is like silk."

The low throb of hunger in his voice melted her, but Isobel held herself in check, standing up to continue her disrobing. She peeled off her garments bit by bit, her voice low and lingering over the description of each delicious step of the process. He watched her with hungry eyes, anticipation heightening the fierce pleasure of Isobel's seduction.

When at last she was naked, Isobel walked toward him slowly, letting his gaze drink her in. As she climbed onto the bed, his hand went to the sheet covering him, shoving it downward, but she reached out and stayed his hand.

"No. Not yet. I'm not finished." She leaned down and kissed his lips. "Let me make love to you." He made an inarticulate noise as her lips moved across his face. "Have I told you what I felt when I first looked at you?" She smiled down into his eyes as she skimmed her thumb along the flaring line of cheekbone. "I wanted to touch you like this. To kiss you." She pressed her lips softly to the skin she had just touched. "To feel you — to know you in all sorts of ways that a lady should not want, though I was too unknowing at the time to even realize what my desire was."

"Sweet heaven. Isobel . . ." he said thickly, but she stopped his words with another kiss.

She kissed his cheeks, his chin, his forehead, with featherlight touches, nuzzling into his neck, taking his earlobe between her teeth to worry it gently, pulling a sharp hiss of pleasure from him. His hands moved restlessly on her, stroking her legs and hips, roaming upward to cup and caress her breasts, his hands so hot they seared her flesh.

Isobel slid downward, her mouth exploring his chest as her hand roamed lower, moving between his legs to cup and stroke. Jack moaned her name, digging his hands into her hair. Pushing the covers aside, she straddled him and sank down upon him. His hands went to her hips as she began to move, hurtling them both ever deeper into the spiraling grip of passion. Jack gazed up at her, his face sharp with need, his eyes hazed and dark with desire. She saw it in his face as the pleasure took him, and his response sparked the explosion of her own passion.

She gripped the headboard under the force of the cataclysm roaring through her, and when it was done, leaving her limp and trembling, she sank down onto the bed beside Jack. He curled his arm around her and pulled her to his side.

"Jack, no, be careful."

"I don't give a damn." His arm was like iron around her, and he buried his face in her hair. "I want to hold you."

And since that was what she wanted, too, Isobel gave in. She pressed herself against his side, her arm looping over his waist, and they clung together, spent and fulfilled.

To occupy Jack's restless mind as he convalesced, Isobel offered to show him the accounts of the estate. To her surprise, he took to the idea, so she brought up the account books, explaining to him all the different aspects. Exploring the business of the estate clearly held Jack's interest more than any book or game had done.

Isobel could not suppress the small spark of hope in her heart. Surely his interest in the numbers, his enjoyment of his rides about the estate and his talking to the crofters, were proof that he was happy here. Surely that meant he might not want to leave Baillannan. She knew she should not count on his staying. It would be foolish beyond measure to fall in love with this man. Love, after all, was not part of their bargain. However, their "bargain" mattered less and less to Isobel with each day that passed, and she was discovering that wisdom had little to do with love.

Isobel stepped out of Jack's room, closing the door softly behind her. The sound of voices rose from a room down the hall; one voice, rising above the other two, was clearly that of Jack's mother. Frowning, Isobel turned toward Millicent's bedroom.

"But Jack would not mind!" Millicent cried, the rest of her words drowned out by the other agitated feminine voices.

"Shhh!" Isobel rushed into the room. "What in the world is going on in here? I just convinced Jack to lie down for a nap."

The three women went silent and turned to face Isobel. Jack's mother sat clutching a bottle filled with a dark amber liquid. A maid beside her was wringing her hands, and Aunt Elizabeth faced Millicent, hands on hips, her eyes flashing fire.

"Isobel!" Elizabeth turned, relief mingling with guilt. "I am sorry."

"They are trying to take my little restorative away." Millicent appealed to Isobel. "I cannot imagine why. I wasn't doing anything wrong." The picture she presented would have been more convincing if her words had not been slurred and her face flushed, with her hair straggling down on one side.

"I feel wretched." Elizabeth came forward. "It was that vexatious old Angus McKay. He brought some of his whiskey to Jack the other day — as if that lethal brew of his would revive an invalid. More likely to put one in a grave, I'd think! Foolishly I set the bottle down in the office. I thought Jack would be pleased to know that Angus was concerned about his health. It never occurred to me that Millicent might go in there and find it." She cast an accusing glance at the other woman.

"She hid it from me!" Millicent started to rise, then sat back down with a plop.

The maid reached for the open bottle tilting precariously in the woman's lap, but Millicent grabbed it with both hands. "You leave that alone! It is mine. Jack would not mind."

"Jack most certainly would mind," Isobel snapped, striding forward. She jerked the bottle from Millicent's grasp, heedless of the liquid that sloshed out onto the floor, and thrust it at the maid.

"Louisa, take this down and pour it out. Auntie" — Isobel turned to Elizabeth — "if you would be so kind as to excuse us, I would like to have a word alone with Mrs. Kensington."

"Of course, dear, of course." Elizabeth shooed the maid from the room before her, casting another apologetic look back at her niece as they left.

Millicent, who had been staring at Isobel openmouthed, surged to her feet. "What do you think you're doing? You have no right . . ."

The older woman swayed on her feet, and Isobel put her hand on Millicent's shoulder, pressing her firmly back down into the chair. Millicent tried to shrug Isobel's restraining hand away and when she could not, she set her chin and gazed up at Isobel like a mutinous child.

"You have no right . . ." Millicent repeated.

"I have every right, and well you know it." Isobel dropped her hand from Millicent's shoulder. "Mrs. Kensington . . ."

"Yes, Mrs. Kensington?" Millicent replied haughtily, then let out a little giggle and pressed her fingers to her mouth. "How silly. We are both Mrs. Kensington."

"Yes, we are." Isobel sighed and squatted down to look her mother-in-law in the eyes. "Millicent. You are my husband's mother, and for that reason I shall treat you with respect. But I must be frank with you."

"Must you?" Millicent wilted. "You — you

are going to send me away, aren't you?"
Great tears welled in the older woman's
eyes.

"No, of course not. You are welcome here.
Baillannan is your son's home, and now it
is yours, too. Where you live is entirely up
to you and Jack."

"He will not want me." Millicent began to
cry. "I have been a terrible mother, and he
hates me. He has every right to hate me."

"He does not hate you. He has taken care
of you all these years despite the . . . the
problems between you."

"I know." Millicent sniffed, dabbing at her
eyes. "He is a wonderful man. So like —"

"No." Isobel cut her off, wrapping her
hand firmly around Millicent's wrist. "Do
not compare him to his father. Whatever
you feel for your husband, Jack is not like
him. He tries very hard *not* to be like him.
Sutton Kensington left you. Jack has not."

Isobel pinned Millicent with her gaze,
grasping her hands firmly, as if she could
somehow infuse the woman with her determination. "You and I both know you like to
drink. And you do not act well when you
have drunk too much." Millicent crumpled,
and Isobel squeezed her hands. "No, now
look at me. This is important. You have an
opportunity, a wonderful opportunity, to

start a new life with your son. You could be happy here with us."

"Yes." Millicent nodded eagerly. "Yes, I am happy." She sniffed. "Elizabeth is very kind." She looked significantly at Isobel.

"Yes, she is. I am not so kind. You may choose to fight me. You can try to ferret out liquor wherever you can; you can pout; you can blame me or argue with me. But I promise you that you will not win. Or, if you choose to, you could join me. You can try to be the mother you wish you had been. You could be strong and fight whatever it is that impels you to drink. But either way, you will *not* drink alcohol in this house. I will not allow you to embarrass Jack or hurt him."

Millicent blinked, and her mouth opened and closed. Finally she whispered, "Yes. I want that. I do, truly."

"An excellent decision, Mother." Both women whirled at the sound of Jack's voice. He stood, leaning against the doorjamb, a trifle pale, but with a faint smile on his lips. "You and I don't stand a chance against Isobel, I fear. She will pull us into propriety however we might struggle."

"Jack! Whatever are you doing up?" Isobel popped to her feet. "You said you were going to nap."

"I was trying to," he protested, giving in easily as she put her arm around his waist and turned him around to lead him back down the hall to their bedroom. Jack curled his arm around her shoulders and bent closer to murmur, "You are quite the little tartar."

"Oh, hush, and come back to bed."

He pressed his lips to her hair, and she felt the breathy touch of his chuckle. "With you? Always."

Jack's mood improved as his strength returned, and once he was well enough to move about the house, his strength multiplied by leaps and bounds, though even he had to admit that his shoulder was not yet healed enough for him to start riding again. Isobel hoped that he would be content with that for a long while. She dreaded the thought of his riding out across the estate, exposed to whatever person might want to harm him.

They did not talk about the shooting after their initial conversation. Jack seemed content enough to dismiss the incident as an accident, an errant shot by a poacher, and Isobel did not express her own doubts on the matter. Coll had reported to her that he had found fresh scrapes and marks on the rocks at the top of the hill where the rockslide had occurred, evidence, he thought, that some sort of lever had been used to pry the rocks from their base and send them tumbling down to the path below. The thought was a spear of ice through her chest. She could see in Coll's eyes that he, too, thought someone had set out to kill Jack.

She could not bear to think about who could have done such a thing. Coll did not believe that any of the men he knew was the culprit. If one of them was capable of murder, it was far more likely he would have attacked Donald MacRae, the Earl of Mardoun's hated steward. It was absurd that any of the crofters would have tried to do away with a man whom they were beginning to know, even like. Only one man so thoroughly disliked her husband. One man who would benefit if Jack died.

But it could not be Andrew!

Isobel could not believe it of her brother. The boy she had loved and taken care of from birth could not have turned out a murderer. Yes, he could be resentful and sullen; he harbored a grudge. But his ill will came out in small, spiteful acts and thoughtless pranks, such as bringing Jack's mother here or encouraging her to drink too much.

He would not resort to cold-blooded killing.

Guiltily, she knew she should tell Jack her suspicions. She should let him know what Coll had found. But every time she steeled herself to address the issue, she could not do it. If even she could suspect Andrew, how much more would Jack believe he had done it? She could not turn Jack so completely against her brother without any real proof.

No matter how bad it might look for Andrew, there had to be another explanation. Coll might turn up evidence of another suspect, or that it had actually been an accident, however unlikely it seemed. In the meantime, Jack was safe here in the house, where she and Hamish could keep an eye on him. Isobel would make sure she was with Jack when he took a stroll outdoors. And Coll now made frequent patrols over the estate, looking for anything or anyone out of place. When Jack insisted on riding again . . . well, she would face that when she came to it.

Jack declared himself strong enough to take a walk outside the house, and after only a minor protest, Isobel gave in, strolling with him to the bench on the promontory above the house. They sat there for several minutes, enjoying the caress of the May sun on their backs as they looked out across the loch.

"I should like to explore the castle again," Jack commented, gazing at the remains of the tower rising in the distance.

"Yes, we should go. I'll have Cook pack us a cold lunch to take."

Jack cast her a sideways glance and smiled. "You cannot guard me forever, you know."

"I am sure I don't know what you mean." Isobel gave him a haughty look. "If you do not care for my company, I shall not force it upon you."

Jack chuckled and took her hand, bringing it to his mouth to kiss. "I care very much for your company. And I look forward with great anticipation to a picnic with you at the castle."

When they returned to the house later, Jack's mother informed them with great regret that they had just missed their cousin's visit.

"Gregory? Was Andrew with him?" Isobel asked, her stomach clenching.

"Not the boys. Cousin Robert." Elizabeth's eyes twinkled as she added, "Millicent thought him quite handsome."

"Cousin Robert?" Isobel asked in surprise.

"Yes, he has such a nice bearing," Milli-

471

cent commented. "I could see at once that he was a military man. He looks a good deal like Gregory, I thought."

"Yes, I suppose he does. I've never thought of him in that regard."

"Robby took after his father," Elizabeth agreed, apparently in better humor with her cousin than usual. "Uncle Fergus was a good-looking man, though never as handsome as my father. A poor imitation, more like."

"He came to inquire after your health, Jack," Millicent went on. "He was most sorry to have missed you."

"Mm. No doubt."

"I think he primarily came to complain about Greg and Andy." Elizabeth chuckled. "Gregory is certain there is a secret room in the cellar of their house, and the treasure must be in it."

"Is there a secret room?" Isobel asked.

"I have never heard of one. Robert says Gregory wants to smash holes in the wall, looking for it."

"Oh, my."

"It sounded terribly exciting," Millicent said. "A priest hole, perhaps." She frowned faintly. "Though Colonel Rose was certain the family was never Catholic, even secretly."

"No," Elizabeth agreed regretfully. "I never heard any stories like that either. Gregory thinks my father hid there after he landed, but I am certain he came here. Why would he have stayed at Fergus's house?"

"Yes, one would think there would be ample places to hide in this house," Millicent commented. "I got lost the other day when —"

Isobel sat bolt upright. "A hidden room!"

"Yes, dear." Her aunt looked at her oddly. "That's what we were talking about. But Robert is convinced there isn't one."

"No, no, I mean here. Do you remember, Auntie, how you said you saw your father walk *into* the fireplace?"

Distress creased Elizabeth's face. "Yes, I know it sounds a little mad, but I — perhaps I was mistaken. But I remember so clearly him walking down the hall and into this room." She pointed toward the massive stone fireplace jutting out from the wall.

"Into the fire itself?"

"No. I — he couldn't have."

"Isobel, what is it?" Jack leaned forward, intrigued. "What are you thinking?"

"Weren't priest holes often beside a fireplace?"

"I suppose so; it would be easier to hide a secret room with the width of the —" Jack stopped, standing up and turning around to look at the fireplace. "You think there is a priest hole there?"

"But the Roses weren't Catholic, at least not after the change of religion."

"Maybe not a priest hole. But what about a hidden passage? There are stories about secret staircases and walkways in the old castle."

"Oh, yes." Elizabeth nodded her head. "There was supposed to be a tunnel out to the sea caves, so that they could escape a siege of the castle. Do you think they put one in this house when they built it? I have never heard of it."

"Maybe they were able to keep a secret." Isobel went to the fireplace, Jack by her side. "I suspect in the 1600s, there were still times a Rose might need an escape route. Or a secret entry."

"Do you remember which side of the fireplace your father was going into?" Jack asked.

"I — I'm not sure. It's so long ago. I peeked in from the hall."

"It does stand out a good bit beyond the mantel." Jack rapped along the protruding wall beside the fireplace until it echoed hollowly. "There seems to be a slight crack here, where the stone of the fireplace be-

474

gins." Jack ran his finger down a line. "But how would it open?"

Isobel joined him, followed by Elizabeth and Millicent. Isobel pressed at one carved decoration, then another. "There might be some mechanism, a lever or —" She leaned closer, peering at the corner of the marble mantel. "Look at this rosette." She pointed to a carving of the familiar Rose emblem. "There's a hole in the center of this flower."

Jack joined her, rubbing his finger gently over it. "Yes. It's odd."

"A flaw in the marble?" Aunt Elizabeth suggested.

"But the hole is so perfectly round, as if it had been drilled."

Jack went to the opposite corner and inspected the matching rosette. "No hole on this one." He turned back.

"Also, it's rather large for a flaw, almost the size of —" Isobel stopped, staring at Jack. "Almost the size of your watch key."

"What?" Millicent looked confused.

Elizabeth, however, drew in a sharp breath. "Isobel . . . do you think . . ."

Jack's eyes lit up as he pulled the key from his vest pocket. "Perhaps that is why your father wanted to keep the key. He did not need the watch, but he needed the key to turn something else. It would be a clever way to conceal it." He inserted the watch key into the hole. It fit perfectly.

With a glance at Isobel, he tried to turn the key. At first it did not move, but as he applied more pressure, it did.

"Papa's key had a longer handle," Elizabeth said. "I remember; it looked a little odd."

"That would make it easier to turn — more leverage." With a click, a narrow section of wall opened along the edge of the stone, swinging slowly out to reveal a small, semicircular chamber.

"It *is* a priest hole!" Millicent exclaimed.

"No." Jack picked up a candlestick from the mantel and held it closer to the chamber. "It is a staircase."

28

"Secret stairs!" Elizabeth's face glowed and she clasped her hands together in excitement. "Where does it go?"

"I don't know." Isobel peered down into the dimly lit spiral of stone steps.

"It must go outside," Elizabeth said. "A secret entrance to the house."

"One where he wouldn't be seen coming or going," Isobel agreed. "It would make sense. He could escape the notice of the soldiers that way."

"I intend to find out where it goes," Jack said, stepping forward. He turned as Isobel grabbed the other candlestick from the mantel and started after him. "Wait. We have no idea what's down there. It could be unsafe. Isobel, perhaps you should —"

She cocked an eyebrow at him. "If you think I am letting you have all the fun, you clearly suffered damage to your head as well as your shoulder."

The two older women, taking a look down the narrow, steep steps, reluctantly agreed that they would wait here for news, so Jack and Isobel went down alone, their flickering candles creating eerie shadows against the old, gray stones.

Turning around on itself in a dizzying fashion, the staircase seemed endless, the steps above and below them fading into darkness. The air was close and musty, the rock walls splotched with lichen and sometimes glistening with moisture. Isobel tried not to think about stepping on a slick patch of stone and tumbling down. The staircase, she hoped, was so narrow one would knock into one wall or the other rather than hurtling down the steps.

"How far down does this go?" Jack asked finally. "Surely we have gone more than one story."

"I think it must lead into the cellars. Perhaps it just goes to a larger secret room. It could be where Malcolm hid."

Finally, his voice rising with anticipation, Jack said, "There's a dirt floor below."

He trotted down the last few steps, Isobel right behind him. The steps ended, with no door, at a low-ceilinged passageway barely wide enough for two people to walk. It stretched out in front of them into utter blackness.

"A tunnel!" Isobel clutched Jack's hand as they started forward.

"Beneath the house?"

"I think so. Either we are below the cellars or the cellars lie on the other side of this wall. I think it's an escape route."

"You think this goes to the caves on the shore?" Jack asked.

Isobel shrugged. "The caves are some distance from here, farther than they are from the castle. But they wouldn't have had to build the tunnel all the way to the sea. It could end anywhere."

Soon the tunnel narrowed so that they had to walk single file, and the ceiling was low enough that Jack had to bend his head to pass through. The walls of stone gave way to braces of timber. Isobel could not help but think uneasily of the weight of the earth above their heads. The tunnel could be a hundred and fifty years old, and it appeared not to have been used since Malcolm came through here some sixty years ago — if, indeed, he had even used the passageway. How much might it have deteriorated? It was easy to envision rot in the support timbers.

Jack's steps slowed, and he held the candlestick higher, letting out an oath. "It's caved in."

"What? No!" Isobel cried in frustration, and Jack turned so that Isobel could see past him.

A few feet in front of Jack, the tunnel was choked with dirt, stones, and broken timbers. They would not find where the passageway came out.

When they emerged from the staircase, Millicent and Elizabeth were predictably impressed with their description of the tunnel, though they did deem the cave-in a disappointment.

"Will you explore the caves to find the other end?" Millicent asked.

"I don't know. They are a great distance from here. In any case, Gregory and Andrew are already searching the caves for the treasure. If there is an entrance there, they might find it." Jack frowned as he said it, and Isobel could not help but feel a spurt of amusement. Clearly Jack had developed a jealous interest in the tunnels that the treasure had not spurred.

"The entrance could be anywhere," Isobel pointed out. "It just needs to be far enough from the house to make one's escape undetected."

"The entrance could be near the loch, I

suppose," Elizabeth said.

"Or the castle ruins," Jack suggested.

Elizabeth nodded. "If there truly was a tunnel to the caves from the castle, digging one from here to the castle would mean one could go all the way to the sea without outside notice."

"I fear it is too dangerous to search the castle ruins." Isobel sighed. "No doubt it was fine when this house was built, and even in our grandfather's day it was probably safe enough. But it has deteriorated a great deal in the last sixty years."

"That's true." Elizabeth frowned. "There was another cave-in there when you and Andrew were children."

"It might be possible to climb down on ropes," Jack mused.

"There would still be the danger of it collapsing on top of you," Isobel pointed out. "Please, Jack, promise me you will not try that."

"I won't. I've more fondness for my skin than that. But if we were to shore it up, it might be possible to search there in the future."

"In the meantime," Isobel put in, "I think the best place to search may be the attic." At the others' puzzled looks, she went on, "When I was cleaning the attic, a number of the chests had papers in them as well as possessions — letters and lists and documents. Cousin Robert took a few chests and I got rid of a fair bit of clothing and such, but most of the papers I just stacked together. Also, there is a good portion of the attic that I never even touched. There might be original plans for this house that show the tunnel. Or letters, instructions, a will. Obviously knowledge must have been passed down in some fashion if our grandfather was using the passageway. If he had lived, he probably would have told my father." She turned to Elizabeth. "Do you think Papa knew of its existence?"

"I don't think so." Elizabeth shook her head. "He never said anything to me, and you know your father was not a secretive man. I know my memory is not always certain, but I cannot believe I could have forgotten it if your father told me about a tunnel. Nor did Mother speak of it; it would not surprise me if she didn't know. The Roses tended to be a secretive lot. My grandfather was said to be very tight-lipped about anything concerning the family. This could have been something they would not let slip to anyone but the heir. Even spouses could have been excluded."

For the next few days, all four of them

spent much of their time searching through the accumulated papers of the Rose family. Isobel had the servants bring down the chests of papers she had set aside when she was cleaning the attic, and Elizabeth and Millicent began to sort through them while Isobel and Jack started with the papers stored in the household strongbox, then moved on to the records in the office.

When nothing of any use turned up, they returned to the area of the attic that Isobel had not yet cleaned. Isobel stumbled upon a trunk containing a number of things belonging to her father, among them some childish notes written by her and her brother that made her eyes mist a bit with sentiment, and she set the chest aside to go through at a more leisurely pace.

After a week of such efforts proved futile, Isobel's aunt and Millicent returned to their needlework and conversation, and Jack was speaking of taking up his daily rides again. Even Isobel's interest began to flag.

Andrew returned from town, declaring that it was simply too boring to continue living in Cousin Robert's house. Isobel realized, with a pang of regret, that she felt more apprehension than happiness at her brother's homecoming. He was, predictably, thrilled at the notion of the tunnel and insisted on trying out the secret stairs and exploring the underground passage.

Looking at her brother's eager face, hearing his easy laugh and droll depiction of the misadventures he and Gregory had experienced in their search for the treasure, Isobel told herself that her suspicions must be wrong. Still, she could not help but hope that Andrew would soon grow bored and head back to London.

The morning after Andrew returned to Baillannan, Jack sent a servant to his room asking Andrew to join him in the office. Predictably, it was almost an hour before Andrew strolled in. He flopped down carelessly in a chair and stretched his legs out in front of him, ankles crossed, the very picture of unconcern. Jack felt an urge to grab the young man by the collar and jerk him upright, but he refrained. He sat down across from the young man and regarded him steadily for a long moment.

"I assume you must have had some reason for sending for me," Andrew said finally, shifting in his chair. "It's like being called down by the headmaster."

"I wouldn't know."

"No. I suppose you would not." The ghost

of a smirk touched the corner of Andrew's mouth.

"It is time you returned to London," Jack said without preamble.

"London!" Andrew jerked upright.

"Or Edinburgh. Wherever you prefer. As long as it is not here."

"You are tossing me out of my own home?" Andrew surged to his feet.

"My home, Andrew. I believe we have discussed this before."

"I grew up here! I belong here!"

"Yes, yes, I know. And I am an interloper."

Andrew clenched his fists, his face flooding with color, but Jack merely cast a sardonic look at his doubled-up hands.

"Really, Andrew? Do you want a dustup?"

Andrew glared at him, jaw set, then stepped back, opening his hands. He gave a half shrug. "Of course not. I don't engage in street fighting."

"Naturally."

"You can't be serious." Andrew moved restlessly around the room. "If you are still on about that little mistake I made regarding Mrs. Kensington, I can assure you it will not happen again. I had no idea it would prove to be such a contretemps."

"No. This is not about my mother or your

attempt to embarrass us. It is about your sister."

"Isobel!" Andrew looked at him sharply. "You're never telling me Isobel wishes me to leave."

"Surely you know her better than that. She loves you, and she feels that she has failed you, given the man you have turned out to be." Andrew's eyes flashed, but he said nothing, and Jack went on in the same cool, inflexible voice. "Perhaps your hope that evening was to show Isobel what a mistake she had made in marrying me. Or perhaps you did not think at all about the effect it would have on your sister; that would be typical of you. But the fact remains that you caused her a great deal of distress."

"Why should Isobel be distressed because your mother cannot hold her liquor?"

"Your pettiness shamed her. You embarrassed a guest in her house, and she feels responsible. It is a harsh blow to someone who loves as deeply as Isobel to find that the person she loves is not worthy of it."

"As if you are!"

"I don't claim to be worthy of Isobel. I am, however, able to protect her. And that is what I am doing."

"She doesn't need to be protected from me. I would never hurt Izzy."

"No? You already have many times over. Do you think it did not cause her pain to see you waste your life drinking and gambling? That it did not hurt when you were too busy carousing in London to come home to visit the women who loved you? You did not spare a single thought for them when you threw away their home!"

"Isobel managed to keep Baillannan, didn't she?" Andrew said sulkily, turning away.

"By offering herself to a stranger! Good God, man, your selfishness is beyond belief. You have been blessed with everything a man could wish for, not least a family who loved you and raised you with tenderness and care. And you threw it away." Jack stopped, drawing a deep breath. "I saw Isobel when you returned to Baillannan yesterday. She looked at you, not with joy, but with worry and unease. I understand that you dislike me, and frankly I don't care. But when you attack me in whatever juvenile way you concoct, it wounds Isobel. I refuse to allow you to do that."

"So you are her great protector," Andrew sneered. "Her knight in shining armor."

"I am her husband." Jack's voice was cold and filled with finality.

"Does Isobel know about this? Is she

aware that you are throwing her flesh and blood out of his home?"

"No. And she will not know. *You* will not tell her." Jack came forward, looming over Andrew. "I do not wish Isobel to be distressed. You will tell her you have decided to return to London. She will not be surprised. Take a few days playing at finding your treasure if you wish. But within a week, I want you gone."

"How am I supposed to live?"

"I understand that you still hold a fund whose income should be enough to sustain you."

"A pittance."

"As long as you do not lose your principal, it will be quite adequate. In addition, I will see to it that you receive a monthly stipend." Jack held up a warning finger. "That stipend will stop the instant you write to Isobel, begging her for money or describing your woes. It will stop if you go to her whining that I have tossed you out. You will visit Baillannan once a year — two if you choose — to visit your aunt and sister. If you do not, that will stop the money as well."

"I am sure Isobel would be pleased to know you are managing her life for her."

"Isobel is well capable of managing her own life and most of ours as well, and I am

488

sure she will continue to do so. But I intend to make sure that she is not made unhappy over you. I will not let you place her in a position where she is torn between her brother and her husband. Do you understand?"

"Of course I do. I'm not dim."

"And do you agree to my conditions?"

"Yes, damn you. Yes." Andrew whirled away. He stalked to the door, then turned his head back to look at Jack. "Cousin Robert was right about you."

"Mm. No doubt he was right about you as well." Jack watched coolly as Andrew stomped out the door.

Jack dismounted and tossed the reins to a groom. Andrew's return to the house had spurred him to resume his rides. Isobel had, predictably, fussed, but even she had to agree that he could not live his entire life without venturing outside. He had ridden out for the first time today, and he had felt exposed, like a bug on a stone wall, uneasily aware of the hills and rocks around him, where any number of attackers could be hiding. He had made himself keep to a canter, neither glancing over his shoulder or shortening the length of his ride. He was determined to make it clear that he was not a man to be frightened away.

Still, he admitted, at least to himself, that he let out a sigh of relief when Pharaoh trotted back into the stable yard. Jack went inside, where he was disappointed to find that Isobel was not at home, and neither his mother nor Elizabeth had any idea where she had gone. He wriggled out of an invitation to sit and converse with them, instead making his way to the office.

It was foolish, he told himself, to feel vaguely aggrieved that Isobel had gone off without him. After all, it was not as if she had to live in his pocket all the time. They were adults; they had separate lives. That they had been in each other's company almost constantly the last couple of weeks did not mean they would continue to do so. Still, he could not help but wonder where she had gone and why she had taken off the first moment he'd left the house.

When he stepped inside the study, he saw the folded, sealed piece of paper on the desk, his name printed in large letters across the front. Curious, he slipped his finger beneath the seal, breaking it, and unfolded the note. There in Isobel's elegant hand was written:

Dear Jack,

I have gone to the castle. I await your arrival. Pray do not tarry. I can say no more, but I think you will not be displeased.

All my love,
Isobel

He read the missive again, a faint smile hovering on his lips, and his thumb ran over her closing words: "All my love." She had never said such a thing to him before, had she? What could she have arranged at the castle? He spent a pleasant moment envisioning the surprise; then, tucking the note into his pocket, he started out the door.

Hamish was lurking about, as he always seemed to be these days. "Coat, sir?"

"I think not. It's too fine a day."

"Indeed. And where might you be going on such a lovely day?"

"You have become oddly curious about my habits." Jack gave him a quizzical look.

"Sir." Hamish stiffened. "I thought Mrs. Kensington might inquire of me about your whereabouts. Of course, if you do not wish me to know . . ."

"No, no. No need to prune up on me." As little as Hamish seemed a butler in other ways, he possessed a butler's unerring ability to convey wounded feelings. "Should my

491

mother ask, tell her that I have gone to the castle to meet the other Mrs. Kensington."

"Ah, Miss Isobel." The butler's face cleared. "Very good, sir."

Jack strode along the path to the castle, his steps quickening as he neared it. Isobel had spoken of taking a cold lunch to the castle one day, and he pictured her now, spreading out a blanket to arrange a picnic. He smiled, thinking that he could come up with more entertaining uses for a blanket.

The path emerged from the trees, and ahead of him the remaining walls and columns rose from the ground like old, bleached bones. He stopped, glancing around in bafflement. There was no sign of either blanket or Isobel. The place appeared quite deserted.

He strolled forward at a slower pace until he reached the edge of the foundation. He turned to look out across the green expanse of grass where the castle floor had collapsed. Rubble filled one end, timbers sticking out into empty space. A beam stretched out over the hole, and at the splintered end of it, a patch of color fluttered. Jack strode forward, fear suddenly clutching at his vitals.

He had wanted to go explore the ruins, even talked of climbing down into the cellars. Surely the surprise Isobel had mentioned would not be such an expedition. She could not have ventured —

His thoughts broke off as the colorful scrap resolved into a recognizable object — Isobel's light-red shawl was caught on the edge of the ruins.

"Isobel!"

He charged forward, his heart thundering in panic, and threw himself down at the edge of the gaping hole. He peered over the edge, relief flooding him when he saw no sign of Isobel in the rubble beneath him. In that moment he felt the ground beneath him shift, the edge crumbling away beneath his hands.

Frantically, he twisted around, grabbing for purchase and encountering nothing but slippery grass and stone slick with lichen. With a loud groan and crack, a timber gave way beneath him, and he felt himself slipping inevitably down. His grasping fingers found the timber as he fell, and for a moment he swung there, pain throbbing through his shoulder.

Trap! It had been a trap. Then, as his fingers slipped down the rough wood, sliced by splinters, and he fell into emptiness, the full reality of the betrayal shot through him. Isobel had lured him to his death.

29

Isobel returned from Meg's, her heart light in her chest. Jack had returned from his ride unscathed; Coll had met her as she walked up from the loch and reported that he had seen nothing unusual in his long-distance surveillance of Jack's ride.

"Miss Isobel!" Hamish appeared at the end of the hall. "Are ye back already, then?"

"Yes. Meg sent Aunt Elizabeth more tonic." Divesting herself of her bonnet and gloves, Isobel extended the bottle to him. "Put it in the stillroom for me, would you?"

"Meg? No, I meant the castle. Are ye back from the castle?"

"The castle!" Isobel smiled. "No. Why would you think that?" She turned away. "Where is Jack?"

"At the castle, miss." Hamish stared at her in confusion. "He's gone to meet you."

"What? Why would he — Are you sure?"

"Of course I'm sure." Hamish scowled.

"It was himself who told me. I asked where he was going when he started out the door, just like you told me, and he said he was going to meet you at the castle, if his ma should ask."

"Did you send a servant to follow him?" Isobel's voice rose.

"No, miss. He was going to meet you. I thought there was no need."

Terror speared through her, and Isobel whipped around, calling over her shoulder, "Send for Coll. Immediately! Tell him to come to the castle."

Not waiting for the butler's response, she ran out the door and down the path. At the castle she was met with a silent, empty tableau. Sucking in air, trembling all over from exertion and fear, she turned this way and that, looking for Jack. He was nowhere to be seen. Shadows from the tall trees were already stretching across the ground. It would be dusk before long. She wished she had thought to bring a lantern with her.

Her breath stopped when she caught sight of her shawl draped over one of the broken timbers, and for an instant she could not move.

"Jack!" Her voice came out as a croak, and she tried again, shouting as she ran toward the gaily fluttering shawl, "Jack! Are

495

you here? Jack!"

Tears were streaming down her face by the time she reached the edge of the hole. The yawning pit was larger than before; clearly another section had fallen in. "Jack! Where are you? Please, please, answer me." Tears choked her voice, and she could not hold back the sobs as she sank to her knees, edging forward to peer over the edge. "Jack!"

"Isobel?" A figure stepped into view, covered with dirt and stone dust, and Jack turned his face up to her.

"Jack!" She began to laugh and cry all at once. "Thank God! Oh, thank God. Jack." Her hand slipped, and suddenly the ground before her crumbled. She plunged downward.

"Isobel!" Jack lunged forward, arms outstretched, and Isobel slammed into him, knocking him over and sending them both to the ground. His breath went out of him with an oomph, and for a moment they lay there, stunned, struggling for air.

Isobel was the first to move, pushing up to her knees. "What are you doing here? Why did you come to the castle — why are you grinning at me like that?"

"From relief." He laughed, sitting up and pulling her into his arms, squeezing her to him so tightly she could hardly breathe. "I thought — God, Isobel, I thought you wanted me dead."

"What!" She jerked back from him, her face flaming with fury. Sweeping the tears from her cheeks, she exploded, "Here I am, thinking you were dead — and you assume I tried to kill you! How could you think such a thing of me? Do you think I shot you as well?"

Isobel scrambled to her feet, her fists clenched. Jack followed quickly, reaching out to take her arms. "No! Never. I mean, not until a few minutes ago. You think I wanted to believe it? But you wrote me a note, asking me to meet you here. And there was your shawl, hanging there. I ran to the edge, thinking you had fallen in. I realized, too late, that this had been planned. It was your hand! I've just spent a hellish hour thinking you wanted me dead."

"It couldn't have been my hand. I didn't write you a note."

He reached inside his jacket and pulled out a folded piece of paper, extending it to her.

"Jack, your hands!" Isobel took his hands, turning them palms up. "They're scraped raw."

"I've had time to pick out the splinters,"

he said wryly. "I thought of wrapping my handkerchief around one, but I fear it is as dirty as the rest of me. Here, don't cry again."

"I'm not crying," she said disdainfully, then sniffed and wiped at her cheeks. "I am just so . . . so *furious.*"

"I know." He bent to press his lips against her forehead. "Read the note."

Isobel unfolded the paper and held it up to the narrow strand of light slanting in through the ruined ceiling. She scanned the words, her stomach turning to ice, and she sank to the floor, her knees suddenly too weak for her to stand. Her voice was barely above a whisper. "It is very like my writing."

"I know. I've seen enough of your ledgers to recognize it."

"I did not write it." She could not bear to say the rest of her thought — how few people would be able to copy her writing.

"I know you did not." Jack squatted down beside her, taking the note from her nerveless fingers and sticking it back into his pocket. "No doubt anyone with access to the house could have looked at your ledgers, too."

"No doubt. Oh, Jack!" She threw her arms

around his neck, burying her face in his chest.

"It's all right. It's over." His arms were tight around her. "No need to worry now."

"There is a need. There is a need until you are safe."

Isobel clung to him, unable to utter the thoughts and fears tumbling about in her head, as the shadows gathered above them.

Suddenly a voice sounded in the distance. "Isobel? Where are you?"

Jack stiffened, but Isobel sprang to her feet. "Coll! We're down here! Be careful! It caved in, but we are all right."

"You're not hurt?" The voice sounded much closer now, and in a moment Coll peered over the side of the hole, haloed by light. When he saw them, he grinned and held the lantern out to illuminate the area beneath him. "You look like a couple of ghosts, all that white dust on you."

"I am sorry we are not presentable enough for you," Isobel retorted tartly, and Coll chuckled. "Now, do you suppose you could get us out of here?"

"I'd like to, but I came running when Hamish found me. I didn't think to bring a rope. I'll get one, and a lad or two to help pull you up. Here — just a minute." He stood up and was gone for a few minutes, returning with a broken-off branch, from which most of the smaller stems had been stripped. Hooking the lantern over one remaining stem, he lowered it to them. "At least you'll not be in the dark the whole time." He stood up. "And, Izzy, try not to pull the rest of it down on your head while I'm gone."

Isobel muttered something beneath her breath and turned to Jack. He stood watching her, the lantern he had retrieved from Coll in his hand.

"I think I am beginning to believe that Munro does think of you as a sister." Jack smiled and took her hand. "I want to show you something. I've been poking around a bit."

"You decided to go exploring?" Isobel asked in astonishment as she followed him.

"I didn't see much point in sitting about waiting to starve to death. Or for someone to come put a bullet in me again. I hoped I might be able to find another way out. And I did find something. I think when the timbers and stones gave way beneath me, it knocked a hole through a wall behind them."

He held up the lantern, illuminating a partially collapsed wall. Behind it, crude stone steps stretched downward.

"Another secret staircase?"

"Your ancestors were obviously enamored of the idea. I don't know if it was secret; there's not enough wall left to be certain. The stairs were half hidden by timbers, but I shoved them aside enough to see down into it. There is a subcellar beneath this one."

"The dungeons?" Isobel's eyes widened. "You're thinking this is where the tunnel might have come out?"

"You said yourself that the castle was as likely a destination as any. I would have explored it, but it was black as pitch down there."

"We have light now."

With a conspiratorial grin, Jack started down the steps. Uneven and rough, these stairs were little more than graduated blocks, with barely half a flight of them, ending in a long, narrow room. What had once been rows of large barrels lined one wall, a few still intact. At the far end of the room was a short wooden door.

Jack tugged at the rusted iron ring halfway down the door. At first, the door would not budge, but then, with a loud scrape, it lurched open a few inches. Keeping a cautious eye on the wall and ceiling around it, Jack pulled at the ancient door until the space was wide enough to slide through.

He almost stumbled, but recovered and went down the three steps onto the lower floor. They were now in a larger vaulted chamber, empty but for a few bits of wood, iron, and leather and a wheelbarrow with a cracked wheel that listed against one wall.

"Well" — Jack surveyed the room — "no tunnel and no more doors."

"I'm not so sure." Isobel pointed to a strip of decorative stone that ran at eye level across the opposite wall. Taking the lantern, she went to the strip and held the light up to it. Carved into the stone every few feet were rosettes. "Look."

"Roses. Just like the fireplace." They paced beside the wall, peering at each stone flower, all thoughts of murder attempts and collapsing ceilings fleeing their heads.

"Jack." Isobel pointed to the small, cylindrical hole in the center of one of the flowers.

He pulled out the watch key, inserted it into the hole, and began to turn. With a click and a thud, part of the wall separated a fraction of an inch. Digging their fingers into the crack, they tugged it open, releasing a scent of dank, dusty air. Jack held up the lantern, revealing the chamber inside. The room was simply but almost elegantly furnished, with tapestries and even a mirror hanging on the walls, giving it a cozy, lived-in appearance.

The pleasant scene was spoiled, however, by the skeleton stretched out in the middle of the floor.

He lay on his face, one arm stretched out and the other bent back to the scabbard at his waist. He was clad in the Rose tartan, buckled with an empty sword belt. And rising from his back, wedged between the ribs, was a long, thin dirk.

Isobel sucked in her breath. "Oh, my God. *Malcolm.*"

30

"Are you certain?" Jack asked.

"Look at the dirk in his scabbard. It has the Rose symbol on the hilt; Malcolm is wearing it in the portrait at Baillannan. You've seen it. Over there, leaning against the wall — I dare swear that is the same claymore he is holding in the picture. He is the right size and he's wearing our tartan. Obviously he knew about this place and how to get in. We can take the ring on his finger and show it to Aunt Elizabeth to be certain. But I know it is he."

"So he never left Baillannan."

"No. The Redcoats must have seen him and followed him into the castle."

"Yes. Or perhaps common thieves." Jack pointed to a small, ornate coffer sitting beside the bed, lid open and empty. "They stabbed him. Took the money from the chest and fled — odd that they did not take the ring as well."

"It would have implicated them in his murder if they were found with it," Isobel pointed out.

"Yes, perhaps that is it. Well . . . Andrew and Gregory will be disappointed to find the treasure has been stolen."

"No doubt." Isobel stepped into the room, feeling as if she were trespassing on sacred ground. "I suppose this was where he hid from the soldiers." She walked over to the chest of drawers, where a washbowl and a pitcher stood. Beside them were two decorative combs such as women wore in their hair. "How sad. Perhaps this was their 'spot,' the one he mentioned in the letter to my grandmother."

"Then she knew about this room all along? About the key? Your aunt is right; the Rose family is indeed tight-mouthed if she never told her son or daughter." Jack paused. "But if she came to meet him and found his body like this, surely she would not have left her husband lying there."

"It could have happened after she left." Isobel frowned. "Though when he never showed up after that, one would think she would have come down here to see if she could find a clue, at least, of what had happened to him."

"He might have had the only key and she

entered it only with him. But, no — any watch key this size would fit, as we've proved."

"I think he kept this secret from everyone. It would have been the best way to ensure his safety. Maybe these combs were gifts he had bought for Cordelia but he never got the chance to give them to her." Isobel sighed. "I suppose we'll never know."

"I would have thought this connected to our tunnel, but there's no other door."

"Perhaps it's hidden. Look at the inside of this door; it would look exactly like the wall when it was closed."

"Very tricky people, your ancestors." Jack glanced speculatively around the room.

At that moment, they heard the distant sound of a man shouting.

"Coll!" Isobel exclaimed, starting toward the door. "He will wonder what has happened to us. We'd best go."

"Very well. We'll come back another day and search for the tunnel." Picking up the watch key and the ring, they left the room.

"Oh!" Elizabeth drew in a quick breath as Jack extended his hand to her, the ring he had removed from the skeleton lying on his palm. She covered her mouth with her hand, tears springing into her eyes. "Papa's ring!"

"Then you recognize it? You know it was Malcolm's."

"Yes, yes, of course. Where did you find it?"

"We found him, Auntie." Isobel put her arm around her aunt's shoulders and guided her to a chair to sit.

"Found him? No, how could — Oh! You mean you found his body?"

Isobel nodded. Jack went down on one knee beside the older woman and took her hand in his. "I am sorry, Aunt Elizabeth, but we came upon a hidden room in the cellars of the castle. He was there, along with this." Jack held out the watch key to her.

"Yes." Elizabeth plucked the key from his hand. "This is the key to his pocket watch. He was killed, wasn't he? I don't know why I'm crying. I've always known he must have died or he would have returned to us. But it's hard, thinking of him lying there all those years and us up here, never knowing it." She took the ring and ran her thumb over it. "This was the crest of his mother's family. She gave it to him. I should give it to Andrew. Where is the boy?"

"Andrew went riding, Hamish said," Isobel replied. "When I see him, I shall tell him you wish to talk to him." She stood up. "If you will excuse me, I must go speak to . . . to Coll."

Jack looked at her curiously, but Isobel avoided his gaze as she slipped out the door. She did not go to find Coll as she had claimed, but strode down to the office and opened the strongbox, taking out a small purse of coins. Tucking them in her pocket, she made her way to the stables and, taking a seat on a bench, waited until her brother trotted into the yard.

"Hallo, Isobel," he said, his eyebrows shooting up in surprise. "What are you doing out here?"

"I came to see you."

Andrew dismounted, handing the reins to a groom, and they walked out into the yard. "What is it? Why do you look as if you have been rolling about in the dirt?"

"Mayhap it is because I fell into the cellars at the castle."

"What!" Andrew gaped at her. Isobel grabbed him by the arm and pulled him over to a tree, away from the stables and the house.

"Yes. Well you might stare. *I* got caught in your trap, as well. Did you not think of that or is it that you simply don't care? How could you do such a thing? I have known you since you were a babe, but you are suddenly a stranger to me."

"What are you talking about?" Andrew shifted uneasily, and whatever doubt Isobel might have had evaporated. "Do what thing?"

"You know exactly what I'm talking about. You wrote that note to Jack. Lured him to the ruins."

"I did not."

"Don't lie to me, Andrew. Your face gives you away. I always thought it meant you were too honest, too good to lie convincingly, but now I realize I must have been fooling myself all these years."

"That's a terrible thing to say!"

"It was a terrible thing to do," Isobel shot back. "Did you think I would not know? Who else but you could copy my hand that well?"

"It was just a lark. A jest."

"A lark! To set a trap for a man! What about the other times? Were they just larks, too? Was it a jest when you sent the boulder down upon him? Or shot him?"

"What! You've gone mad. I never did any of that." He faced her indignantly.

"*I've* gone mad! This isn't a joke. It isn't a lark. And you are not a child any longer.

Don't you realize that Jack could have been killed!"

"That is all you care about!" Andrew's face reddened. "He strips me of my inheritance and I come home and find that he has taken my sister from me as well! He has bewitched you. I understand that you had to marry him; I don't blame you for that."

"Well, thank you." Isobel's voice dripped sarcasm.

"But why did you slave away at his bedside when he was wounded? Why did you work so hard to nurse him back to health? Don't you understand? Everything could return to normal if he was dead."

Isobel lashed out, her hand landing against his cheek with an audible crack. "Get out!"

Andrew stared at her, openmouthed, the mark of her hand red against his skin.

"I want you to leave this house! Now."

"My house?" he asked incredulously. "You are tossing me out of my own house?"

"It is not yours. You have never loved Baillannan. You have not lived here since you were at university; the only reason you even visit is because you have spent all your money. You did not *lose* Baillannan. It was not *taken* from you. You threw it away with both hands because you were too foolish and irresponsible to be entrusted with it.

Now go!"

"Where will I go?" he asked blankly.

"I don't know. Go to Edinburgh. Go to London. It does not matter to me. But I want you to leave today. Now. You have an income from the Funds if you do not squander it away."

"But that is not enough to live on."

"It is enough to live, just not in the style you prefer. Do you not understand that Jack is bound to realize you are the one who tried to kill him? That the note must have been written by someone close enough to me to know my hand? Someone who could sneak my shawl out of the house and plant it there?"

"I didn't —"

"Stop! Just . . . stop." She held up her hand. "I do not know what Jack would do to you, and I don't want to find out. You are my brother, and God help me, I cannot see you wind up in gaol or transported. Here." She thrust the coin purse into his hand. "This is all the gold I have in the strongbox. It will get you back to the city. Now go. I cannot bear to see you. Just go."

Isobel turned and fled back to the house, tears streaming down her face.

If Jack found Andrew's sudden disappearance from the house odd, he said nothing about it. For her part, Isobel avoided the topic assiduously. Even Aunt Elizabeth barely fretted about it, for she was much more interested in the discovery they had made in the ruins of the castle. Given her certainty that the bones they had found were those of her father, Jack had them brought up with all the dignity they could manage, and Malcolm was buried beside the kirk in the family plot.

Jack and Coll spent most of the next few days deep in the task of shoring up the sub-cellar ruins to ensure safety when they started their search for the tunnel. Apparently the prospect of finding the ancient secret was enough to make them forget their disapproval of one another, and they spent most afternoons at the castle, digging in the dirt, as Isobel termed it.

The matter of Andrew and his attempts on Jack's life sat between him and Isobel. Though neither was eager to talk about it, their silence on the subject weighed upon them, bringing an unaccustomed constraint to their relationship. The night brought an end to all such awkwardness, and they came together in a passion so fervent it tasted of desperation. But come the morning, the lack of ease made its appearance again.

Fretful and restless, Isobel tried to set herself once again to the task of going through the old papers, but she could not keep her mind on the task. Guilt pricked at her; if she had only acted on her worries earlier, Jack would not have been lured to the ruins. She should have told him what she suspected; she wanted to ask him if he blamed her for not revealing her suspicions; it ate at her that she could not summon the courage to talk to him about any of it. If she told him, if she brought the subject out in the open, she feared what might happen.

However much he had let her see inside him the past few weeks, he did not like to reveal his pain. He was not one to invite discord into his life or to engage in drama. What if what she had done — or, rather, failed to do — turned him away from her? What if he decided the nights with her were not worth the turmoil?

Jack might decide that he had had enough of this life, that his bargain did not require staying at Baillannan, that London would be a far more peaceful — and safer — place to live. Isobel did not know what she would do if that happened. Despite her best intentions, she had done what she had been determined not to — she had fallen in love with her husband. Now she was not sure she could face the price she would have to pay for that mistake.

"There." Coll drove the last nail into the brace and stepped back to survey his work. "That's the last."

"You think it will hold?" Jack, who had had his shoulder to the crossbeam, holding it steady as Coll hammered, moved away, wiping the sheen of sweat from his brow.

"Oh, aye, it will hold well enough. Whether that brace is enough to keep the roof from caving in is another matter." At Jack's sharp glance, Coll laughed and shrugged. " 'Tis the best we can do, and I think it is sturdy enough. But I am a Scot, so I expect the worst."

Jack rolled his eyes. He found, strangely, that he was beginning to like Munro. The longer he was around him, the more he realized the truth of Isobel's words: the two of them were like kin. Nor could he suspect him of murder now that Coll had come to his rescue twice.

His would-be assassin was Isobel's brother, obviously. Andrew had come to mind immediately as the one most likely to be able to imitate his sister's handwriting, and Andrew's fleeing the house had confirmed Jack's suspicion.

At first he had been furious and considered hunting the man down to have it out with him. But an evening of reflection convinced him that the ticklish situation was better left this way. The man was Isobel's brother; he could do nothing to him without bringing hurt to her.

Isobel knew. She had an air of sorrow about her that Jack did not know how to breach, except at night in the warmth of their bed. She had not questioned her brother's departure — or, indeed, talked about Andrew at all — proof enough that she understood the implications of Andrew's precipitous departure. But knowing Andrew's guilt and wishing her brother to suffer for it were entirely different things; it would cause her pain for Andrew to be brought to justice. He was out of their lives, and for Isobel's sake, Jack could live with that.

"Will you be looking for the door now?" Coll asked, pulling Jack back from his thoughts. Jack turned to see the other man casting a speculative look around the walls of the room. "Do you really think there's an opening here?"

"I am almost certain of it. Somewhere in here, there is a little hole and a fine line through the mortar between the stones."

Coll wandered closer to the wall. "We might cast our eyes about a wee bit before we leave."

Jack chuckled. "It's tempting, but Isobel will have my head if I sneak a glance into the tunnel without her here."

"You are right about that." Coll sighed.

"However, there's nothing to say I could not go to the house and ask her to join us." Jack rolled down his sleeves and grabbed his jacket. "There is time before tea, after all."

Coll grinned. "True. There is a place or two above I can work on while you're gone." He bent and picked up his tools, following Jack out of the room.

Jack left him shifting the debris and climbed the rope ladder to the surface. Dusting himself off as best he could, he shrugged into his jacket and turned toward the house. To his surprise, Robert Rose was sitting on the remains of one of the stone walls. As Jack walked toward him, the man stood up, giving him a stiff nod.

"Mr. Rose."

"Mr. Kensington." Robert cleared his throat. "I have come about a . . . a matter of some delicacy. A family matter, actually."

"Very well." Jack's curiosity rose.

"I am not one to go against my own, but

in this case, I believe it is my duty to do so."

"Yes?" Jack said when the other man did not go on.

"The fact is — I am aware of my cousin's whereabouts. I am here to take you to him."

"Andrew?" Jack asked, surprised. "He is still here?"

"Yes. That is what I am saying. He came to me for help, you see, when Isobel tossed him out."

"Isobel tossed him out?"

"Yes." Robert frowned at him. "You do realize what he did, don't you?"

"Yes, of course. I just did not realize . . ." Jack pushed aside the warm feeling the thought engendered in him; that was something he would consider later, at his leisure. "That's not important now. Why have you come to me?"

The older man blinked. "Why? Well, I — Don't you want to find him? He tried to kill you."

"Much as I would enjoy the thought of thrashing Andrew, I cannot see that it would serve any purpose. I cannot think of anything to do with him that would not grieve Isobel. Tell him to go; I won't pursue him. I won't go to the authorities. I will not even spread it about London that he is a would-be murderer. I just want him gone from my life and Isobel's." Jack swung on his heel and started toward the house, leaving Robert staring after him.

"Wait!"

Jack turned around. Robert was hurrying after him down the path, his face filled with alarm.

"You don't understand." Robert came to a halt in front of Jack, pulling out his handkerchief and dabbing at the sweat on his upper lip. "He will not go. That is what I am trying to tell you. I advised him to leave the country, to go to America or India and make a new life for himself, but he refused. I even offered to give him the money to do so. He will not go. He —" Robert drew a deep breath. "He is determined to kill you."

"What?" Jack stared. "When everyone will know he is the one who did it?"

"He is not rational, I tell you. He has an obsession, an *idée fixe,* that if you were dead, all his problems would be over. That is why I had to tell you despite my blood tie to the lad. I could not in good conscience allow him to commit murder. He is hiding in the caves, plotting his revenge. I can take you there; perhaps between the two of us we can make him see reason. And if not . . ." Robert squared his shoulders. "Well, if not, we will simply have to take him to the magistrate."

"The devil!" Jack cast a regretful look toward the house. "Oh, very well."

"Come, we should hurry." Robert started purposefully away from the house.

"Wait. I should tell Coll."

"Coll? Why?" Robert scowled. "This is a family matter. We don't need that interloper. And we cannot wait. I don't know how long Andrew will remain there. If we miss him, we won't know where he is." Robert took Jack's arm, and he seemed so agitated that Jack gave in, letting him steer him toward the cliff.

Jack followed Robert down the path that led in an easy manner around the highest point, then down to the seashore. They strode along a narrow beach between the rocks and the sea, and after several minutes, Robert turned right, skirted a large rock, and Jack saw a yawning hole in the cliff before them. Jack had to duck down to enter the mouth of the cave, but once inside, he was able to stand up straight. It was dim, the only light coming in through the cave opening, but Robert picked up a lantern by the entrance and lit it.

"Do people come here frequently?" Jack asked.

Robert turned, holding a finger to his lips, and pointed back into the cave. Jack trailed after him across the damp floor. The path rose, then flattened out, going through a long, narrow passage before opening up into a large vaulted cave. Columns rose from the ground and seemed to drip from the ceiling, highlighted eerily by the circle of light from the lantern. Robert set down the lantern, motioning silently for Jack to stop, then went quietly ahead by himself, disappearing into another opening on their right.

Jack waited, glancing around him with interest. They seemed to be in some sort of central chamber, and he could see two other tunnels branching off ahead besides the smaller opening Robert had entered. He would have to come back with Isobel and explore the place. Jack was gazing back the way they had come when the scrape of a boot drew his attention, and he turned around.

Robert had returned and was standing a few feet on the other side of the lantern. In his hand he held a pistol pointed straight at Jack's heart.

31

Isobel stood at the window of the sitting room. In the distance, above the trees, she could see the top of the single stone wall still standing at the castle. She wished she had gone with Jack and Coll to the ruins this morning. She certainly was not getting anything done here.

Her aunt and Millicent were rummaging through one of the chests Isobel had brought down from the attic. Since the discovery of her father's body, Elizabeth had taken to looking through everything she could find that might pertain to her father and his demise. She had found nothing, but she had not given up, and she was now deep into a trunk of Isobel's father. Isobel had tried to enter into the project, but she had soon lost interest.

"Oh! This box!" Isobel turned back at her aunt's pleased exclamation and saw Elizabeth pulling a rectangular wooden box from the trunk. "Isobel, look."

"I remember that." Isobel walked over and sat down beside Elizabeth. "It used to sit on Papa's desk. It was lovely."

The top of the dark mahogany box was inlaid with a rose done in pieces of paler wood. Elizabeth opened the box, but it was empty, and she closed it. Smoothing her hand across the design, her voice soft with nostalgia, Elizabeth said, "It was my mother's. John and I loved it when we were little; she would never let us touch it. It was a wedding present, I think from her sister."

"She and Malcolm must have loved each other very much," Isobel said. "You could tell that in the note he wrote her, even though it was brief."

"No doubt. I don't remember how they were together; I was so young and I never thought about things like that. But she felt it deeply, I'm sure; she would never talk about him or his death. It was too painful. Sometimes I would see her sitting in front of the fire, just staring into it and turning her wedding ring on her finger, over and over."

"What a lovely inlay." Millicent leaned closer to admire it, and Elizabeth handed her the box. "Oh!" Millicent's eyes widened in surprise. "It's heavier than it looks." She trailed her fingers over the pieces of wood fitted together. "It reminds me of one Jack's father had. It had an inlay of wooden pieces — angel's wings, they were. His was not nearly so fine, of course, just a cheap sort of thing. But it was clever. It had a secret bottom."

"Really?" Intrigued, Isobel leaned over. "How did it work?"

"I'm not sure I remember." Millicent handed the box to Isobel. "Sutton's little chest was heavier than it looked, too. That is what made me think of it. It was because of the extra compartment that one couldn't see."

"What if this one does, too?" Elizabeth's eyes sparkled. "Perhaps that was why Mother never let us touch it."

"Do you think it might?" Millicent looked intrigued, and she tilted her head to the side, thinking. "Now, what was it that made it open? Sutton never would tell me how it worked, but Jack figured it out, the clever boy. There was a little pin that released a spring. Let me think. Oh! One of the pieces lifted out. You pushed it aside a tiny bit and you could pop it out. Then he slid something to one side."

"We'll have to see if Jack can open this one." Isobel ran her forefinger over the inlay.

"If this one had a hidden drawer, I would think Grandmother would have saved that note in here instead of sewing it into her Bible."

She stopped. The faintest bit of roughness was at the edge of one of the petals of the rose. Leaning closer, she used her fingernail and discovered that the piece seemed just the faintest bit loose. Remembering what Jack had done when they were searching her grandmother's room, Isobel took a pin from her hair, carefully inserting it into the crack. She gave a little twist of her wrist, and the petal popped out.

Elizabeth gasped, and Millicent exclaimed, "Look at that!"

Isobel pushed and pulled, twisted and turned, and finally the center of the rose slid over into the empty space of the petal. A pin popped up, released by the movement, and something clicked in the bottom of the box. Isobel tugged and the bottom slid out, revealing a folded piece of paper.

"Isobel!" Aunt Elizabeth breathed. "What have you found?"

"I don't know." Isobel picked up the piece of paper. Below it, resting on the velvet-lined bottom of the drawer, was a watch key. She looked up at her aunt, who was staring back at her, stunned.

"It's just like the key you found in the cellars!" Millicent cried.

"Not exactly, but I'll warrant it fits just the same."

"Then Mother did have a key to the stairs. Why did she never say anything?"

Isobel shook her head, filled with foreboding. "And why did she never use it on the door in the cellar?"

"Perhaps she did not know one could get into the cellars that way," Elizabeth suggested. "She might have only known about the stairs."

Isobel opened the long paper. This was a more formal piece of writing than the note she had found in Cordelia's Bible. The lines were straight, the writing slow and careful.

"It's dated just a few days after Culloden," Isobel said, her eyes dropping first to the bottom of the page, where a signature slanted across the page. "And it's signed Fergus Rose."

"Who?" Millicent asked, confused.

"Cousin Robert's father. Malcolm's brother," Elizabeth explained. "Tell us what it says, Isobel."

Isobel stared at the page, hardly able to take it in. When her aunt said her name again, Isobel replied, "It's a confession." She swallowed and began to read aloud,

" 'I, Fergus Alan Rose, on this day did conspire to end the life of my brother, Malcolm Dennis Rose, Laird of Baillannan —' "

"What!" Elizabeth clapped her hand to her mouth, her eyes huge. "My uncle killed Papa?"

"That is not the worst of it." Isobel stared at Elizabeth in consternation. "It goes on to say: '. . . aided and abetted in this endeavor by Cordelia Fleming Rose, wife of Malcolm. Having agreed upon this course of action with my sister by marriage, I followed my brother to his assignation with the harlot, and there, in concert with Cordelia Rose, I did take his life with my blade.' "

Isobel dropped the letter into her lap and stared at her aunt, unable to form a coherent thought.

"The harlot?" Millicent asked, wrinkling her brow. "Who is that?"

"I have no idea. 'His assignation with the harlot.' He couldn't have meant Malcolm's wife. Malcolm must have had a —" Isobel sent an apologetic look to her aunt. "He must have had a mistress." She stopped, struck by a thought. "That note wasn't sent to his wife! That was a letter to another woman, telling her to meet him at 'their place.' No doubt the cellars."

"But why did Mother have it?"

"I don't know. But she must have found it, intercepted it, something."

"That was why she killed him," Elizabeth said flatly. "That was how they knew he had a tryst."

"She killed him out of jealousy," Millicent said.

"Uncle Fergus killed him from jealousy, as well. He was always a bitter, mean man. He resented the fact that your father, Isobel, inherited Baillannan and all that went with it. I know it from little comments he would make about only the oldest son inheriting. He would have felt the same way about my father." Elizabeth sighed. "Sad to say, I am not surprised to learn he killed my father."

"Auntie, I am so sorry." Isobel reached out to take Elizabeth's hand.

"You have done nothing to be sorry about." Elizabeth was pale, but she no longer looked as if she might faint. "No wonder Mother never wanted to talk about him. She hated him."

"And loved him, too," Millicent put in sadly. " 'Tis easy enough to do both."

"What will Robert say?" Elizabeth shook her head. "He will be appalled. With all his insistence on honor and duty and the family name, and now he finds out his father killed his own brother?"

"I wonder if perhaps he does not already know it," Isobel mused.

"You think he's known all these years? Surely his father did not tell him."

"I don't know, any more than I know why his father would have written down such an admission. No one knew; they had gotten away with it. Yet he wrote a confession and gave it to my grandmother."

"It is odd. It gave her a great deal of power over him," Millicent mused.

"Yes, but she could not use it without revealing her own involvement," Isobel said.

"Perhaps that was the point." Elizabeth paused, organizing her thoughts. "Mother and Uncle Fergus did not get along well. She tolerated him and he, her, but they were never more than civil to one another. I — I loved my mother; you must understand that she loved John and me, and she was never cruel or hurt us. But she was not an easy person; she was . . . indomitable. And she was clever. I can think of no nicer way to put it: she was cunning. Fergus was much the same, at least in regard to his cunning. I do not think that they trusted each other. They might have allied themselves in this one thing, but they would be suspicious that the other might betray them."

"You think this confession was meant to be a way to keep them both in line?" Isobel offered. "It makes sense. Neither of them could accuse the other of murdering Malcolm without ensuring his or her own downfall as well."

"But why did your mother not sign it, too, Elizabeth?" Millicent asked.

"I don't know. I would have thought Uncle Fergus would have demanded it."

"What if she signed one as well?" Isobel asked. "One that Fergus would hold over her head just as she held this over his."

"A perfect stalemate."

"Is that why you said you thought your cousin already knew about this?"

"No, I hadn't thought of that when I said it. It was just — I could not help but think of how Cousin Robert was when I was clearing out the attic. He was willing to take all those things in the attic, not only his father's things, but other trunks as well. He even came over to help me go through them one day. He spent all his time in the attic opening trunks and glancing through them, then moving on to something else. I thought it was just because he did not want to be bothered with anything that did not interest him, but maybe he was searching for this."

Isobel waggled the confession in the air.

"He was most odd about Mother's room, wasn't he?" Elizabeth added, frowning.

"Yes, he offered to help me clean it. He was very keen."

"I remember. He claimed he was fond of Mother. I knew that was a lie, but I thought he was pretending to feel the proper thing."

"What if he was the one who searched Cordelia's room?"

"What? When? What are you talking about?" Elizabeth looked uncertain. "I don't remember that."

"No, I did not tell you. I'm sorry. But it hardly seemed worth mentioning. It didn't appear that anything was missing. But after the wedding, when I went into Grand-mother's room, I was certain someone had gone through it. That was why Jack and I searched her room and found that note from Malcolm."

"So while Robert was here for the wed-ding, he sneaked in and looked through the room?"

"I don't know, but it is certainly possible. He would have had ample time and every-one was down at the barn. It would have been easy to have gone undetected. And before that . . ." Isobel straightened, her voice speeding up a bit. "One night Jack was sure someone had tried to get into the house. He chased them, but they were gone by the time he got down there. He thought it was Coll, which I knew was ridiculous, but I was afraid he would start investigating the men — you know, the ones fighting the Clearances."

"Oh!" Elizabeth brightened. "You're talking about the night the spirits were on the island. I remember that."

"Yes. Exactly." Isobel jumped to her feet, thrusting the confession into her aunt's hands. "I must tell Jack about this."

"That is a good idea," Millicent agreed, nodding happily. "Jack always knows just what to do."

Relieved, Isobel sped down the stairs and out the front door, not even bothering to grab her bonnet or gloves. She ran the whole way to the castle, and she could not help but remember the day last week when she had run this same path, filled with fear for Jack. The thought gave her a cold feeling deep in the pit of her stomach. Just as she reached the ruins, Coll climbed out of the ruins.

"Isobel!" he said, startled. "Where is Jack?"

"I thought he was here. What do you mean?"

"No, he went to fetch you. We finished the shoring up, and we were thinking of searching for the entrance to the tunnel." Coll grinned. "Interested?"

"Yes, but, no, not now. You said he 'went to fetch' me?"

"He left to get you, but then I heard him talking to someone out here. I was curious; I thought I heard him mention Andrew. So I thought — well, I knew you wouldn't like it if Jack took off after Andrew. So I stuck my head up to see what was going on. And he was walking off with your cousin — the colonel, not Gregory."

"Cousin Robert?" Isobel stared at him.

"Yes. Why are you looking at me like that?"

"They were talking about Andrew?"

"I think so. What is it, Izzy? They won't get into a brawl if Mr. Rose is with them, surely."

"I don't know." Isobel took a step back. Everything inside her was humming with warning. "Where did they go? Did you see?"

"They headed over there." Coll pointed. "They were headed for the caves, I assume. Isobel, what is going on? What are you afraid of?"

"I don't know! It makes no sense. But it seems like such a coincidence — we found out that Robert's father killed Malcolm."

"Fergus? His brother?" Coll stared at her, slack-jawed.

"Yes — Oh, I haven't time to get into it now. But I feel — something is wrong, Coll. I can't think why Cousin Robert would have tried to hurt Jack, but —"

"We shouldn't be standing about here talking, then. Come on. I know the caves like the back of my hand. I can take you in the back way and get you out to the shore in half the time it'd take them." He whirled and started running toward the cliff, with Isobel right behind.

"It was you?" Jack regarded Robert Rose in astonishment. "You were the one trying to kill me? You wrote the note? You shot at me?"

"Well, no, that fool Andrew wrote that for me. He was happy to play a trick on you — he likes to pretend that he did not know what the result of his prank would be, but we all know he'd be glad enough to see you dead. And he is bird-witted enough not to realize he would be found out immediately. But the rest of it — the planning, the preparation, the rockslide — that was all me. I was always something of a marksman."

"Good God."

"You did not suspect that, did you?" Robert smiled smugly. "You southerners. London dandies. Think you know everything. Some old Scotsman could never get the best of you, could he?"

"You think I should be impressed that you are a killer?"

"I am a soldier!" Rose retorted. "And a soldier does whatever is necessary to protect his home."

"How the devil are you protecting your home?" Jack had little interest in conversing with this madman, but he knew his best hope was to keep the braggart telling his story. Perhaps if Robert talked enough, Jack could manage to distract him — or think of something, anything, that would give him an advantage. "It isn't as if I invaded."

"That is exactly what you did! You invaded Baillannan. You changed everything. You stole the Rose land. And you had the audacity to marry my cousin!"

"You want to kill me because I married into your family?"

"No, you fool." Robert shook the gun at Jack for emphasis, and for a moment Jack thought that he was done, but Robert did not fire. "I killed you so that Isobel would be free."

"Did you ask Isobel if she wanted to be free?"

"Her. She doesn't know what she wants. Like all females, she's distracted by a handsome face. At first I was furious, but then I realized — she had done what she had to do, what a true Rose should do, to keep Baillannan. She's a silly lass, but she knows her duty, unlike her brother. I saw that my plans were not ruined. I could still bring it about. If you were dead, she would inherit the land. And she would be free to marry my son."

"Gregory is in favor of this scheme?"

"Gregory?" Robert chuckled. "You think he knows anything of this? He would be of less use than Andrew. At least Andrew resents you. Gregory cannot even see that you spoiled his chances."

"Does he want to marry Isobel? I never had the impression that he thought of her that way."

Robert said dismissively, "He is my son, and he will do as I tell him."

"Has it not occurred to you that you could rid Isobel of me and she might not agree to marry Gregory?"

"That won't happen."

"Mr. Rose, I don't think you've thought this matter through," Jack said in an amiable tone, moving a step closer and leaning in toward him, his hands spread out, palms up.

"Do you think to mock me?" The older man's face reddened.

"No, indeed not. But I must point out that Andrew knows you persuaded him to write that note. At some time he will realize that it is in his best interest to tell everyone that. Also, it will be a trifle difficult for you to explain how I left with you and wound up dead in this cave."

"Who is to know that you were with me?"

"Coll Munro, for one. He was working with me at the ruins, you know. He would have heard us." In fact, Jack had little faith that Munro had been close enough to hear them, let alone identify whom Jack had been talking to, but Jack had mastered lying long ago.

His words obviously rocked Robert for a moment, but the old man recovered quickly. "It doesn't matter. No one would take Munro's word over mine. Even he would never think I killed you. He'll believe it was Andrew, too. They all will. I shall just say Andrew surprised us, and before I could do anything, he shot you."

"You think Andrew will go along with this? He may have fled town, but they will find him. He isn't one to cover his tracks."

"He won't need to." Robert smiled. "You see, sadly, I will be duty-bound to try to stop his attempt to murder you, and he and this gun will be found on the shore, among the rocks."

"You plan to kill your own cousin? For this scheme of yours?"

"I did not set out to, but you have the very luck of the devil. I had to enlist Andrew's help, and I know full well he is a weak reed. He could never keep his mouth closed about it. Thank God he ran, practically admitting his guilt. Even better, he ran to me for help. I didn't lie about Andrew being here, you know. He is in the cave behind us, though he's in no position to move at the moment."

"He's here?" Jack looked beyond Robert, and what he saw there almost stopped his heart.

Isobel was creeping down one of the tunnels toward them, Coll Munro beside her.

"What do you mean Andrew's here?" Jack raised his voice, taking a long step forward.

"Stop!" Robert shouted, and shook the pistol at Jack again. "Stop right there or I will shoot you."

"What difference does it make? You are going to shoot me anyway. Besides" — Jack smiled derisively, casting a pointed look at the older man's hand — "you are trembling like a leaf. You haven't the nerve to kill me."

"Of course I will," Robert blustered, putting his other hand under his arm with the gun to steady it. "I've already shot you once."

"From a distance," Jack retorted scornfully. "Easy enough to take aim from a hundred feet away or to send a pile of rocks tumbling down upon me." He walked steadily toward Robert as he spat the words out, and Robert backed up uneasily. "But up close? Looking right into my face? You haven't got the nerve to kill a man that way." Jack stepped past the lantern. "Go on, do it. Shoot me."

Robert lifted the gun, sighting down it.

"Jack, no!" Isobel darted forward.

Startled, Robert jerked and turned toward her. Jack threw himself forward, knocking Rose to the ground and sending his pistol tumbling harmlessly across the floor.

"Och, Sassenach," Coll said as Isobel ran to Jack. "I'm getting a wee bit tired of saving your British hide."

Jack began to laugh as he stood up and wrapped his arms around Isobel, hugging her to him as tightly as he could. "It wasn't you, Munro. It was Isobel who saved me. Always."

32

"You mean he was going to kill that nice young Andrew?" Jack's mother asked in shocked tones. Jack and Isobel had returned from the cave a few minutes earlier and related their story to Millicent and Elizabeth, leaving both of the women astonished. "I can't believe it."

"Yet you are not surprised he wanted to murder me," Jack commented drily.

"Oh, Jack! You know what I mean."

"Stop teasing your mother," Isobel said. She sat beside Jack on the sofa and had yet to let go of his hand since they had walked out of the caves. "I know exactly what you mean, Mrs. Kensington. And, yes, Cousin Robert had Andrew there, tied up and gagged. He had heard everything, and as you can imagine, he was quite terrified."

"Poor Robby," Aunt Elizabeth murmured. "He must have gone entirely mad. And he told me *I* was losing my mind. What will happen to him now?"

"I don't know," Isobel admitted. "Coll took him and Andrew back to Kinclannoch to tell Gregory. It is all such a tangle."

"I think Baillannan has seen enough scandal for a while," Jack said. "Gregory apparently knew nothing of it; it seems unfair that he should have to suffer for his father's misdeeds. The best thing is to make sure Robert is far away from here. I think what Robert said about Andrew would work well enough for himself — relocating somewhere in the colonies."

"Will he go?" Millicent asked.

"I think he'll have no choice," Jack replied grimly.

"And he was also the one who tried to break in here?" Millicent frowned. "I don't understand. What did searching your grandmother's room have to do with harming Jack?"

"I think they were only connected through being set off by Jack's arrival at Baillannan," Isobel said. "Cousin Robert tried to explain it to me afterward. He seemed to think I would see the sense of it. When Jack came here and I started cleaning out the attic, I gave Cousin Robert some things of his father's. Among them was Cordelia's confession, just as we guessed, along with a letter from his father to Robert in which Fergus ordered him to destroy both confessions. That is why Cousin Robert was so eager to look through the attic, and when he did not find what he wanted, he tried to break into the house, but Jack thwarted him. Later, during the wedding feast, he had ample time to search Grandmother's room, but, of course, he still could not find the confession. That is when his obsession with Jack and the inheritance apparently started."

"He always had the nonsensical notion that you would marry Gregory," Elizabeth said.

"Yes, and when he made up his mind that Gregory would come into the family land if he killed Jack, he became absolutely driven to do it. He convinced himself that Jack would reveal the scandal and only his death would keep it quiet."

The room fell into silence for a moment, as everyone digested this thought. Then Elizabeth said, "Does anyone know what happened to the treasure? Was there one? Did my mother and Uncle Fergus take it?"

"Mr. Rose was adamant that it was never there," Jack told her. "The letter his father left said that he opened the chest after Malcolm was killed and found it empty. He was apparently quite bitter about it, as that was to have been his reward when he and Malcolm's wife formed their pact. Fergus would take the treasure. Her little boy would get the land, of course, as he was Malcolm's heir, and she would have the satisfaction of punishing her husband's faithlessness."

"Did he say who the other woman was?"

"Not a word. Or so Cousin Robert claims. If Fergus said anything different, we will never know; Cousin Robert told us he burned the letter and the confession after reading them."

They continued to rehash the events of the afternoon as they consumed their afternoon tea, and afterward, still not quite able to settle down, Isobel and Jack strolled outside. Their steps turned inevitably toward the castle.

"You have been very good to my mother," Jack told her, wrapping his arm around her shoulders and pulling her to his side.

"She is your mother. She deserves my respect. And I can scarcely claim that my family is without flaws."

Jack smiled faintly. "I cannot deny that, I suppose."

"Your mother has been good for Aunt Elizabeth. She has seemed much improved lately, don't you think?"

"She is happier, more at ease. That helps, but —"

"I know. I don't expect her to be as she once was. But I am grateful that she is more settled."

They had reached the castle, and they stopped, gazing at the ruins in the slanting light of the late-afternoon sun.

"I wonder what we will find down there now," Isobel mused. "Another door? The other end of the tunnel?"

Jack looked at her. "We could find out now, you know."

"What about Coll? He will be incensed if we do not wait for him."

Jack's eyes danced. "There is no need for him to know."

Isobel laughed. "You are a corrupting influence."

"I know."

They climbed down the rope ladder, and lighting the lanterns Jack and Coll had left there, they made their way to the room they had discovered. Knowing now exactly what they were looking for, it did not take them long to find the small keyhole on the wall opposite the entrance to the room. With a twist of Jack's key, a section of the wall separated, and Jack pulled the door open, the rusty hinges groaning.

The tunnel beyond was narrow and low ceilinged, but its resemblance to the tunnel they had found at Baillannan was unmistakable. They made their way along it, hand in hand, the light of their lanterns bobbing before them, revealing the tunnel bit by bit, until finally it ended, just as the other one had, in a pile of rubble.

"It *was* connected," Jack said, raising the lantern to survey the damage.

"They did it to hide the evidence of their crime, didn't they?" Isobel said in a hushed voice. "Cordelia and Fergus. Left the body lying there — her husband, his brother — still warm."

"And destroyed the tunnel to make sure it was never found. I expect so." Jack curled his arm around her shoulders and pressed a kiss to her hair. "You Roses seem to be a bloodthirsty lot. And jealous. I shall have to remember that."

"Jack!"

He chuckled, turning around and leading her back down the tunnel. "I think I'll take my chances."

"You always do," Isobel scolded. "I could not believe that you dared Robert to shoot you today. My heart nearly stopped."

"I could tell he did not have the courage to pull the trigger." Jack shrugged. "I saw you, and I was afraid you'd startle him and he would fire in a panic. He could have hit you."

"He was much more likely to hit you! His pistol was aimed straight at your heart."

"His hand was wobbling so that he was likely to miss even if he did summon the nerve to fire. He might have wounded me, but that is all."

"All!"

"His pistol would have been empty, and I had little doubt that Coll would have been able to subdue him." Jack grinned down at her as they stepped back through the door. "Then you would have nursed me back to health again. I trust my luck; I always have." He reached out and caressed her hair. "My luck brought me to you, didn't it?"

"Jack, promise me." Isobel dug her hands into his lapels, looking up at him entreatingly. "Promise me that you will not do anything so foolhardy again. I could not bear it if —" She broke off, her eyes suddenly swimming with tears.

"Here now," he said softly, brushing his knuckle along her cheek. "Don't cry, love."

"I cannot," she said brokenly, "I cannot keep our bargain." She closed her eyes, the tears spilling onto her cheeks, and she leaned her forehead against his chest.

"Our bargain?" He stiffened. "You mean our marriage?"

"Yes. Yes!" She raised her head, her face blazing in something close to defiance. "I swore we would go our own ways, that I would not try to hold you or keep you here. You could go off to London, and I would not care. But I cannot, I cannot let you go. It will break my heart!"

She buried her face in his shirt, giving way to sobs. Jack relaxed, sliding his arms around her, a smile curving his mouth. "Shh, don't cry now." He rested his cheek against her head, cradling her to him. After a moment he said, "Is London entirely forbidden? I should like to show it to you, you know, as you've shown me Baillannan. We could go there in the dead of winter perhaps; I'll warrant it's bitter cold here in January."

Isobel pulled back, staring at him. "What are you saying? What do you mean?" She swiped at the tears on her cheeks.

"I am saying, my love, that I am not going anywhere unless you are with me." He gripped her shoulders, gazing deep into her eyes. "The other day, when I thought you had betrayed me, lured me here to kill me, I realized that it did not matter. I was as good as dead if you did not love me." He bent and kissed her tenderly on the mouth. "I love you, Isobel."

"Oh, Jack!" Isobel threw her arms around his neck, laughing and crying all at once. "I love you. I've loved you for so long, and I dared not say it." She pulled back, looking at him with shining eyes. "I cannot take it all in."

"Don't worry. You have plenty of time to do so. You are my wife, and Baillannan is my home. And I am not going anywhere, unless you go with me."

Isobel smiled and went back into his arms. "That is a much better bargain."